Praise for *The Perfect Girl*

"A wonderfully addictive book with virtuoso plotting and characters—for anyone who loved *Girl on the Train,* it's a must-read."
—Rosamund Lupton

"With tightly drawn characters, a fascinating storyline, and absolutely exquisite narration, *The Perfect Girl* is sure to keep readers up all night. Gilly Macmillan proves once again to be a master of the written word and is quickly becoming one of my go-to authors. Literary suspense at its finest."
—Mary Kubica, *New York Times* bestselling author of *Pretty Baby*

"I DEVOURED *The Perfect Girl*. An incredible page-turner with awesome characters and suspense. Bravo."
—Kate White, *New York Times* bestselling author

Praise for *What She Knew*

"What an amazing, gripping, beautifully written debut. *What She Knew* kept me up late into the night (and scared the life out of me)."
—Liane Moriarty, *New York Times* bestselling author

"Tightly focused and fast-paced. You won't rest until you really know what happened."
—Lisa Ballantyne, author of *Everything She Forgot*

"Gilly Macmillan introduces some smart variations on the [missing child] theme in her debut mystery. . . . Macmillan enlivens the narrative with emails, newspaper headlines, passages from professional journals, even transcripts from Inspector Clemo's sessions with a psychotherapist. But her best move is to include vicious blog posts that go viral."
—*New York Times Book Review*

"A nuanced, completely addictive debut."
—*People*

"Readers will have a tough time putting this one down."
—*Publishers Weekly*

"A terrific debut."
—*Reader's Digest*

THE
PERFECT
GIRL

Also by Gilly Macmillan

What She Knew

THE PERFECT GIRL

GILLY MACMILLAN

wm

WILLIAM MORROW

An Imprint of HarperCollinsPublishers

A trade paperback edition of this book was published in 2016 by Piatkus, an imprint of Little, Brown Book Group, a Hachette UK company.

P.S.™ is a trademark of HarperCollins Publishers.

HarperCollins books may be purchased for educational, business, or sales promotional use. For information please e-mail the Special Markets Department at SPsales@harpercollins.com.

FIRST WILLIAM MORROW EDITION PUBLISHED 2016.

Library of Congress Cataloging-in-Publication Data has been applied for.

ISBN 978-0-06-247676-0 (trade paperback)
ISBN 978-0-06-265431-1 (international edition)
ISBN 978-0-06-256748-2 (library edition)
ISBN 978-0-06-266231-6 (Target edition)

16 17 18 19 20 OV/RRD 10 9 8 7 6 5 4 3 2 1

To my family

THE
PERFECT
GIRL

SUNDAY AND MONDAY

An Evening of Summer Music

Sunday, August 24, 2014

7 P.M.

Holy Trinity Church, Westbury-on-Trym, Bristol

Zoe Maisey and Lucas Kennedy

play

Brahms, Debussy, Chopin, Liszt & Scarlatti

"You won't want to miss these two precociously talented teenagers making their Bristol debut— this promises to be a very special evening."
—Bristol Evening Post, *"What's On"*

In Aid of the Family Bereavement Society

Tickets: £6 for adults, £3 for children.
Family ticket £15.

Please contact Maria at maria.maiseykennedy@gmail.com
for bookings and details of future performances.

SUNDAY NIGHT

The Concert

ZOE

Before the concert begins, I stand inside the entrance to the church and look down the nave. Shadows lurk in the ceiling vaults even though the light outside hasn't dimmed yet, and behind me the large wooden doors have been pulled shut.

In front of me, the last few members of the audience have just settled into their places. Almost every seat is filled. The sound of their talk is a medium-pitched rumble.

I shudder. In the heavy heat of the afternoon, when I was sweaty and tired after rehearsing, I forgot that it could be cold in the church even when the air was oven hot outside, so I chose a little black dress to wear this evening, with skinny straps, and now I'm feeling the chill. My arms are covered in goose bumps.

The doors to the church have been closed, sealing out the heat, because we don't want outside noise to disturb us. This suburb of Bristol isn't known for its rowdy inhabitants, but people have paid good money for their tickets.

And it's not just that. The thing is that this concert is my first performance since I left the Unit, and my first performance as part of my Second Chance Life.

As my mum said, only about a hundred times today, "This performance must be as perfect as it's possible to be."

I glance at Lucas, who's standing beside me. Only a millimeter or two of air separates us.

He's wearing black trousers that my mum put a crease in this afternoon, and a black shirt. He looks good. His dark brown hair is just about tamed into neatness, but not quite, and I think that if he was bothered to, he could make those girls who are still lame enough to read vampire romance stories wilt.

I look good too, or I will when the goose bumps subside. I'm small-boned, I have pale, clear skin, and my hair is long and very blond but thin: cobweb-caught-in-sunlight hair, which looks amazing against my black dress. In the right light my hair can look white, and this gives me a look of innocence.

"Like a baby deer, fragile, delicate" was how the prosecutor described me, which I thought was quite nice, though it still hurts me to remember that she added "but don't be fooled."

I flex my fingers and lace them together to make sure the gloves I'm wearing are fitting extra snugly, the way I like them, and then I put my arms to my sides and shake them, to get my hands moving. I want my fingers to be warm and flexible. I want them pulsating with blood.

Beside me, Lucas shakes his hands too, slowly, and one at a time. Pianists catch hand shaking from each other like other people catch yawns.

At the far end of the nave, in front of the altar, the grand piano stands on a low platform, its hammer and string intestines reflected on the underside of the propped-up shiny black lid. It's waiting for us. Lucas is staring at it, completely focused, as if it represents a vertical glacier that he has to ascend with his bare hands.

We have different approaches to nerves. He becomes as still as possible, he starts to breathe through his nose, slowly, and he won't respond to anybody.

In contrast, I fidget, and my mind can't rest because it has to run through the things I have to do, in the order I have to do them in, before I begin to perform. It's not until I play the first note that the concentration I need, and the music itself, will wrap around me, pure and white like a shroud, and everything else will disappear.

Until that point, I'm sick with nerves, just like Lucas is.

Beside the piano, a lady has been introducing the concert, and now she gestures toward us, and then sort of scrapes and bows her way off the stage.

It's time for us to go on.

I pull my gloves off quickly, and drop them onto a table beside me where the coffee and catechism leaflets are, and Lucas and I walk together down the aisle as if we're play-acting a wedding. As we do, the heads of the audience turn to look at us, each row triggering the next.

We walk past my aunt Tessa, who's in charge of a camera that's been set up to record our performances. The idea is to replay them later, to analyze them for imperfection, and identify areas where improvement can be squeezed out of us.

Tessa is squinting a bit nervously at the camera as if it might turn around and lick her face, but she gives us a thumbs-up. I love Tessa; she's like a much more chilled-out version of my mum. She has no kids of her own and she says that makes me all the more special to her.

The other faces in the church smile as Lucas and I walk

between them, creasing deeper into expressions of encouragement as we approach. I'm seventeen now, but I've known this
look since I was a little child.

Mum describes these sorts of people as our "supporters."
She says they'll turn up to watch time and time again if we
play well, and they'll tell their friends. I don't love the supporters, though. I don't like the way they come up to you at
the end of a concert and say stuff like "You have such a gift,"
as if piano playing isn't something that you work on day in and
day out, if you want to make it perfect.

You can almost see the word "genius" flashing up like a
neon sign in their minds, temptingly bright. Beware that sign,
I would say to them, if they asked. Be careful what you wish
for, because everything has a price.

In the front row of the church, the last pair of faces I focus
on belong to my mum and Lucas's dad. Or, to put it another
way, my stepdad and his stepmum, because Lucas and I are
stepsiblings. As usual, they're wearing the too-bright expressions of parents who are disguising a level of ambition for their
children that could choke you.

Lucas is ahead of me by the time we get to the end of the
aisle and he's already taking his seat as I step up onto the platform where the piano sits.

We're going to start by playing a duet. It's a crowd pleaser,
the brainchild of our parents. Plus, they think it'll help us to
calm our nerves if we play together at the beginning.

Lucas and I would both rather play alone, but we humor
them, partly because we have no choice, and partly because
we're both performers at heart and a performer wants to perform, needs to perform, loves to perform.

A performer is trained to perform.

So we'll do it, and we'll do it as well as we can.

As I sit down at the piano, I keep my back straight and I'm smiling for the audience even though my insides have constricted and twisted so they feel like a ball of elastic bands. But I don't smile too much. It's important that I look humble too, that I get my performance face just right.

There's a bit of fuss while Lucas and I get settled and adjust the piano stools. We already know that they're perfectly positioned, because we tried out the piano before everybody arrived, but still we fiddle about with them, the spacing of them, a tiny height adjustment. It's part of the performance. It's nerves. Or showmanship. Or both.

Once we're both sitting perfectly, I place my hands over the keys. I have to work hard to control my breathing because my heart is hammering but my focus sharpens onto the music that's ahead, all of me waiting to hear those first notes now, like a starting gun at the beginning of a race.

The audience is hushed. Just a cough from somebody that echoes around the vaults and columns. Lucas waits for the sound to disappear and, in the absolute silence that follows, he first wipes his palms on his trouser legs and then he positions his hands over the keys.

Now that smooth run of black and white stretching out beneath our hands is everything and I watch his hands as intently as an animal ready to pounce. I mustn't miss his cue. There's a beat or two more of perfect silence before he arches his palms and his hands bounce lightly: once, twice, three times.

Then we're off, in perfect synchrony.

We dazzle when we do this; everybody says so. The energy two players produce can be electrifying when it's right. It's a tightrope act controlling the power, the tone, and the dynamics, because all of it must be perfectly balanced, and it wasn't so good this afternoon when we got tired and cross with each other while practicing in the heat, but tonight, it's brilliant. It's seamless, beautiful, and we're right in the music, both of us, and I'll admit that doesn't always happen. Mostly doesn't happen.

In fact, I'm so into it that at first I don't hear the shouting, and not hearing the shouting means that I don't realize that what's just begun is the end.

But I wish I had realized.

Why do I wish that?

Because, six hours later, my mother is dead.

MONDAY MORNING

SAM

At 8 A.M. Tessa still hasn't stirred, but I've been awake since dawn.

I'm a criminal lawyer, with a heavy workload. I often work late and usually I sleep heavily until my alarm goes off, but today I have a hospital appointment that's been burning a hole in the page of my diary for more than a week, and it's on my mind the minute my eyes open.

The curtains are drawn at my bedroom window, darkening the room, and light filters around them in lazy, unpredictable curves as they move with the breeze from the river. If I opened them, I would see the wide expanse of the floating harbor outside, and the colorful mixture of modern apartments and old warehouses and boathouses that bundle together on the bank opposite.

But I don't.

I stay where I am and I notice that the breeze is so soft that it barely disrupts the stillness of the room. They promised us a storm last night, but it never came. There was just a short, violent rain shower, followed by a dusting of drizzle, which offered a brief respite from the heat, but only brief, because now it's thickening again.

Tessa arrived in the rain, in the middle of the night.

She apologized for disturbing me, as if she hadn't just made my evening. She said she'd tried to phone. I hadn't noticed because I'd passed out on the sofa in front of the TV, with the remains of a special chow mein on my lap, and the letter from the hospital on my chest.

When I opened the door to her, I noticed dark smudges of exhaustion on the damp skin underneath her eyes, and she stood very still when I embraced her, as if every muscle in her body was stretched too tight.

She said she didn't want to talk, so I didn't press her to. Ours is a quiet, respectful affair; we don't ask for or expect a comprehensive emotional download from each other. We're more in the business of providing refuge for each other, and by that I mean a strong, safe place to reside, a place where we are almost certainly what two less reserved adults would call "in love," though we would never say that.

I'm a shy person. I moved from Devon to Bristol two years ago, because it's what you do if you want to avoid spending your whole life and career among the same small circle of people, in the area you grew up in. Opportunities in Bristol are much greater, and I'd cut my teeth on Zoe Guerin's case, so I felt ready for a change.

But it hasn't worked out too well for me. My cases are more varied, and the workload is more intense, that's true, but new friendships haven't come easily because I have to work all hours, and you don't meet too many potential partners when you're doing prison visits and court attendances. So when Tess and I ran into each other, just in the street one day, it felt like a godsend. She was a familiar face, we had shared history, how-ever difficult, and we slipped quickly into a pattern of snatching time with each other, just coffees and drinks at first, and then more. Tessa is married, though, so that's where things have sort of stalled. We can't move on unless she leaves her husband.

Last night, after she arrived, she flopped on my sofa as if the stuffing had been knocked out of her, and I brought her a cold beer and discreetly slipped the hospital letter into a drawer on my way to the kitchen, so she wouldn't see it. I didn't want it to mar things between us, not until I was sure. Not until I'd got through today's appointment. It was fairly easy to disguise the numbness in my left hand. Nobody at work had noticed it either.

She sipped her beer and we watched a Hitchcock film, in the dark, and the black-and-white images on the screen made the room flicker as if it was animated. Beside me, Tessa re-mained still and quiet as she watched, once or twice rolling the cold drink across her forehead, and I snuck a glance or two at her when I could, wondering what was wrong.

Tessa doesn't share the white-blond hair, pale skin, and re-fined features of her sister or her niece—her looks have none of their hauteur—though she does share their sharp blue eyes. Tess mostly wears her thick, silky strawberry-blond hair tied back, and the open features on her heart-shaped face and her lightly freckled skin make her look approachable and kind, and her eyes often dance with humor. Her figure is athletic, her attitude is practical and no-nonsense. For me, she is beautiful.

As I look at her now, in the warm darkness of my bedroom, she's lying with her hands on the pillow beside her face, fin-gers curled in beside her lips. Only the sight of the tarnished gold wedding ring on her finger spoils the picture for me.

After a while, I ease myself out of bed, because I want breakfast. So I'm riffling through a pile of laundry on the floor to locate something to wear when my phone vibrates.

I snatch it up quickly, because I don't want it to disturb her.

The screen tells me that it's Jeanette calling, my secretary. She's always at her desk early, especially on a Monday.

I go through an internal fight with myself, wondering whether to answer it or not, but the truth is that I'm a conscientious chap so the battle was really lost as soon as the phone started buzzing. I answer the call.

"Sam, I'm sorry, but there's a client turned up for you here, at the office."

"Who?" I ask, and I mentally shuffle through the deck of some of my more notable clients, trying to guess which of them might have pitched himself or herself off the good behavior wagon and back into the mud this time.

"She's only a girl." Jeannette tells me this in a stage whisper.

"What's her name?" As I ask I think, It can't be, can it?, because I've only had one client who was a teenage girl.

"She says she's called Zoe Maisey, only you knew her as Zoe Guerin."

I take myself out of the bedroom, into the en suite, shut the door and sit on the side of the bath. Here, the morning light streams in through the frosted window, yellowing the room, assaulting my dark-widened pupils.

"You are joking?"

"I'm afraid I absolutely am not. Sam, she says her mum was found dead last night."

"Oh dear God."

Those three words express in only a paltry way my utter

disbelief, because of course Zoe is Tessa's niece, and her mother, Maria, is Tessa's sister.

"Sam?"

"Can you put her on the phone?"

"She's insisting she wants to see you."

I calculate that because my appointment isn't until late morning, I probably have time to deal with this, at least partly.

"Tell her I'm on my way."

I'm about to hang up the phone when Jeanette adds, "And she's with her uncle," and my insides take a swan dive yet again, because Zoe's uncle is Tessa's husband.

SUNDAY NIGHT

The Concert

TESSA

When you don't have kids of your own, people have a tendency to give you things to look after. I think they assume that you're lacking in outlets for any nurturing instincts that you might have.

On the night of Zoe's concert, the child substitute that I've been given to be in charge of is the camera. I'm supposed to be looking after it throughout the duration of the performance, so that I can record the show in its entirety. It is, I'm told by my sister in a pedantic way, as if I'm lacking in mental capacity, an important job.

Shall we deal with the reasons for my childlessness straightaway? Let's do it. In spite of the fact that I'm a successful professional and happy in my skin, it's what people always seem to be most curious about.

So here goes: "Unexplained Infertility" is a thing. It's an official thing in spite of its unofficial-sounding title, and I have it. My husband, Richard, and I didn't discover it until we were in our thirties, because we left having kids until after we'd gone traveling and established our careers.

After we found out, we tried IVF and went three rounds

before we gave up. Surrogacy: I didn't fancy it; not brave enough. Adoption: same reason. They'd never pass us now anyway, not with Richard's drinking.

As for being somebody who's lacking in nurturing instincts, I could snort with laughter over that, because I'm a vet.

My practice is in the city center, lodged where several of Bristol's most contrasting neighborhoods meet. On an average day, I probably see between twenty and twenty-five animals that I prod, probe, stroke, reassure, and sometimes muzzle in order to treat their health and sometimes their psychological problems. Then I might reassure, or advise, and very occasionally stroke their owners too if there's bad news.

In short, I nurture, all day, most days of the week.

But you know there's a bit of irony here, which never escapes me when I'm with my little sister, especially when I'm roped in to help with her family, as I am tonight.

You see, when we were growing up, Maria was the naughty girl, compared to my Perfect Peter. She had lots of potential as a child, especially musical potential, which got my parents excited, but she never met their expectations.

From a very young age she was feisty, and funny, but when she hit fourteen she began to run wild. While I burrowed into my bedroom in the evenings, studying hard, my heart set on vet school, her desk, on the other side of our room, would be covered only in makeup she'd discarded after getting ready for a night out. She stopped studying, she stopped playing classical music, and she had fun instead.

She didn't see the point of the rest of it, she said, in spite of the fact that my dad's eyes bulged when she spoke like that.

Boyfriendless, much plainer, and less socially adept than my beautiful little sister, I loved living vicariously through her and I think she liked that too. She whispered her secrets to me after she got home in the small hours: kisses and drinks and pills taken; jealousies and triumphs: adventures, all of them.

But then, to all of our surprise, aged just nineteen she met Philip Guerin at a music festival. He was twenty-seven and had already inherited the family farm, and she just took off and went to live with him there, and shortly afterward she married him. Just like that. "Living the dream," my mother said sarcastically, as she actually wrung her hands.

Zoe followed soon after. Maria had her when she was just twenty-two, and I think it was after that that the reality of life on the farm with a small child began to rub the shiny edges off her a bit. But she didn't quit, to give her credit. Instead, she began to put all her energies into Zoe, and when Zoe's extraordinary musicality presented itself as plain to see when she was all of three years old and began to pick out tunes on the piano at the farm, Maria made it her mission to nurture that talent.

That was before the accident, of course, when things went very wrong for them. But my point is that in the meantime, having done everything right all my life, and studied hard, and followed the rules, I am married, sure, but I've ended up with no children. I've come to terms with it, but Richard isn't coping so well, especially after a dramatic professional disappointment, which coincided with me refusing to go for IVF round number four.

So here we are tonight. I'm helping my sister and Zoe, which is something I love to do when Maria will let me. I'm looking forward to the performance, because Zoe's playing has almost regained the standard it used to be, before she went to the Unit, and I'm sure she's going to blow everybody away tonight, and I'm hoping I won't mess up the job of recording everything.

I've had a meager thirty-second tutorial from Lucas, the son of my sister's newish husband, on how to operate the camera. Lucas is a film and camera buff, so I was in good hands, but the tutorial wasn't really enough, because by instinct I'm a bit of a technophobe, and even as Lucas was saying them, I felt his words swimming uncontrolled around my head like a panicky shoal of fish.

I could do with my Richard being here to help me, but he's let me down again.

Just an hour ago I went to find him when it was time to get ready for the concert. He was in the shed at the bottom of our garden, supposedly working on building a model airplane, but when I got there I found him squeezing out the dregs of his box of wine from the shiny bladder inside. He'd ripped the cardboard away and he was massaging and twisting that silvery bag as if it was a recalcitrant udder, holding it over his tea mug.

As I stood watching in the doorway, a few pale drops of liquid dribbled from the bag into the mug. Richard drank them immediately and then he noticed me. He made no apology and no effort to hide what he was doing. "Tess!" he said. "Do we have another box?"

Even from the doorway I could tell that his breath stank and his speech was slurred, and although he was trying to behave like a civilized drinker, somebody just enjoying a glass of white on a Sunday afternoon, shame wandered across his features and exaggerated the tremor in his hands. The balsa wood model he was ostensibly there to make lay in its box, all the precision-cut pieces still in perfect order underneath the unopened instruction manual.

"In the garage," I said. And I left to go to the concert on my own.

So now I'm here with a camera that I'm not sure is working properly, a pounding head, and a disappointed heart, and I'm telling myself that I mustn't, I must not, give in to temptation and go and see Sam after the concert tonight, because that would be wrong.

SUNDAY NIGHT

The Concert

ZOE

Lucas hears the shouting before me.

He stops playing first, but I don't notice immediately because we're in the middle of a complicated passage of music that always pulls me through it with the unstoppability of a freight train.

When I realize that his hands have stilled, and that I'm playing on my own, I keep going at first, glancing at him because I wonder if he's forgotten his part. We're playing the duet from memory, and that happens sometimes: your brain just freezes.

So I'm expecting him to pick up the melody at any moment, I'm *willing* him to remember, because this concert must be perfect, and I'm doing that right up until the moment when I work out that he's properly stopped, because a man is standing in the center of the aisle.

So I stop playing too and, as the last vibrations from my chords die away, I look at the man, and I think I might recognize him.

The expression on his face is smudged out of normal. It's in no way appreciative of our playing, it's red with rage; the tendons on his neck are straining so much that they look like extra bones.

"It's a travesty!" he shouts. "A travesty! It's disrespectful!" His words ricochet around the space, and one or two people stand up.

He's staring at me and I realize that I do know him.

I know him because I killed his daughter.

The piano stool makes very little noise when I stand up, because even though it tips over, it's on a square of crimson carpet that breaks the sound of its fall so that it's a dull thud only.

My mother rises from her seat. She knows the man too.

"Mr. Barlow," she says. "Mr. Barlow, Tom, please," and she starts to walk toward him.

I don't stay. I'm too afraid of what he might do to me.

I leave the stage, my hip clashing painfully with the edge of the piano, and I flee toward the back of the church, away from him, to where there's a doorway behind the altar that takes me out of his sight. I shove through it, then clatter down slippery stone steps into a tiny room where there's just a sink draped with stained cloths and I crouch in a corner, shaking, drenched yet again with the cold sweat of my remorse, with the impossibility of this life of mine, of second chances or fresh starts, until eventually my mum finds me.

She says words that mean nothing but are an attempt to make me feel better. She says them to me in a hushed voice, and her hand smooths the hair on my head, smooths it lightly down my back. She says, "Shush now. Shush," but I'm not sure if that's because she wants to comfort me or because she wants my sobbing to quiet down so nobody else can hear me.

Fifteen minutes later—it takes that long for us to be sure

that they've got rid of Thomas Barlow and his raging grief—she leads me out of a back door, through the graveyard, and toward the car.

There's no question that I'll perform now. I'm still shaking, and the notes are all jumbled in my head anyway.

Outside, I take in the fact that the night is deeply dusky and warm, and that feels like a balm after the cold air inside. I notice a strong smell from the glowing white roses that hang over the churchyard gate, and the dark fluttering of bats that swarm from a high corner of the church tower. Around us, as we walk in the tired grass, gravestones whose cadaverous foundations have failed them lean against each other for support. I see a Celtic cross, the contours of lichen-covered stone mounds, writing everywhere, words of remembrance, and, above us, the dark, pointed leaves of the yew tree greedily sucking away the last of the light.

From inside the church we hear the sound of Lucas beginning his Debussy. The show must go on. The sound is a warm bath of notes at first, then a river flowing. It's something beautiful, which I wrap around me to shield me from what's just happened.

It diverts me from looking down at the edges of the path where there's a plaque that has been recently laid. "Amelia Barlow" is inscribed on it. "Aged 15. Beloved by family, cherished by friends. The sun shone brighter when you were alive." There are freshly tended flowers planted around it.

We didn't know that her family had laid a plaque for her there. We would never have hired that church as a venue if we'd known, never in a million years. Continents would have drifted and re-formed before we'd have done that.

For the whole drive home my mum says almost nothing,

apart from, "It doesn't matter. We can reorganize the concert, and you'll be ready for the diploma. You're already ready."

My mother: who never talks about what really matters, and who is trying to reassure me, because although public musical performance at the child prodigy level was my downfall tonight, she believes it's ultimately going to be my salvation. She believes that it was the catalyst for our second life, and that it will also be the fuel that will propel it into a stratosphere that is a gazillion light-years away from our life so far.

And perhaps I should have listened harder when she spoke because it was the last time she ever truly reassured me, the last time I felt the frustration of our inability to connect with each other prickle the air between us.

Perhaps I should have emerged from the cocoon of my own misery to ask her if she was OK, even though that was the one thing we hadn't been for the past few years. We hadn't been OK.

But I wish I had. Asked her, I mean. I wish I had.

MONDAY MORNING

SAM

In the bathroom of my flat, after ending the call with Jeanette, and feeling a coruscating dread at the thought of having to break the news to Tessa, I sit for a moment longer and remember when I was first introduced to Zoe Maisey, or Zoe Guerin as she was known then.

My first encounter with Zoe was more than three years previously, when I lived in North Devon, and the introduction came in the form of a phone call from the Defense Solicitor Call Center, because I was the solicitor on duty when she was arrested.

The call came in at nine-thirty in the morning, about eight hours after the accident had happened. They described Zoe and her situation as follows:

"Juvenile, appropriate adult present, charge is death by careless driving, two fatalities, another critically injured, ready for interview at Barnstaple Police Station and your Duty Solicitor number is 00746387A."

I phoned the custody suite at the police station right away, identified myself, and asked the custody sergeant to put Zoe on the phone.

"Hello?" she said.

I introduced myself. "Don't tell the police anything about the accident," I said. "I'm on my way. I'll be about forty-five minutes. Don't start any interviews without me."

And in reply she said, "OK," in a voice that sounded quiet with shock, and she had not a single question that she wanted to ask me.

I drove through the countryside to get to the police station. It was a beautiful, cold morning. I passed white frosted fields bordered by hedges that were a couple of feet thick, sturdy and sinuous at once as they partitioned off the surrounding fields, and stripped of leaves by the winter but so dense that the shadows they cast were deep horizontal bands. The blue-gray ocean, surprisingly calm, was visible here and there where clefts in the landscape revealed it, and Lundy Island was clear as day offshore, peaceful, ancient, and cold.

In the custody suite in Barnstaple the sergeant handed me a charge sheet.

"She won't have her mother with her," he said. "She refused, even though Mum's here. Social worker's just arrived. She didn't want a brief either but the social worker overruled her."

I scanned the charge sheet. It wasn't quite as they'd said on the phone. The charge was: "Death by careless driving" but there was an addition: "while under the influence of alcohol."

It was a shocking charge for anybody to face, but for a fourteen-year-old, whose life had been stretching out lazily before her just hours earlier, still packed with potential, it was nothing short of horrific.

"Has she been interviewed?"

"Not yet. Social worker just arrived."

The police weren't allowed to interview Zoe without an

"appropriate adult" present because of her age. If she'd refused to have her mother with her they would have had to wait until a social worker came on shift this morning.

The custody sergeant wore a tight black police top with a high collar and short sleeves that gripped muscular arms, and literally talked down to me from his desk, which was on a raised platform. As he spoke, he tapped efficiently at his keyboard, eyes glued to the screen of his computer monitor.

"I've just had the handover, so I'm acquainting myself with the details, but she was brought in at about four-thirty after a couple of hours at the hospital."

I pitied Zoe her hours in the cell. Even my clients who'd been to prison said that they hated being in police custody more than anything. There's no routine, just four walls, a mattress on a shelf, a toilet that may or may not be properly screened, and a pair of eyes on you at all times, either directly or via the camera.

"Why didn't she want her mother?" I asked him. I was wondering if this girl had been in care, or lived with her father, or was bereaved.

"We're not entirely sure. Best guess: ashamed."

"Ashamed?"

He shrugged his shoulders and spread his hands wide, palms upward. "Mum's been sitting in reception since Zoe arrived."

There had been a lone woman sitting in reception on my arrival, with white-blond hair and fine features. She was huddled in a corner, and shuddered when the electronic doors ushered in a cold draft with me, and met my eye with the clear gaze of somebody who's waiting for nothing good at all to happen and has had no sleep to speak of.

It was a common expression in the waiting rooms I frequented: at police stations, in courtrooms, nobody's looking forward to what's going to happen.

That nice-looking woman, who'd been shut firmly out of her daughter's life at that moment, was my first clue that this case was going to be far from straightforward.

I had no picture in my head of Zoe before I met her. I'd had enough experience by then to know that criminality takes all kinds, so you could never predict what your clients would be like, though if I'd had to hazard a guess I might have told you that the girl I was about to meet would be a mature fourteen-year-old, probably a bit rough around the edges, probably a seasoned drinker, maybe a dabbler in the local drugs scene, definitely a party girl.

The girl I met wasn't like that. The police had taken her clothing at the hospital as evidence, so she was wearing an outfit that the A & E nurses must have had to cobble together for her: oversize gray sweatpants and a blue zipped-up fleece top. She had a dressed wound on one temple and long white-blond hair, a shade paler even than her mother's, which sparkled with tiny, glittery fragments of glass from the accident.

She sat in a molded plastic chair that was bolted to the floor; her feet were drawn up and her arms were wrapped around her knees. She looked disheveled and very small. Her cheek-bones were fine, her eyes were a bright, clear blue, and her skin was as pale as the frost outside. Her hands were tucked into the sleeves of the fleece, which looked grubby on the cuffs: stains from another life that the hospital laundry hadn't been able to get rid of.

Beside her sat a woman who wore the stoic expression of a seen-it-all social worker. She was middle-aged, with hair cropped short and sharp, and a face that was deeply grooved and grayish from what I would have guessed had been twenty cigarettes a day for twenty years. She had deposited a neat pile of gloves, hat, and scarf onto the interview table.

I introduced myself to Zoe and she surprised me by standing up and offering me a timid handshake. Unfolded, she revealed herself to be of medium height and very slight, totally swamped by the borrowed clothing. She looked exceptionally fragile.

We sat down opposite each other.

It wasn't the beginning of her nightmare—that had happened hours earlier—but it was the moment when I had to begin the delicate process of trying to help her to understand precisely how grave her situation might be.

SUNDAY NIGHT

The Concert

TESSA

I'm feeling pretty certain that the camera is actually filming when Zoe and Lucas start playing their duet because there's a red light flashing in the bottom right-hand corner of its screen and a counter appears to be frenetically keeping track of the seconds and milliseconds that are passing.

Zoe and Lucas look great on the podium, as ever: a sweet vision of teenage perfection. They are yin and yang, blond and dark, an ice princess and her swarthy consort.

I'm one of the first to notice Tom Barlow because the camera tripod and I are positioned just at the side of the aisle, quite near the entrance, so that I can stand up and tend to it without blocking anybody's view.

I don't recognize him at first, and by the time I do it's too late to do anything.

Later, I wonder what might have happened differently if I'd acted at that moment, whether I could have stopped him and changed the course of things, but it's pointless speculation because, like the rest of the audience, I do nothing more than watch, openmouthed, as he shouts, his spittle flecking the air in front of him.

Zoe is the last person in the church to notice him, and when she does, fear jerks her limbs like she's a puppet on strings, and she scrambles to get off the stage. I don't blame her. Tom Barlow looks like a man possessed, and he's a big man.

When Maria stands up and makes a feeble attempt to pacify him, he's having none of it. "You have your daughter," he says to her, and the words seem to strike her like blows. "Don't tell me what to do. You have your daughter."

"I'm so sorry, Tom," she says, but he scythes her down with his reply: "It's your fault," he says. "It was your fault."

And then there's a muddle, as people begin to leave their seats and surround Mr. Barlow, and he sinks to his knees and begins to sob, and it's an awful, wrenching sound, a sound to make the hairs on the back of your neck stand up.

I know who he is, because I recognize him from the trial, of course. Zoe's trial took place in a closed court, because of her age, so I never went inside the actual courtroom, but I was still there every day, in the waiting room reserved for families of the accused, and I saw the families of the victims outside the courthouse in the street, day in, day out, huddled in groups.

We kept our distance, to avoid any scenes, but I'm certain I recognize Tom Barlow because his face was in the local paper too. He and the other parents were pictured prominently, black clad and riddled with grief at the funerals of their children.

In the mayhem at the concert, Maria follows Zoe off stage, though before she does there's a tense exchange between her and her newish husband, Chris, during which he seems to question her and she shakes her head vigorously. Maria meets my eye as she goes, she looks stricken, and I mouth, *Do you want me to come?* She signals that she doesn't, so I sit down where I am. I'm keen not to draw attention to myself. Others are kneeling beside Tom Barlow, looking after him, so I don't need to. Best if he doesn't see me at this point. There's a possibility that he might recognize me.

I wonder how Tom Barlow knew Zoe was here tonight. Since leaving Devon, she's changed her surname, broken links with the families, with everything. We all thought she'd left Amelia Barlow's family a hundred miles away.

If we're unlucky enough that Tom Barlow and his wife and their remaining children have moved here too, it won't be long before people make connections. Bristol, it seems, might not have been far enough away for my sister and Zoe to move to escape the tragedy, and Bristol is a place where news travels fast. Within certain circles, there are often only a few degrees of separation between anybody in this city.

Chris Kennedy doesn't follow Maria and Zoe. Instead, he goes to stand beside Lucas, who's still sitting at the piano. Both of them watch the dying throes of Tom Barlow's meltdown with shock and disbelief on their faces and I feel leaden as I think of all the stories that are now going to have to be told, all the truths uncovered, and I think sadly of the impossibility of my sister's shiny, happy new life continuing as it is.

Zoe, our dear Zoe, has caused domestic bliss to implode yet again.

When Mr. Barlow has been cleared away, mopped up off the floor like a spilled drink, it's decided that Lucas will continue to play alone. As the audience settles into this news I double-check that the video camera is still recording. In the screen, I can see Lucas, and I think I've framed him quite well. I can also see Chris Kennedy in profile and he sits completely still, staring front and forward. Only a small fold in his forehead and the utter stillness of his features betray the incomprehension that he must be feeling. .

SUNDAY NIGHT

After the Concert

ZOE

The thorny, spiky, typical silence in the car as Mum drives me home means that I get a bit of a chance to pull myself together, because my mum doesn't like crying. It's the kind of silence that we often share, Mum and I. She grips the steering wheel with white knuckles while she drives. When I try to talk to her, she shushes me and tells me that she needs to think.

I stay quiet, but the silence is demolished when we pull up in the driveway, because the stone walls of our big, grand house are thumping with the kind of sounds that me and Lucas can pretty much only listen to surreptitiously on our iPods.

It's popular music, the kind that the kids in the Secure Unit listened to. Here, in this house, it's usually a treat that's severely rationed so that Lucas and I don't break our diet of classical repertoire, which allows us to "develop our musicality."

Mum hurries into the house and I follow her. The volume of music means that Katya, the au pair, is oblivious to us and she doesn't notice us until we're in the sitting room, standing right behind her.

She's on our sofa, with my baby sister, Grace, on her knee,

and right beside her, so close it looks as though he's stuck to her, is a boy who I know from school, called Barney Scott. Grace is laughing loudly because Katya is holding her arms and bouncing her up and down, but when she sees us she reaches out to my mum, and Katya and Barney leap up off the sofa and stroke down their rumpled clothing and make a totally impressive recovery.

"Hello, Maria, hello, Zoe," Katya says, and hands over the baby.

My mum is speechless at these blatant transgressions of the rules of the house: the music, the boyfriend, the baby downstairs after bedtime. She clutches Grace as if we've just heard that a landslide's about to sweep the five of us and the descendants of all mankind into the ocean.

"I hope you don't mind me asking Barney here, but his dad is a doctor and Grace was very unsettled," Katya says. Her full-on Russian accent and her deadpan face, cheeks like slabs of limestone, both give the sentence instant gravitas.

I look at my mum. Even she's not insane enough to fall for the dad-as-doctor line but I can see that Katya has scored a big, fat bull's-eye with the "unsettled" comment.

Grace is the Second Chance Baby, the Miracle Baby; she is a Gift to Us All. She is half of Mum and half of Chris and therefore a product of what Lucas calls their Perfect Union. As Chris said at her naming ceremony, she has "a lovely, sunny disposition" and is a "joy," and she "helped us all to start again."

What this means is that Katya's comment has adeptly maneuvered my mum's psyche down the path it most likes to travel, which is to exist in a state of fear for Grace's health.

So my mum ignores the fact that Grace looks ecstatic, and

is shiny with a sheen of overstimulation, and she takes her immediately upstairs to settle her, with Katya in her wake, and I'm left in the room on my own with Barney Scott. It's weird for me because we would never normally be alone together, absolutely no way. This is because, at my school, he's a Popular Boy.

Barney Scott scrunches his face up and I think that he's trying to smile at me. It makes me wonder what he and Katya thought they were going to get up to, because surely only guilt would make him do that.

"Hey," he says.

"Hey," I say back.

"Back early then," he says.

"Obviously."

"Huh." He's nodding his head like a plastic dog on a dashboard. "Did you . . . ah . . . did you play well?"

Barney Scott is not interested in how I played, though I suppose I'm impressed that he's making the effort to ask. He's the type of boy who posts things online like "On the Downs. 8 P.M. BBQ, Booze, and Bitches" and thinks that's hilarious, and he's probably right because girls like Katya, or the Popular Girls at school, then actually turn up wearing microscopic shorts with the pocket patches hanging out over their foreign-holiday-tanned thighs so they can get drunk and be groped.

"It was OK," I say. Barney Scott doesn't need to know what happened, and I want him to go away.

He obviously doesn't want to be with me either. "I'll wait outside," he says, waving at the door to the hallway like I don't know where it is.

"OK," I say, but, as I watch him go, what I'm desperate to

say to him is that I kind-of-sort-of-maybe had a Popular Boy in love with me once, or at least in lust, so I'm not as stupid or pointless as they all think I am, I'm not.

My very own Popular Boy was called Jack Bell and he acted like he liked me. A lot. Unfortunately, there were obstacles to us going out, and the biggest one was Jack's twin sister, Eva, who was the Most Popular of All the Girls at school. Eva lost no time making it clear to me that her brother was not "in love" but was "playing the field" instead. The girl he really liked, the one he wanted instead of me, Eva said, was her best friend, Amelia Barlow.

And even though the word of Eva Bell was God for most of the people around me at that school, I didn't believe her, because I saw the way Jack Bell looked at me and even now, when I think of that, I get a dissolving feeling inside me. I might be socially awkward, I know I am, but I'm not stupid.

But what I have to do is to shut that dissolving feeling down quickly, because Jack Bell, like Amelia Barlow, is buried now, and the ache of that is too sharp for me to bear.

The sitting room window has been thrown open but the heat inside is still stifling. I hear Barney Scott crunching on the gravel outside and see him leaning against our front gate, waiting for Katya.

I want my mum to come down, but I don't want to disturb her while she settles Grace. I'm starting to feel sick with fear thinking about what will happen when Chris and Lucas get here, because they're going to want to know what the hell Mr. Barlow, back there in the church, was shouting about, and if nothing is to ruin the Second Chance Family, then me and Mum need to work out what we're going to say.

MONDAY MORNING

SAM

I have to wake her, because I have to tell her about Maria and Zoe, yet no part of me wants to.

"Tessa," I say. "Tess." There's a thin sheet covering her, and its sculptural white folds describe the lines of her body so closely, it's as if somebody had carefully laid it there, like the first damp bandages of a plaster cast.

She's alert quickly, eyes wide open; she's heard something in my voice.

"What?" she says, and it's a whisper; she hasn't moved yet.

I want to swallow the reason I've woken her up, never speak of it. I don't want to do this to her.

"I'm so sorry," I say, and the words make me feel terribly, throat-clearingly formal. They steal an intimacy from us.

And in the moment after I tell Tessa that her sister is dead, and she sits up, her eyes searching mine for confirmation of the truth of what I've said, I have the strange realization that she resembles Maria more closely than I'd ever noticed before.

And after a time where I hold her tight while shock takes hold of her, and I experience what I can only describe as an ache in my heart, in spite of the clichéd awfulness of that phrase, I have to let her go.

And that heartache, that hard pinch of a feeling, is not something I can indulge. It's a shallow, oil-slicked puddle of self-indulgent emotion compared to the oceans of grief that Tess's family have been through, and will now go through again. Just to totally overkill the metaphor: their grief could fill the Mariana Trench.

I gather up Tess's clothes for her and she dresses silently. When she's finished, I ask: "Do you want to come with me? To see Zoe? And Richard?"

His name seems to me to hover bulkily in the air between us, but it's the least of her worries at this moment.

"I should go to the house first," Tess says. "I need to see . . . and the baby . . ."

She can't finish her sentence; her words are choked with shock and incomprehension. We have very little information, just that Maria died at the house, but we don't know how. I understand that it's up to me to look after Zoe for now, whoever she's with.

"Shall I drop you there?" I ask. I'm worried about her driving.

We're standing on the communal landing in my building now. It's a small, bright space, with floor-to-ceiling windows over the busy commuter road below, no lift, just a functional metal staircase that winds its way down to the ground floor and the car park, and it's airless and stifling.

"No," Tess says. "You need to go to Zoe. I'll come later." And then she's gone, sandals clattering on the steps.

SUNDAY NIGHT

After the Concert

ZOE

Lucas's Debussy piece lasts for fourteen minutes, and his Bach is nine minutes. If you add to that the time he'll need to mix with the audience afterward, and then the drive home, and assume that since Mum and I took the car, Aunt Tess will be bringing them in her VW bus, which doesn't go above 36 mph without belching out black smoke, then I think Mum and me originally had about an hour and ten minutes to talk before Lucas and Chris arrive, minus the time it took discovering Katya and Barney on the sofa and the minute that Barney could stand to be in the room with me afterward, leaving us about fifty-eight minutes.

I wait on the sofa, stretched out, while Mum is still upstairs with Grace. My hip aches painfully from the bang against the piano and I pull up my dress to examine it and see a dark bruise forming there already. It's tender to the touch. The sight of it makes tears spring to my eyes and I shut them, and lie back down, and try to breathe, the way I've been told, to blank my thoughts, to focus just on the sensation of inhales and exhales instead.

It's hot. Our Second Chance House is a big old Victorian

pile and it usually feels damply cold to me, whatever the weather, but this summer's been so hot for so long that the heat's gradually built up and tonight feels like a culmination of that, as if the house has finally reached a rolling boil and the air inside is hot like jazz music bouncing off a dripping ceiling in a packed-full club, or like the picture of a red sun pulsating over shimmering orange ground in the portfolio-sized photo book about deserts that my dad gave me when I was little.

From upstairs I can hear the sound of the musical mobile that hangs above Grace's crib being wound up, then its tinkly noises begin, repetitive and familiar, soul-destroyingly plinky.

Katya appears suddenly in the doorway and looks at me without saying anything.

"He's outside," I say.

"I know. I just texted him. Your mother is settling Grace."

"I know."

Katya stands in the doorway for longer than I'm comfortable with and I lie there silently willing her to go away.

"I tried to be your friend," she says and I just don't, utterly don't have time for this right now. She has no idea.

"Thanks, Katya," I say. "*Spasiba.*" I say that because it really annoys her when I try to speak Russian. I get out my phone and scroll around it and try to look like I'm actually expecting to get a message from a real person.

"Zoe, you are your own worst enemy."

"Original," I say.

"Excuse me?"

"I saw what you were doing." I suddenly feel vulnerable in my prostrate position—it's funny how one moment you can feel glamorously hot and worn out like a panting diva in an old film and the next you realize you probably just look stupid—so I sit up and look properly at her over the back of the sofa. "With Barney. I saw where his hand was."

She makes an expression that mixes disgust and sadness at my amoeba level of existence.

"Inappropriate," she says. "Totally. Ugh." She has a habit of using Americanisms, which makes her sound like she's hosting the Eurovision Song Contest.

And I'm about to say how I'm not the one who's inappropriate and what she did was inappropriate, and has my mum even said that she's allowed to go out with Barney tonight anyway, but her phone pings and we're both trained to be silent when a phone pings—this is a Major Characteristic of Our Generation, my aunt Tessa says: the veneration of the ping of the phone—and so we're both silent while she reads the text.

"Barney's waiting," she says, and she turns so fast that the wispy ends of her hair fly out in a fan shape and she's disappeared before I can organize my riposte.

I lie back down. I'm happy she's gone. From upstairs the circus mobile is still crunching out its tune and I know what my mother will be doing. She'll be sitting on the floor beside Grace's crib, being as still as possible and stroking the baby's forehead. She can do that for ages, and tonight it makes me feel super tense because I feel like the time we have left before Lucas and Chris get home is on one of those kitchen timers that click madly like a bomb that's going to detonate until they make a screechy buzz that Lucas says sounds like a small bird being strangled.

And then I notice a thing. I notice that my phone browsing, which I basically did for show when Katya was looking at me, has actually turned something up. I have a notification and the sight of it makes my stomach ball up prickly and tight like a hedgehog, because there it sits, just like it used to: a number one, in a red circle, on the corner of the panop app.

It's an app I shouldn't even have on my phone. It's forbidden, because it was, according to Jason, my key worker at the Unit, and I did have to agree with him, definitely part of my downfall, because Eva Bell and Amelia Barlow and their cronies used it to torment me.

So I should have stayed away from it, but when I came out of the Unit, I couldn't resist downloading it, just to have a look, because I was curious about what happened to the people I used to know. I left one life when I went into the Unit, and when I came out I had another life completely, in another place, and nobody would talk about the old one, and panop was my only way back there. So I downloaded the app, and sometimes I sneak a look to see what people are doing. It's anonymous you see, if you want it to be.

Grace has gone quiet upstairs, but I estimate it'll be another ten minutes at least before my mum appears. With my heart pounding, I click on the app. A question fills the screen:

Did you think you could stay hidden forever?

SUNDAY NIGHT

The End of the Concert

TESSA

At the end of the concert, the crowd has an edge to it, an atmosphere, like a kind of low-level static. Lucas's performance hasn't succeeded in washing away the unease caused by Tom Barlow's scene.

As Lucas takes his bow, I check my phone and I have two texts:

Maria: Don't say anything.

Richard: Where are you?

I reply to neither of them. I'll do as Maria says, she knows I will, and Richard can wait. I imagine he'll have made it out of his shed and back into our house, and have suddenly worked out that he's alone.

When I look up, Chris is by my side.

He's brusque: "Maria's taken the car and I want to get home, but I think I need to stay for at least a few minutes. People will be expecting me to."

He's probably right, so I say, "I'll wait. I'll give you a lift whenever you're ready."

He makes no direct reference to Tom Barlow's outburst.

We don't know each other very well, Chris Kennedy and I, because Maria has always kept him to herself, like a piece of treasure that she'd found, and no wonder really, because she'd been through hell.

When Zoe was convicted, Maria's marriage fell apart and she was left on her own to pick up the pieces. Zoe spent eighteen months in jail, and in that time Maria had to cope with the transition from farmer's wife with a talented, beautiful child, a musical prodigy no less, to single mother with a teenage child with a criminal record.

She moved from Devon to be near me in Bristol, settling into a rented flat in the only area of the city she could afford, and starting work as a secretary at the university, a job that Richard got her, and that she could barely hold down at first, so powerful was her depression.

It was the piano that changed everything, as it always had done throughout Zoe's life.

Zoe's father would have none of it; he blamed her piano playing for much of what had happened before. He said it had led to her being different, being above herself, and that had in turn led to the bullying, and the accident.

The rest of us took a different view: that piano could help Zoe rediscover herself, repair her self-esteem, and provide her with a path for the future. Her talent was so ferociously strong that none of us could bear to let it rest, and, after all, what else did she have left apart from that and her intellect?

On advice from Zoe's therapist at the Unit, we encouraged Zoe to start playing again when she came home, and after a couple of months of practice on a keyboard that Richard bought for her, and the shlonky pianos at her new school, and with the help of some lessons from a teacher that Richard found and I paid for, Maria entered her tentatively into a low-key, local competition to help her recover her form.

It was a repertoire class that Zoe entered. It was non-competitive, and there were only two entrants. The other was Lucas.

Zoe played brilliantly that day, considering. She rose to the occasion.

I sat with Maria, and Chris Kennedy sat just a seat away from us. We were the only people watching, apart from the adjudicator, who would not declare a winner, but would give feedback to the players.

After Zoe's performance, Chris leaned over to us and asked who Zoe's teacher was. Maria answered him, and it wasn't long before I felt like a lemon and took Zoe to find a cup of tea while they chatted intensely in the corridor outside the performance hall, and Lucas skulked around the perimeter.

Chris and Maria exchanged phone numbers that day, ostensibly to share information about Lucas's piano teacher, whom Chris declared to be "the best in the southwest, and the only teacher for a talent like Zoe," and they met up soon afterward.

It became apparent very quickly that Chris was extremely good for Maria. She began to dress better and to take care of herself. She smiled. She moved Zoe to the new teacher, who cost Richard and me twice as much, but we were happy to pay. When Maria finally declared that they were in a proper relationship, it felt a little bit as if Chris had saved her.

However, in spite of all that, and even though I've met him on numerous occasions for social events, Chris still feels like a bit of a stranger to me. The only semi-intimate conversation I can claim to ever have had with him was when we met on the train to London once, by accident. It was just after Grace was born because I remember the way he seemed to glow when he spoke about her.

Chris was on his way to be the key speaker at a backslapping networking lunch for successful entrepreneurs, millionaires who want to be gazillionaires. His description, not mine, and delivered with a healthy dose of irony. I was on my way to a conference about feline hyperthyroidism.

After we met on the platform at Bristol Temple Meads, he kindly bumped me up to first class, where he laid his business tools out lavishly across the table that was between us: *Financial Times*, BlackBerry, iPhone, laptop, speech notes.

While he made a business call during which he stared out of the window and said things like "Well, as soon as it gets to market, it's a matter of how I judge that," and "Yup, yeah sure, indeed. This all plays back to . . . yes, well, it'll raise hairs, won't it, but it is the fact we've got to get into it," I sat in front of him feeling intimidated and not daring to eat the flaky sausage roll I'd bought for breakfast, or to get out my *Hello!* magazine.

Still, I didn't need the magazine, because after the call Chris and I chatted all the way, about my work, about his, and about baby Grace, who'd just been born. "Maria is such a natural mother," he said. "I'm a lucky man, after everything." And I'd felt happy for my sister, because who would have believed that she could have had this turn of fortune after Zoe's trial.

"Do you know what I loved about your sister, when I first met her?" he asked.

I shook my head. When Chris first met Maria she'd been a shadow of the girl boys trailed around after while when we were at school.

"She's a beautiful woman, obviously," he said, "but what I noticed most of all were extraordinary qualities of sweetness and poise, as if she just knew who she was. She was like a fine piece of porcelain; I couldn't believe my luck."

I smiled at the fondness in his words and the emotion, but my first thought at that moment was that Chris didn't know Maria very well; that he'd met a version of her that was clubbed by antidepressants and shock and he'd mistaken those qualities for frailty and composure.

Obviously, I kept that thought to myself at the time, but it did make me wonder whether Maria had since concealed what I thought of as her true personality traits. Had Chris ever got a full, no-holds-barred view of her robustness, her intelligence, or her humor, the qualities that were innate to her, that would surely reappear even a little bit once she and Zoe began to recover? Or had she kept those under wraps purposefully, not wanting to spoil the dynamics of this relationship, or the good fortune of this second chance?

I was brave then. I asked Chris about his first wife. Pure nosiness, but who isn't curious about the uncommon circumstances of a man bringing up his son alone? I'd asked Maria about it, of course, but she was either badly informed on the subject or incredibly discreet because she said very little except that Lucas's mum had died from illness when he was ten and that it had shattered him and his father. Chris had apparently not had a significant relationship between Julia's death and meeting Maria.

In the train, emboldened by a surfeit of caffeine on an empty stomach, I said, "Has it helped Lucas get over his loss, to be part of this new family?"

"Very much so." Chris's answer was swift and sure.

"How did his mother die?"

"She had a terminal brain tumor, a particularly savage one." He spoke in quite a clinical tone, but his hand twitched on the table and he began to turn his BlackBerry over and over in his palm.

"Oh. I'm so sorry." And I was. I felt a blush creeping up my neck and across my cheeks. "I shouldn't have asked."

"I don't mind. Lucas was devoted to her, of course, but it wasn't easy toward the end. She wasn't very stable. I, we, Lucas and I are so very grateful that Maria agreed to marry me. She's a wonderful woman, your sister. I'm a lucky man."

That day on the train I wondered if Maria had done the right thing keeping Zoe's past from Chris. Surely, I thought, that can't last. I resolved to advise her to tell him, when the moment was right, when he would surely understand. But the conversation never worked like that, because when I brought it up Maria was appalled. I was not, ever, ever to consider interfering in her and Zoe's life like that, she told me. She had found her soul mate and she was going to do everything she could to make it work for her and for Zoe. I was to stay quiet about their past and keep my nose out of their business.

And so I did, but in the concert hall on this stifling night I wonder again if that decision isn't destined to bite us all.

I dismantle the camera and tripod setup clumsily, and when I join everybody who's enjoying a post-concert drink I notice that the atmosphere still isn't quite the usual one of satisfaction, where the audience appears to bask in the pleasure of exchanging opinions about what they've just heard. Tonight it seems more conspiratorial. People are huddling, and some are discussing Lucas's performance, but most, I can tell, are talking about the outburst.

I strip the plastic wrap from two plates of food that have been laid out on a trestle table at the side of the room. Each has a selection of little snacks on them, which Maria made herself.

Lucas appears beside me, and he looks white. "Well done," I tell him. "You played beautifully." I say this even though it isn't entirely what I believe, and I touch his arm lightly because he's a nice kid and I always seem to have this urge to reassure him even though he's incredibly composed; maybe because he's incredibly composed.

"Is Zoe all right?" he says.

"I think so. She's with her mum. I'll call them in a minute."

"Should we go home?"

"I'll drive you and your dad back very soon."

"Do you . . . ?" He wants to ask me about what happened, I can see that written all over his face, but I say, "Let's talk about it later, OK?"

He looks at me, and now he's wearing that inscrutable gaze of his again, and after only a fraction of a pause he begins to help me.

Chris peels away from the crowd discreetly after about twenty minutes, and we find Lucas sitting in a pew in the church, doing something on his sleek little tablet, which he hastily slips into his music bag.

In my VW bus, they both seem huge: all knees and hunched shoulders.

We travel mostly in silence.

MONDAY MORNING

SAM

Zoe and I didn't talk for long that first time we met at the police station in Barnstaple. I mostly wanted to introduce myself, to reassure her as much as I could, and explain to her that I was there to help her. I wanted to try to gain her trust before detailed questioning began. And I didn't want to start that until I'd spoken to the officer on the case, to get disclosure.

I met him in the custody reception area. After a brief handshake, we took a seat in a room similar to the one that Zoe was waiting in. He had a broad, whiskery face and Punch and Judy red cheeks. His uniform was tight around the belly.

He handed me the charge sheet and told me that he was going to make an audio recording of the disclosure too. That's sensible, it's a record of what's taken place so there's nothing to argue over later, because that's my job, to find holes in the evidence: procedural or actual, it doesn't matter, either can serve my client.

He told me what they had, all of it. The police don't have to do this, they can be slippery, and disclose in stages, drawing the process out if they're inclined to. I've had disclosures that dribble out over hours, interspersed with exhausting client interviews where we're forced to run a "no comment" defense because we don't know what they're going to pull out of the bag next.

Zoe's disclosure was forthright, succinct, and the content was as depressing as possible.

When you get a good, honest exchange with an officer in this situation, normally it restores your faith in your profession, boosts you up for the daily grind of criminality, because that well-behaved, professional exchange between you both feels like an honorable thing; it pushes away the thoughts of the shysters and the ambulance chasers, the doughnut munchers and the baton wielders. You become two men, in a room, upholding the law, and there's a purity to that, a kind of distinction, which is a very rare thing on a day-to-day basis.

In Zoe's case, it made things only slightly more bearable, because the facts of her arrest were so unremittingly grim.

"She'd got herself out of the car when we got there," he said. "But she was definitely the driver. We Breathalyzed her at the scene, seventy-five mg."

My heart sank because that reading was well over the limit. She must have consumed a great deal of alcohol to be that drunk, even given her small size.

"Three passengers in the car," he continued, deadpan, though it was tough stuff to read out, even if you're a professional. "Front passenger dead at the scene, rear left-side passenger dead at the scene, rear right-side passenger transferred to Barnstaple Hospital."

He caught the question in my gaze but shook his head.

"Died half an hour ago. Massive bleed to the brain. Family agreed to turn her off."

"Christ."

"I've seen some scenes, but this was really bad. And there was music pumping from the car, you could hear it on approach, made for a strange scene, spooky."

I imagined the black night, starlight above, headlights parked at a crazy angle, a steaming engine, crumpled bodywork, shattered glass and the stereo still blasting out a loud driving tune to the broken bodies inside, only two out of the four of them producing wisps of misty breath in the cold darkness.

"She consented to a blood test at the hospital," he continued. "Confirmed she was well over the limit."

"Zoe consented?"

"And the doctor."

I might have had something to work with if Zoe alone had consented to a blood test, because of her age. It was another situation where she had to have an "appropriate adult" advising her. I was pretty sure the police had this one taped, but made a note that it was something to check.

"Road traffic report?"

"Ordered."

"How long for that?"

"As quick as we can make it—end of the week probably."

At this early stage in proceedings, part of my job was to be sure that the police had the evidence they needed to prove all the elements of the offense that the prosecution would present at court. We would need all the test results and paperwork in before I could make a proper judgment on that, but the heaviness in his voice and the apparently rigid adherence to protocol told me that as far as this area of the investigation was concerned, things weren't looking good for Zoe. If I was going to find a defense for her, I suspected it was unlikely it would lie in the procedural detail, or the facts of the accident, or the quality of her treatment afterward, because, so far, the police appeared to have done everything by the book.

"You're going to have to bail her. You can't keep her in, she's too young."

I wondered if he was going to argue this, because of the severity of what Zoe had done, but he didn't.

"We're probably happy with that, subject to conditions, of course."

"Good. We can discuss conditions. So you're charging her with 'Death by careless driving while under the influence.'"

"Sorry," he said, but he meant "Yes."

We stood. Our chairs didn't move because they were bolted to the floor. A firm handshake and he said, "It's a bad one, this. It's a shame. She's just a kid."

I nodded. I agreed with him, but I wondered whether the families of the children who died would feel that way.

Before I left the room, I said, "Does she know? About the fatalities?"

"She knows about the first two, but not about the girl who died at the hospital. Sorry."

That word again.

SUNDAY NIGHT

After the Concert

ZOE

I shut the panop app and my hands are shaking, because this is what used to happen when it all began.

In rehabilitation sessions at the Unit, Jason, my key worker, liked to stress this, and liked to make me go over and over it until he'd satisfied himself that I understood:

"What must you avoid, Zoe, when you leave here?"

"Social media."

"And which social media in particular?"

"All of it."

"And especially?"

"Well, that question doesn't make sense if we've already agreed that I'm avoiding all of it."

"Humor me."

"Panop."

"Well done."

"Can I have a gold star?"

"Don't be cheeky."

Jason was, basically, mostly awesome. He didn't take any crap from anybody.

My IQ has been officially measured as 162. This puts me

in the category of "exceptionally gifted." It means that I beat Einstein and Professor Stephen Hawking, who scored 160.

But the problem is, a high IQ doesn't necessarily mean that you're clever enough to avoid being a massive teenage cliché. Which is what I was, or what I became. Before my descent into "teen tragedy," that is.

When Jason looked over my case notes with me, at our first-ever session, this is what he said: "For somebody with a genius-level IQ you've made some pretty interesting decisions, haven't you?"

At that point, I didn't know that he was going to be as close as I would get in that place to having a knight in shining armor, because I'd only been at the Secure Unit for a week, so I said, "Screw you," which was a phrase I'd already learned from the kids on my corridor.

I didn't like the look of Jason with his film premiere facial hair, or the sound of his voice, which was boring and nasal like he had an adenoidal cold, or the stewed tea he put in front of me in a stained mug. I thought "Screw you" was a good response, but it turned out that Jason had a bit more life experience than me. Go figure.

Panop is an app where you can anonymously ask questions of others. This is what you read on the page where you can register for an account:

> Hey! Welcome to panop!
> We hate to do it, but we need to start with a word of caution . . .
> We know that some people can sometimes get ugly and transform into trolls when they get online and we're asking you nicely: if you sign up,

don't troll up. Don't do it. Ask anybody a question, but keep it nice. If you can't be nice, don't
sign up.

And if you sign up and you get asked a nasty
question, don't answer it! In fact don't respond
at all. Panop people (ppeeps!) should know their
own minds, and they should be nice. We're all
about amusement, entertainment, and good
times online!

Happy asking . . .

After I signed up to panop, aged thirteen, a brand-new
pupil in Year Nine at Hartwood House School, do you want
to know what the first question I received was?

It was this: R u a hore?

I thought it was a mistake. It even took me a few hours to
work out that it was a spelling-challenged attempt to write the
word "whore." I was that naive.

I didn't realize that I'd been seen talking to Jack Bell the
Popular Boy, who was supposed to be the exclusive property
of his sister Eva and her posse of Popular Girls at my school.
I didn't realize I wasn't supposed to talk to Jack Bell, because
nobody had explained to me that by virtue of his parents'
money and his boy band hair and low-riding jeans, Jack Bell
was Social Gold Dust, and that, as a recipient of the Year Nine
Hartwood House School music scholarship, I was automatically granted the status of Social Pond Life.

Being a music scholar meant that my parents could not
afford the school tuition, so I was not part of the Entitled. I
wasn't much better than a beggar. Everybody knew that I paid
for my schooling with my piano playing, and it subsidized my

ugly uniform too. I had to turn out at every concert and open evening, and be in every brochure, hands poised over the keyboard and smiling serenely as if the very act of being a pupil at Hartwood House School had bestowed me with any talent and opportunity that I might be so lucky as to have.

I know by now that it's possible to overcome the status of Social Pond Life if you work very hard and are prepared to make a multitude of fundamental compromises of the soul, but at the time I wasn't sharp enough even to recognize that possibility.

So I found myself talking one day, during the first few weeks of term, to Jack Bell. And Jack Bell and I got on well, or I thought we did. I didn't realize that other people were watching and judging, and testing me in fact. I didn't realize that Jack Bell was nothing more than a bright white lure dangling in front of me, blinding me to the dark, wide, gaping jaws of the beast behind, and that those jaws were lined with stiletto-sharp teeth.

There was so much I didn't realize then. "You couldn't have," said Jason. "You were naive, that's all, and probably a bit unfiltered too."

Jason, bless him, was the master of the understatement, because I was just as dumb as Forrest Gump, dumber perhaps, because I didn't even work out that what I should have done was run.

But, while I'm sitting there with my phone in my hand, remembering all of this, what totally blows my mind is that I get a text from Lucas right then. This is the most activity I've had on my mobile for days, weeks, months even. Check your email, is all it says, and although he's not exactly the master of sensitivity, I thought Lucas might at least have asked me how

I was, or something. But I do check my email anyway, and there is one from him.

The only thing the email message says is "Please read this," and then there's just a PDF attachment called "What I Know." The title of it freezes my blood for an instant, but I try to stay calm, because there's no way he could know about me, is there? It's probably just one of those lists of stupid or funny things from the Web, which is the kind of thing he usually sends me and which makes Mum and Chris annoyed because I laugh out loud unexpectedly when I read them and that is apparently "very rude to the people around you."

I open the attachment. It's a script, written by Lucas. Lucas is obsessed with film. He's not really allowed to watch any of the films he wants to in our house, but I know he's built a proxy website so when he's at school he can bypass their Internet security and watch films on his tablet there. I won't tell, but I know. Lucas is clever in his quiet way.

I start to read.

"WHAT I KNOW"

A SCRIPT FOR FILM

BY LUCAS KENNEDY

Dear Maria and Zoe,

I'm sending you this to
explain a bit about how things
were before my mum died.

This is a film script I wrote to
tell the story of what happened to me,
my mum, and my dad, before we met you,
and I hope you will read it.

Please read it.

Love from Lucas

ACT I

**INT. PRIVATE HOSPITAL ROOM. VERY WELL
APPOINTED. NIGHT.**

A woman, JULIA, in her early thirties, but
looking much older due to her condition,
lies completely still in a hospital bed.
She was clearly beautiful once, and there
are traces of this in her fine, symmetrical
features and long dark hair, which spreads
out over the pillow, framing her face.

We might see a vase of flowers, and just
one or two get-well cards around the side
of the room, which is immaculately clean,
extremely well appointed, and brightly lit.
JULIA is getting the finest medical care
available.

Beside her bed sits her son, LUCAS, 10
years old, who is holding one of her hands
in both of his. He is a lovely, wide-eyed,
dark-haired little boy. Mostly, his head
hangs low, though at times he looks up
and pulls her hand carefully to rest on
his cheek, and when he does that we might
see a tear fall. As her voice-over (V.O.)
begins he raises his head to look at her,
and adjusts her hair on the pillow so that
it looks nice.

When JULIA speaks her voice is warm. She
sounds like somebody who you would like to
have as a friend.

>   DYING JULIA (V.O.)
>   This is not how I would have liked
>   to meet you. I would have liked
>   to have been on my feet, with
>   my hair brushed, and at least a
>   little bit of makeup on. And I
>   would have preferred not to be
>   wearing a nightie. If you had come
>   to our house, I would have invited
>   you in and offered you a cup of
>   tea and a biscuit, or maybe even
>   a fresh muffin if Lucas and I had
>   been baking that day. We could
>   have chatted in the sunlight at my
>   kitchen table, and it would have
>   been nice.

The camera is traveling around the bed
so we see JULIA's frailty, her pale skin
and the stillness of her body. She's not
breathing independently.

>   DYING JULIA (V.O.)
>   The end isn't far away now, as you
>   can probably see, and a big part
>   of me is desperately grateful to
>   have Lucas here with me, because

I never want to have to leave
him; but I will admit that there's
another part of me that's relieved
that it's nearly over, because
what I can't stand any longer is
watching Lucas watching me die.
It's been a brutal, lingering
process, in spite of my efforts
to hasten it. But we're nearly in
the closing stages. I've already
had one massive heart attack, you
see, and I'm about to have another,
which will be fatal.

We see a "Do Not Resuscitate" order pinned
to the end of JULIA's bed.

           DYING JULIA (V.O.)
Is that a heartless thing to do?
Lucas wept when they explained
what the DNR order meant, and
he screamed at the doctors. But
it's necessary, so that things
don't drag on, and so that my
boy doesn't suffer more than he
needs to. You see, I had an idea
that in spite of my best efforts
to leave him cleanly, my lovely,
intuitive boy might find an
excuse to come home from school

early on the day I did it, that
he might beg for me to be saved,
whatever state I was in.

**INT. CHRIS AND JULIA'S BEDROOM. DAY. A FEW
HOURS EARLIER.**

JULIA lies on her bed in a sumptuous,
tasteful, and beautiful bedroom. She's
already unconscious. Beside her lie
multiple bottles of pills, all empty. One
of her hands is loosely draped over a
bottle of water. An envelope is on her
chest. "To whom it may concern" is written
on the front of it. We hear frantic
knocking on the bedroom door.

> LUCAS (out of sight)
> Mum? Mum! Mummy! Are you in there?
> Mum!

We hear the sound of the door being kicked
in an increasingly frenzied way, and
then a different kind of thudding, as if
somebody is throwing their entire body
weight against it. After that, silence.

LUCAS (out of sight) (CONT'D)
Yes, hello, ambulance, please,
yes, and fire brigade. Please come
quickly. It's my mum.

**INT. PRIVATE HOSPITAL ROOM. VERY WELL
APPOINTED. NIGHT.**

We find JULIA and LUCAS in exactly the same
positions as before. We also see a younger
CHRIS standing on the other side of the
door, looking through it, at JULIA and
LUCAS. He has the palm of his hand on the
glass. He looks full of despair.

DYING JULIA (V.O.)
That's my husband, Chris. He's
as distraught as our son at this
moment. He wants to be with me
too, but he's allowing our child
time to say goodbye in his
own way.

The camera has made a full circle of
the room now, and we see JULIA's
monitoring machines, slowly beeping.
One of the readings seems to falter,
before settling back into a steady
rhythm again, and LUCAS stares at it,
alarmed. He gestures to CHRIS, who

calls a NURSE. She bustles in, checks
things, then lays a hand on LUCAS's
shoulder to reassure him. He sits back
down and now CHRIS sits behind him.
It's a vigil.

          DYING JULIA (V.O.)
No, don't worry. It's not quite
time yet. There are a few more
moments, and while I have them,
I want to tell you my story.
It's the story of Chris and me,
of our life, and the baby we
had together, who we named Lucas.
And I'm going to start the story
when Chris was just fifteen
years old.

INT. A YOUNG MAN'S BEDROOM. NIGHT.

A teenage CHRIS is sitting at a desk
surrounded by books and papers, and
he's working in longhand on a pad of
paper, writing furiously, pausing only
to check facts in a textbook or
cross-reference some notes. We might
see that the room is quite dark apart
from a single lamp illuminating his desk.
A bare bulb hangs from the ceiling,
but it's broken. The room isn't quite

squalid, but it's not comfortable either.
We might see that a clock on CHRIS's
desk shows that it's past midnight.

> DYING JULIA (V.O.)
> Christopher Kennedy was an only
> child in a family where he had a
> mum and a dad, but where crack
> cocaine was sometimes the third,
> and always the most unpredictable,
> parent in the house.

We hear violent shouting coming from
outside the room, and the unmistakable
sound of somebody being struck. CHRIS
winces, but keeps working; he's used to
this. Seconds later, a door slams and the
sobbing we hear is a hopeless, defeated
sound, like the whimpers of a beaten dog.
Then we hear CHRIS'S MOTHER call to him.

> CHRIS'S MOTHER (O.O.S.)
> Christopher darling, come and help
> me. Please, come and help me.

CHRIS pauses to listen. We see various
emotions working across his face, and at
first he puts his pen down and appears
to be about to get up, but then his
expression changes to one of resolve. He
reaches for a pair of headphones, which

he puts on before resuming his work. With
him, we hear piano music soaring, and the
sobbing is drowned out. CHRIS's expression
changes to one of calm focus.

> DYING JULIA (V.O.)
> Chris knew, from a very young age,
> that the only person who could
> help him get anywhere was himself.
> So he became self-reliant, and he
> put in hours of work.

**INT. THE WILLS MEMORIAL BUILDING, BRISTOL
UNIVERSITY. DAY.**

CHRIS is attending a graduation ceremony.
We hear his name called and see him
walking up onto the podium to collect his
graduation certificate. The large audience
applauds.

> DYING JULIA (V.O.)
> Chris's hard work paid off. He
> graduated with a first-class
> degree in computer science from
> Bristol University, at age 19, one
> of the youngest ever to do so. And
> after that, he kept his head down,
> and things continued to go well
> for him.

INT. CHRIS'S OFFICE IN THE COMPUTER SCIENCE DEPARTMENT AT BRISTOL UNIVERSITY. NIGHT.

We might see city lights sparkling outside, through a small, high window. It's a poky space, with a desk and a very plain student-type sofa crammed into it.

> DYING JULIA (V.O.)
> The University of Bristol gave him an office all of his own to develop his ideas in. If he stood in the right place, he could even see a view. And he didn't rest on his laurels, because before long Chris had an idea that made some other people very excited indeed.

We see Chris staring at his screen. He writes an email and we can see the text: "I think I've bloody done it." He clicks the "send" button.

INT. AN OFFICE IN THE HOME OF AN INVESTOR. NIGHT.

An older, wealthy-looking man sits at a desk in a room that looks the way you might imagine a gentlemen's club. He

receives Chris's email. He smiles when he
reads it and composes an email in reply.
It says, "WE'RE GOING TO MAKE A KILLING."
He presses "send."

**INT. CHRIS'S NEW OFFICE AT THE UNIVERSITY.
DAY.**

CHRIS's new office is bigger and lighter,
and the view of the city is extensive
and impressive. The only thing that
remains the same is the sofa, looking
a little older and scruffier, but still
there.

CHRIS lies on the sofa, he's wearing a
headset, and is on a call.

> DYING JULIA (V.O.)
> Chris got upgraded to a new office
> by the university, and deservedly
> so. His business idea was a good
> one. In fact, it was a great one,
> and he got a particularly tempting
> offer from an investment fund to
> turn it into a business.

CHRIS is speaking on the phone via his
headset, and, as he does, sits up in
excitement.

> YOUNG CHRIS

An order for five thousand? That's
good. That's very, very good, a
great start, solid ...
> (listens)

Sorry? Fifty thousand? Are you
joking? I thought you said ...
> (listens)

Fifty thousand? That's, well that's
just incredible.

> DYING JULIA (V.O.)

And the business began to do so
well, so quickly, that he didn't
need the support of the university
anymore. He set up on his own,
and the investment fund gave him
enough support that he could even
afford to hire an assistant.

INT. A COFFEE SHOP. DAY.

CHRIS is sitting at a small table with a
sheaf of papers in front of him. A young
woman, JULIA, enters and approaches the
table.

> JULIA

Hello? Are you Chris?

                    CHRIS
Yes! Hello! Julia?

                    JULIA
Yes. It's me. Should I?

                    CHRIS
Yes! Sorry! Please! Take a seat.

CHRIS jumps out of his seat and pulls out
a chair for JULIA. It looks like a bit of
a hasty gesture from a man who perhaps
isn't used to displaying polished manners,
and is clumsy enough that people at other
tables notice, one or two maybe smiling
discreetly at his display of keenness.
CHRIS and JULIA sit facing each other and
he stares at her, forgetting to speak.

                    JULIA
So . . .

                    CHRIS
Yes!

                    JULIA
Here's my CV.

                    CHRIS
Right! Yes! Thank you.

CHRIS skims down the CV quickly, as it's
only one sheet.

                    CHRIS (CONT'D)
          Looks great. Perfect. Do you have
          any questions?

                    JULIA
          Oh! Me? OK, well, I was wondering
          if I was experienced enough for
          the position?
                    (realizing)
          Oh, gosh, sorry, that's such a
          stupid thing to say. I'm so sorry.

CHRIS is jolted out of his infatuated
stare and bursts out laughing.

                    CHRIS
          That is the worst interview
          technique I've ever heard!

                    JULIA
          I should go. I'm sorry. This is the
          first job I've ever applied for. I
          don't know what I'm doing.

                    CHRIS
          No! No—sorry, I didn't mean to
          upset you. Stay, please. Let's
          talk about the job. And I should

probably ask you some questions.
Before we start, would you like
something to drink?

DYING JULIA (V.O.)
I had a hot chocolate. With cream
on top. And so did he.

EXT. A PRETTY STREET. A FINE, COLD EVENING.

The camera moves along the time-worn
slabs of a fine old pavement toward the
well-lit window of a restaurant. It's a
small place, and at a table tucked into
the window we see CHRIS and JULIA, one
on either side of an intimate table, both
noticeably better dressed and less awkward
than they were at their first meeting.
Candlelight glints off the wineglasses
they're sipping from, and they both lean
back as the waiter arrives with plates of
food, though they don't take their eyes
off each other. They look warm, cozy, and
very happy.

DYING JULIA (V.O.)
And it wasn't too long before
Chris was having to interview for
a new office assistant, because I
was promoted to the position of

fiancée. He swept me off my feet.
He expressed feelings for me that
were so intense they were like
nothing I'd experienced before.
It was intoxicating. And with all
the optimism of young love, we
felt that we owned our lives, and
our city, and that anything was
possible, and that a future without
each other would be impossible.

Inside the restaurant, once the waiter
has moved away, CHRIS takes a small box
from his pocket and hands it to JULIA.
She opens it and it is, of course,
a ring, a beautiful diamond ring. We
see her delight, and how much this moves
her as well. We see her mouth the word
"yes," and then the camera moves away
from the restaurant window to show the
street once again, and this time we
might notice pretty Christmas lights,
before the camera moves out farther
still, up and over Clifton Village to
show us the Suspension Bridge, lit up
spectacularly, and looking ethereal as
it hangs over the deep gorge. It's a
romantic, gorgeous scene and we might
even see a full moon hanging over it too,
looking crisp and hopeful in the winter
night.

> DYING JULIA (V.O.)
> It was one of the happiest nights
> of my life.

INT. GOLDNEY HALL ORANGERY IN CLIFTON, BRISTOL. DAY.

CHRIS and JULIA are standing in the middle of a fine Georgian room lined with floor-to-ceiling sash windows overlooking a beautiful garden. Chandeliers hang above them and under their feet the floor is made from slabs of soft golden stone.

> DYING JULIA (V.O.)
> Chris and I arranged the wedding together, every detail. He wanted the very best.

JULIA takes CHRIS's hand.

> JULIA
> Do you think it's too big?

> CHRIS
> I think it's perfect.

And we can see from the excitement on JULIA's face that she does too, but she wanted him to say it first.

INT. GOLDNEY HALL ORANGERY. DAY.

The orangery is lavishly decorated for a
wedding ceremony, and a modest number of
people are gathered at one end, seated
around CHRIS and JULIA, the bride and
groom, who stand before them and hold
hands as they face each other and say
their vows.

> DYING JULIA (V.O.)
> Of course the room was too big
> for our little ceremony, but Chris
> invited a lot of colleagues to make
> up for the very small number of
> family both of us had. His parents
> weren't there. He said that his
> family meant nothing to him, that
> he didn't want to talk about them.

We see the crowd consists of a large posse
of well-dressed professional folk watching
the ceremony.

> DYING JULIA (V.O.)
> My mother came. Alone, because
> since my father abandoned us
> when I was a baby, she said she
> preferred it.

We see a rather lovely woman, JULIA'S
MOTHER, sitting at the front, where she
has a good view of her daughter. She is
dressed extremely plainly, wears only a
little makeup but has beautiful flowers
in the lapel of her jacket and wears a
carefully positioned hat.

              DYING JULIA (V.O.)
She was grateful to Chris for
paying for the wedding, because
her budget wouldn't have run much
past two dozen sausage rolls and
a cash bar at the social club,
and it made her proud to see me
entering a marriage that had so
much more hope than her own,
because, if truth be told, I had
figured prominently at her wedding,
in the shape of a large bump, and
was a source of shame to both
parties. But we'll gloss over that.
And I was glad she came, because
I loved her very much, and sadly
she died shortly afterward, but it
meant the world to her to know
that I was happily married before
she went.

We see a smile creep across JULIA'S
MOTHER's face and then the camera swings
around to show us what she sees: it's the
bride and groom leaning in to kiss each
other as the crowd claps.

When they break away from each other
CHRIS stands with his arm around JULIA,
squeezing her tight and smiling broadly.

                    CHRIS
        My wife! I've got a wife!

And everybody laughs while JULIA looks a
little embarrassed but very happy.

SUNDAY NIGHT

After the Concert

ZOE

I stop reading because I hear my mum coming down the stairs, finally. The script is quite interesting, but it's mostly just a love story between Chris and Julia so far and it's told in the voice of Lucas's dying mum, which I find really weird, so I'm not one hundred percent fully interested if I'm honest, also because I don't see what it's got to do with me.

Really, I'm not exactly sure why Lucas was so keen for me and Mum to read it.

I put my phone down, in fact I push it down the side of the sofa cushions because the panop thing is still making my palms sweat a bit so I don't even really want to look at it, and I go and wait in the hall for my mum as she comes down the stairs, her hand trailing on the polished banister. When she gets to the bottom, she first puts her finger on her lips to keep me quiet so we don't wake the baby, and then beckons me to follow her into the kitchen.

I follow her in there, and she gets a wineglass out of the cupboard and pours herself a hefty slug from a bottle that starts to drip with condensation now that it's out of the fridge. I wait, listening to the glass chinking on the granite, and I straighten my dress, because since we've been in the Second Chance Family she likes me to look nice, and I think I'm probably a bit mussed up from lying on the sofa.

She drinks deeply, twice, then she says, "Zoe," and I say, "Yes," and I'm full of fear because this is the moment that she and I have to come together, so that we can decide what we have to do. From the railway-station-sized clock on the kitchen wall I estimate we have about seventeen minutes left to do it in before Tessa and the men get here.

"I think . . ." Mum says, and with her fingers and her palms she makes a motion that smooths her cheeks up; it's a temporary facelift. And in spite of everything, a tiny part of me glows, because I feel a little bit happy that we're going to do this together, that we're going to do anything together in fact, because that hasn't really happened for a very long time.

And my heart's pumping like the loud techno music beats that make cars shudder, because now's the moment, but then she says, and her tone is as bright as Grace's mobile: "Do you know what I think would be nice? I think we should make some bruschetta for the boys."

MONDAY MORNING

SAM

At Barnstaple Police Station, when I returned to talk to Zoe after the disclosure, I found her in exactly the same position as before, curled up in her plastic chair, social worker sitting silently beside her.

Zoe watched me come in and sit down, hungover eyes following me like a cat's under that glass-spangled hair.

"Hello again," I said.

"Hello."

"Now. Have you let anybody know that you've been arrested?"

"They phoned Mum."

"Would you like your mum to be in here with us?"

"No."

The social worker's lips pursed, but she remained quiet.

"Can you tell me why?"

"I didn't want her to know."

"She's outside, Zoe, she knows you're here, and she knows why. You're not going to be able to keep this a secret from her."

An immediate firm shake of her head, so I didn't push it. A

fragment of glass fell out of her hair and onto the table in front of her and she put a finger on it, curious, almost hypnotized by the sight of it. It looked like a small diamond.

"Don't," I said, but I was too late. The glass cut her finger and she pulled it sharply away and put it into her mouth. The little shard skittered away across the table and onto the floor.

"I'll get the first-aider," said the social worker.

"It's OK," Zoe said. "It's nothing." She held her finger up to show us just a tiny bead of blood welling there, then she sucked it away.

The social worker rummaged in her bag and handed Zoe a tissue. We both watched her wrap it tightly around her finger until the tip went white.

"Well, if you change your mind at any point, then we can call Mum in. What about your dad?"

Another head shake, even firmer this time.

"Do you feel well enough to talk to me now?" Close up, she looked worse than I'd thought. They told me that she'd puked at the hospital.

"Yes."

"Your welfare is important to everybody here, so you must let me or . . ."

"Ruth," said the social worker.

"You must let me or Ruth know straightaway if you're too unwell to talk, or for any other reason. Ruth is here to support you, and I am, as I've told you, a solicitor, and that means that I want to make sure you get the right advice to help you in your situation and also to help you understand anything that happens this morning or that happened last night. And, most important, and this is why you need to tell us if you're not coping at any point, I need to make sure that you completely understand what effects any statements or responses you give to the police might mean."

"I'm OK."

I wondered where this stoicism came from. I didn't yet know about the piano, about her capacity for discipline and self-control, and her hunger for excellence, but the intelligence was beginning to emerge. There was sharp clarity in those eyes.

"Do you live locally, Zoe?"

"Between Hartland and Clovelly, at East Wildberry Farm."

"Near the Point?"

"Yes. That's where we were going."

"In the car? To the Point?"

"To the lighthouse."

"Why?"

"Because Jack said I could use his dad's car to drive Gull home, but only on condition we went to the lighthouse on the way."

I thought of Hartland Point lighthouse, because I knew it well. To get to it you had to sneak past some locked gates and descend a rubbly, steep cliff path to the shore, where black rocks lined the edges of the tide line like shark's teeth and the lighthouse sat on an outcrop that was fortified by a sea wall, to save it from being beaten away by waves. It was no longer occupied and the light was about to be decommissioned entirely. There were empty buildings beside it, where the lighthouse keepers used to live.

Four drunk teenagers planning to go down there on a dark, cold night sounded like a bad business to me.

"Why did Jack want to go to the lighthouse?"

She calculated something behind those eyes before she replied. "I don't know."

I changed tack. "How do you know how to drive?"

"My dad taught me, on the farm."

"Why were you driving when Jack was old enough to have a license?"

"Jack was pissed. He was too pissed to drive."

"But you were drunk as well."

"I wasn't. I only had a spritzer."

"According to the police your blood alcohol level was twice the limit."

"I wasn't drunk."

I left the denial for now. I'd tease that out later. If she somehow didn't know she was drunk, we might have a defense to build there.

"Why did Gull want to leave the party?"

"Because she got sick, and she wanted to go home."

"Sick from drinking?"

"I think so."

"Were you with her?"

"She came to find me when she got sick."

"Are you friends?"

"She's my best friend."

"And where were you when she came to find you?"

"With Jack."

"Where were you and Jack?"

"In the bedroom."

I wrote this down while the social worker shuffled in her seat, and I wondered if it was defiance that I heard in her tone. I was going to need to know every detail later, but for now

I decided that I wouldn't push her, because when I looked at her I could see that she was fading, and I thought she might throw up.

"I think we should take a break, because I don't believe you're well enough for an interview this morning. But before we stop, is there anything else you want me to know, Zoe? We're going to talk lots more, but is there anything you want me to know now?"

"It's Gull's birthday today," she said, and she began to cry.

SUNDAY NIGHT

After the Concert

ZOE

"Bruschetta?" I ask Mum. This is a perfect example of why she's insane to deal with sometimes. We all ate before we came out, so nobody will be hungry when they get back from the concert. I'm one hundred percent sure that Key Worker Jason would say that making bruschetta at this moment is a classic example of displacement activity.

"Yes, I think we will," she says. She's not actually listening to me at all; she's just answering herself. She crosses the kitchen, her shoes tapping on the stone floor. She's still wearing her heels from the concert. She heaves open the door of our fridge. "Now let's see . . ." she says. "Have we got what we need?"

My mum has a very big fridge. It's big enough that you could stuff a body inside it. Lucas says that. He once said, "Do you think if we put Grace in the fridge she would stop crying? Or at least we wouldn't be able to hear her."

I laughed really hard at that, partly because Lucas doesn't often make a joke when we're all together, so I thought it would be good to laugh, to encourage him, and partly because I pictured Grace in the fridge in a Tupperware box, just like my mum stores all the leftover food. And I don't mean that in a morbid way—everybody always thinks I mean things morbidly—it was just funny.

"Black humor," said Jason the Key Worker to me once, taking off his glasses and massaging his frown lines so deeply it was like he was looking for something lost in there, "can be a tool to deal with your emotions and you'll hear it a lot while you're in the Unit, but you have to be very, very careful, Zoe, about how you use it when you're back in the outside world."

Mum went white as a Mini Milk lollipop when Lucas said that, and even whiter when I laughed ultra loudly. At the time, Grace was so tiny that she just spent most of her time draped over Mum's shoulder with slimy bubbles popping out of her mouth.

Chris went ballistic, which isn't really a good description of him being cross. When my dad used to go ballistic he would shout, and his hands would fly everywhere, and once he threw a baked potato on the floor and it exploded everywhere, and him and Mum and me killed ourselves laughing.

Chris isn't like that, he's far too polite. His version of ballistic is that he just went a bit rigid and said to Lucas, "Could we have a little chat?" and they left the room and I heard the sound of them talking on and on in Chris's study down the hallway. In the kitchen my mum put on Radio 3 and said, "You didn't need to laugh like that," and I felt ashamed. When Lucas and Chris came back in, Lucas said, "Sorry, Maria, what I said was inappropriate," and Mum said, "I understand it was only a joke, Lucas, but I appreciate the apology. It's fine," and Chris pointed out that if he wasn't mistaken, that was Barenboim playing Beethoven on the radio, so we all listened to that.

Mum has pulled a packet of small, plump tomatoes out of the fridge. They're the size of big marbles. "Please can we talk about Mr. Barlow?" I say to her. She begins unwrapping the packet and pulling out the tomatoes; they're blooming with redness and still attached to their stalk.

"Yes! OK, yes!" she says, but then, "I think these are small and sweet enough that we won't have to skin them. Pass me some garlic, will you, please? We're going to need, let's see, probably two large cloves or three small ones."

In the pantry, I find the garlic, a chunky plait of fat papery bulbs hanging from a shiny metal hook. It's cooler than the kitchen in the pantry and I feel like staying there, resting my head on the marble surface where there's a chocolate fudge cake in a tin. Quietly I open the tin and stick my finger into the icing in the middle of the cake, where I won't leave a trace. I scoop deeply and it's productive. I suck the chocolate off my finger and then smooth the icing over so nobody will notice. Easy.

I try to think of ways to talk to Mum about Amelia Barlow's dad.

When I come out of the pantry I push the garlic cloves (two big ones) across the granite island toward her. It's a large island, and the granite is a dense, polished black. Chris and Mum spent three weeks choosing it. Chris brought loads of samples home and he said it was her choice, but I know she would have preferred something lighter, like the one where the pattern looks like grains of sand, in beiges and whites, with just a sprinkle of black in there. She went for the ebony granite to please him, for sure, because they always try to outdo each other to see who can please the other one the most. Lucas says they're probably eternally trapped in a cycle of mutual congratulation now, that they'll be doing it until death does them part. He says it's because they're both afraid of being alone.

When I went to Gull's grave it was black granite too, but it had silver shreds speckling it. I think Gull would have liked that; she loved a bit of bling, and definitely not in an ironic way. The churchyard had a view of the sea. Gull's grave was black sparkling granite against the so-green fields and the freezing gray ocean, which, on the afternoon we went to visit, was churning out huge, violent waves like a warning, and the wind was so strong we had to turn our backs to it.

The headstone would have cost a fortune, my mum said. More than Gull's family had, because she was a scholarship girl at Hartwood House School like me. The only difference was that she won her scholarship because she was good at sports. We bonded over it. It meant we could be Social Pond Life together.

I wanted to spend more time at Gull's grave, but it was important that we mustn't be seen, because people would have been angry. I had to wear a beanie hat to cover up my ice-maiden hair. I had to wrap a scarf high up around my neck.

Mum is holding a large knife and she's sawing at a baguette with it now, using precise, quick diagonal cuts. I'm looking for an opening in her activity so I can say something, but I don't think I'm going to get one, so I just say, "Mum."

"This is yesterday's," she says, "so it's a bit stale, but that's fine."

"Mum."

"It's probably better actually. For bruschetta." She says it the Italian way: "brusketta." Chris would like that. He took her to Italy for two weeks before Grace was born, and when they

came back, Mum pronounced everything the correct Italian
way. She had lots of time to read the phrase book, she said,
and improve her Italian, which was the silver lining of twisting her ankle on her fourth day there. My mum puts a lot of
store in silver linings. Go figure.

I estimate that there will be three more noisy crumb-
scratchy slices to cut until she's finished. Then she'll have to
acknowledge me. The sawing sound is relentless, but finally
the knife goes down onto the granite with a clatter and the
serrated edge catches the light as it falls. There are crumbs everywhere and a neat, stacked pile of bread, cut on the diagonal
like in the magazines.

"Mummy," I say again. I know I'm too old to call her
Mummy, I know that, but she's not listening to me. "Mummy.
What will we tell them?"

She swallows and does multiple blinks, which is a sign of
tension for her, and begins to brush the crumbs off the granite,
cupping one hand at the edge and sweeping the crumbs into it
with the other. Her movements are fast, but not as efficient as
usual. She's being hasty, and crumbs are falling on the floor.
I notice she's drunk two-thirds of her glass of wine already;
she must have had a good slug when I was in the pantry. The
glass is sweating so much it looks thirsty itself.

"We're going to tell them it was a mistake," she says
brightly. "That we don't know the man and that he made a
mistake!" I can see small patches of damp under each armpit
and a single lock of hair that's fallen onto her forehead and
looks greasy from the heat. She'd hate that, if she could see it.

"But you said his name."

"Don't argue with me, Zoe. Just! Don't! I need to *think*!"

Her voice is shockingly shrill and it makes my spine snap straight.

She blows at the greasy bit of hair, she can feel it, and it rises and then falls back onto her forehead, right where it was before.

"God, it's hot!" she says, and she gets a fresh tea towel out of the drawer where they all sit perfectly clean and pressed and folded, and she dabs her forehead with it. Her hands are definitely shaking, and I'm suddenly suffused with the loneliness that's been my real punishment since the accident. I'm riddled with it. It eats me up like a cancer; it spreads into my brain and makes me feel as though I'm going mad. I'm lonely because I'm never allowed to talk about it in the Second Chance Family, even though it happened, and it's a part of me, and I can't change that. I'm so freaking lonely, it's even worse than it was before it happened. But on the subject of loneliness it's best to be absolutely silent.

So I sit on a stool on the other side of the kitchen island from my mum, and watch while she starts on the tomatoes, chopping them into tiny, tiny little pieces, minuscule pieces that she heaps up into a moist fleshy mountain on the edge of the cutting board, and then she grabs handfuls of basil from the plants she has in pots in the middle of the island, and she starts to rip them up, and the little shredded pieces tumble into a white bowl.

"You see, you always *rip* basil, Zoe. You never cut it, because that crushes its edges. Tear it to let the flavor out gently," she says. But the tearing she's doing is not gentle, it's rough, and I can see that the torn little leaves are bruised.

She never did this kind of cooking instruction before we

lived with Chris, but she never seems to stop doing it now. I think it's because he loves it when she does it. He says it's "part of a proper upbringing" and he can't wait for Mum to teach Grace the "alchemy of cooking" and he says that Lucas should listen when Mum is sharing her knowledge.

But I don't want my mum to talk to me like this when it's just me and her and so I can't help it, as she gets started on the garlic, unwrapping the nubbly cloves, starting to chop them in half, I get tearful again. I have to breathe deeply because I know she won't want me to cry because that's against the rule of Preferably No Crying (subgenre: especially when Chris might be on his way home), but I'm overwhelmed with it and I have to start breathing through my nose to try to stop it, but that doesn't work, so I'm silently convulsing when I hear the knife stop after just a couple of firm chops. The smell of the garlic is pungent.

"Sweetheart," she says and for the first time since we crouched together in the room at the back of the church I think I might be able to hear a bit of warmth in her voice again, and I look at her, and her face is worn out, the way mine feels, but then we hear two little beeps from a car horn, which is what Aunt Tessa always does when she arrives at our house, and I see in Mum's eyes that she's as aware as I am that time has just run out, because they're back.

"Leave it with me," she says. "Just don't admit to anything. *Nothing at all.* Promise me?"

Her chin goes up and I can tell she wants to go and meet them at the door, but she's waiting for me to agree.

I nod and then I say, "Wait!" and she turns back to me. I come toward her, where she's hovering at the entrance to the hall, and I tend to the front of her hair so that the little greasy strand is hidden, and she looks smooth and lovely, just like Chris will want her to.

"Thank you," she says, and she adjusts the strap of my dress on my shoulder, tucks my hair behind my ears and I reckon we might, maybe, just still have a second or two to talk, but then she says, "Go and wash your face. Quick as you can. And when you come down, you can oil and toast the bread slices."

SUNDAY NIGHT

After the Concert

TESSA

I park on the street outside Chris and Maria's house. There are so many beautifully manicured shrubs in their driveway that I always avoid parking on it because I'm afraid my VW bus will cause them fatal damage if I have to perform any sort of reversing maneuver when it's time to leave. There are also two stone pillars to avoid, which grandly frame the entrance to the drive, chipped and old in golden stone, and I don't want to be the one to topple them.

The gravel crunches as we walk across it, three abreast, and Maria opens the door as we get there. She shares Zoe's ice-maiden looks, only her hair's much shorter than Zoe's, cropped into a bob. Considering everything, she looks reasonably composed.

She focuses her attention on Chris, stepping toward him in a light movement.

"Hello, darling," she says and she places the palm of her hand on one of his cheeks and plants a kiss on the other, which he offers with a practiced motion, though it looks, tonight, as if it might need a little oiling. Maria and Chris are always dancing around each other like this, their actions reminding me of choreographed mime. They're somehow able to fit an appropriately socially smooth movement to almost any situation. If I tried to kiss Richard like that, one of us would somehow be in the wrong place and there would be an awkwardness of some description. Sam might be a different matter, though I can't know that because our relationship has never been for public consumption; we've never had to present a face to the world because anything to do with us is an entirely secret, private thing.

I wouldn't have got out of my car at all except that I thought Maria might need some solidarity tonight. Normally, I would have just dropped the boys off and legged it.

Chris says nothing, once he's taken receipt of his kiss, but he looks at her carefully.

"How was the concert?" she asks, as if nothing untoward had happened at all.

Chris looks at Lucas, who clearly has to scrabble around mentally for an answer, because his mind is elsewhere.

"Fine," is all he comes up with.

"Bit of work needed on the Scarlatti, I think, but otherwise not too bad," says Chris, and Maria says, "Well, I'm sure you did brilliantly," and when she turns to go into the house Chris steps forward quickly and follows her with his hand on her lower back, as if guiding her in.

Lucas gives me a "ladies first" gesture, but I hate that kind of formality. Instead, I link my arm in his and I say, "Help an old lady in, would you?" and he doesn't smile but nor does he protest, and I hope he doesn't notice the deep breath I'm taking as we cross the threshold and the heavily glossed door clicks shut behind us.

Ahead of us, Chris is saying to Maria, "Darling, could we have a quick word?" but she's ready for that.

"Can it wait?" she says. "I'm afraid I've got to see to the bruschetta."

SUNDAY NIGHT

After the Concert

ZOE

I wash my face, and I'm careful not to get my hair wet. I reapply a little bit of makeup, then I brush my hair until it's silky. I want to shower and change my clothes, to rid myself of the concert, and of Tom Barlow, of Katya and Barney and the message on my phone. I want to curl up in my bedroom, which is my refuge, my nest, my safe place, but I know I can't.

In the mirror I look like I always do: white hair halo, blue eyes, skin like wax. "Like a princess," Jack Bell said as he held my chin and gently tilted my head up toward his. People always say I look like a princess. Lucas refuted that when I told him. He says it's a white middle-class fantasy (subgenres: Northern European and North American) that princesses are small, blond, pale creatures with barely formed features.

Jack Bell called me a princess at a party he had at his house, on the night of the accident. Then he pulled my hand to him and put it on his stomach.

"Zoe Guerin," he said. "Why's your name French?"

"My dad's family was French about a hundred years ago," I said.

"I bet you know the exact date, don't you?" He was mocking me because I always had my hand up to answer questions at school, but I didn't mind.

I could feel under my palm that Jack Bell's stomach was muscly. Even though it was so cold outside that the fields were beginning to glow white with a night frost, he was just wearing a T-shirt. I'd been watching him shed layers of clothing as he danced, waiting for the looks to come my way. And they did: a look and then a smile, and now we're close enough that my hand is on his stomach, my fingers splaying a bit wider.

I liked Jack Bell, even though he could be mean sometimes, like when he ignored me at school if he was in a group with his friends. In spite of that, I really liked him. If I'm honest, I thought about him all the time.

Jack Bell played the male hero in every fantasy I had. In my mind, we were husband and wife, friends for life; we were a perfect cadence at the end of a piece of music: harmonious, satisfying, whole, meant to be.

I think that's why it shocked me in a way, the actual touching of him, because Jack Bell was so much in my mind then that the real feel of him was strange. His breath smelled of alcohol and his skin was sweaty, and I wasn't sure I liked it, but still my fingers widened on his abdomen.

"Come with me," he whispered into my ear.

I looked for Gull. She was across the other side of the room, talking to one of Jack's friends, laughing at something he'd said.

Jack took me into a room just down the corridor. It was a bedroom. He shut the door and put his hands on my waist and then ran them up my sides, crinkling the folds of my dress. It felt like hot water was pouring through me. The intensity of it made me push him away a little.

Jack Bell smiled and took me to the bed. "Sit with me," he said and so I did, and we were side by side on the extra-bouncy mattress. I tried it out, laughing as I bounced higher. "Come here," said Jack and we kissed for a minute all awkwardly because we were sitting next to each other. It was my first ever kiss. His hand touched one of my breasts and I jumped. Jack said, "Where's your drink? Let me get you another drink."

I'd had one spritzer already, and I knew I couldn't have any more alcohol. That was essential because I wasn't even used to it, and I shouldn't have even been at the party because I had a piano competition the next afternoon, so I said, "Just a Coke, please."

"Are you sure you wouldn't like something stronger?"

"Coke is good."

"Sure?" That smile tempted me to say yes, but I didn't.

"Just a Coke."

"You always know what you want, don't you, Zoe? Did you want me to notice your figure in that dress?"

A little thrill of guilt passed over me when he said that, because I did want him to notice me, but I also thought he was wrong in a way, because I was never *sure* what I wanted, never ever. I'm still not.

"Will you check on Gull?" I asked. "She might be wondering where I am."

"Yep," and he stared at me for just a moment before he left the room and the door shut softly behind him. I fell backward onto the bed, and stared up at the ceiling and wondered why, if this was one of life's moments, it felt bad and good all at the same time.

And just the memory of that moment still gives me a powerful sensation of falling, even now.

I'm pulled away from it, though, all of a sudden, because I'm distracted by movement. Something is flying around the bathroom.

At first I think it's a moth, and I turn off the bathroom light quickly, because I don't want it to bombard the light and flap around me, but as my eyes adjust to the darkness I'm surprised to see that it's a butterfly, because they don't usually fly at night. It seems to like the darkness because it settles on the edge of the mirror and closes its wings.

The reflection of the butterfly in the mirror transfixes me. Its ragged-edged wings look as if they're made of striated layers of dark iridescent powder, which reflect and absorb the light from the chandelier in the hall in uncountable numbers of tiny, unreliable glimmers. It's like a living shadow.

I stand very still and it rewards me by opening its wings wide, just for a second, revealing brilliant color—a flash of deep red and patches of blue, black, and yellow—and I know at once it's a peacock butterfly. When I was little my dad and I would watch out for butterflies in our fields, and we would name them all. We had a book, so if we didn't know what one was, we would try to remember it and look it up when we got home. I was obsessed with them, I thought they were the most beautiful creatures in the world, and it's why my nickname is "Butterfly," though Mum doesn't call me that any longer.

After the butterfly closes its wings again, I stand and watch it for a few moments more, hoping it'll give me another glimpse of color, but it doesn't. Sounds from the garden drift up through the open window and remind me that I need to leave the butterfly, and the mirror, and the room, because I need to rejoin my Second Chance Family.

A final check in the mirror shows me that my eyes now look as dark as pools of oil, and again the shoulder strap of my dress has slipped. I pull it up and I make my way back downstairs.

The chalk-cool tiles in the hallway feel lovely again, but I need to put on shoes because bruschetta usually goes with other Italian dishes and sitting down at the table, and Chris prefers that we're not barefoot at dinner.

What would he have thought of my dad, I wonder, but I never dare to ask Mum. What would Chris have thought of my real dad, who couldn't have cared less about formality; who sat on rugs with his back against the sofa and watched TV with me, fish and chips on our laps; who made us toasted sandwiches so we could eat them over the Monopoly board, who never cared what you wore on your feet when you ate. "Her father never had any boundaries," my mum said in a family reintegration meeting at the Secure Unit, "and look where that got us." Her mouth was drawn tight but uncertain like zigzag patterns on a line graph, and I wanted to say, "But you never minded that," but I didn't dare.

When I get down the stairs, I find that everybody's in the kitchen. My heart has begun to pound again, and I don't have the courage to go any farther than the doorway of the room. Everybody has their back to me apart from Mum.

"Zoe!" she says and she reminds me of the open-winged butterfly, twinkling bright, sharp, and pretty. "Could you toast the bread?"

She's holding a crystal glass tumbler, which is Chris's Tom

Collins tumbler, and there's ice in it, which chinks against the sides, and an inch of clear liquid, which I know is gin. My mum adds club soda and it fizzes. A Tom Collins is what Chris always drinks before supper on the weekend.

"Hi, sweetie," says Tess as she turns around, and she gives me one of her huge hugs and while she's doing that she whispers into my ear, "It'll be OK."

Over Tess's shoulder I can see Lucas is at the table. He mouths some words at me and I think he's saying: *Did you read the email?* I kind of shake my head, because obviously I didn't finish it, and I don't know why he's so obsessed with it all of a sudden.

I look at Chris last, but he's busy opening the bifold doors so that one wall of our kitchen is thrown open to the garden, and he's putting on the garden lights.

They throw up great yellow beams from the base of the trees that are out there. There's a young silver birch that he and my mum planted—a crane had to lift it into the garden—but my favorite is a big old cedar tree whose trunk is huge and gray and forms chunks of dry bark like scabs that you can pick off.

My mother pours olive oil into a small white round dish. The green-gold ooze reminds me of petrol. She hands me a brush.

"Just on one side," she says. "Not too much, not too little."

I'm concentrating so much on the movement of the brush, the initial resistance of the bread, then the soaking in of the oil, that it makes me jump when Chris puts a hand on my shoulder.

"Zoe," he says, and his voice sounds extravagantly rich and wraparound as if we were shut together in a confessional, he behind the screen in robes, me about to unplug the so-long-repressed words to purge my disgrace. I sense his body behind mine, and I feel myself straighten up. I don't think Chris has ever touched me before. He's careful, careful around me like he's read a how-to manual on being a non-creepy stepfather. "Now tell me," he says, "are you all right?" His hand falls away practically before it's landed.

Across the island, over the sea of stripped basil, I meet my mother's eye, but she looks away. Her earring swings from her lobe—finest pieces of gold interlinked. From behind her, Lucas is staring at us. In front of him, in a row, are little tea-light holders that I suppose he's meant to be filling, and a bag of candles. Aunt Tessa isn't meeting my eye; she's busy adding oil and balsamic vinegar to a bowl where the chopped tomatoes and pummeled basil wait damply.

"I'm sorry," I say. "I don't know what came over me."

"Did you know that man in the church?" Chris asks me.

"No," I say to the baguette slices.

"I beg your pardon?"

"No," I say it more loudly. I shake my head.

"Did you know him, Maria?" Chris asks my mother.

She turns on her heel and gives Chris full, bright eye contact, just like she did with Jason the Key Worker when she had to explain to him why my dad wasn't coming to family reintegration meetings anymore. My mum is a brilliant actress. She could give Meryl Streep a run for her money.

"I thought I knew him, darling, but I don't think I did," she says. "I must have made a mistake. Would you like one of these? They're from the deli." She puts a small plate of shiny green olives on the island.

"I'm not hungry," says Chris. "I have no idea why you're cooking at this time of night."

"I'm hungry," says Tessa, who's using Mum's femur-sized pepper grinder to season the bowl of tomatoes. "Starving, actually."

"But you called that man by his name," Chris says to Mum and I feel as if his words somehow have substance in the heat, that they're glutinous like the dregs of the oil in my bowl. I keep my head down and I finish brushing the oil, in slow strokes, and then I start to place the bread on the oven tray.

"I thought he was somebody I knew." My mother has turned away; she's getting another wineglass down, pouring some for Tess. "But, on reflection, I think I was wrong."

She glances at me. "Olive oil side down," she says, and I start to turn the bread slices over, one by one, so they look untouched again, as though there's not a drop of oil on them.

SUNDAY NIGHT

After the Concert

TESSA

The glass of wine that Maria pours me is tiny, because she knows I'm driving. I'm grateful she's remembered, in spite of what's going on, because it's not the sort of thing you can easily bring up in front of Zoe. I take the glass from her and reach for one of the olives.

"It would be lovely to eat."

I am hungry, actually, but I'd be saying it even if it wasn't true. I don't know what Maria's playing at exactly, but she's definitely buying time.

Chris, for the first time in my experience, looks lost. Their kitchen is vast, cavernous compared to the small space that Richard and I share at home, and he stands in the middle of it, glass in hand, lit up as brightly as our surgical theater at work by the halogens, and somehow wrong-footed by Maria's unexpected assertiveness.

Light glances off every surface in this room, all of them shined or polished or brushed, and I understand why my sister always looks so put together. There's nowhere in here where you won't see some version of yourself reflected back at you, nowhere where others will be able to watch you in any way other than forensically.

When I look at Chris, whom I've always thought of as a benign king of his castle, I can clearly see that he's wrestling with a dilemma.

I recognize this easily because I see it frequently in the owners of pets I treat. The biggest and trickiest dilemma that many of them face is whether to continue prolonging the life of their animal or to end its suffering. Some people want me to make the decision for them, though I can't do that. Some break down, while others wrestle silently with it, faces contorted by the effort of not showing emotion in public, knuckles white around a limp dog lead or on the handle of a cage, objects that might soon just be mementos, and this is what Chris looks like.

Chris's dilemma is this: to assert himself, or to back down for now, to play a longer game. He has this dilemma because I don't think he believes Maria.

I wouldn't.

While he cogitates, Maria takes the lifeline I've thrown her. "How hungry are you?" she says.

"Absolutely bloody starving," I say. "I could eat a horse." This is the kind of joke we unashamedly make at the clinic. Among the vets and support staff we have a competition to use as many animal-related sayings as possible.

Chris takes a long sip of his drink and walks over to gaze out at the garden. It looks magnificent. It's a huge plot for the location, with a couple of fabulous mature large specimen trees and a view from the end of it across the city.

"I'll lay the table out here, shall I then?" he asks Maria.

"That would be lovely. We could use the new lights."

Chris says to me, "Would you like to phone Richard? See if he can join us? That would be nice."

I'm surprised by this because Chris is well aware of Richard's proclivity for drink. It's an open secret in the family. His question gets Maria's attention too. She looks at him, and then she says, words crisply clear: "Richard's got summer flu. Best let him sleep it off. I don't want Grace to catch anything."

Chris's eyes narrow because all three of us know that the chances of Richard having summer flu are very, very small. I'm sure I'm not the only one among us who is imagining Richard right now, passed out somewhere, stinking of booze, and depression; catatonic with it.

"What about me?" We all turn to look at Lucas because it's not often that he addresses a room full of people. Lucas is a one-on-one person. He's usually only comfortable with an audience if he's sitting at a piano, insulated by his performance.

"Doesn't it matter if I get flu? Or Zoe?" He says it really deadpan. He has a surprisingly deep voice.

Maria's eyebrows raise and she exhales sharply.

"That's very rude!" Chris snaps.

"No, no, it's OK. It's a reasonable question," Maria says, her hands up, palms outward. "I thought it would go without saying that we don't want either of you to get sick. Of course we don't."

"Apologize!" Chris crosses to the table where Lucas sits and leans over it, head hovering closer to his son than it needs to. In the civilized confines of this room, with the smell of oil-brushed baguette toasting and the drifting scent of somebody else's barbecue through the open doors, this stands out as a gesture of aggression. Lucas's head jerks back. He reads it the same way I do. There's surprise on his face.

"I'm sorry, Maria." Lucas says it to her nicely enough but drops his gaze quickly afterward, and turns his head away from his father a little, and begins to insert candles into their holders, each one making a small sound as it lands. I'll admit, I'm shocked. Zoe has her back to them at the grill; she doesn't see it. Maria has been watching with eyes that look blank.

"Sweetheart," Maria says to Lucas, and for the first time I see her composure wobble. Her voice rattles like pebbles in a jar. "It's fine, really. Could you possibly pop those out on the garden table for me when you're done? It might need a wipe first. And if you're starving, Tess, I could whip up some chicken Parmigiana? If you'd like that?"

Two things strike me. First, nobody whips up chicken Parmigiana. It's a beast of a recipe, involving breadcrumbs and eggs and dunking and bashing of meat and then sauces and grilling and baking. It's a labor of love, to be prepared starting at five in the evening, not late on a Sunday night. I wonder if my sister can really be trying to cook herself out of this situation, because it's surely a doomed effort; she can't keep cooking forever. My second thought is, it's my favorite dish, and Maria knows that.

"That would be amazing," I say, and she gives a small nod.

"Great! I hoped you'd want some! We can have an impromptu supper in the garden!"

It's strange, because I'm not normally the focus of her hostess charm. It's a new skill, which she's developed since being with Chris, and usually I watch her from the sidelines, exempt from being its target myself. The pre-accident Maria ran her household as a take-us-as-you-find-us affair, with a shoe-strewn hallway and a kitchen where you'd have to shift the Sunday supplements to find a space to sit. It was relaxed and informal.

It was everything that Chris, bless him, isn't.

SUNDAY NIGHT

After the Concert

ZOE

I can't handle raw white meat. It's to do with the accident and the things I saw, and Mum knows this, so she gets Lucas to bash the chicken breasts flat.

While he pounds them in a crashing slow-motion rhythm that I'm guessing would equate to about forty beats per minute on the metronome, I lay the outside table with Chris. He wipes it down and I set out shiny cutlery and wineglasses and spread Lucas's tea lights out along the length of it so they look pretty.

There are also wide terra-cotta bowls on the table, containing yellow citronella-scented candle wax, and Chris lights the thick wicks with a long, chunky match that flares in the darkness. The candles smoke blackly at first but then give off a scent that prickles my nostrils in a nearly nice way. Chris looks at me across the table and more or less repeats the question he asked earlier, only he says it slower, as if he wants to give his words more meaning.

"Zoe, are you absolutely sure you didn't know that man?" he asks me. "In the church?"

I look him in the eye; both of us lit by the flicker of the

candles, and also by the aqueous blue sheen of the swimming pool lights, which somebody inside the house has just turned on.

"No," I say. "I don't think so." If I know anything, it's that I must do as my mother says. She's basically a human shield between the world and me. But I'm tempted to tell him the truth; I can't deny it. There's a part of me that wants Chris to know, but only if he could handle it. My real dad couldn't.

"Are you sure?" Chris's voice isn't pressing, and there's an encouraging elasticity to his tone of voice that almost coaxes the truthful answer out of me, but the impulse goes when he adds: "You reacted very strongly," and that sounds sharper.

"I was afraid of him," I said. "He looked crazy."

In the silence I can still hear the steady pounding of Lucas's meat tenderizing and I'm not sure if Chris's breathing is actually audible, but I feel like I can hear it as loudly as if his lips were centimeters from my ear. For a moment he studies me like I'm the Mona Lisa or something.

"You would tell me the truth, wouldn't you, Zoe?" he asks. "You know it's important that we're all honest in this family?"

"Of course," I say, and I know I should keep my eyes on him, that's the kind of thing you talk about in the Unit, how you should keep your eyes on people so they don't think you're being shifty, but I can't help it, I let mine slide away a bit, because Chris's voice is like caramel and sometimes I want to feel his arms around me in a hug, just like my dad used to do. The urge to tell can be strong.

But Chris turns and strides toward the kitchen. "Lucas!" he calls out. "Isn't that done yet? Are you trying to give me a migraine?"

"How flat does it have to be?" I hear Lucas ask my mother.

Inside the kitchen, framed by the huge rectangular door opening, the scene looks like something out of an advent calendar
window: people preparing food together, talking together.
Lucas holds up a bit of roadkill flat chicken for my mother to
inspect and she says, "That's fine, darling. Perfect," and I have
to look away.

I don't like the pool lights being on at night, because it
becomes a death trap for insects. I think of the butterfly I saw
earlier and I wonder if it's still on the mirror and why it didn't
fly toward the light like the moths out here are doing. They're
diving like kamikaze planes toward the candle flames and
spinning in circles on the lit-up surface of the pool. There are
midges out here too, I can feel them nipping at my arms and
making my scalp itch.

I slip off my shoes and sit on the edge of the pool and let
my feet hang into it.

I'm not happy about the lies I've told Chris, but they're just
the usual ones, so they create a low-level unease that's man-
ageable because it's nowhere near becoming what my mum
would call "an incident."

Around my shins ripples shoot off toward the pool edges,
distorting the light and creating shadows and dancing shapes
within the water. A small bird dives down and takes a mouth-
ful of water right in front of me, or maybe it's an insect that's
drowned. The bird is gone before it arrived; its flight is the
most elegant thing to watch.

"Did you see that?" I say, because I can hear somebody
coming out of the house, and yet more lights come on, this
time a string of bulbs that hang over the pergola that our
table is under. They cast a soft white glow into the leaves that

cluster above it, and show up the delicate yellow roses that my mum insists on pruning herself twice a year. She's pleased with them this year because they're managing to repeat flower after what Chris called "a truly fabulous display" in June, and I think of them as trying very hard to please.

It's my mum who's coming now and she's carrying a plate of bruschetta and a pile of napkins.

"Paper napkins, I think, for a garden supper," she says. She hasn't heard what I said and I don't repeat myself.

We sit around the table and Chris pours wine: a full glass for him and Mum, but just a half for Lucas and me. Tessa covers the top of her glass. "Water for me now, I think," she says. "It's so hot."

You'd think I'd steer clear of alcohol, wouldn't you, but you see Chris insists that Lucas and I get used to "being around alcohol in a civilized way," so for us to be offered half a glass of something fine that he's selected is not unusual. Only half, mind you, because anything more would be "excessive." Not something he has to spell out for me, but he doesn't know that.

"Tuck in," says my mum, and all our hands reach out toward the bruschetta apart from Chris's.

"To you, darling," says Chris, raising his glass to Mum, "the only woman I know who can whip up a feast like this on a Sunday night. What a treat." He's sitting at the head of the table, so all of our heads turn toward him as he speaks.

"Thank you," she says. "Won't you have a bruschetta?"

"I'm saving myself for the chicken," he says. "As I said, I'm still full from the concert."

"Of course," says my mum, and she breaks a tiny bit off her

bruschetta and nibbles at it. She raises her own glass. "Can I just say how lucky I feel that we can all be here together to-night. It's very special."

We all drink. Nobody speaks. Beside my mum on the table is Grace's baby monitor, the green light steady like a snake's eye.

"So," says Aunt Tess in the silence that briefly follows, "guess which animal I treated for the very first time this week," and she's about to elaborate on this, but she's inter-rupted by the doorbell.

Only it's not just the doorbell, there's also a pounding on the door, as if Lucas were still bashing the chicken breasts, and then the bell rings again urgently. All of this noise registers on Grace's baby monitor; it sends the lights shooting off the scale and back down again, and then we can hear the unmistakable sound of her snuffling.

"Who the hell can that be?" says Chris. His chair squeaks as it drags across the pressure-washed flagstones. "I'll get it."

Mum is up too. "I'll get it," she says, "you relax," but she's too slow off the mark because Chris is already marching into the house and the hissy intercom is telling us that Grace is revving up for a full-blown yell and he says to Mum, "See to the baby."

MONDAY MORNING

SAM

Right after the car accident, Zoe remained on bail for a couple of weeks while the police gathered evidence. I met with her and her parents during this time to discuss strategy for what might happen next. I hadn't yet had sight of any of the papers that the Crown Prosecution Service was preparing, but it was important to get Zoe's story complete.

The family came to my office in Bideford one morning, dressed smartly. Sometimes families hold hands with each other when they arrive; sometimes husbands pull chairs out for their wives or children to sit down on. Zoe and her parents weren't distant with each other exactly, but neither did they seem close in that way.

It was my first meeting with Mr. Guerin, Zoe's dad, and he was clearly very uncomfortable. I imagined that he was more used to being out on the fields than in an office, dogs and livestock his usual companions. He looked older than his wife, though perhaps that was because he was weathered.

"We were away that night," he said. "We went to my sister's house near Exeter because her husband was just back from a tour in Afghanistan, and they were having a party. Zoe told us she wanted to stay with Gull for a sleepover, for Gull's birthday treat, you see. That's all we knew of it. First we heard was the phone call from the police when they got her in the hospital. We didn't know Gull's parents were away, see, and they didn't know we were. The girls lied to us."

Zoe's head hung down as he spoke, though I noticed that she snuck one or two glances at me, watching my reaction to her father's words.

"She'd never even been to a party that we knew," he continued. He was warming up, almost as if he couldn't stop speaking now, as if he'd been waiting to unburden himself of this story. Beside him, his wife and daughter sat silent as his words filled the space between us all. "She had trouble making friends at the new school, some girls weren't very nice to her, Internet bullying that's what she told us. She was bullied, Mr. Locke, and we want to know if that can be a defense against what she's done."

So this was what he'd been working up to, a spark of hope that the family thought they'd discovered, and which they were sheltering and nurturing with cupped hands.

"They sent her messages through an app, called panop. They bombarded her with awful, vitriolic stuff," said Maria Guerin. She sounded instantly more articulate than her husband, and I could tell she wasn't born and raised around here. I wondered how hard it had been for her to manage as a farmer's wife, because the rural community can be a difficult one to find acceptance within if you're an outsider.

"We didn't know about it." Mr. Guerin added this.

"What kind of messages?" I asked Zoe.

She looked at me, holding something back.

"Give him your phone, Zo," said her dad. "You can see it all on her phone."

She pressed a button or two on her phone and pushed it across the table. It was such a typical young teenage girl's phone: metallic pink, with stickers on the back of it, musical notes.

On the screen I could see the messages that Zoe had received. The content of them jolted me. They were nasty, taunting, shocking messages. They oozed with clever, calculated malice, and targeted every aspect of her figure and her personality. They left me momentarily speechless.

When I looked up, Zoe had her eyes on me, but she dropped them and a flush crept up and over her cheeks.

"Who sent these?" I asked.

"They're anonymous," Maria answered me.

"Do you know, Zoe?"

"I don't know."

"You must have some idea," said her dad. I could tell this wasn't the first time he'd said this to her.

Maria put her hand on his. "Don't shout. There's no need to shout. Not here."

He pulled his hand out from under hers and ran it through his hair in frustration. He had proud aquiline features, which lent dignity to his weather-beaten skin. Maria withdrew her hand to her lap.

I wondered what Zoe would tell me if it were just her and me in the room. I wondered what she hid from her parents.

"Do you feel that these messages affected your behavior on the night of the accident?" I asked her. This was important, because it could lead to a possible coercion defense.

"I didn't get any that night."

"Which tells me," her father raised his voice again, "that somebody there that night was sending them. It's not rocket science. I might not have degrees coming out of my ears but it's common sense, isn't it? Common bloody sense. They lured her there, and they bullied her into doing something she wouldn't have done otherwise."

"They didn't." Zoe's voice was soft and quiet.

"What?" he said to her.

"They didn't bully me into it! I decided to drive. I chose to drive. You taught me, Dad, you taught me yourself. I decided to drive, but I didn't know I was drunk. I swear it."

Both of Zoe's parents were about to speak, but I raised my hand to silence them. I had to intervene because we needed to make rational, careful decisions; the law doesn't legislate for feelings.

"Tell me about that, Zoe," I said. "Talk to me about that, because that can be a valid defense."

SUNDAY NIGHT

After the Concert

ZOE

It's just me and Lucas at the table after everybody else has gone; we're sitting opposite each other, candle flames and a pile of bruschetta between us. There's a scratchy noise still coming through the baby monitor, so I turn off the sound.

"Did you read the script?" says Lucas.

"I read a bit of it, but I only had time to look at the beginning. It was sad."

I think of my phone tucked under the sofa cushions, and I wonder if I can expect more panop questions when I retrieve it. Before, when things were at their worst, the messages used to come through all the time, question after question, sometimes I could get ten in five minutes, each one shoveling away at my foundations in a different way.

Who do you think you are?

Are you sick you filthy bitch?

Crying yourself to sleep yet?

How does it feel when everybody hatehatehate
hatehates you?

Do gay bitches cry gay tears?

Actually that one really didn't make sense given that the
basis of what they were accusing me of was prostituting myself
to Jack Bell, but it was miserable to read anyway. And iron-
ically, because I've got what Jason the Key Worker called a
"finely honed sense of irony," it was the panop messages that
made me so keen to go to *that* party: the one where I became
a princess for just a moment or two in the hands of Jack Bell.

The messages were supposed to put me off going near
him, but they didn't, because I'm also what Jason described as
"stubborn" and "driven." You don't win piano competitions
at the level I play at unless you're both of those things.

So when Jack asked me to his house party just a few weeks
before Christmas, and grudgingly invited Gull too because I
said I couldn't come without her, especially because it was her
birthday the next day, there was a part of me that thought,
Suck on that, Eva Bell and Amelia Barlow. Because I was
pretty sure they were sending the messages, them and their
minions.

I take a sip of my wine and say to Lucas, "Shall we top up,
while they're not here?" It feels like a daring thing to say, and
I should know better, of course I should, but I say it because
I want to jolt Lucas out of his flatness and get him to joke
around with me a bit. I want to do something that'll make the
memory of the church go away.

Lucas gets the bottle and refills our glasses, but no higher
than Chris originally poured them.

"Will you read the rest of the script?" he says.

He dips his index finger into his mouth and then begins to run it around the rim of his wineglass. A note, high and pure and piercing, sings out from it. I do the same to my finger and my glass.

"I will," I say, so he doesn't feel bad.

The sound from the glasses has momentum now. Our fingers scoot around and around. He's chewing his lip, and he doesn't answer right away, and I don't want him to cry or anything like that because the script makes him think about his mum.

"Does this count as a repetitive noise?" I ask him. Repetitive noises are irritating to other people, I'm told, if my foot gets the urge to tap up and down on the stone floor of the kitchen, or if I click my fingers in time to some music that only I can hear in my head.

"Nah," Lucas says. "It's C sharp."

I have perfect pitch, so I know that his glass is making C natural and mine is making E flat, but I don't correct him because nobody likes a smarty-pants.

"What's in the rest of the script then?" I ask him.

"It's just . . . You need to read it."

"It was quite hard to read on my phone."

He stops with the glass abruptly then, and the whining note dies away slowly. I stop mine too and clamp my hand on top of my glass, to stop the vibrations instantly. Then the sound of the greedy, flapping filters in the swimming pool becomes our soundtrack. Lucas is passing his finger through one of the candle flames now, and I can see the edge of it blackening.

"Can you show me on your iPad? After supper?" I ask him.

Lucas's eyes look artificially twinkly because the fairy lights

are being reflected in his dark pupils. Usually they're flatly
dark; unknowable vats of Lucas thought.

"Maybe," he says. "But you could just read it on your
phone, it's not that hard."

It's a bit weird to be here with Lucas, with wine, just us
two, because there are rules about us in this house.

We first moved in right before Grace was born. Mum and
me lived in a scuzzy flat before then, where she survived
mostly on Prozac, and Lucas and Chris lived in a different big
house. We could have all fitted into their old house, but then
it wouldn't have been "a fresh start."

What I'm remembering now, though, is the talk that Lucas
and me had to have with our parents when we all moved in
together, which was unbelievably excruciating. The gist of
it was—can you guess?—that me and Lucas were not under
any circumstances ever to consider starting a relationship
with each other because above all we had to "respect the
new family." The only practical result of this was that we
had to agree not to go into each other's bedroom unless an
adult was present. I had a fully hollow internal laugh when
they said that because it was so like the Secure Unit it wasn't
even true.

Afterward, when we were alone, Lucas said they were
hypocrites, and controlling, and didn't trust us. Then he asked
me if I'd ever thought about him in that way and I said I had,
and he stared at me like he wasn't expecting that answer at all.
So I added to my answer. I said, "Only once." He never told
me if he'd ever felt the same, maybe because I was too nervous
to ask. He just went to do his practice and, while I listened
to it, I thought about how some people could rape you with
their eyes in the Unit, even if they never touched you at all.

"I sent it to your mum too," Lucas says. "The email."

"Why don't you just tell me what's in it?"

"I don't know how to; it's best if you read it."

When he says this, his voice is so unexpectedly strange and serious that it makes a shudder run through me, deep and cold.

SUNDAY NIGHT

After the Concert

TESSA

It's Tom Barlow at the door. I hang back in the hallway, by the door of the coat cupboard, and watch Chris greet him cautiously.

Tom Barlow is highly agitated, just as he was in the church: face and neck red, emotions burning him up with the intensity of a forest fire. Chris stands in the doorway, blocking it mostly, and gently tells Tom Barlow to calm down and that he's certainly made a mistake, and come to the wrong house. Chris's voice is calm and measured; he's very much in control.

I stay in the shadows, watching, and I sense Maria upstairs, trying to listen as she soothes the baby. I'm pressed up against Chris's fishing rods and his winter work coats: great swaths of cashmere, smelling faintly in the heat despite being wrapped in dry cleaner's plastic.

Chris remains patient even when Tom Barlow refuses to listen to what he's being told. Chris doesn't invite him inside, but asks him if he'd like to take a seat on a bench that is just beside the ornate front porch, overlooking the driveway.

"Perhaps," Chris says to Tom Barlow in a tone that's calm but which I think could be dangerously patronizing, "I could fetch you a glass of iced water?"

Tom Barlow is having none of it.

"She needs to answer for what she did," he shouts at Chris, and then, just like in the church, his phrases seem to circulate on a loop as if the energy that's driving him to these desperate acts is taking so much out of him that he can do nothing more. He repeats it. "She needs to answer," he says, "she needs to answer for what she took from me."

"Who?" says Chris. "To whom are you referring?"

And Mr. Barlow rocks backward and forward on his feet, disbelief etched more deeply on his face every time I can catch a glimpse of him. He practically spits out his reply. He says, "Zoe Guerin, I'm referring to Zoe Guerin. Who the hell else would I be referring to?"

These two sentences seem to paralyze the air around Chris and Mr. Barlow, and the two men remain standing face-to-face, speaking not at all. I imagine that Mr. Barlow is watching a variety of emotions, and, most important, realizations work across Chris's face, because right at this moment Chris must be coming to the conclusion that Mr. Barlow has indeed come to the right house and that Maria has lied to him.

From upstairs there's absolute silence. Maria has stopped shushing the baby, and I wonder if she's heard what I've heard because if she has, then she'll know that the game is up.

When Chris moves again his actions are swift. With both of his hands, he shoves Tom Barlow backward violently and, as Tom Barlow staggers across the gravel, stones crunching, Chris says, "How dare you?"

I emerge from my nook then. I run down the hall toward them, and I step out on the front drive.

"Hey," I say, as gently as possible. Tom Barlow has recovered physically and is standing and staring at Chris with intense hatred and not a little disbelief. I put a hand on Chris's arm.

"Hey," I say, "Chris, stop, it's OK."

Chris's jaw is clenched and rigid and his arm is solid with poised muscle. Tom Barlow is breathing through his nose, nostrils flaring and jaw set, squaring up to this threat of violence, this added outrage, and he looks as if he might charge Chris. It's scary, primitive stuff, dogs with hackles up; a hair's breadth away from turning into a nasty fight. I step right between them, my back to Chris, and I say to Tom Barlow, "Would you like to talk?"

His eyes flick across my face and I think he recognizes me.

Behind me, I feel Chris move forward and I put my arm out behind my back until my fingers make contact with him, telling him that I want him to stay there. "Talk to me?" I say again to Tom Barlow, and I keep my voice soft.

For a moment longer he glares over my shoulder, chest heaving, unable to take his outraged eyes off Chris, but then a sort of collapse takes place within his eyes. Tears well, huge droplets that flatten on his cheeks, smearing them. "Come with me," I say, "we'll talk about it."

I take his arm, slowly, because dogs can still bite even after their hackles have gone down. I look at Chris. "Go inside," I say, and I'm shocked at the anger that's on his face, but my priority is to move Tom Barlow away, to prevent him from confronting Maria or Zoe, and from making things any worse than they are already.

Chris doesn't move.

"Go. Inside," I repeat.

He takes one small step backward, his gaze still locked on Tom Barlow, and he says, "I will phone the police if I see you on my property again." Even then Chris doesn't go in. He stands, long arms by his sides, in the middle of the elegant circle of gravel that shapes his driveway and he's framed by flowerbeds full of manicured topiary and shrubbery, beneath which the shady undergrowth hisses with a discreet watering system to ensure that nothing dries out.

Above him, in an upstairs window I see Maria, with Grace in her arms. She's holding the blackout blind aside, and gazing down at us, but then, as her husband finally turns and enters the house, she drops the blind and is invisible to me again.

SUNDAY NIGHT

After the Concert

ZOE

Lucas notices my shudder. His eyes pass over my bare shoulders.

"Do you need a sweater?" he says. "I can get you one."

"No, thank you."

"Are you sure?"

"It was just a little breeze."

There's a tiny bit of movement around us now, though it's hot, velvety air that arrives from somewhere unseen in the darkness. It doesn't refresh.

"Someone walk over your grave?" he asks.

"Probably," I say, but that's the kind of comment that I have to work hard to keep my composure in the face of.

I put my finger in the candle flame to distract myself, and because I want to do what he's been doing, but it hurts immediately, and I pull it away. Lucas laughs and then we're silent again and I think about how much I couldn't bear it if he wasn't in this house with us. My mum's not warm anymore, not since the accident, and Chris isn't warm. Grace is warm but in a fuggy, baby way, so it's only Lucas who feels truly personality-warm to me, who seems to see things a bit the same way I do, even if he doesn't say much.

"Lucas," I say, but he's begun to talk at the same time as me.

"Do you ever think of giving up piano?" he says, and that is such a totally, unbelievably, jaw-droppingly, incredible, unexpected, shocking thing for him to say that even I'm lost for words.

"Why?" I ask. I can't conceive of giving up piano. Piano playing is like an addiction for me. It's a path I have to walk down, water I have to drink, food I must consume, air I need to breathe. It's the only thing that can take my head some-where safe and everybody tells me it's going to give me "a bright future."

"Don't tell my dad I said that," he says. He sees my surprise and it's made him nervous, but I'm a loyal person.

"I won't." I put those words out there quickly because I want Lucas to know that I'm on his side, but I have to ask again: "Why?"

"I didn't say I was doing it." He's backtracking.

"But why are you thinking about it?"

He tips back his chair. "Because it's part of what's not right."

"Piano?"

"No."

"What's not right?"

"This. Any of it."

"What do you mean?" I can't believe I'm hearing this, be-cause Lucas practices longer and harder than me on the piano and he never complains.

He's holding up his fingers now, making a rectangle shape and looking at me through it. I know what he's doing; he's framing me for a shot because he's obsessed with films. He does it a lot, and it really annoys Chris.

"Is it because you want to do films?" I ask. I know he does, we all know he does, but he doesn't talk about it because Chris says it's not a proper career.

He drops his hands. "I do want to make films; it's not only that, though. Sometimes piano feels like it's just a cog in a machine. Like it doesn't mean anything for itself, it's just for appearances. I hate that. Don't you hate that?"

And those words make me actually gasp, as though the air I've just breathed in is scorching hot, because they really, truly shock me. I would never give up piano. I just would never give up, because we have to move forward.

I have an urge to get up from the table and turn away from him, because I don't want him to see my eyes go filmy with tears about this, so I stand up sort of awkwardly in the way you do when you're rushing but your knees are a bit stuck under a table, and as I do that I manage to flip up the plate of bruschetta with my hand.

So it rains bruschetta. Gobbets of chopped tomato and basil and oil splatter the tablecloth and Lucas and the floor. It's all over his black concert shirt and it's on his face and hair. I couldn't have done a more efficient job of spreading them everywhere if I'd used a spray gun. And because I don't know what else to do, I laugh. I'm bad at laughing when bad things happen. It's just a sort of reaction that I can't help. It got me into trouble in the Secure Unit once, because that's the kind of place you really don't want to laugh at people. I won't tell you what they put in my bed that night, and the night after.

Lucas looks me right in the eye, and the super-serious expression he had a few seconds earlier stays there for just an instant before it dissolves into a nicer one and he laughs. So I laugh again too, really loudly, like "that's hilarious" sort of laughing, which means that when Chris speaks from the doorway it's the most massive shock ever because I didn't hear him coming, and it makes me scream, short and sharp.

"What are you both doing?" he says. He's using a voice that I've never heard before. It's icy cold.

Lucas says, "Sorry," and I say, "It was my fault. I'm really sorry," and I have one of those moments again where one minute you're all standing there laughing in your dress, and you feel good because you're having a nice time with somebody, and the next minute it's all back down to earth because you're still just you and you're worthless, and probably worse too.

Chris sees it.

Chris, who's never said a bad word to me, though I suppose he's never really said much.

To Lucas, Chris says: "Get yourself cleaned up."

To me, he says: "Stop behaving like a slut in front of my son. Don't think I don't see you doing it."

The silence that follows those words makes my skin crawl in cold, fluid patches, as if somebody was moving around me and blowing on it, because I don't know what to do. I stay really still and I focus on the slap, slap of the water in the pool against the filters, and I crunch the skin on the back of my lips between my teeth. My nose tingles with the early warning signal that tears are coming and once again I fight that urge, as silently and as discreetly as possible.

Chris looks as though he's expecting me to answer, but I can't think of a single thing to say, because my brain is confused by the uncertainty of it all. I didn't know I was behaving like a slut, or perhaps I did know, and I've therefore purposely done something shameful, but if that's true then I wonder, should I admit to it?

I feel like I'm naked. Chris's words remind me of the panop messages I used to get, they remind me of the girls who used to bait me, and they remind me of the Unit. Those words don't belong in this house. I say, "I'm sorry, Chris. I didn't mean to. Truly, I didn't."

"You're on thin ice, young lady," he says. "Go and look after the baby and ask your mother to come down. I need to speak to her."

I walk past him and Lucas without looking them in the eye at all, and I try to keep my head straight up and make sure that my walk isn't at all like a slut's walk, and when I'm inside the house I start to run and I don't stop until I've pounded all the way up the stairs and I'm standing on the landing outside Grace's room, where I stop.

SUNDAY NIGHT

After the Concert

TESSA

"I know you," Tom Barlow says. "Don't I?"

"I'm Zoe's aunt. Tessa Downing."

"You were at the court." He recognizes me, even all these years on.

I nod.

"I'm so sorry for your loss," I say. The words are hollow with my inability to make things right for him. My only hope is that he can hear my intention.

We're standing on the street outside Maria's house, but I want to move him farther away. It would be too easy for him to walk back into the house from here, or to go around the back and find Zoe in the garden. Now that the secret's out, I think my greatest fear is that he could do her some harm. It's an exercise in damage limitation at this stage.

"Would you like to talk?" I ask him. "We could sit in my car? Or walk?"

I'm trying to remember what I know about this man, to separate the descriptions I read of him in the newspapers from the other families. As far as I remember, Tom Barlow is, or was, in property. In fact, his profile wasn't all that different from Chris's. He was a self-made businessman, and proud of it. If Chris and Tom Barlow had met under other circumstances they might have got on well. Amelia, who died in the accident, was not the Barlow family's only child, but she was their only daughter. I remember photographs of two young boys, the image of their sister, clutching the hands of their parents in the photographs of the funeral.

"I need a smoke," he says, and he sinks down onto the stone wall that borders the front of Chris and Maria's garden, containing the dense foliage at their boundary. It's not as good as moving away from the property, but at least if we sit we won't be visible from the house.

He pulls a cigarette from a packet and offers me one, but I shake my head.

"Do you mind?" he asks me, and the question, in the midst of all this, almost makes me laugh. How is it that manners are so strong that they pervade all situations? I've lost count of the times that people have apologized to me for crying when I've just euthanized their pet.

"Not at all," I say. "Of course not."

Tom Barlow leans forward and hangs his head. His hands clench between his knees and his cigarette dangles from between his knuckles, the rising smoke making him turn his head a little to the side, away from me.

I notice that he has a monklike area of thinning hair on the crown of his head that he's tried to disguise with careful use of hair product of some sort. It tells me that he didn't start his day thinking about Zoe, that what happened has probably been as much of a shock to him as it has been to us. You almost certainly don't take time with hair product if you're consumed with rage and indignation.

We sit in silence because I don't want to inflame him again by saying the wrong thing, and after a few minutes, when the cigarette is half smoked, he reaches into the pocket of his shorts and hands me a crumpled piece of paper.

It's a flyer, advertising Zoe's concert.

"Through my door," he says. "This morning. Through my front door, onto my doormat, in my house. In my own home. I only came because I couldn't believe it actually would be her."

I hold the flyer in my hands. I have no idea who distributed it, but my best guess is that it was one of the busybody organizers from the church.

"If we had known," I say carefully, "we would never, ever have let this happen. Please believe me."

"We came here to escape from it," he says. "We sold everything, we moved the boys, we lost money, we started again. It hasn't been easy."

His voice cracks and I think how the same words could describe Zoe and Maria's flight from Devon to Bristol, but of course I don't say that.

I want to put my hand on his back to comfort him, but I'm not sure that's a good idea, so instead I say, "I'm so, so sorry."

"We buried her in Hartland," he says, and I think again of the newspaper pictures, where the backdrop to the black-clad processional figures was the tiered gray stone spire of Hartland Church, built toweringly tall to act as a landmark for sailors, to save lives centuries before the lighthouse at the Point ever existed. "So we couldn't bring her with us when we moved, but we had a plaque laid, at the church in Westbury. We chose a plaque with the boys."

And so I understand the awfulness of it now. Zoe has played a concert at a church where one of the victims of the accident she caused has a memorial plaque. Zoe has tried to rebuild her life on the site of her victim's memorial.

"Mr. Barlow—" I say. I try to choose the words I'm going to say next extremely carefully, but he cuts me off.

"Who is that man?" he says. "That's not her dad."

"No. Maria's remarried. That's Zoe's stepdad."

"Does he know? Does he know what she's done? What she is? Does he know that and still treat me like shit on his shoe?"

He studies me as I try to word my answer, try to work out what is the least incendiary thing I can say, but I'm too slow and he sees the truth.

"He doesn't know, does he?"

"I think—" I begin, but he interrupts me.

"I feel sorry for your family," he says. "Living with a murderer."

He stands up and I do too. I feel things slipping out of my control again. "Please know that we are truly, truly sorry," I say.

"People should know. She needs to pay."

"She has paid for what she did," I tell him. "She's a changed person."

"What? Twelve months in a cushy detention center somewhere doing her GCSEs? How does that make up for what she's done?"

He gestures his hand at Chris and Maria's house, at its immaculate grandeur, and disbelief at the injustice of it all runs rampant in his expression.

"We have nothing!" he says. "And she has all of this. She shows off with her piano still and she lives in a mansion like nothing ever happened."

"That's not true," I say. "She's been punished. This destroyed her life too. Be fair . . ."

But that was the wrong thing to say. "Be fair?" he asks, and he snatches the program from my hand and reads from it: " 'You won't want to miss these two precociously talented teenagers making their Bristol debut—this promises to be a very special evening.' "

There's nothing but disgust in his tone.

"People need to know," he says, "and I'm going to make sure they do."

"Is it so wrong for her to have a future?" I ask. I'm desperate now. My ability to remain calm is slipping through my fingers.

"Why should she have one when we don't?"

He screws the paper up and hurls it at my feet and then he turns away and begins to walk down the street, away from the house, shoulders slack and head bowed, toward the streetlight that's making the top of the mailbox at the end of the road shine a slippery red.

"What are you doing?" I call after him. "What are you going to do?"

He disappears around the corner.

I look at the house, and I wonder what's happening in there, and I look at the corner that Tom Barlow has just disappeared around, and I decide to follow him.

SUNDAY NIGHT

After the Concert

ZOE

Chris's words have made me shake. I'm used to being called bad things, but not by him.

On the landing, I notice the butterfly again. It's come out of the bathroom, and now it's high up in a corner flapping uselessly against the walls. I don't like it doing that, because I imagine the sparkling dust on its wings being dislodged every time it makes impact, a microscopic shower of irides- cent powder falling like sand through an hourglass, weak- ening the butterfly little by little, until it won't be able to fly any longer.

It makes me think of my life, and of the damage I've done, and I think that I've been lucky so far, because when things have gone wrong, and when the sand in my hourglass has run through and time has run out for me, I've been able to pick it up, turn it over, and start again. But I wonder if that's ever going to be possible now. I wonder how many chances a person can get.

I ease open the door to Grace's bedroom. My mum is lying on the bed that's in there, on the other side of the room from Grace's crib. Grace is lying with her. As I adjust to the darkness, I see that they've turned their heads toward me, that their eyes are darkly reflecting the light from the hallway.

"Mum," I whisper. "Chris wants to talk to you. Shall I look after Grace?"

I don't mention what he's said to me because I don't want anything else to go wrong for my mum today, especially not if it's my fault.

Normally, Mum would leap up if I said that. She always goes quickly to Chris. She's super attentive to him. Chris gets first-class service, because the Second Chance Family is a First-Class Operation, just like Chris's business, and just like my and Lucas's standard of performance. Chris and Mum set a lot of store in that.

Mum doesn't leap up, though. As I walk through the inky darkness of the room toward them, I see that she and Grace are lying together like a bear and its cub. My mum isn't trying to get Grace to sleep; she's playing with her. Mum runs the side of her finger down over Grace's temple, and Grace reaches for Mum's hand and holds it in front of her face. Mum uses a fingertip to dab Grace lightly on the nose and Grace giggles.

I approach them quietly because I want to be on the bed with them. There's a little space just below where Grace is lying and I perch there cautiously. Mum is against the wall. Grace kicks me gently with her feet. The room's hot and she's just wearing a nappy and I feel her warm toes on my bare leg. I move them a little because that's near where the piano bruised me earlier.

"Chris wants you," I whisper to Mum.

"Lie with us," she says.

My heart begins to beat so freaking loudly when she says that that I feel like I might hyperventilate. Mum shuffles over toward the wall and pulls Grace gently with her, leaving a thin sliver of space along the edge of the bed. I lie down, my head beside Grace's, and she celebrates with some monster kicking, and then by taking a hank of my hair and giving it a pull. I don't mind though, I'm used to it. Grace tries to sit up, but my mum whispers, "Gracie-girl, lie with us, come on," and, miraculously, Grace does.

We lie for a minute and then Mum says, "My girls," in a voice that's warm and sweet like hot chocolate, and she nestles her head into Grace and reaches across her to put a hand on my cheek and her thumb runs down my temple too, and for the first time in a gazillion years I forget all the things that have gone wrong, and I just relax and lie there and feel her hand on me and Grace's wriggly body between us, and if I couldn't hear the butterfly still flapping on the landing, reminding me of my hourglass life, it would be just like heaven.

SUNDAY NIGHT

After the Concert

TESSA

What are the odds that Tom Barlow would be living only a few miles from Chris and Maria's new house? Long. Just as the odds are that Zoe would be playing a concert at the very church where Amelia is remembered.

But if you work in the business that I do, you know that long odds don't always make any difference at all. Somebody always makes up that small percentage of people to whom un-likely or desperate things happen, and there's actually nothing to say it can't be you.

Tom Barlow doesn't jog for long. He gets in a car around the corner from Chris and Maria's house, and when I realize that I still have my bag over my shoulder and my keys are inside it—Maria's hostess skills have failed her tonight, my bag wasn't taken from me on arrival—I turn back swiftly and get my car, even though I fear that I'm going to lose him. But I don't. When I trundle around the corner, his car is only just pulling out, as though he's had to sit in there for a few minutes and pull himself together before leaving, or perhaps make a phone call.

We leave the wide, leafy, sedate lanes of Chris and Maria's

neighborhood and drive farther out into surburbia, retracing some of the route back from the concert. On a long street in Westbury, which seems to go on forever, Tom Barlow pulls into the driveway of a modest semidetached house that looks as though it was built in the sixties, and I'm able to park in a space opposite. I keep my head back so that he can't see my face, but I have a view of his house.

It has a large picture window in the front, and through it I can see the sitting room. There are two sofas and a TV, plus some gaming equipment. The walls are painted a plain magnolia. There's not much else, apart from a poster-sized family photograph on the wall, where the kids are small, and Amelia is sandwiched between her little brothers, who appear to be twins. The sparse furnishings make the room look more functional than loved.

Tom Barlow stays sitting in his car for a good few minutes before he gets out. In fact, he stays there for so long that a woman, whom I recognize as his wife, opens the door and looks out inquiringly.

He gets out of the car and holds her in a long, tight hug.

"I thought that was you. Are you all right?" I hear her say. "What's wrong?"

I can't hear his reply, but he shakes his head as if to say "Nothing's wrong" and then she pushes him away from her so that she's holding him by the shoulders, and she smiles at him. "I love you too," she says. From the doorway, one of their boys watches, bare-chested, wearing just pajama bottoms. Tom Barlow puts his arm around his son on the way into the house and, as the door shuts, the child starts an explanation about how it was too hot to sleep.

On my way there, I thought I would ring on the doorbell

and try to speak to the family, to convince them that Zoe should be allowed a chance to rebuild, that she and Maria are entitled to their privacy, and entitled to move on. But I can't do that now because I'm pretty certain that nobody else in his house knows what Tom Barlow has been doing that evening. Not yet, anyway, and I don't want to be the one to tell them.

SUNDAY NIGHT

After the Concert

ZOE

The light that's been gently creeping into Grace's bedroom from the hallway suddenly disappears. Mum and me turn our heads toward the door to see why. A man-sized silhouette blocks the doorway and at first it's hard to tell whether it's Lucas or Chris. He steps away after a small pause, without saying anything, but it's enough to rouse my mum. She lets out what I think is a quiet moan, and then eases herself up off the bed. Gracie-girl doesn't want Mum to go. She gives a bit of a whimper herself, but I distract her by making my fingers flutter right in front of her face and she grabs for them.

You never know when Grace is going to accept me as a Mum substitute. Sometimes she's happy to; other times she just yells blue murder until she gets Mum back. It's the same with Lucas. And even with Chris. Mum is definitely Grace's favorite. Oh, and Katya. But, to be honest, I'd rather gloss over that because it massively annoys me.

When Mum has left the room, she pulls the door softly behind her so that it's almost completely shut but not quite, as if she wants to keep us both just the way she left us. Grace is sort of sleepy now. She turns her body to me and I put my arm around her so that her head can nestle into the side of me, and I sing to her, a little tune that my dad used to sing to me when I was little.

I think about my dad a lot. He's a farmer. He couldn't cope after the accident, because he said it was Mum's fault, that she pushed me too hard with the music, that it had turned me into somebody I should never have been trying to be. He said that I should never have gone for a music scholarship in the first place, because it wasn't for people like us. I should have stayed at the local school and grown up just the way he did: safely, at the farm, in the heart of the community.

"But you *love* listening to Zoe play," my mum said in the last reintegration meeting at the Unit that Dad ever attended. "You always said I was right to push her."

"Not at this cost," he'd replied, and he put on his coat and said, "I'm sorry, Zoe," and then he left, even though Jason asked him not to and talked to him in the corridor outside for ages.

I didn't see my dad for nine months after that, the time it takes to make a whole new human being. I went back to see him at the farm when I got out of the Unit, but only once. We had an OK day and Granny Guerin came around with some scones, but Dad was mostly sad and awkward, and when he went out to see to the cattle Granny Guerin said he never did know how to put a feeling into words and that was just the way he was, but she knew for sure that he loved me and he always would.

I wanted to tell him that I was still the same girl as before the accident, I was still his girl. I wanted to say that I wasn't a bad person, I'd just done a bad thing, by accident, but on that day his silence meant that I found it hard to put anything into words too. Perhaps it's catching.

Granny Guerin saw that I had a lot of words stored up in me, and she said, "I know your mother thinks I've abandoned you both, but he's my child and I must protect him. I'm just doing the same as what your mother's doing for you. Know that he loves you, Zoe, I can't promise anything more than that now, so I won't, because I don't like to raise expectations. But time can heal things, my darling."

But on the train on the way back to Bristol I also thought about how time destroyed everything on the farm, how part of my dad's life was just keeping things fixed that time had broken. And I imagined Dad, with his red farmer's cheeks and furrowed brow, and I thought how everything about him looked more or less exactly the same as it did before the accident, except that now the farmhouse didn't feel cozy like it used to, and his eyes were full of sadness. If I was going to be über-dramatic (vampire-romance fans: be alert! This is your moment!), I would say that his eyes were wells of tears.

I don't know exactly what happened to my parents when I was in the Unit. I only know that they found it too difficult to go on together. Jason said that a traumatic event within a family can make it very difficult for a marriage to continue, and that was something I might just have to accept. Cracks in a marriage, he said, can become chasms if they're shaken by trauma. I told him he was almost sounding like a poet. He told me it would benefit me if I could learn to take things seriously.

By the time I came out, Mum had moved all our stuff from the farm and found a flat in Bristol, and started a job that my aunt Tessa got for her through her wunderkind husband, Richard the Rocket Scientist, who's fond of a tipple.

We weren't going to dwell on the past, Mum told me, we were going to look forward, to try to start something fresh. My dad would be OK, she said, I could go and stay with him on the holidays. But she cried every night, and she was crying when she woke up some mornings too, until she met Chris.

SUNDAY NIGHT

After the Concert

TESSA

When the door has shut behind Tom Barlow and his wife, I don't hang around for long. I put the bus into gear and trundle off down their road, but I park again when I'm around the corner, out of their sight, because I want to think.

Once I've turned the headlights off, I notice that the darkness is musky and thick with humidity. I can smell barbecue from somebody's garden, and a cyclist whizzes past me on a road bike, making me jump.

My phone's in my back pocket and I squirm to get it out. Richard has tried to ring me again so I phone him back. He takes about half a second to answer.

"Tess!" He knows it's me because nobody else phones our landline.

"Hi."

"Where are you?"

I try to judge the level of his intoxication from the extent to which he's slurring his words. I figure that he's close to being blotto, and he's clearly feeling paranoid.

"I was at Zoe's concert," I tell him. "And then I went back to Maria's house. I had to give Chris and Lucas a lift."

I don't tell him anything more about the evening. Richard's not good at absorbing other people's problems when his own have swelled up enough to fill his mind entirely. His response to what I've said will tell me precisely what his mood is like.

Richard is either a self-hating drunk or an overambitious drunk, but I'm never sure which I'm going to get when he hits the bottle. Neither option thrills me. The self-hating is profoundly tedious because it's a circular, defeatist state of mind, but then the overambitious is bad because it's simply delusional, consisting as it usually does of a series of promises that Richard will never keep.

"I've let you down again," he says, and I get my answer right there: tonight Richard is suffering from drunken self-hatred, and he would like me to shore him up in this.

"It's all I ever do," he says. "Why don't you leave me, Tessa? Just leave me."

It's a good question, that, and it's one I've asked myself on numerous occasions, and in fact Sam has asked me that question too. "Why don't you leave him?"

The answer is that I like Richard, even now. We've been together for many, many years, and I loved the man I married.

We first met when I was doing my large animal placement as part of my training, and Richard was doing his PhD at the university engineering department. It was the gentlest, easiest start to a relationship you could imagine. We just got on as if we'd always been friends. We laughed together; we discovered we liked doing the same things. I loved his gentle intelligence, the way he thought before he spoke and was never mocking or snobbish.

We moved in together into a tiny attic flat, which nearly had a view of the Clifton Suspension Bridge, only four months after meeting, and we both studied like mad and made each other cups of instant coffee and lived on vats of chili con carne and baked potatoes that we took turns to make.

Our flat was an unfurnished place, and we slept together on a cramped futon and sat on deck chairs to watch TV because we didn't have enough money to buy a sofa. It was good practice for the traveling we did after we'd finished studying. Richard and I went around the world with backpacks for a year, and then lived for a time in Kenya, where we both managed to get work.

We married when we got back to the UK, and had our reception in the Clifton Pavilion at Bristol Zoo. It was still a happy time for us then, because it wasn't until a few years after that, after we'd got ourselves properly established back in Bristol, with new jobs and a new house, that things began to slip and slide, almost imperceptibly slowly, into something much less than what we had dreamed of.

So now we find ourselves a somewhat sourer version of the couple we imagined we would become. Richard has no work, and we have no children, and the resulting bitter disappointment has mostly turned him into a depressed, drunken, foolish version of my beloved bridegroom. However, there are hours, days, weeks, when the man that I loved reemerges, and I find that these are enough to keep me with him. To part would be to acknowledge that alcohol has managed to destroy us, and I'm just not ready to do that yet.

To Sam, I just say, "I can't, not yet," and as I say it I feel like a clichéd cheating spouse. But it's not to do with wanting to keep the status quo; it's to do with not being able to let go of what Richard and I had, the perfect idea of us, even though our reality has fallen so far from that.

To Richard, on the phone, I muster all my reserves in an effort not to lose my temper, and I just say, "Did you find the lasagna? Because you should eat. I'll be back later." Then, before he can suck me farther into his misery, I hang up and start the engine.

SUNDAY NIGHT

After the Concert

ZOE

Beside me, really peacefully, Grace falls asleep. I love her when she's asleep because she looks perfect: all that energy tucked away temporarily inside her silky smooth exterior, recuperating, so it can explode out of her when she wakes up later. Grace has such simple needs. Wake, give love, receive love, refuel, expend energy, sleep. I love that about her. Her energy is monumental, though; she could power the Hadron Collider.

I want to stay on the bed with Grace and sleep with her for the whole night. I've done that sometimes. If I've heard her wake up in the night before Mum or Chris do, I've gone in and taken her into the bed in her room with me. It gives my mum a break, and in the morning when Grace wakes I just get up with her before it disturbs Mum, and I change her and quickly make up the bed, because sleeping with her would be frowned on as "deviating from the routine." When I've done that, I take her to Mum and go downstairs and start to get her bottle ready. Grace loves to go in Mum and Chris's bed. It must seem as big as a football field to her, and she spreads her arms and legs out and nuzzles her head down into their duvet and then looks up to see if anybody is laughing.

Once I heard Chris say to Mum, "She's energetic, isn't she, for a girl?" as if he was a bit worried about that, but Mum said, "They all are at that age, that's nothing to worry about." I didn't hear the rest of the conversation because they kissed and I slipped away.

It would be a burning apocalypse, a red-rimmed sunset and the horsemen pounding so fast that they were almost on top of me before I watched those two snogging for longer than I had to, one of his hands all tight on her hips, puckering her silky pajama bottoms, the fingers of the other running down to find the place where her buttock meets her thigh.

I might have just stayed there with Grace that night, and things could have gone somehow differently, but Lucas is in the doorway making the same dark shadow as his dad did earlier, and he says, "Zoe, you need to come."

I pick Grace up as carefully as I can. Her limbs are warm-heavy-floppy, and I cradle her head on my arm and then lay her carefully in her crib. For a moment it looks like she might wake up again, because she tenses when her back settles onto the mattress, but then she relaxes and her head falls to one side, and I pull the thin cotton sheet just up over her legs because I don't want her to get too hot. Her chest makes tiny rise and fall movements, which I can just see in the darkness and her lips are puckered as if she's expecting a kiss from a prince.

Lucas is waiting on the landing. He's noticed the butterfly, which is still flapping in the high corner, and its wings have reached a pitch that is as fast as the fastest trill I can play on the piano. I wonder how long it can go on.

"Can you save it?" I say to Lucas.

"It's too high up."

"Why doesn't it fly to the light?"

"Only moths do that. Butterflies don't like artificial light."

He reaches out to turn off the light switch and in the darkness the butterfly's wings hush, as if it feels relief.

I look at Lucas and smile, but he's looking at me in a really intense sort of a way, which isn't that unusual for him, but what he does next is.

He kisses me.

It's especially clumsy at first, because I'm so not expecting it. He puts his mouth over mine and kisses me like I've never been kissed before, not even by Jack Bell, because it's fearsome, super-hot kissing, like in films.

It only lasts a few seconds and then he pulls away from me and I don't know what to say.

"Zoe," he whispers. "I know about you. I've known for a long time, but my dad doesn't. We need to stay with him and stay with your mum, we mustn't let them be alone, do you understand? They mustn't be alone. And listen, this is important, you need to get your mum to read my email."

"But we're supposed to look after Grace," I say.

"This is more important. Come on . . ."

He starts to walk down the stairs, but then he turns and looks back up at me because I'm still standing at the top, understanding nothing.

"Come on." He offers his hand to me, palm open and ready to be held.

"Why can't we leave them alone?" I ask him.

"Because."

"Because what?"

I can't see the expression on his face, so I don't know what he's thinking in the few seconds before he answers. "Dad can be mean sometimes."

And I don't know what to say to that, so I take hold of his hand and squeeze it a little, and follow him down the stairs.

We find Mum and Chris in the kitchen. They're standing with the island in between them. Chris has his hands on the granite as if he's about to try to lift it up. On the other side, Mum is stuffing hunks of white bread into the top of her food processor, which is whirring and rattling at top speed and pulverizing the bread into fine crumbs.

My mum has been crying. Her mascara has smudged a bit around her eyes.

"I thought I told you to look after Grace," Chris says to Lucas and me.

Obviously we're not holding hands anymore. Lucas dropped my hand before we got to the kitchen door. We've got the usual six feet between us.

"She's asleep," I say.

"Where is she?" Mum asks, fluttery-panicky, as if I'm stupid enough to leave Grace on the bed on her own.

"I put her in the crib. On her back. I put the sheet just on her legs."

"Oh! She might be too hot like that. Where's the monitor?"

I fetch it. It's on the table outside, amid the debris of the bruschetta, which hasn't been cleared up yet. I wipe a bit of tomato off it and turn the volume on. Grace is quiet. Inside, Mum takes the monitor from me. "It's nineteen degrees in her room," she says to Chris. "Do you think a sheet is OK?" Grace's monitor tells you practically everything about her bedroom, although it does stop short of videoing her.

Chris hasn't moved. I've barely dared to meet his eye, but

I can see that he's moving his jaw a bit, clenching and un-
clenching it.

"I don't know why you're asking me, darling," he says, and
he sounds mean. "Because it seems you don't even respect
me enough to be honest with me about who you and your
daughter are."

My mum detaches the lid from the blender very slowly
and decants the breadcrumbs into a wide, shallow dish. She
takes a very deep breath in, she practically inhales a reservoir
of air, and then she lets it out through puffed cheeks. All the
time, she's smoothing the breadcrumbs flat with the side of her
hand, so they're ready for covering the chicken breasts.

"Here's what I suggest," she says. "I suggest that we sit
down with some food and talk about this as a family. There
is something that Zoe and I would like to explain to you
both, but I would like to do it properly, the way we always
do things."

"Isn't it a bit late for that?" says Chris.

My mother straightens her back and walks to the fridge.
She hefts open the dungeon-sized stainless-steel door and
takes out a box of twelve organic, free-range eggs. Her lip
wobbles as she walks back to the island, and when she gets
there, she raises the box of eggs high into the air and slams it
down on the island, hard.

"Only," she says to Chris, facing him over the denuded
basil plants, the egg box in front of her looking as if it's been
crushed, oozing egg white and yolk in every direction, "if you
don't care about these two children, about that baby upstairs,
and about everything else that we have built up together.
Only if you want our lives to end up like this!"

And she opens the lid of the box. The slimy, shattered carcasses of eight or nine eggs lie within it, and I have to look away because I don't like to see things all smashed up.

"Is that what you want?" she says to him. "Is it? Is this what you want?"

She's scooping her hands into the egg now, dredging up bits of broken eggshell and showing them to him on fingers that are dripping with the slimy insides. It's disgusting. Some of it has fallen down the front of her silk shirt.

"Have you gone mad?" Chris asks her. "Look at yourself. Have you gone totally stark raving mad?"

They face each other in silence, in a kind of still, mute combat.

Lucas steps forward and starts to take the egg box away, but just as he's got it in his hands Chris says, "Leave them," and Lucas does. He slides the box back onto the counter in front of my mother and steps away, his movements as careful as if he were performing an operation.

My mother says, "Mad? Is that what you think this is?"

The wrecking of the food isn't something that makes me think my mum has gone mad, because that's the kind of thing my parents used to do when they rowed, before the accident. Food got thrown, maybe a mug, there was shouting, then it was all over, all cleaned up, all settled back to normal, hugs on the sofa.

What's freaking me out now, apart from the obvious, which is that Chris is about to know all about me, is that Mum never behaves this way around Chris. Around Chris she's like the butterfly. When it's appropriate she sits, wings closed tight, demure and tidy, patient, twitching almost indiscernibly until the moment when he's ready for her to spread her wings and show how beautiful she is, and then she's gorgeous, admired.

But only when he wants her to be. And that's it. She never, ever gets out of control. The Second Chance Family is not like that.

"Do you know what mad is?" my mum says. Now she's leaning forward with her hands on the granite, and she's fully facing up to Chris. The greasy lock of hair has fallen back over her forehead and the only kind of butterfly she looks like now would be an injured one, circling on the ground, wings shredded and useless, waiting for a foot to put it out of its misery.

"Mad is this! All of this!" She gesticulates theatrically, spreading her arms wide.

Chris looks at her, and then at us, and then at the used, empty wineglass in front of my mother on the granite, which narrowly escaped being knocked over by the egg box.

"You're drunk, Maria," he says to her. "It's not attractive."

"I am NOT drunk," she says.

Chris raises his eyebrows slightly. "I think we both know that you are," he says.

"Don't patronize me!"

"I'll take you upstairs," he says. "We'll talk about this in the morning."

"No!" Lucas says, and that gets all of our attention. "Where's Tessa?" he says. "Isn't she having supper?"

Chris and Mum stare at Lucas for a moment as if they're only just remembering that he and I are here. Then Mum says, "Tessa popped out for a few minutes, but, yes, let's have our supper." She runs her forearm over her forehead and then looks at her hands as if she can't understand why they're covered in gunk.

"Dad?" Lucas says to Chris, who's still staring at my mum.

"Out," he says to me and Lucas. "Out of this room. Now!"

And he bellows that in a way that makes my hands go up to my ears and makes me feel like the world has turned dark and I'll never be able to see again, and I open my mouth because the only thing I know to do now is to scream.

SUNDAY NIGHT

After the Concert

TESSA

When I get back to Maria and Chris's house I park on the
street again and then I let myself back in, and the first thing I
hear is a scream. It's long, and high-pitched, and it makes me
hurtle down the stairs into the kitchen.

Zoe is screaming. She has her hands over her ears and her
mouth open wide and she's screaming as if something's unbearable.

Maria stands at the island and says, "Stop it, Zoe, stop it!
Stop it! Will you stop it!" but it's not until I have Zoe wrapped
tightly in my arms that she does stop and I feel her body go
limp against mine. Lucas hovers beside us, anxious. Chris
looks on aghast.

Something's gone wrong; that's obvious. I think Chris has
confronted Maria. She looks awful: smudged eye makeup,
a dirty shirt, red eyes, and there are eggs smashed on the
counter.

"Come with me, honey," I say to Zoe, and I usher her
toward the door, and upstairs into the sitting room, which is
decorated as if the family regularly entertains minor royalty,

which, for all I know, they do. I sit her down and, although it's too hot for hugs, I keep my arms around her for all the long minutes that it takes for her body to stop shaking.

Zoe's a convicted killer. There are no two ways around that. Tom Barlow would probably qualify that farther by saying that she is a murderer. But she's still my niece. She's the baby I visited within hours of her birth all those years ago, a scrumpled-up scrap of a thing, at that moment full of all the potential in the world. She's the toddler I took to the beach and made a sandcastle with, she's the girl I took to the zoo and helped to be brave when she wanted to feed the lorikeets but was afraid of the feel of them when they landed on her hand. She was the nine-year-old I cheered on when she made it to her first regional piano final in blinding style, making me swell with pride even though I'd bitten my fingernails to the quick.

She was the child I loved and thought about and took an interest in.

And so, in spite of what she's responsible for, I love her still. Zoe made a stupid mistake one night of her life, which has had the most terrible consequences. But I will always love her. Somebody has to.

I know Maria loves her too, but Maria is closer, obviously, and the fallout from Zoe's actions has fractured Maria's life before and might now fracture it again and that, however much you love somebody, is complicated. They are tied to-gether too tightly for their love to be easy. But I think Zoe has a good heart. I believe her story about what happened all those years ago, on the night of the accident, and I want her to know that somebody loves her after the accident just the same way they did before it. I think she deserves that.

And so, as my body gets hotter, and damper, from the close contact with hers, I wipe her tears gently as they fall, and I just hold her, and I whisper to her that I'll always be there for her, no matter what, and that I love her to bits, and when she's calmed down enough I encourage her to lie down and I slip back downstairs to see what's happening.

SUNDAY NIGHT

After the Concert

ZOE

When Aunt Tess has gone downstairs I'm alone in the sitting room once more and I think about everything, mostly about how I've stuffed things up again because you shouldn't just scream.

"Screaming might feel like an outlet to you," said Jason, "and of course it is in a way, but there are other ways we can channel feelings. We can leave the room, we can ask for a timeout, we can point out that what's being said is making us feel very uncomfortable or anxious rather than just displaying it. These are better strategies than screaming."

"What about howling like a wolf?" I asked him.

Jason smiled, but he didn't run with it, not that I thought he would, but I liked to try to make him smile.

"Let's talk about what you could do instead," he said, and he started to try to teach me, yet again, how to be a functional human being.

It's funny, I thought I was one before I went to the Unit, but by the time they've counseled the hell out of you, you understand just how freaky you are.

The night I went to Jack Bell's party I didn't feel freaky, I felt as though I was about to enter the realms of the Popular.

What happened in the bedroom with Jack is something that I've had to talk about a lot with Sam, my solicitor, and at the trial, but that was really all about alcohol levels and issues of (new word I had to learn) culpability.

I didn't ever get to remember that bit of the party as something that might have been nice for me.

When Jack came back to the bedroom at the party, he brought me a pint glass full of Coke, which I told him was overkill and that made him laugh.

Jack handed me the glass and I took a big long drink, swallowing and swallowing until I made bug eyes and the bubbles tingled my nose, just to make him laugh.

"You never do anything by halves, do you?" he said.

"Is that Diet Coke?" I asked him. "It tastes funny."

"What are you?" he said. "Some kind of Coke connoisseur? Yeah, it is, so it tastes different. Do you want me to get you another one?"

"No," I said. "It's fine. I like it."

He sat very close to me, and he put his hand over mine, and pushed his fingers between mine.

"I've never heard you play piano," he said. "I should one day."

I didn't really know what to say to that. Piano is, and always has been, a private thing for me, although it makes me a public person, and the sight of his fingers on mine suddenly brought to mind my mum's hand, placing my fingertips on the keys, pushing them down, in the days when her hands were much bigger than mine, when my hands were far too small to stretch to an octave.

Jack interpreted my silence as coyness, as flirtatiousness.

"Perhaps I'll come to a concert next time," he said, "sit in the front row . . ." He leaned toward me and ran his fingers from just under my ear all the way down my jawline to my chin. "Or would that put you off?" he asked, and he leaned in even farther then, and put his mouth on mine and his hand dropped to my chest.

I pushed him away a bit, because the intensity of the thrill was sort of frightening, and Jack was older than me and bigger than me.

"I heard you play like a demon," he said. "Like you're possessed or something."

That made me laugh. "I don't know about that," I said, but inside I thought that maybe I did, sometimes, when I was really into the music. You don't really know how you look when you're playing well, because the concentrating and listening are everything.

It's a hard thing to explain to somebody without sounding weird, so I drank some more of my Coke to cover up how awkward I was feeling, and Jack's eyes were on me all the time, even when he downed his drink all in one go.

"What are you drinking?" I asked him.

"Cider. Do you want to try? I can get you some."

I shook my head.

"It's good," he said, and he took my Coke from me and put it on the bedside table, and put his drink beside it, and then he sort of climbed on top of me a bit and pushed me back onto the pillows, ever so gently, and he started to whisper something into my ear, words that you dream of, when there was a knock on the door.

"Shhh," he said.

"Zoe?" It was Gull.

"I have to," I said.

"Don't," he told me, "I want you."

But I couldn't abandon Gull; it just wasn't something I could do. Jack saw it. He rolled away and onto his back with a grunt of irritation.

"Gull," I said.

I went to the door. It was locked, although I hadn't noticed him do that, but the key was there, so I opened it, to find her slumped against the wall.

"Where've you been?" she said. "I couldn't find you anywhere."

She looked disoriented and her voice was slurred.

"Sorry," I said, as she leaned heavily on me. "Gull? Are you OK?"

And she puked, all over the floor.

"Oh fuck!" said Jack. "Get her to the bathroom."

He kind of manhandled Gull down the corridor. I sat by her as she threw up, again and again, into the loo. Jack went to clear up the mess on the floor, and I realized quickly that I should have locked the door to the loo because before I knew it Eva Bell was standing in the doorway, shoulder to shoulder with best friend Amelia Barlow, and both of them were looking at us with absolute disdain.

"Should have stayed in the library, girls," she said, "if you can't take your drink."

I heard once that Eva and her friends bought mixers to drink while they were getting ready for parties just in case there's not enough alcohol when they get there.

"Shut up," I said, but my heart wasn't in it because Gull was puking so hard it was making her cry.

"My mum's going to kill me," she said, and I gathered her hair up and held it back from her head.

"She doesn't have to know," I said.

"I want to go home," said Gull. She grabbed hold of me unsteadily. "I need to go home. It's my birthday tomorrow."

"What have you been drinking?" I asked her. I didn't tell her it was so late that it was already her birthday, because that probably would have made her more upset.

"Somebody spiked my drink. I swear, somebody spiked it."

We had cycled to the party, sharing Gull's bike. It was four miles, mostly downhill. The plan had been to walk home with the bike, but I could see that that wasn't going to happen. Gull was pulling herself up on me now and I didn't think she could even manage to walk.

Jack said, "I can drive you home." He was looking a little nervous now, as if vomit and neediness weren't on his agenda tonight.

Amy was right beside him, hanging off him a bit like Gull was off me only her body was pressed against his, and when he said this, her eyes and Eva's shot lasers at me. Amy was not very drunk, or if she was, she was holding it well.

"How much have you had?" she asked Jack. "Why don't you let them walk home? She lives nearby, doesn't she?"

Amy was right. Gull's family had a small, modern home in Hartland where the washing-up was never done and even the dogs didn't bother licking the grease off the floor. Her mum and dad were the warmest people you could meet, it's just they didn't care about that kind of stuff. They cared about Gull. Every penny they had, every ounce of love and effort, went to her.

"She runs like the wind, our girl," her dad would say, "like the wind," and my dad would mutter, "He used to run like the wind too, Gull's got it from her dad."

Gull's real name was Linda, but her parents, surprised by a baby when they'd given up hope of having one, began to call her Gull when, as her dad said, "She squawked like a gull at all hours, what else were we supposed to call her?" "We used to laugh," he said, "she squawked so loud. You'd have thought we was throttling her, not getting her a meal and cleaning her ladyship up."

Gull didn't like people to know where she lived, because of being a scholarship girl like me. We didn't live in big houses like Jack and Eva Bell and Amy Barlow and the other kids at our school. We lived in normal houses where there was mud, and stuff was old, and animals lay beside fires and there was single glazing.

"She can't stay here," Jack said. "My parents are coming home first thing in the morning."

"I'm not drunk," I said. "If I can borrow a car I can drive her home."

"You can't drive," Amy said.

"My dad taught me how."

Jack had a look in his eyes suddenly. "We could drop Gull home and then go to the lighthouse," he said. "Have you ever done that?"

"No," I said, but I was suddenly seduced by the glint in his eye, and I said, "but I'd like to."

Amy said, "That's a stupid idea, Jack. Let her drive Gull home and bring the car back. Then she can go home on the bike."

Jack ignored her. "It's very cool," he said. "You can climb up to the top. I know a way. We could take my dad's car."

And I got this incredible idea of the lighthouse, with its strong beam of light raking the waves below, and I heard powerful music in my head, classical music, rising like the spray on the rocks. I knew there was a shipwreck there too, which you could see when the tide was low, basking on the stony shore like rusted orange skeleton bones abandoned after a violent death.

"You should go with them, Ames," slurred Eva. She was drunk, definitely. "Make sure Jack doesn't cop off with piano girl. He's pissed enough he just might."

"Shut up," said Jack.

A boy called Douglas appeared behind Eva and slipped his hands around her waist and buried his head in the back of her neck.

"You coming too then, Eva?" Amy said to her.

"Somebody needs to hold the fort," she said, "if Jack goes off. You go, make sure he behaves himself."

She turned to Douglas, and her body seemed to slide up his and they kissed so long and hard that I was totally embarrassed, and in that moment it seemed that it had been decided that I would drive Gull home.

And I remember finishing my drink while me and Gull sat on the bed waiting for Jack to find the car keys, one arm around her and the other holding that pint glass of Coke. And I remember Amy glowering as if she would rather be anywhere else but with us, but didn't know what else to do.

And I remember helping Gull to the car, and helping her in, and then getting into the car myself and starting the ignition, and I remember how it felt powerful and smooth, quite unlike the truck I'd driven on the farm.

But I shut down the memories there, because this is the bit where it gets painful for me.

I think about how I'm in the sitting room on my own, again, and I wonder if I should go downstairs and apologize for screaming like I did, because "apologies are always good and always necessary," but I think my mum might want me to stay away so she can keep things smooth.

Lucas lingers in my mind: the kiss, the fact that he knows. How does he know? I wonder. Why hasn't he said? His request that I read his email comes back into my mind. I remember where my phone is, and I dig down under the sofa cushions and find it.

MONDAY MORNING

SAM

The choice that I gave to Mr. and Mrs. Guerin and Zoe, when we met to discuss her case on that freezing cold morning in Bideford, was a difficult one.

Zoe could go to her initial hearing at court and plead guilty. The court would look favorably on this, as it avoided a costly trial and was an admission of culpability. It would probably keep her sentence to a minimum, though she was unlikely to avoid something custodial.

Or Zoe could turn up at her initial hearing and make a "special reasons" plea. She would have to admit that she drove the car, and caused the accident, but could ask a judge to decide whether she was guilty of knowingly driving when drunk. If you accepted Zoe's explanation, it would appear that somebody spiked her drink at the party, most likely the boy she was with, Jack Bell, who was also one of the victims. We would have to prove that in court, though, and that would be a tough call, especially as three of the key witnesses were dead.

"Well, we'll do that then," says Mr. Guerin when he heard this option. "That's a plan then."

People who are in the system for the first time are always

tempted to mount a defense, because it feels like a chink of light, a way of minimizing the damage they've done, the guilt they feel, and the harm to their reputation and that of their family.

Maria could see pitfalls: "Well, wait a minute, what if they don't believe her?"

"It's the truth, isn't it?" her husband said.

Maria didn't speak; she was waiting for my reply.

"If the court doesn't accept that defense, then Zoe risks a tougher sentence than she might have got if she pleaded guilty."

"But it's not on her conscience then, is it?" said Mr. Guerin. "If she pleads guilty it's like telling the world that our daughter accepts that she murdered those children. Murdered them, Maria."

Zoe was shrinking into her chair.

Maria ignored him. "It's a gamble, then." She directed this at me.

"It would be a gamble, yes."

"Would she have a chance of getting less of a sentence if the judge accepts the plea than if she pleaded guilty in the first place?"

"I doubt it, no."

"But we wouldn't have it on our conscience," said Maria. "It would be a similar sentence but it would be proven that she didn't know she was drunk, that it was just a normal accident."

In my view, this is what you call clutching at straws, but this family was obviously trying to clutch at anything.

Mr. Guerin was on his feet now, standing at the window of my office, which had a view of the waterside, where the tide was low that morning, leaving the boats mostly stranded on the mud. A low, immovable gray sky waited patiently above the scene while this family considered their options, and it dulled and flattened the landscape across the harbor. Below it, seagulls hovered and circled, just as they did every day.

Mr. Guerin had his back to us, but when he spoke his voice was firm, and it was clear that he'd made a mental U-turn.

"It's not worth the risk," he said. "What if they don't believe her?"

"I'll tell them the truth," said Zoe.

"You've killed people, Zoe," he said. "Who's going to believe you?"

Quite apart from the hopeless resignation in his tone, and the effect it had on his daughter, this statement got to me because Philip Guerin was exactly the kind of man who was likely to be on a jury in this part of the world, and while I knew that there would be no jury in a youth court, where Zoe would be tried, it was an attitude that could well be shared by the magistrates or the judge.

"They'll believe her." Maria was suddenly adamant. "We can coach her. They'll feel sorry for her, she'll be a good witness, and perhaps we can get some of the other children in the witness box."

"No," said Mr. Guerin. "I'm fed up with you coaching her. You've coached her enough, Maria. We wouldn't be in this mess if you hadn't coached her so she got a music scholarship. She'd be at the local school, which was good enough for me by the way, but not good enough for your daughter. If she'd gone there, none of this would have happened. It's going to that jumped-up school and trying to keep up with the kids there, that's why this has happened. No. I won't do it. She should plead guilty and take the consequences for what she's done, pay for it, and then perhaps we can get some forgiveness one day."

"I don't agree," said Maria. "Think of Zoe. Think of us!"

"I am thinking of her. And of the other families. I grew up with Matt." His voice choked. I recognized the name of Zoe's friend Gull's dad.

"I know you did," Maria said.

"I won't put him and Sue through a trial."

"We have to give Zoe a chance to clear her name."

"No! Gull was their only child, you know that."

"I'm not willing to jeopardize Zoe's future to save the feelings of the other families."

"Sometimes, Maria, you have a hard heart," said her husband. "What future does Zoe have now anyway?"

I wanted to jump in and defend Zoe, but Maria was on her feet now too, and both of them were seemingly oblivious to Zoe.

"How is it having a hard heart to protect your daughter?" Maria spoke quietly but with a vehemence that was startling.

"And what if it doesn't protect her? What if it goes wrong and she goes to jail for longer than she would have if she pleaded guilty?"

They were facing each other across the table, although it was hard to see Mr. Guerin's expression because his back was to the window now.

"Zoe," I said, because it was definitely time for me to calm things down and I wanted to remind these two adults that their child was listening to them. "Do you understand what the decision is here?"

"I don't want to go to prison, but I don't want to make it worse for the families," she said. "I'll say I'm guilty."

As there was a sharp intake of breath from Maria, Mr. Guerin came around the table and put his hands on the back of Zoe's shoulders. He had huge, red, dry, callused hands, and they made Zoe look smaller and more fragile than ever.

"Well done, girl," he said.

But I looked at Maria and at Zoe, who watched her mother anxiously, and I didn't think this decision was made yet.

SUNDAY NIGHT

After the Concert

TESSA

When I get back downstairs, there's nobody in the kitchen. On the island, the box of smashed eggs lies untouched, and the mess from it drips silently off the side of the granite down onto the golden stone floor.

I go outside. Lucas and his father are standing at one end of the swimming pool, their faces washed blue and yellow by the lights, and at the other end of it, sitting on the end of the squat diving board, is my sister, the tips of her toes in the water.

Maria's breakdown after the accident was a slow burn. It began when Zoe was sentenced and taken to the Unit, which was when Maria stopped having a purpose, and when the adrenaline that had taken her through the trial, and the months leading up to it, crashed. She'd been closely involved in every detail up to then, liaising with Sam and with the rest of Zoe's legal team, discussing defense strategies. Adrenaline fueled her. She lost weight, she more or less lost her husband because they disagreed so strongly, and still she focused only on the case. She continued to be a tiger mother.

But the minute that Zoe was taken down, Maria ceased

to cope, because suddenly there was nothing to do. There was just an empty farmhouse, a husband who slept in another room, and a silence that sat with them, twiddling its fingers, looking from one of them to the other, whenever they were in a room together.

"Philip couldn't bear it," Maria told me. "It shamed him. He felt he'd failed her, failed at making a family."

I think she was right. Philip Guerin had been a doting father while the going was good, but nothing in his life had prepared him for what Zoe did, and while Maria became a dynamo, he retreated, shut himself down. Perhaps it was because he, like the families whose children died, had been rooted in that community for decades. Perhaps that meant he felt the loss of those three young folk more than Maria did. Perhaps it was because he was weaker than she was. Whatever the reason, it was shocking, his inability to cope. He didn't even protest when Maria moved out and came to Bristol to be near me, to make that fresh start with Zoe.

In the dense night air, on the end of the diving board, Maria has pulled her skirt up around her thighs. Her shoes have been discarded and lie poolside, one on its side. Her legs are bare and thin. Her toenails are painted a deep black-red.

When she sees me, she calls out to me, in a voice that I barely recognize, so strained is it.

"So," she says, "I've told my husband what happened to Zoe, his stepdaughter. I've told him that Zoe has been convicted of a crime, and do you know what, Tess: I think he's going to dump us."

Chris turns to me.

"She's drunk," he says. "She's totally lost her mind. I can't get any sense out of her."

I start to walk around the edge of the pool and Maria struggles to her feet. I can't quite understand how Maria could have got so drunk so quickly, because I reckon I've only been out of the house for about forty-five minutes, an hour tops. Though perhaps, as she says, she isn't.

"Don't come near me!" she shouts. "Nobody come near me!"

I almost laugh at that because the diving board is not high and the tone in which she says it makes it sound like a threat, as if she were teetering on the edge of the Clifton Suspension Bridge, hundreds of feet above the Avon Gorge. But I don't laugh because Maria looks like a broken puppet and Chris looks desperate, and I don't want to do anything other than help them to get through this evening, in the hope that once they do, they'll find that they still have a future together.

"Maria," I say.

She staggers to her feet, skirt tight around her thighs, making her wobble. "Don't come near me!" she repeats.

So I stop, halfway around the pool. I wonder if in fact Chris is mistaking instability for drunkenness, if the real explanation is that years of ghastliness have just reached their peak and now threaten to topple her sanity. When she got pregnant with Grace, I did worry about her, that she might not cope with the pressures of starting all over again, but she seemed to sail through that, just as she'd sailed into her new role as Mrs. Christopher Kennedy, mother to Zoe, stepmother to Lucas, and now I'm wondering whether that was a Band-Aid, masking wounds that I know run very deep.

Chris says, "Maria, come off there, please. Let's talk; let's eat. Like you wanted to."

"No," she says. "Because the eggs are broken, so I can't get the breadcrumbs on the meat." She sounds pathetic now. She looks at me. "I'm sorry, Tessa," she says.

"It's fine," I say. "Of course it is. Don't be silly."

Teetering now on the end of the board, Maria has noticed the stain on her shirt and she starts to rub at it, and when that doesn't work, she begins to unbutton it.

"For Christ's sake, Maria!" Chris's voice explodes around the pool. "What are you doing?"

Lucas turns his head away because before we know it she's pulled the shirt off and is standing there in just her skirt and bra, a complicated, lacy bit of apparatus which holds her breasts firm and pert. Her body is perfectly taut. I think that her bra probably cost more than my entire outfit.

"Oh, I'm so sorry!" she shouts at him. "I'm so sorry that I'm not perfect."

Chris marches around the pool toward her.

"What are you doing?" she calls and she's taunting him. "Coming to tell me off? Coming to tell me to behave like a good girl? Coming to tell me I'm useless?"

He pauses at the end of the diving board, unsure what to do.

"Maria!" I call. "For God's sake!"

And Maria, in a gesture that's at once melodramatic and extraordinary, turns around, pinches her nose and lets herself fall back into the pool, and, for a moment or two, we all just watch the splash subside and see that she's sunk to the bottom, where she floats for a second or two, eyes shut.

It's Lucas who gets her out. He jumps in fully clothed and pulls her up to the surface, and they both swim together to the side, where he helps her up the steps, and she's gasping and coughing, but by the time they're both out, Chris has gone indoors. Turned and walked away, as if he's too disgusted to deal with her at all.

I take her sobbing, wet body from Lucas and send him inside to change, partly because he needs dry clothes, but also because I've got to strip her out of her sodden skirt and I don't wish her humiliation to be any worse.

I hold her, just as I held Zoe minutes earlier, and I'm persuading her to try to get out of her wet clothing when Chris reappears. He has a large towel with him, and a change of clothes for her. He holds the towel open and Maria looks at it for a moment before walking slowly toward him and letting him envelop her with it.

He wraps the towel around her and holds her tight in his arms. The water from her soaking skirt still swarms down her legs in rivulets. She's shivering.

"Maria," he says. "My Maria. Come on. Let's get you in the shower."

She looks up into his face and nods. "I'm sorry," she says, "I don't know what came over me."

"Let's talk about it," he says. She shuts her eyes and leans against him.

"I think it's probably best if you go home now," he says to me. "We're all right. We'll be OK."

"Are you sure?" I say. I want to get Maria's agreement, but she's huddled into him, shaking, seeking the warmth from his body, because the air around us is beginning to lightly shift and buffet.

"I'll look after her," he says. "Are you OK with that, honey? If Tess goes?"

He puts a finger under Maria's chin and lifts it gently

and she looks up at him and nods. Her smile is hopeful but precarious, threatening to break into pieces like the paper napkin that's fallen into the pool, and floats there, slowly disintegrating into many different pieces in the softly eddying water.

SUNDAY NIGHT

After the Concert

ZOE

When I get my phone out, I see that panop has notified me again. It says:

> How could you think you could keep it a secret?
> I've known all along.

And I understand suddenly that it has to be Lucas sending me the messages, because who else could it be? It's Lucas and he's known for a long time like he said, and he's kept that totally secret from me. And in a way that's a relief because it's not somebody from back then, but it's frightening too.

I'm confident enough that I'm right to send a message back:

> How do you know?

I want to know how he found out and I want to know what it means to him, because I didn't get the chance to ask him. I want to know why he kissed me. Was it real? Or did he just want to find out how it feels to kiss a killer? Lots of teenagers get off on that kind of stuff actually, and although I don't think Lucas is that kind of boy, you can never be really sure about anybody.

I also want to know why he's using panop to contact me, because that's horribly, awfully freaky, but Lucas is a super-tech computer person so I suppose it's not that surprising that he's found out about me. I close panop, because I'm still curious to have another look at Lucas's email. I open my inbox and I find it, but I can't read the attachment straightaway because for some reason I have to download it again as my phone is always such a fail and needs upgrading.

While I wait I try to control my breathing, which has become fast and shallow. To distract myself, I scroll around my phone, and I see that his email is surrounded by about twenty other unread emails, none of them personal.

The only one that interests me is a Facebook notification, where I can see what Katya is doing. When she first arrived, Katya was really friendly to me, like a cat rubbing up against your legs, and she wanted us to be friends on Facebook; that was before she worked out that I was Social Pond Life and had no proper friends, either online or in real life. What being her Facebook friend means is that I can see when she changes her profile picture, and in fact she's just done that. She's just changed it from the vampy Kardashian pout that she put up last week and now it's a picture of her and Barney Scott together, all nostrils and foreheads and sunglasses, all teeth and chins and my heart kind of sinks because they look sexy and funny and cool like teenagers are supposed to look.

There are no photos of me online from the trial because the press weren't allowed to report my name or publish photos of me, which was a saving grace, as my mum said at the time.

The only photos of me online now are from a stupid website that my mum runs to manage my profile. In those photos, I'm always groomed and wearing a concert outfit. I'm never drunk, or stoned, or sexy, or funny, or wearing sunglasses. My tongue doesn't loll out rudely like a pop star. The only prop I have in any of my online photos is a shiny silver trophy, which my mum will soon be snatching from my hands so that she can take it away and get my name engraved on it, for perpetuity, just like my criminal record.

I can hear somebody coming. Chris takes the stairs up from the basement two at a time, passes the sitting room door, and continues up to the second floor. "Sshh," I want to say, "don't wake the baby," but I would never dare. That phrase is in my head because it's what he and Mum say all the time to me and Lucas, and once somebody has said something one thousand times, it's in your head forever. I just let my mouth form the words silently instead. He reappears again quite quickly, holding bundles of things, heading back down. He doesn't look at me, he doesn't know I'm watching, and I wonder what's happening.

I think it's best if I stay away from downstairs, though, because I'm messing everything up tonight. So I close the Facebook email and go back to the one from Lucas.

The attachment is downloading so slowly, which is incredibly annoying. I think about the title of it, and it makes my heart start to beat a little faster because now I wonder what "What I Know" is referring to, and if the script is going to be about our life now, after it's talked about his mum, and if it will tell me how Lucas knows about me. I kind of take a mental deep breath because I'm always wary now of people turning on me and I wonder if Lucas is about to. People can, even if they've kissed you, even if they've kissed you deeply.

"It's complicated, that," Jason told me once when we were talking about what happened with Jack Bell, "because you'd be surprised how easily people can mix up feelings of love and hate. You wouldn't think they can, but they do, and it's because they're both strong and sometimes frightening emotions."

I had to agree with that, because although I've never told anybody about it, I fully remember what happened in the car right before we crashed, right before they died.

We argued. I was driving super slowly, and I mean super slowly, because it was icy out and I was still struggling to handle the car. In the rearview mirror I could see Gull's head lolling and Jack said, "Come on! Let's go to the lighthouse now—all of us—you can look after her, Ames—you won't mind, will you?"

"No," I said, "I think I need to get Gull home."

I suddenly felt odd then, queasy and dizzy, and the road ahead seemed to have a life of its own like a ribbon twisting in the wind. I blinked and it steadied. Ahead in the lights I could see frost-tipped hedges, and I knew that around the corner, just after the junction to the lighthouse, was the lane where Gull's parents' house could be found.

I clasped the wheel carefully, hands at ten to two, and in the back Amy said, "For God's sake, Zoe, you're driving like such a girl."

"She is a girl," said Jack. "She's doing fine," but then he leaned over to me and whispered in my ear, "Though you could probably speed up a little bit."

He turned on the car stereo and cranked up the volume

until it was blasting out. "'Highway to Hell,' ACDC," he said and he gave me a massive grin, which I just loved. As the music pumped around the car I put my foot down a little. Jack peered into the back seat. "Gull's asleep," he said. "Come on, let's just go to the lighthouse."

"No, no," I said. "We should take her home. Actually, I don't feel so good myself." In fact I felt disorientated and strange and uncertain, because suddenly the hedges we were driving between somehow didn't look familiar and I wasn't sure where I was.

"Oh, relax," said Jack. He was thumping the tops of his legs in time to the music. "You won't believe how awesome it is at the lighthouse, honestly, I'm telling you."

Amy said, "What are you planning to do with her there anyway, Jack? She's just a pathetic little slut, you know."

I heard that loud and clear and I turned around for just a second to say something to her, to tell her that her comment proved that she was the bitch who was sending me the panop messages, but as I did Jack said, "Zoe! You're missing the turn," and I looked back around at the road to see the turn to the lighthouse but as I did I hit the accelerator by mistake and the car surged forward just as Jack reached out to turn the wheel away from Gull's house and down the lane that led to the lighthouse, and it was only a millisecond before there were no memories anymore because there was only blackness, until I woke up to hear somebody phoning for an ambulance, and then the rest of my life started.

I remember all this as if it's a slow-motion film while I'm watching the attachment trying to download, achingly slowly, like death by volcanic ash burial, when Tessa comes upstairs.

"Hey," she says. "Mum slipped into the pool. She's fine, but we're not going to do dinner because it's getting a bit late, so I'm off home."

"Did she go for a swim?"

"No, it was more of an accident."

My mum is clumsy like me, but I think that this really takes the biscuit, as Jason would say.

"Do you have to go?" I ask.

I don't want her to go. I really don't. Aunt Tessa is sort of my best friend these days, and it's like she can read my mind because she says, "Do you want to come and stay the night with me?"

And I do, I really, really so badly do, but I know that Mum might need me here and I don't want her to be alone if there's going to be an argument or "a talk," so I say, "I'm fine. I'd better stay."

She hugs me again, warm and lovely, and pats my back while she's hugging me in the way that she's always done. I feel a tear slip down my cheek. Just one.

"I'll call you in the morning," she says. "Be strong, Butterfly, you've nothing to feel bad about. Nothing. Remember that. You've paid for what you did and you have a right to a life."

I stand behind one of the heavy drapes and watch from the front window as she crunches down the drive. She turns once to look back at the house before she disappears from sight.

MONDAY MORNING

SAM

Zoe did not plead guilty. Against her father's wishes, and guided by her mother, she pleaded not guilty and went for the special reasons defense instead. It was an unusual defense—I had repeatedly warned the whole family of that—but, at first, it seemed that we might be successful.

Zoe went into the stand and presented herself fairly well when speaking about the events that had taken place that night. She showed that she had terrible regrets, and she admitted her guilt by accepting that she had been the driver, but assured the judge that she wasn't knowingly drunk. She agreed that she'd had a drink when she arrived at the party, a spritzer, but insisted that she'd asked only for Coca-Cola after that, and repeated her conviction that her drink must have therefore been spiked.

It wasn't until Eva Bell, Jack Bell's twin sister, and a witness for the Crown, took the stand that any chance of success we might have had was ruined.

The Crown called Eva Bell to give evidence that Zoe knowingly drank an excessive amount of alcohol, and Eva couldn't have been a more successful witness.

There was a minimum of people in the courtroom, because of Zoe's age, and we'd been there for a week already hearing testimony from experts about the site of the accident, the condition of the car, and the blood alcohol levels, so some of the tension had left the proceedings to be replaced by boredom. The walls of the courtroom were clad in wooden strips and there was no natural light, so it felt a bit as though we'd all been buried underground for a week. Zoe had agreed to her mother attending but didn't want her father to be there, because she was embarrassed that she'd ignored his preference for an early guilty plea. If she'd done done what he wanted, there would have been no trial.

Eva Bell arrived with her own mother. They were ushered into the court from a waiting area separate from Zoe and her mother, a service the court provided to minimize ugly scenes. They sat alone on a bench across the aisle from the prosecutor.

In contrast to how Zoe had described her, which was as some kind of tormentor, Eva Bell presented as demure, intelligent, and, most of all, incredibly sad. Her mother sobbed audibly as she gave evidence, and Eva did not once look at Zoe.

It didn't help us that the prosecutor was a woman who you'd like to make godmother to your children. She led Eva down a gentle path of questioning that was devastating to us.

"Were you with your brother Jack when he got a drink for Zoe?"

"Yes, I was."

"In your view did Jack add anything to the drink that was alcoholic?"

"I poured the drink myself, so I know he didn't."

"Did you pour the drink from a bottle?"

"Yes, but I had to open it."

"So you don't think the drink was spiked?"

"No. I saw him carry it to the room they were in. If he spiked it, he would have had to do it in front of her."

I saw the panic on Zoe's face during this testimony and I willed her to stay calm, because of course the story that she'd told the court directly contradicted this.

"And did you see Zoe taking a drink earlier in the evening?"

"Yes."

"And what did she drink?"

A tiny stumble in Eva's composure here, but it could easily be read as grief by the judge.

"She drank," Eva said, "vodka and coke."

"Did you make that for her?"

"No. She made it herself. And she was generous with the vodka."

"And did you see her refill her glass?"

She pursed her lips, before replying, "Yes, yes, I did," and Maria's gasp was audible throughout the entire courtroom.

And the prosecution hadn't finished there. Another girl, a friend of Eva and Amelia, testified to the same thing and there was nothing we could do to contradict it. It was their word against Zoe's, and they were in the majority.

SUNDAY NIGHT

After the Concert

TESSA

As I drive away from Chris and Maria's house, I feel absolutely wrung out. It's eleven o'clock at night and I need my bed. I send a text to Sam, who I hope isn't waiting up for me, to say that I won't be coming around because I need to go home and sleep. We didn't have any sort of definite arrangement, but he knew I went to the concert alone, and that I might have an opportunity to visit him afterward, so I feel I owe him the courtesy of letting him know at least.

I always feel guilty when I see Sam, and that's never easy, but I don't seem to be able to stop myself going back to him, because, although I love Richard, I'm tired of his joyless existence.

We've tried everything to lift Richard's spirits: a chemical cocktail, a course of therapy, a holiday, hobbies, a different diet, exercise, and more. And we've tried all kinds of different combinations of the above, but, in the end, none of them have worked.

Richard's black dog is his constant companion, and he leavens the intensity of their relationship with alcohol. If I have a role in his life anymore, it's to make sure that while he's in the teeth of the dog, the rest of his life doesn't disappear. I do this because I hope that his depression will lift one day. If it never does, I've made a very bad call. His addiction will have got the better of me. It's ironic, really, as it's my life's work to cure and to rehabilitate.

It means that I dread going home. I dread it every day. I dread the monotony of his despair and the way that he can leach the colors from everything. I dread his inability to enjoy even a hot cup of tea or the smell of a freshly plucked mint leaf. I sympathize with his feelings, because I understand depression, or at least I think I do, but I dread it too, with every cell of my body.

It was why I was extremely happy for Maria when she met Chris. She was in the teeth of the black dog too up until then, put there by Zoe and by the shock of the loss of their world on the farm in Devon. You don't think of farming families imploding, or I never did. There's something about the continuity of their way of life that makes it seem, from the outside, more stable than the choices the rest of us have made. But clearly, I was wrong. So when Maria met Chris and things between them developed, I was glad for her, and I was glad for Zoe; in fact, I was unbelievably relieved.

Richard hasn't found the thing that will allow a slice of light to pierce the darkness in his head yet, and if I'm honest I'm not sure why the darkness ever fell so completely. He had disappointment at work, for sure. He was passed over for a prestigious appointment, which should have been his, because he was never good at playing the politics in his department, but others have survived that kind of thing without succumbing to such a complete breakdown.

I sometimes wonder whether our childlessness has deprived him of what might have been a source of happiness.

Would the Richard who worked so enthusiastically in his department, who loved to travel, who decorated our house, and so carefully planted up our garden in the early years, and dreamed of blooms and sunshine in the summer, have been saved by becoming a father? Would that have made the difference? Or would I have spent my time explaining to our confused offspring why Daddy wasn't getting out of bed today, or hadn't smiled even though it was Christmas.

I'll never know; it's just something I wonder about when I'm looking for reasons. Alone, I'm not enough to anchor Richard in the present, and so of course I wonder if a family would have been.

So many "what if"s. It's something that must roll around Zoe's head too. What if I hadn't got in the car that night? What if I hadn't gone to the party? When Zoe was in the legal process, surrounded by lawyers and court papers and police reports, the thing that got to me was how her case bowed every head. Sam would talk about that too. How the police handled her with kid gloves, how everybody around her was sunk by the misfortune of her situation.

Maria would have felt the "what if" factor then too. What if I hadn't tried to save face? What if I'd let her plead guilty in the first instance? What if . . .

I park in the driveway of my house and, when I let myself in, I find that it's completely quiet, though a light glows from the landing upstairs.

Richard is in our bed, on his back. He's asleep and his snoring is loud and persistent. The bedroom is clear of bottles, but I find one stuffed into the poky dark area at the bottom of his cupboard. The neck of the bottle is still damp and smells of fresh wine. My heart sinks because it probably means he stashed it there before passing out on the bed, and that probably means that his bladder is full but he'll be too drunk to feel it. I sigh because it means I'm going to have to wake him.

I spend a good ten minutes shaking him into a state resembling consciousness so that I can persuade him to pee. He manages it, unsteadily, lurching along the landing like the drunk he is, words slurring and sliding out of his mouth, as clumsy as his physical movements. When he's done, he passes out on the bed again, exactly the same as before, and I'm left with aching arms and a pounding heart from supporting him down the corridor, from talking him through what he's got to do, and from dodging the amorous advances that he always makes when he's this far gone, but which we both know won't amount to anything once he's horizontal again.

Down in the kitchen I clear up the mess he's made heating and eating the lasagna and I lock the back door, which he's left wide open to the stifling night air.

Then I sit at the kitchen table, now scrubbed as clean as my surgery at work, and think about the conversation that he and I will have in the morning, an old conversation, where we both know our lines by heart. It's a conversation about going to rehab, and how I want him to, and how he doesn't feel it's necessary because he feels he can get better on his own, and when I think of that, and of Tom Barlow, and all the things Maria will be having to explain to Chris tonight, weariness and loneliness saturate me and make me cry, just for a moment or two. And suddenly I crave company, not sleep, so I do what I shouldn't: I try to phone Sam.

SUNDAY NIGHT

After the Concert

ZOE

A short time after Tessa has gone, Lucas comes into the sitting room where I'm lying with my phone watching his PDF fail to download quickly. He tells me that we're all going to talk in Chris's study. He's changed his clothes and his hair is wet.

I start to say to him, *How do you know about me?*, but he puts a finger to his lips.

He holds out a hand to pull me up and I get a frisson of electricity when I touch it. I wonder if this means he's my friend, or my boyfriend, or neither, but I don't dare ask him and now isn't the moment anyway.

When I was in the Unit I made friends with people who I can't tell my mum about; actually, I can't tell anybody in the Second Chance Family. In the Unit, I sometimes felt like it was easier to make friends than at school. You have crime in common, after all, and I know that sounds stupid, and it doesn't make things easy always, but it does "level the playing field," as Jason the Key Worker used to say.

My friends in the Unit were Connor (breaking and entering, repeatedly) and Ellie (common assault, three strikes and you're out). They were what Jason called "Revolving Door Cases."

"You're categorically *not* a Revolving Door Case, Zoe," he said. "Cat-e-gor-i-cal-ly not." He pronounced each syllable separately to make his point. Jason didn't have much apart from verbal tricks to make his points. And laser eye contact. No PowerPoint presentations for him. Just me and him, in a room with a barred window to the outside, and a reinforced sheet of glass in the door, and a table and two chairs, which were bolted to the floor.

I would be wearing my lovely Unit attire of green sweatsuit bottoms and top and Jason would be in jeans and a T-shirt. Unless it was winter, when a little line of snow rimmed even the barbed wire coils outside, until a sharp wind dispatched it into soft whorls and then blew it into every crack and crevice in the building. Then Jason might wear a short-sleeved sweater over his T-shirt which, if I'm honest, made him look like a sad nineties pop star having a quiet night in.

"Put the f★★★★★g heating on," shouted Ellie from her cell, all night for the first night when it got cold. "Turn up the f★★★★★g heat, you f★★★★★g c★★★s, I'm freezing my f★★★★★g tits off in here." Her language was so bad it fully made me blush.

She banged her door too that night, an ear-splitting rhythmic pounding with a metallic edge that made me press my hands down hard on my ears. You could make a good racket if you banged the door with a tin cup. The next day we got extra blankets, which had "HMP Dartmoor" printed on them and were thin and gray and made me wonder who had slept under them before, and whether they were Revolving Door Cases who'd revolved all the way into an adult center. You only have to be eighteen to go into an adult prison.

The reason I wasn't a Revolving Door Case, according to Jason, was because of my family, which meant that I had a chance when I got out. My mum, he said, was determined to make a fresh start for me, determined to help me. I also had a talent, he said, with my music, my mum had told him all about it, and they had agreed that they couldn't think of any better way to rehabilitate me. Revolving Door Cases had no chance. They would go back into lives of abuse, and deprivation and neglect, and they would be reoffending and back in court before they knew it, their families watching dully, looking drowned by the inevitability of it all, if they bothered to turn up at all.

Lucas's PDF still hasn't downloaded by the time we all troop into Chris's study. It's on sixty-five percent with five minutes remaining. I'm thinking that because Chris's study is where our Wi-Fi hub is, that it might download a bit quicker once we're in there, but I forget all about that as soon as we get into the room.

It's not a room I normally go into. It's Chris's sanctuary; it's where he talks to Lucas when they need to "chat." Lucas never looks happy when he's going in there. My mum goes in there sometimes, but usually only when she's bearing a gift of some sort for Chris: a cup of tea, or coffee, or a Tom Collins if it's after six o'clock. I've been in once or twice, and when I do, I usually look at the frame that's on the wall behind Chris's desk. It's a black frame, about twelve inches square, and in the middle of it, mounted on a black background, is a single computer chip. Chris invented it and it's the reason he's minted. Chris was like Midas when he made that chip; it made everything turn to gold.

Not that you'd think that from the look of his study, because it's really plain. My mum always wants to decorate it, and sometimes she brings swatches of things home: new fabrics for Chris's sofa, or for curtains, but he always refuses. The sofa he keeps in there is one that he had in his office at work when he invented the chip back in the day. He says he's "not a senti-mental man" but he "can't let go of that sofa." It's a lucky sofa for him.

I get that, because I have a lucky hair ribbon that I wore at my first piano competition. I don't wear it anymore because my image has moved on, but I always have a little feel of it before a competition or a concert. I touched it before the concert tonight, not that this helped me much. The ribbon is black and velvety; it looks like nothing much and the ends are a little frayed now, but the feeling of it is a lucky thing for me.

Beside the rank sofa, Chris has two club chairs, which my mum did persuade him to buy, because she said he ought to be able to have meetings in the home office without it look-ing like an Ikea showroom. Opposite the rank sofa, against the wall of the room, Chris has a big long desk, which is surrounded by bookshelves where there are tons and tons of books about computer coding and stuff like that, including three books that he has written.

Chris is very, very clever, my mum told me when she came home after her first date with him, and a basic knowledge of genetics will tell you that that is probably why Lucas is too. Lucas once told me that his mum was clever too, though she never got a chance to show it before she died, but I couldn't really have that conversation with him because it made me think too much of Gull.

"A student with exceptional potential," the prosecution said about her in their summing up, "a bloom cut down before it could flower," which I thought was a bit much, but that was definitely something I was not allowed to point out, though I think if Gull had heard it she would have snorted, definitely.

She always snorted like a pony on a cold morning when she heard something blowsy like that.

I sit first, on the sofa. The cushions tilt backward so I have to perch on the very edge of them if I want to preserve any kind of what my mum would call "suitable decorum." I'm careful to cross my legs at my ankles, not my knees, and I tug down the skirt of my dress so that it's covering as much of me as possible. Unfortunately, that does make the top of my dress ride down a bit so I have to wriggle a little to cover myself up as best as I can, and I can tell that Chris's eyes are on me under a frowning brow.

Lucas sits on one of the club chairs and, as he settles into it, I see a resemblance to Chris that I don't always notice. Lucas's looks mostly favor his mum, that's obvious. There are no photographs of her anywhere in our house apart from Lucas's room, but I've been in there and I could see how much they look like each other.

Chris is holding Grace's intercom and, as he puts it down on his desk, he jogs the mouse of his computer and the huge screen comes to life. On it, frozen in super-high definition, is an image of Lucas and me sitting at the piano in the church. Lucas is looking toward the camera and I'm playing, bent over the piano, one of my hands poised over the next note, the tips of my hair brushing the keys.

In the foreground is Tom Barlow, or rather the back of him, and it's him that Lucas is looking at.

This is the moment it all started to happen and, as my mum comes into the room, she gasps at the sight of it.

MONDAY MORNING

SAM

The judge didn't accept Zoe's special reasons plea.

He found against Zoe, he stated, because he simply didn't believe that she would have been monitoring what she drank that night. No matter that we'd explained that she was a conscientious person, a good student, that she'd had a piano competition the following day. We might not have convinced him anyway, but Eva Bell and her friend's testimony, which so strongly contradicted Zoe's claim that Jack Bell had spiked her drink, certainly put the knife in Zoe's back, and twisted it too.

Zoe stood up in the courtroom as the judge spoke to her.

"I find," he said, looking at her over a pair of reading glasses, "that as you were only fourteen years old on the night of the party, there was no reason for you to monitor closely how much alcohol you were able to drink before driving, because you were not legally able to drive a motor vehicle. I find that you did drink freely during the course of that evening and that you don't actually know how much you had to drink. Therefore, regrettably, I find that while you might not have known exactly how much you had to drink, you knew you were too drunk to drive that car."

He sentenced her to an eighteen-month detention and training order. It meant that she would probably serve nine months, or thereabouts. I felt that wasn't too bad in the circumstances, but her family would never get the satisfaction of proving that Zoe had done what she did only because she was unwittingly drunk. She met nobody's eye as they took her down.

My goodbye to her mother was muted and painful. Tessa was there too, because I remember them standing together outside court looking desolate. Zoe had no other supporters with her that day.

It took me a while to get the trial out of my system. I felt a sense of failure in some ways, because I wondered whether I should have insisted more on a simple guilty plea at the first hearing. It could have resulted in a more lenient sentence. In the end, we took a legal gamble and lost, and Zoe paid the price. I wondered if she took any satisfaction afterward from knowing that she did, at least, tell the truth, or whether it was a regret or, worse, something to resent.

It wasn't until two years later, after I'd moved to Bristol to broaden my criminal practice experience, that I ran into Tessa by chance. We recognized each other immediately and met for coffee the following week. Things developed from there. Until we reached last night.

Now, as I watch Tessa ease her VW into the Monday-morning traffic outside my apartment, on her way to find out how and why her sister is dead, it's clear to me that things might just become very complicated indeed.

SUNDAY NIGHT

After the Concert

ZOE

It goes weirdly well. You wouldn't think it, looking at Lucas, who's got a face on through the whole thing like he's about to have a medical emergency on a TV daytime drama.

Once my mum has got over seeing Tom Barlow, and me and Lucas, frozen on the screen, she takes control in a way that I think is totally impressive, considering.

She isn't wearing her normal Second Chance Family clothes when she comes down. She's in a pair of leggings and a loose T-shirt. Maybe that's what makes me relax a bit, because she's dressed more like she used to dress, before it happened and when we still lived with my dad: still pretty, still nice, but way more casual. She's taken the makeup off her face and tied her hair back. The short, soft sleeves of the T-shirt make her arms look fragile and thin, and without foundation the dark circles under her eyes resemble small bruises. My mum, I realize, is very tired.

As she stands in the doorway, Chris gestures toward the chairs and the rank sofa. I think she's going to sit down beside me, but she doesn't. She takes the club chair opposite Lucas and Chris is left with the spare sofa seat. When he sits down, the weight of him makes the sofa cushions sag heavily and I become even more extra self-conscious about my bare knees and shoulders.

"Sit up, Zoe," is the first thing my mum says as she looks at me with eyes that are red-rimmed and empty of everything except the bottomless look she had had permanently for a long time after the accident. "You're hunching."

I notice that Lucas adjusts his posture too, when she says that, but my mum's oblivious. She focuses her whole being on Chris, like he's the last animal of his kind on earth.

"Thank you for listening," she says. "Zoe and I do have some proper explaining to do, we owe that to you both and I'm grateful to you for listening . . ." Mum does a bitter-looking swallow then, and tears begin to slip from her eyes, though she doesn't pay any attention to them. It makes me want to cry myself and I have to work very hard not to.

Mum doesn't notice that, though. She's sitting ramrod straight in the chair and she fixes Chris with her eyes, which I once heard him tell her were beautiful.

Chris doesn't do poetic description—"I'm just a computer scientist!" he sometimes says when Mum is asking him to make a decorating choice. "You're the creative one!"—so "beautiful" was probably an adjectival stretch for him. I could add to that description. Mum's eyes are pellucid, arctic blue. The blue is washed pale inside the eyes with a darker rim around the edge and, if you look closely, a fleck of hazel lies within one of her irises, like an intruder.

She tells Chris and Lucas the full blow-by-blow story of the accident, of my fall from grace, the way we told it at the trial. It's the version of the story where I'm as much of a good person as a bad one; it's the version where I think I'm doing the right thing when I decide to drive the car. It's the true version.

Chris stands up when she's finished. He hasn't said a word while she talked. On his computer screen the image from the church is still freeze-framed, like Munch's silent scream. She tries to reach for his hand as he walks away from her, but she's too slow. Mum doesn't look at me, she just folds her hands into her lap after that and waits, and so I copy her.

I look at the lights that are on in the room, because it's dark everywhere else now. Chris's desk lamp is dumping a tired circle of yellow onto the surface of his desk, and the glass wall lights that are sculpted to look like flaming torches are glowing, as is the bulb that shows off Chris's famous, framed computer chip. Between them, there's gloom.

"Maria," Chris says, "I'm glad that you've told me. Thank you."

Mum's lips disappear inside her mouth. The tears roll down her face faster now. Chris doesn't look at me. He doesn't look at Mum. He's looking at the computer monitor, as if he's mesmerized by it. He leans forward and uses the mouse to click on the play button, and the film begins to move.

"Travesty!" Tom Barlow shouts. "It's a travesty."

On the screen, in the movie of myself, I finally notice Tom Barlow. I stare at him, then I get up, and I bang my leg against the piano, as I run out of the frame. I look like a fairy tale girl, fleeing from a wolf. Lucas just stays staring, and then my mum is standing up at the front, turning, and she says, "Mr. Barlow, Tom . . ." and Chris clicks "pause."

"I'm just finding," says Chris, "the fact that you lied to me *twice* difficult to accept."

That's therapy-speak, that "difficult to accept" stuff. I've had enough therapy to know it when I hear it. "It's better to describe your emotions than display them," Jason would repeat patiently at our Monday meeting when I'd raged or sobbed my way through the weekends at the Unit, "then people can help you manage them instead of feeling as if they're bearing the brunt of them."

Chris keeps talking and I think that if his voice were a cat then it would be padding quietly and unstoppably toward my mother with unblinking eyes.

"You lied to me about Zoe's history, and I suppose I can understand it, I think I can. What Zoe and you have experienced is obviously . . . well, I'm at a loss for words to describe it just now. You should have told me, but I understand why you didn't, it was a lie by omission. What I cannot understand, what feels like a slap in the face, is why you lied to me earlier, when you denied knowing that man. That was an out-and-out lie and you know how I feel about lying, and I'm finding that very difficult to accept."

"I'm sorry," my mum says. She stands and walks toward him.

"He came to my house!" Chris says. "He's unstable. He needs managing, and he came to this house!"

"I never wanted to lie to you," Mum says.

"You know how I feel about lying. You know it must not happen in my house."

"Our house," I say. I don't know why. It just slips out, because twice he's said "my" house, but I should have kept it in my head.

"You! Stay out of it." He doesn't look at me because he's watching Mum, but his arm shoots out and he points a finger at me while his gaze is locked on hers.

Mum goes right up to him. She looks smaller than usual against him because she has bare feet. She slides her arms around his waist and rests her head on his chest. He's too angry to return the hug so his arms stay in midair, actively keeping distance between him and her. She looks up at him, like some kind of supplicant, trying to bathe her face in the light of him. "I'm so, so sorry," she says. "I panicked. I should have trusted you. I was very stupid, I was insecure."

Mum's arms snake farther around Chris until her hands are linked and I can see his body soften a little at her touch. I marvel a bit at that. Beside me, Lucas is staring at them too, but he feels my eyes turn to him and he looks back at me briefly, and I wonder if I have that power, with him, or if he's in charge.

Chris unpeels my mum's arms from his body and holds her hands in his, between them, as if they might pray together.

"It's going to rain," he says, and he's right because I'm suddenly aware of a sharp, cool breeze that makes the open window rattle and we can hear the foliage shifting outside. "Let's clear up and go to bed."

"Chris." There's a desperate note in Mum's voice that makes my heart tear, because I can tell that she still doesn't know which way this is going.

He hears her desperation too. "We'll talk more," he says, "upstairs." He tucks her hair behind her ear.

"Let's talk here," says Lucas, "all together."

Chris looks at him. "This is probably something Maria and I need to discuss alone at this point."

I agree with him, although I know Lucas doesn't want us to leave them, but I don't understand that, and I want Mum to have a chance, so I say, "I'll clear up," and, as rain begins to smatter onto the windowpane, I stand up.

"I'll do it, you go to bed," I say.

When I reach the doorway I turn and I look for a moment at them both standing there and I say, "I'm sorry, Mummy and Chris."

SUNDAY NIGHT

After the Concert

TESSA

One of the tube lights under my kitchen cabinets is flickering silently. It needs replacing.

Sam doesn't answer his phone, so I leave a message to ask if I can come over, although I wonder if he's asleep. I apologize for potentially disturbing him. We're very polite to each other, Sam and I, though it's not formality. I think it's fear that we'll lose each other.

I put my phone down on the kitchen table and watch as the screen dims to black. I roll my shoulders back to ease the tension that's grabbed them in a pincer grip.

The room is stuffy and the smell of Richard's lasagna still lingers; it's cloying and it feels as though it will make the back of my throat catch. I get a glass and turn on the tap at the sink, waiting for the warm water to run through until it's cold before I fill it, and then I drink it all in one go. I look out into the darkness of our garden, and see the shape of Richard's shed at the end of it, and remember how I found him there earlier in the day.

Even though I know that the homes and the streets of

Bristol will be full of people having normal, comfortable Sunday evenings, I feel as though I'm the last person on earth.

And suddenly I can't stand to be in my house any longer. I grab my bag and leave. I'll just take my chances and go and turn up at Sam's flat, because there's nowhere else I can bear to be.

I'm halfway there, and about to pull over and try to phone him again to give him some warning, when I remember that I've left my phone at home, on the kitchen table, and I just can't face going back to collect it, not now that I'm nearly at Sam's.

No matter, I think. It won't do Richard any harm to not be able to contact me for a while, to understand how it feels to have a spouse who is utterly unavailable for support. It won't do him any harm to feel frightened in the morning because he has to cope with the unreliable actions of the person he's supposed to be sharing his life with. If I go straight to work in the morning I can manage without it, and Richard can always phone there to track me down. I'll tell him I stayed at Maria's or with a friend.

I surprise myself a little with these sharp feelings of spite toward him, but the thing is, you need energy to cope with an alcoholic spouse, and I have none tonight, so the malice creeps in.

Rain begins to fall as I drive. It's not heavy, but it's persistent and my windshield wipers creak noisily across the glass.

The city center is empty and I find a parking space easily near Sam's apartment building.

Before I go up to Sam's flat I sit in the car for a moment and I wonder whether I should go back to Maria's house and check on them, before I remind myself that she's an adult and I mustn't interfere.

I wonder what Tom Barlow is doing or thinking. I wonder if he's lying awake beside his wife and stewing, or whether he's online, searching for more information about Zoe, and her new family.

Raindrops spatter on the roof of the bus with a tinny persistence, like a fusillade of toy guns. My thoughts have become exhausting enough that I decide I've had enough of sitting in the car. I step out and run across the wide pavement that separates the road from Sam's building and I don't stop until I'm safely under the partial cover of the meanly proportioned porch, and I press the buzzer for his apartment.

SUNDAY NIGHT

After the Concert

ZOE

Outside, the surface of the pool has gone crazy rough with the rain that's coming down. Under the table there's a fox gulping down bruschetta that he must have pulled off the table. He runs away when he sees me. First thing I do is mostly close the big doors to the kitchen because the rain has come into the room and run all over the stone floor and it's slippery as hell. I grab as much as I can from the table and bring it inside, tripping through the rain and getting soaked.

Lucas is standing in the doorway to the kitchen when I turn to make a second run into the house, and now the rain's falling hard enough that it pings off the plates and back up into my face. I'm not unaware that this could be a romantic moment, that it could be the point where the soaking wet heroine is caught and embraced by the hero. But that doesn't happen.

"We mustn't leave them alone," Lucas says.

"Can you help me?"

"Come back in."

"I said I would clear up."

I want to do just this one thing right tonight. I'm going to make the kitchen sparkle for my mum, and then, I've already thought of it, I'm going to go and lie with Grace again so that Mum isn't disturbed in the night.

"Why aren't you listening to me?"

"Because you looked deranged," I say, though that's not precisely true.

I put the plates down by the sink, and I'm hoping Lucas might help me, but he just stands there.

"How did you know? About me?" I ask.

"I played piano at a competition in Truro once," he said. "You were there. You beat me. I remembered you." A crooked smile.

"When?" I try to remember because there's a competition in Truro that I entered most years throughout my childhood, but I have no memory of Lucas.

"It was years ago. You beat me so I remembered your name and I thought I recognized you. I got the rest off the Internet."

"But my name wasn't allowed to be reported."

"You can piece it together if you look hard enough."

It makes sense that he remembers me from piano. Except for the children we saw year after year at competitions, I only ever remember the kids who beat me, which is probably why he recalls me, but not the other way around.

"But Chris?" I ask.

"I was just with my mum at the time. We were spending a week on holiday, and it was bad weather so we entered the competition on a whim, for extra performance practice."

"Oh." I let that hang there because I don't know what to say since Lucas never talks about his mum. Then I think of something.

"How did you know about panop?" I ask.

"I saw you had it on your phone. It wasn't difficult to find your account."

He must have had a look on my phone one day. I'm always leaving it on the piano by mistake, where it's hard to spot against the black shiny wood. He could easily have seen me put in my passcode too.

"It's what they used to send me messages on," I tell him. "The people at my old school. They bullied me."

"I'm sorry," he said. "I only wanted to get your attention. I thought if you knew I'd kept your secret you'd believe in me."

"Did you read the old messages that people sent me?"

"No. I couldn't do that."

I'm grateful for that.

"Believe in you about what?" I ask, because that was a strange thing to say.

"The script."

"You didn't need to do that. I would have read the script anyway."

I feel like he's being really weird and kind of selfish about the script with everything else that's happening.

"I'm sorry," he says, but he sounds a bit impatient when he says it and that annoys me too because the messages he sent really scared me. "Come in. Let's go upstairs." He catches my arm, and I try to shake his hand off but his grip is quite tight.

"You go. I'll come when I've finished."

"Zoe!"

"What? I want to do this for my mum!"

He looks like he wants to reply to that, but what he wants to say is too difficult, so instead he drops my arm, although his fingers have pressed into it by now, and it hurts.

"Fine," he says, and he goes upstairs.

By the time I've finished clearing up, all is quiet and the lights are off everywhere in the house. As I pass Chris's study I can see the steady green light of Grace's intercom, and I realize that they've forgotten to take it up with them, which means there's all the more reason for me to sleep with Grace.

Upstairs, the lights are also off in all the bedrooms and in the hall and landing, and I hear nothing. If the butterfly is still there, it's gone quiet. Only the rain is loud, still hissing and spattering on the glass skylight at the top of the stairwell.

Downstairs, I've laid out all the breakfast things and made everything perfect. I've put my mum's favorite cup out and a tea bag of Earl Grey tea neatly beside it with a spoon. I've put a mug for Chris beside it with a tea bag of English Breakfast, because that's what he likes.

In my bedroom I change out of my wet dress and put on a T-shirt and pajama shorts. I dry my hair with a towel. I take my iPod from my bedside table. One rule in this house is that Lucas and I must listen to recordings of the repertoire that we're playing before we sleep. It helps us to remember the pieces, imprints the detail of them on our minds.

I creep into Grace's room. She's lying in her crib, on her back, head to one side. Her little fists are loosely clenched. She's got one of them in her mouth, and the other is just touching the mad soft hair on the back of her head. It's how she always sleeps. She's very quiet and I know I shouldn't but I pick her up and bring her into the bed with me. I place her between me and wall, so she won't fall out. She doesn't stir at all and I inhale the smell of her.

Carefully, I put my headphones in, and start the music play-ing on my iPod. Chopin. A nocturne.

As the music swells, I think about my baby sister beside me and think that if there's one way that I can pay back the world for what I've done, it's to take care of her as much as I can, to make sure that she doesn't make the mistakes that I did, to help her not to hurt people. It's a vow that I made when I first met her in the hospital, and it's a vow I repeat to myself all the time.

I settle down and cover myself in just a sheet because it's still warm in her room, and right before I fall heavily asleep, with the Chopin relaxing me through my headphones, I notice on the clock beside the bed that it's a few minutes after midnight, which means it's Monday now, not Sunday anymore, and I hope that Monday might be better.

SUNDAY NIGHT

Midnight

TESSA

Sam and I watch a Hitchcock film and I relax. I curl up into him once we go to bed. After the events of the evening I feel as if I'm finally in a safe place, a place where I don't need to be a carer, or a supporter, or anything to anybody else. I can just be me.

As Sam's breathing settles into the rhythms of sleep, I lie awake a little longer and think about the evening and about how I'm glad I'm away from Maria's house because it's not my life after all, it's Maria's, and she is, after all, an adult who's made her own decisions.

I haven't mentioned what happened earlier to Sam because I didn't want to sully our time together. I wanted the few hours we spent in each other's company tonight to be simple and lovely, and unmarred by the imperfections that have spread like stains across other areas of my life.

But even with the warmth of his body beside mine, and the cocoon of his company sheltering me from reality for a while, I shed a tear or two before I sleep; just one or two.

SUNDAY NIGHT

Midnight

ZOE

I'm hardly asleep when I'm awake again and I hear screaming and for a moment, in my confusion, I think it's me.

But it's not.

The sound is coming from the front of the house and it's high-pitched and frightening.

There's shouting too, and then commotion in the house. Feet pounding.

With Grace in my arms, I run onto a deserted landing, where all the bedroom doors are open and the lights are on, and down the stairs. The front door's wide open too, and I go out and then run-walk across the gravel, feeling the slippery sharp stones digging into the soles of my feet. Katya and Barney Scott stand beside the wooden shed that houses our rubbish bins and they're both drenched with rain, sopping with it, their clothes sticking to them like plastic wrap.

They're looking at the door of the shed, where I can see that Chris is standing in boxer shorts and a T-shirt and has his hand over his mouth.

"Call an ambulance," he shouts. He turns to Katya and Barney. "Give me your phone," he says to them. "We need to call an ambulance."

Grace begins to whimper in my arms because it's dark and wet and there's shouting and she doesn't know why she's awake. She uses her fists to try to brush away rain that's getting into her eyes but grinds it in instead.

"Keep the baby away," Chris says to me, but he's fumbling with Barney's phone so he can't stop me when I walk past him and look into the shed.

On the floor of the shed, lying as motionless as the grave mounds at the church, blood soaking the side of her pale angel hair, is my mother. Her eyes are open wide and they stare at nothing at all.

I am still on my knees beside her when the emergency services arrive. They've taken Grace from me long ago, but they couldn't move me from my mother's side. I have sunk my face onto her neck, her chest; I have taken in the living smell of her for the last time. I have stroked the soft, soft skin on her temple, just like she did to Grace and me. I have whispered things into her ear that I want to tell her. And while I did all that, her eyes still didn't move.

When one of the paramedics leads me out of the shed, and away from my mum's body, I see Chris, and Barney, and Lucas standing there. Katya is in the doorway of the house, holding Grace.

I see an ambulance in the driveway, its back doors wide open, and I see a police car whose lights are slowly flashing. I see that the rain has eased so the droplets of water look like nothing more than fine dust motes in the air, swirling and shimmering, lit up blue against the black night.

I try to run back to my mother's body, to be with her a while longer, because I'm not ready to let her go, but they don't let me do that.

MONDAY

ZOE

I sit in a circle with the others in the sitting room of our Second Chance House and I feel as if I would break if somebody touched me. I feel as if my skin and hair are brittle, as if my teeth will never unclench.

There are some pieces of music I've played which got under my skin and made me feel this way, but that feeling went away after I lifted my fingers from the piano keys.

This feeling doesn't. It sticks, and it reminds me of before.

"Grief blooms," Jason said to me at the Unit in therapy sessions, when they were trying to make sure that I wouldn't have Unresolved Grief over the three deaths I caused. And he was right, because the pain of losing Gull and the others did unfold like a new bud at first, and it took forever before it began to wither.

I have names for all those feelings because Jason told them to me. Adults like to put a name on everything you feel, as if a name can neutralize it. They're wrong though. Some things settle under your skin and don't ever go away, no matter what you call them.

Today, what I'm feeling is even bigger than before. After my mum's death, the grief doesn't just bloom, it bursts out. It creates a mushroom cloud, instantly. It fills the sky that night and envelops us all; it's towering and toxic. It's off the Richter scale.

I feel it.

Chris feels it.

Lucas feels it.

Grace does not. Because she doesn't understand what's happened. She carries on being a baby and we all watch her, passing her from arms to arms, not able to explain to her.

We all sit in the sitting room of our house together like in an Agatha Christie novel.

We are four teenagers, one baby, and Chris.

And a police officer sits with us and stares at the floor, but she's listening to everything we say. I know for sure that police officers always listen.

I want Tessa, and they want to contact her too, to tell her, to get her to come and be with us, but nobody can find her. She's not answering her mobile and her landline rings and rings over and over again, and Uncle Richard doesn't even pick up.

Outside, the drizzle has stopped and so have the flashing blue lights, though the police cars are still there, and we see them as the sun rises up in a hazy, too-bright dawn, which also coaxes our faces from the shadows and shows them sagged and doughy as if we've all been slapped senseless with the shock.

Yellow tape is stretched out across the entrance to our driveway and around the shed where my mum's body still lies.

At first, one of the policemen asks us if it could have been an accident, whether my mum had been drinking.

"I don't know," says Chris. "I just don't know. She'd had a bit of wine, but we'd all gone to bed. We were all asleep."

Chris is upset and flustered, but he's the first to accuse somebody else.

"It was that man," he says. "Tom Barlow. You need to go and find a man called Thomas Barlow."

The police officer encourages Chris to sit back down, tells him that he'll pass the information on, and that Chris will be interviewed in due course, but for now, if it's OK, they'd prefer it if we all stayed where we were.

Lucas begins to sob, and the sound of it is painful and loud. It makes Grace crawl over to him and put her hand on his leg and pull herself up, and he reaches down to stroke her small fingers and sobs some more. She watches his face with an open mouth until it makes her cry too, and then she thumps back onto her bottom on the floor and is full of despair of her own.

Barney Scott's dad arrives and stands in the doorway and says, "I'm so sorry," and takes Barney away after a talk with the police.

Everybody is talking. I remember it from before. Always the talking, and the building of cages with words.

Katya is tear-streaked and squashed out of her arrogant shape and she sits by me and looks like she might want to hug me like you see on TV reports where women cling and wail, but I feel nothing for her and I'm used to feeling things on my own so I edge away to make sure that she doesn't touch me at all.

Later, when dawn has just become proper morning, they ask us if we mind being moved to the police station. They say that the house has become a "scene," and I'm straightaway transported back to court where they kept repeating "scene of the accident" over and over again. I look around instinctively to see if Mum has had the same thought and then I remember: she's gone.

The police come upstairs with each of us in turn to pack what they fully pedantically specify as "a small overnight bag." We all do except Grace, who ends up with a bag busting with stuff, which I pack myself because I don't want Katya to do it.

Standing on the gravel, waiting to leave, feeling the heat start to push back into the day as if nothing out of the ordinary has happened, as if there had been no blue dust rain, and no broken body, I concentrate on the feel of the sharp stones pushing at the soles of my Converse, to try to keep myself solid. But even doing that I can't help myself glancing at the shed, and wondering if my mum is still in there, because the ambulance has gone. A policeman stands in front of the shed door and looks at his phone, and when I ask the question out loud, somebody else tells me that Mum's going to be moved very soon.

"Doesn't she need the ambulance?" I ask, but nobody answers.

They use two cars to drive all of us away from the house, but not before Chris has got angry when he tried to get Grace's car seat out of Mum's car and it got stuck. Normally Mum moves the car seat. After he finally yanked it free, Chris cursed and threw the car seat onto the gravel and stones kicked up and hit the side of the police car, but nobody mentioned that. Instead, I picked up the seat, and put it in the car, and so now I'm holding Grace's fingers tightly as we ride together in the backseat and Katya sits on the other side of me with the bag of Grace's stuff on her knees.

In the car, the police driver tells me that they've finally managed to get in touch with Uncle Richard, Tessa's husband, and he'll meet us at the police station.

As we drive away from the house another policeman lifts the tape at the end of our road and somebody standing on the pavement with their dog stares at us, and my stomach is carved out with the feeling that the only thing I want is Mum, and my head is collapsing around an imploding feeling that my life is shattering again, and I begin to cry. Katya doesn't see because she's looking out of the other window with a face like an Easter Island statue and Grace is fully occupied playing with a piece of gravel that she must have picked up when we were at our house.

And, on top of everything, and through my tears, I feel guilty about that because I think Mum would have noticed it long before Grace might have had a chance to put the stone in her mouth, and I quickly take it away from her before she does.

And alongside that thought, which my mixed-up head is giving space to, my fear is beginning to unfold as fast as my grief did.

Two questions are pushing to the front of my mind and they're frightening me to the point where I start to shake.

One: What if my mum's death was revenge for what I did and they're going to come after me too?

Two: What if the police think I did it?

I'm a convicted killer, after all.

TESSA

When I arrive at Maria and Chris's avenue I'm not allowed to drive down it. I park on an adjoining street and run until I'm held back by the raised arms of a police officer who's guarding the strip of crime scene tape that sags across the entrance to their road.

"I'm family," I say. "It's my sister."

He begins to explain why that's not a good enough reason to encroach on the "crime scene," but I can't stand to listen, because I need to see, and so I duck away from him and under the tape and run the hundred yards down the street until I'm standing at the entrance to Chris and Maria's driveway taking breaths that scorch my throat.

I'm just in time to see a body bag being carried out of the shed, and placed on a gurney. Faintness almost fells me and I have to lean against the golden stone column at the entrance to the driveway. It's the realization that this is true.

Maria's my younger sister; she was always a sprite compared to me, a waif, she was my shadow when we were younger, the one who could make our dad beam even when he was supposed to be cross with her, and now she's gone. Your younger sister is not supposed to die before you, it's not right. As I have no child whom I fear will predecease me, this upsets the natural order of things for me in a way that's unexpectedly shocking. Our parents are both dead, but I didn't feel orphaned until now, because I had Maria.

As I watch the men carry her, I imagine how it feels to them, because I know the weight of a dead body. I've hauled an animal corpse out of the back of a car or off a surgical table on more than one occasion. When all the tissues are lifeless and the heart has stopped pumping, the weight of death is extraordinary. If someone brings a dead animal to us, when we prepare to move the body from our surgery car park into the building for cremation, we usually wait until passersby have gone, to spare their feelings, but the folks with the gurney outside Maria's house take no such precautions. They're not paramedics, because there's no need for paramedics now. These are men whose jobs are rarely advertised, because they collect the lifeless bodies. They wheel the gurney toward the back of a van, which is unmarked. There's no need for an ambulance now either.

The policeman is by my side, and he guides me away, but he's kind enough to support me too and to explain gently that Maria's body is in the care of the coroner now, pending a postmortem investigation, and a murder inquiry has been launched.

And as I take my last look back at their house I think something that I've thought before: "What a waste." And even my skeptical soul can't help but wonder if our family is somehow cursed.

ZOE

I feel safe in the police car in a sort of way because if Tom Barlow hurt my mum, then he can't get me here, but I also feel afraid, because being in the police car feels like it did before.

It's not cold, or dark, and I'm not in my party clothes with shards of glass in my hair and cuts on my face, and I'm not over the limit, but it is a police car and I am being transported.

That's when I get the idea that I need Sam.

I know he's in Bristol now because Tessa told Mum once that she'd run into him and that he lives here now too, like us.

"That's a funny coincidence, don't you think?" she said to Mum, but of course Mum didn't want to talk about it, so Tess had to keep her little smile at the coincidence just for herself.

The only person who can take me to see Sam is Uncle Richard, but I can't mention it to him at first, because when he meets us at the police station he gives me a too-tight hug, but then all he does is try to tell the police that Aunt Tessa didn't come home last night. Nobody listens to him at first, but after he's told them like a thousand times eventually one of them asks him if Richard has any reason to fear for her safety, or if he thinks Tess might have had a reason to have argued with her sister.

"No!" Richard shouts in a too-dry voice that lurches up an octave. "No, she bloody hasn't. How dare you?" Uncle Richard is always fierce about Tess, and my mum says that's because he loves her so much.

I want Sam, because of what I did before. I need him and his advice because I'm scared people will put the blame on me.

I hold my head together enough to put my plan into action because I'm able to put my grief in a box and put my thinking cap on. Jason at the Unit taught me how to do that. "Imagine your grief as a flower that has bloomed," he said in one of our sessions and I was like, "You already said grief blooms."

"Bear with me," he said. "Imagine it."

So I shut my eyes and did; I made my grief into a peony, big and blowsy.

"Now convert that flower into something made of paper."

I opened my eyes when he said that. "What?"

"Hang in there. Do you know what origami is?"

"Of course. Japanese. 'Ori' means 'folding' and 'kami' means 'paper.' First clear reference to paper models is in a 1680 poem by Ihara Saikaku."

Jason leaned back and looked at me. "Zoe-pedia," he said, and this encouraged me to say: "The poem is about butterflies, in a dream, and they are made from origami. Traditionally, they would be used in wedding ceremonies."

I drew breath because there was more I could have said. I thought that I could probably tell him the line of the poem in Japanese because I read it phonetically once, but Jason interrupted me:

"So imagine an origami flower."

In my head, the peony I pictured morphed from a mass of bloomy petals so soft that they could suffocate you into something made of sharp folds and symmetry.

"Now, fold that flower up tight. Fold the blooms back in."

I saw it in my mind. The collapsing of the flower, the neatness of the package I could make it into. It unbloomed.

"Now imagine that you're going to stow that folded-up flower in a box. You'll take it out later, and you'll let it open out again, but for now we're going to fold it away and keep it safe, and see what happens when it's gone for a little while."

It didn't happen right away, but once I'd practiced these thoughts, and finally believed Jason when he said it was OK sometimes to step away from the grief, and the guilt, I discovered that I got my concentration brain back. That's the brain that lets me memorize anything that I see, the brain that connects with the music. It's the brain that Granny Guerin said was like our family's laundry basket: always packed to the brim, always overflowing, you could never keep everything stuffed into it and close the lid.

So on the morning after my mum dies I'm using Jason's advice and putting my grief for her in a box. I know it can't stay there for long, because it's too big, but I also know that it's essential to do it and to have my wits about me. I ask Richard to take me to Sam; I tell him we have to because of what happened to me before. I tell him that Sam knows Tessa from back then, so he might be able to help us find her.

Richard looks at me and says, "Well, he can't be any more useless than they are here, come on then, let's give it a go."

Uncle Richard finds Sam's office address really quickly on the Internet on his phone and when they don't answer his call he says it's probably because it's too early and it's best just to go there.

At first, we have a bit of a problem persuading the police to let us go, because they act like they don't know what to think about it, and Chris and Lucas and Katya just stare at us like they're in shock that we're abandoning them. But Richard is clever, and he knows that the police can't keep us at the station because we're not actually arrested, so they can't stop us leaving, especially if it's just for a little while. He tells them that Sam is a family friend as well as a solicitor and it would be a great comfort to me if I could see him.

The policeman obviously doesn't like it, but when it seems as though he's made all the objections he can and Richard has answered them, all confident, he just asks Richard if he thinks he should be driving. Richard makes a nervous look at me like people always do when drunk driving is brought up, and then assures the policeman that he's going to call us a taxi, which is how he arrived at the police station in the first place. I can tell the question hurts his pride, but he's trying not to be too indignant or cross, because he wants them to let us go.

When we arrive at Sam's office there are people just opening up, but we have to wait for a while because it's Sam's day off, which I didn't think of, and some of the people stare at us a bit as they walk past in their smart business suit clothing while Sam's secretary phones him.

"He's on his way," she says after she's spoken to him. "You're lucky I could get hold of him."

Once Sam arrives it's much better because we can be private in his office and I feel a surge of relief because Sam is somebody who knows every detail about what I did. With him, there's nothing to hide, and I don't have to pretend to be somebody else.

Sometimes I think I'm more happy when I'm with people who know about it. In the Unit, all of us were there because we'd done something bad, so it didn't make me different from anybody else, and that was relaxing in a way, it truly was. And with Sam, I feel like he doesn't judge me, he just helps me. I can say anything to him. With the Second Chance Family it wasn't like that. There was so much that I couldn't say, so much that I had to be ashamed of, even though the verdict at the trial was unfair to me and the idea of that twists and turns inside me every single day.

Sam sits, and we sit too, and in his hot, dark office with a scratchy carpet and framed certificates wonky behind his desk, I know I'm ready to tell him everything that's happened.

SAM

It's déjà vu: Zoe Maisey sits in front of me, and once again she's white with shock. The only difference is that there's no glass in her hair this time, and no hospital outfit. She's wearing a teenage-girl sweatsuit-pajama-type outfit, covered by a flimsy cardigan, which she's wrapped around herself tightly. She's shaking.

Beside her sits her uncle. He's red-faced, sweating, and he stinks of alcohol. I hope he hasn't driven Zoe here because I suspect he's probably still over the limit, but I reassure myself that surely somebody in this family would know better.

But the worst thing is that in spite of the bloodshot eyes and the oily, widened pores, and the untended shock of hair that's just starting to gray at the temples, he's quite obviously a very nice and also a good-looking man. His manner is lovely and gentle, though he's surprisingly posh. I never imagined Tess with a posh husband, but I can see instantly why she married him and I have to stop myself from hating him for this. I must not make comparisons between us. Jealousy would not be appropriate.

"She really needs her aunt," Richard says to me. "My wife.

We've been trying to get hold of her for hours, but she went out somewhere last night and left her mobile at home and we don't know where she is."

I know his name, but he doesn't know that I know it, and I must be careful what I say.

I extend my hand to him. "Sam Locke," I say.

"Richard Downing." His handshake trembles, and his palms are clammy. He gives a two-handed shake, and his wedding ring, identical to Tess's, clashes with my knuckle when he encloses my hand with both of his. "I'm sorry to turn up like this, but I know how much you helped them before. My wife, Tessa, told me about it, and Zoe was desperate."

I wonder why he never came to court in Devon, why he and I have never encountered each other before. I've no time to consider this, though, because he's speaking urgently, almost furtively.

"The thing is, I'm worried about her," he says. "I don't know where she is. I'm sorry, I know it's nothing on top of what happened last night, but it's so unlike her. What if she's come to harm too?"

He's wide-eyed and genuinely worried, but I don't want this conversation.

I glance at Zoe who's looking at me with glazed eyes; I don't think she's taking in a thing that we're saying.

"I'm sure your wife will reappear," I tell Richard rather shortly, because how can I reassure him that I know she's OK. "Perhaps she stayed with a friend last night?"

He begins to respond, but I absolutely can't let this continue, so I turn to Zoe and I ask the question that's been bugging me since Jeanette called me: "Why have you come to me?"

"Because it feels like before," she says. "It feels like before."

She breaks down into such awful, terrible sobbing that it's as if the sound of it alone could wound you. But what I'm wondering, even while she vents her grief, is whether Zoe knows something and knows that she needs protecting.

Richard tries to comfort her. He puts his arms around her and her head falls onto his shoulder. He looks as though he's feeling like death, and when our eyes meet his expression is one of compassion and confusion with a "help me" in there too.

"Why is it like before?" I ask Zoe when her tears ebb a little. "Do you feel responsible in some way?"

Richard says, "Now hang on!"

"I need to ask."

"She's just lost her mother!" Saying it chokes him up.

"And I'm on her side, but I need to know why she wanted to come here."

Zoe is emotionally and socially immature, but she's also exceptionally intelligent. All the reports on her at the trial stressed this. She has the processing capabilities equal to any judge who might sit on her case and she has experience of the system too. Yes, she's in shock, yes, her mother has just died, but she's come to me for a reason and I need to know exactly what that is.

She peels herself from her uncle's shoulder, which is now wet from her tears, and says, "Because I'm afraid."

"Afraid of what?"

"Afraid of Tom Barlow."

I remember him from the trial.

"Why Tom Barlow?"

"They're saying he disrupted the concert yesterday and came to the house afterward," Richard explains as Zoe fixes me with deer-in-headlight eyes.

"Do you think he hurt your mum?"

"I don't know. He's nice."

She always said that at the time: Amelia Barlow is horrible, although her mum and dad are really nice.

"The police say they're going to talk to him," Richard adds.

"If the police know about him, then you mustn't worry," I tell Zoe. "They won't let him hurt you. What?"

She's shaking her head madly. "But what if they blame me?"

I sigh. Zoe's mind has raced ahead down the path of somebody who has a victim mentality. I take a tough line with her in response: "Is there anything to blame you for, Zoe?"

"Oh dear God, you poor child." Richard rubs her back. "You don't have to answer that."

In her eyes I see she understands that I have to ask this, and that she's ready to answer. It's not the first time we've discussed her responsibility for somebody else's death. Zoe and I have trodden these boards before and it doesn't faze us, although Richard looks as though he might puke.

"No," she says, "I was asleep. I fell asleep with my baby sister, my new sister. I went to sleep with her in her room. I didn't hear anything because I had my headphones in."

I'm about to reassure her that if that's the case, then she should have nothing to worry about, and that there's surely no reason for the police to think she would harm her own mother, but Richard interrupts me.

"Tessa went to the concert!" he blurts out, as if the memory is a big fish he's suddenly managed to hook out of the empty lake of his booze-addled brain.

"And she came to dinner with us afterward," Zoe tells him. "She was there."

"Yes, that's right," Richard agrees as Zoe reminds him of Tess's movements, his neurons firing their way out of his hangover now, and putting last night into some kind of order. "She went to the concert, and we spoke afterward and she said she was staying for dinner, but I didn't see her after that."

I did, I think, but I can't say it.

"We had bruschetta," Zoe tells Richard, and tears still fall fatly down her cheeks. "But the police are there now, we're not allowed home."

While I often think of her as having a head that's far too smart for her age, in front of me today she is very much a child and I feel slightly guilty for taking a hard questioning line with her, though really I had no choice.

What I realize is that I'm well beyond my professional remit here. This feels like more of a personal, not a professional, visit, and that makes me feel extremely twitchy. If Tess had been with Zoe, she wouldn't have let her come.

I stand up, look out of the window. I need to order my thoughts.

Various half-formed ideas scud across my mind: Zoe's going to need huge amounts of help, but not the kind that I can give her. She's here because she's afraid, that's all, not because she actually requires legal assistance. My gut tells me that she's not involved in this as a perpetrator, and my gut is usually right, though not always.

But what floods me with apprehension, on top of that, and makes me try to wrench the window open farther, hoping for a gasp of fresh air from the dank gulley separating our small building from the towering block beside us, is the newly forming realization that, even if I wanted to, I couldn't possibly help Zoe in this, in any of it, neither in an official capacity nor a personal one. This is because the fact that I spent the night with Tess means two things: first, that I'm a potential witness, and, second, that our relationship is bound to become known.

I need, I think, a way out.

ZOE

Sam stares out of his office window at the building opposite for a long time, while I sit and lean against my uncle Richard, who smells strangely sweet, and I think about the men who are probably in the Second Chance House now, examining it for clues. I imagine it just like the wreck of the car in Devon: taped off, Property of the Police.

I wonder if the butterfly is still crouched in a high corner of our landing ceiling at the Second Chance House or if, in the darkness, its wings open and shut enough times that it used up its energy stores and fell to the floor. I wonder if the men in white suits will find a small pile of powdery scales and a spindly-legged carcass on the cream carpet of our landing.

After a while, Sam clears his throat, says that he needs to make a phone call, and leaves the room. Richard and I stay where we are, and first he scrolls around his phone a bit, and then he puts it on the table, but he keeps picking it up again to check it and I can tell he's willing Tess to ring.

I just stare at the view that Sam was looking at.

The windows on the building opposite are like little boxes, each one showing you a glimpse into somebody else's day. I watch a lady at her desk neatly slitting envelopes open with a knife, before getting out the letters and unfolding them and then whacking down on them with a big stamp. I can't hear her, obviously, but my brain provides the soundtrack, and the whump of the stamp as it hits the paper is loud in my mind, as well as the sharp sound as the knife slits the envelope, and the slurp each time she sips from a takeout coffee cup. The sounds alternate in my head, crescendoing, building up like the panic I'm feeling, until Sam returns.

I was right to panic, because he's betrayed me.

"I've phoned your dad," he says. "He's on his way."

"No!" I totally and absolutely don't want my dad. He didn't cope with me before, so how is he going to now that it's even worse?

"Don't be angry, Zoe," Sam says. "You need somebody to look after you."

"You don't know!"

"I do know."

He's nodding at me, as if that makes him more right, which it doesn't, and I want to argue about it more, because I'm scared of how my dad will be with me.

I'm staring hard at Sam, thinking of what to say, when Richard's phone rings and Richard lunges to grab it off the table where it's skittering around on the shiny surface as it vibrates even faster than his tremor hands.

TESS MOBILE it says on the screen.

"Oh God, it's you!" he practically shouts, once he's fumbled hitting the screen to answer it. "Thank God! Thank God! Where the hell have you been?"

She's speaking to him urgently; you can hear that down the line, but not her actual words. Richard's face goes slacker as he concentrates on what she's saying.

Eventually, he says: "I'm so sorry, darling, I'm so sorry about Maria, I just can't believe it and I just thought you . . . no, don't worry, I thought something might have happened to you too," he says, and his hand is on his chest, but he fully lies when he says, "God, Tessa, no, I'm not crying, no, I'm not, OK, yes," and then gets back on track when he says, "We're at the solicitor's place, Zoe's solicitor, do you remember him? . . . Because she wanted me to bring her here . . . of course we told the police where we were going, honestly they were in chaos, it doesn't inspire one with confidence . . . no, I didn't think of it like that . . . no, sorry, no, perhaps I should have, but there wasn't time to think . . . yes, she is . . . OK . . ."

He passes his phone to me. "Aunty Tess wants to talk to you. She's OK."

I can't talk to her at first. The sound of her voice, and the way it's strangulated and strange, makes me sob again.

"What happened?" she says.

It takes me a few moments to get my breathing under control, and Richard's arm wraps around my shoulders as I do. "I don't know. She was in the shed. She never goes in the shed."

"When? What time?"

"We went to bed. We all went to bed and Katya woke us up when she got back."

"Did Katya find Mummy?"

"Yes!"

"Zoe, you've done nothing wrong, so don't behave as if you have, whatever you do. I think you should come away from

Sam's office and come back to the police station to be with the others."

"I don't want to be at the station." Like the courtroom, the station is a vipers' nest, a place where I can trip myself up, say the wrong thing, dig my own grave, put myself behind bars.

"I know, I understand, but I'm coming now and I'll meet you there and then we'll find out what's going on and take things from there. You don't need a solicitor. You've done nothing wrong."

"I don't want to be with the police."

"But you don't want them to suspect you've done something either, do you?"

Sometimes people say things to you straight and I like that. I didn't think that coming to see Sam might make me look worse, but I see suddenly that she might be right.

In her silence, I ask, "Where were you?"

"I stayed with a friend. I left my phone at home. I'm sorry I didn't come earlier."

"Will I live with Daddy now?"

She sighs before answering, and it's a hollow sound. "Honestly, I don't know what we're going to do, let's take one thing at a time. Zoe? Are you there?"

"Yes."

"Don't worry about that now. We'll take care of you, OK? I promise."

Sam is nice to me as he walks us out of the building, all of our feet thumping down flights of stairs.

"I don't think I've ever had a client just turn up before," he says. "It's very unusual, really."

Maybe nobody has ever needed you as much as me, I think. We're standing on the steps of his building now, and the soft early morning shadows are already getting shorter and more brutal as the sun rises and starts to superheat the city and turn every surface into a glare.

"Don't be afraid, Zoe," he says. "The police will protect you until they know what's happened. They'll do a better job of it than me."

I'm actually shocked that Sam, who saw how wrong things went for me before, could even think that, let alone say it to me. Until now, he's never been in the category of "adults who don't understand," but he earns his membership badge right there on the steps, and I feel sick with disappointment.

On the drive back to the police station, my mind stays so blank with it all that I notice nothing apart from the fact that the air conditioning in the taxi is broken and Richard's sweat is making half-moon shapes under his armpits.

TESSA

I arrive at the police station at the same time as Richard and Zoe. He practically falls out of their taxi in his haste to embrace me, but it's her I want to feel in my arms first, because she's my flesh and blood.

"Where've you been?" Richard says as I clasp her. "I was so worried."

I'm shot through with irritation at this, because I don't feel as though his concern is for me, but for himself. I'm already cross with Richard anyway, for taking Zoe to Sam. Cross because that's risky for me, but also because it feels risky for her. She doesn't need a solicitor. Why would we compound this desperate situation by publicly seeking legal advice for her? It makes her look suspicious. Richard has no common sense; he shouldn't have given in to her request.

"Later," I say. "For God's sake!"

I don't meet his eye, but from the way he falls in behind Zoe and me, bringing up the rear as we walk toward the entrance to the police station, and then scurrying past us to hold open the door, I think: he doesn't know about me and Sam, and for that, right now, I'm grateful.

As a uniformed officer leads us down a corridor within the police station, we hear Chris before we see him. As we round a corner, his voice is loud, and almost uncontrolled, as he explains to somebody that enough is enough, and the family can't stay at the police station.

"Why are you incarcerating us?" he asks. "What are you doing that's in any way useful?"

We arrive by an open doorway that leads into a small room where Lucas, Katya, and the baby are seated on sofas around a long, low table. Grace's face is tear-streaked and Katya holds her while wearing the expression of somebody who's both physically and mentally exhausted. Chris is standing beside the doorway remonstrating with a female officer who appears cowed by him.

"We're just in the process of opening up the investigation into your wife's death, sir," she explains in a sentence where the words sound very carefully chosen. "If you could bear with us while we do that, we will, of course, keep you updated on everything that's happening. It's a complicated—"

Chris interrupts her. "I understand complexity. What I don't understand is why we're being held here. Why are we *camping* in your police station? What is the plan?"

His voice is louder now and it sets the baby off again.

"You could come to our house," I say. "If you'd like to?"

Chris notices us for the first time, but he barely glances at Zoe.

He looks back at the officer. "Is that allowed?" he says. "Or are we under suspicion?"

She's careful with her response. "You're not being held here, sir, we simply wanted to offer you somewhere to be while your house isn't accessible to you. We thought it might be easier to conduct interviews while you were here, as we'll be needing to speak to everybody soon."

Behind Chris, Grace is having a low-level whine and Katya is bumping her on her knee in a desultory way, which only makes Grace's mouth hang wider in despair. Zoe slips past Chris and goes to the baby, taking her into her arms.

"I have a baby!" says Chris. "And children I'm responsible for. This isn't right! Look at them!"

They are a sight. Their bags are dumped all over the place, and baby paraphernalia has spread everywhere, including a stroller, a nappy-changing mat on the floor, and a half-eaten jar of purée beside a bundle of wipes.

They need help.

"Officer," I say. "They can come to my house, if that's allowed? It's just over in Stoke Bishop."

"I'll check," she says. "I expect they'd prefer you here just for now, but I'll ask."

Only when she's moved away up the corridor do I step toward Chris and, almost as if it's an afterthought, we embrace awkwardly. Chris's grief hasn't weakened him physically; he feels as taut as the skin of a drum.

The police agree to us all going back to my house, and so we make the journey in an assortment of vehicles.

I regret the offer when we arrive there, though, because the reality of having Chris in my house, and the baby, and Katya, and the teenagers, is suddenly overwhelming. A family liaison officer has come with us too. Among them, they make the space feel incredibly claustrophobic even though my home is a good size by anybody's standards. They leave no room for my grief.

Richard notices how I'm feeling; perhaps he's feeling it too. "Go upstairs," he says. "Take a few minutes to yourself."

It's as I'm heading up the stairs that I hear him add, "Take a shower," and I realize that I'm still in the clothes I wore to the concert. He surely won't remember what I put on yesterday, but he's not stupid either and I wonder if his shower comment is supposed to have a subtext or if I'm being paranoid.

As the new fact of my sister's death reverberates around my mind, I take a hard line with Richard: if I cheated, you deserved it. You drank me to it.

I turn on the water in the shower and run it until it's almost too hot to stand. I hear shouting from downstairs, and the baby crying loudly, but I don't want to leave the shower until it's unbearable to stay in it any longer, because there's a part of me that can't cope with any of them, and doesn't want to look into a single one of their faces.

I think of Sam and of my night with him, and want nothing more than to be back there in his flat with him, where the river is our soundtrack and our view, and it's just about us, and Richard is reliably drunk, and my sister and Zoe are OK in their new life, and there are no more complications.

And beyond that, as the water streams down my back, and tears stream down my face, I feel only numbness.

ZOE

We never went to Tess's house much after Mum met Chris, but I love it.

"Every house is a world of its own," Mum said when she and Chris were deciding on all the finishes for our Second Chance House. Mum had so many samples sent, for so many different things, and she would lay them out on the table and move them around like jigsaw pieces, looking to see which ones fitted best together.

We had fabric, stone, wood, and paint samples in all shades of tasteful. Mum went for muted colors and expensive stuff and everything was strokable. She loved her choices. She would smile to herself when each new thing was delivered and looked just right and Chris would say, "You have such a good eye, Maria."

In the end, the world she made looked like a magazine. She loved it and Chris loved it. They never stopped talking about how much they loved it. Grace puked on parts of it and I told them I loved it, but mostly I missed our farmhouse. Katya, when she arrived, took a look around every room in the house and, when we got back to the kitchen, she said, "You have luxury lifestyle," and looked very pleased about that.

Lucas never mentioned it, he just moved quietly around the different parts of the house, and when he settled down anywhere it reminded me of a dark shadow cast over a patch of white sand.

Tessa's house is really different from the Second Chance House, but I properly love it. It tells lots of stories about Tess and Richard.

The main one it tells is that when they were younger Tess and Richard traveled around a lot, and they collected things. Their house is like a display cabinet for all the objects they brought home with them, but it's not posh. It's warm and friendly, and full of pictures as well as objects, and you can pick everything up and hold it if you want to and splat down on their sofa, which has blankets and throws on it, and sometimes a dog that Tess is fostering for work. There are rugs all over the floors too, which you have to be careful not to trip over, because nothing's perfect in their house, so they have curled-up edges and threadbare patches. Bookshelves clamber up most of the walls in the sitting room and the books are arranged in a higgledy-piggledy way, all different sizes and all different heights all over the place and nothing in alphabetical order at all. They're mostly travel books, and science and vet books, but there are lots of novels too and stacks of DVDs.

Tessa goes upstairs when we get back, and Richard tries to make tea for everybody, but nobody wants any, and Chris paces around the place until he stops and shouts at Katya.

"Stop the baby crying. Can you stop the baby crying?"

"Baby has lost mother!" Katya shouts back at him with surprising force. "It is not time to make her be quiet."

Richard looks from one of them to the other and says to Chris: "Say you let me help on this front, what do you need?"

"Baby needs somewhere to sleep," Katya says. "And milk." Richard's kind manner softens her tone, though she still glares at Chris with intensity. I wish I dared to look at him like that, but I wonder what he'd say if I did.

"Are you up to giving me a hand?" Richard asks Katya. "Shall we see what we can fix up?"

She responds by hoisting Grace farther up her hip and following Richard in a huffy way.

Chris turns to me. "Did you actually go and see a solicitor this morning?" he asks me.

I nod. A headache is bringing tears to my eyes, and, because of what he said to me last night, the question feels like a threat.

"Why?"

"I don't know."

"You must know."

I feel my hands start to shake, and I don't know what to say. I'm not ready to talk to him about that stuff yet. It's been secret for so long that I feel like I don't really have a vocabulary for it any more.

"What?" he says, even though I didn't think I said anything.

"I wanted Sam to help me. I know him from before."

Chris is standing in the center of the room, with his arms folded and his hair sticking up because he's run his hands through it so many times this morning. He considers me like I'm an interesting painting.

"There's a lot I don't know about you, Zoe," he says, and I bow my head to break eye contact with him.

In the Unit, I shared my room with a girl who told me how she always did that to stop her dad beating the crap out of her. *It sometimes works,* she said, *but sometimes it doesn't, but it doesn't cost you to try, does it, because people just want to feel like they're the king of you.*

It works on Chris, confirming my view that most people are members of the fully paid-up schizophrenia club. They act one way until they don't. Just like that. Even Jason was all one way around me until he suddenly wasn't.

Chris sits down on the sofa in between me and Lucas, and he reaches out a hand to take one of mine and one of Lucas's, like we're going to pray.

I don't like the physical contact with him but I force my fingers to wilt into his hot palm.

"We're still a family," says Chris, and he chokes on his words, "and I want you to know that I'm here for both of you now."

He squeezes my hand hard, and then he stands and leaves the room without another word.

Lucas and I look at each other. We've not been alone together since it happened.

"I'm sorry," he says.

"Why was she out in front of the house?" I say. "What was she doing there?"

"I don't know."

He bows his head, and that makes me feel angry because I want more from him. I want the connection we had last night.

"It's all going to kick off now," I say, and he rises to my bait.

"What do you mean?"

Sometimes when I'm angry I want to throw all the awful things that I know at people; I want them to feel all the horrible things that I've had to feel.

"You can do that," Jason said to me once when I described the way that Amy Barlow's eyes were open but dead and her ear was ripped half from her head in the back of the car, "you can try to pull me into that scene, and wound me with it, but we both know that it's a space that only you occupy, Zoe, and my job is to help you move on from that safely, not to join you there. It's not my horror. You're punishing yourself if you inflict this stuff on other people because it will only push them away from you."

I ignore Jason's advice this morning and I try to punish Lucas with my knowledge.

"Do you actually know what they're going to do? They'll take us in, they'll question us, they'll take our phones, our computers, they'll make us wait, they'll lock us in a cell, the investigation will go on and on and so will the trial. It never ends, Lucas. No matter what you do afterward, it never goes away."

"We were all asleep," he says. "We don't know anything."

"Were you? Were you asleep?"

"Me and Dad were asleep!" he says.

"I was asleep too. I didn't hear anything."

The thought that I slept while harm came to my mum is a torment to me, because I think how it could have been different if I'd not put my headphones in. Then I might have heard Mum go out, and maybe stopped her, called her back into bed with me and Grace instead. I could have done it, I could have pretended I had a headache, or a tummy ache, or something. She would have come, I think.

I begin to cry again, but Lucas doesn't move, he just stares at the tufted rug, which has repeating geometric patterns on

it that draw your eye around and around in a whirl, and even
when my tears stop, we stay silent and I look at a line drawing
of a building, which Uncle Richard has framed and hung over
his woodburning stove. It's spare and perfect, with orderly
black lines on white like musical notation paper, and a thought
occurs to me.

"Do you think she went outside to see Mr. Barlow?"

"I don't know," he says. "How do you know they'll take
our phones?"

"Because it's what they do."

"But we're not under suspicion."

"I will be."

"Why?"

"Because of what happened."

They tell you that in the Unit. If you've been done once,
they'll do you again even quicker. Makes life easier for them.
Everyone in the Unit feels like life's a conspiracy against them.

"It's not," Jason said when we talked about it. "Although
some people do get stuck in a cycle of crime and punishment,
it's true, but that doesn't have to be you, Zoe. It shouldn't
be you."

"My verdict was unfair."

"I know you believe that, and it might or might not be
true . . ."

"It's true." I think about it every day, the feeling of being
cheated at my trial, the helplessness of nobody believing me.
In the Unit I still felt very angry about it, and although I
still feel that way deep down, I've learned to hide it, because
nobody wants to hear it.

"Let me finish. Regardless of whether your verdict was the

right one or not, you now have to look forward, and you have both the support and the opportunity to escape the cycle."

My support was my mum, and my opportunity was music, which was organized by my mum, so what do I have now?

Lucas says, "It doesn't make sense that they would automatically suspect you."

"It doesn't have to make sense," I tell him.

"It's paranoid."

I'm not going to give him an answer to that. There are things that only I know about this kind of thing. Lucas has no experience.

"Zoe, can you do something for me?" he asks after he's worked out that I'm not going to rise to his comment.

"What?"

"Delete the email I sent you. The script."

"Why?"

"Did you read it?"

"Only the first part."

"Just delete it. I'm deleting it from mine."

He has his phone out now and he's scrolling through it, probably deleting it from his "sent" box.

"Why?"

"It doesn't matter anymore. It's stupid."

"What?"

"Pass me your phone, I can do it."

"No."

He scoots along the sofa, closer to me, and he puts his hand on my leg, which sends a jolt of something through me, but it's not the same feeling I had last night when he kissed me, it's stranger than that somehow.

"I'll delete it for you. Please. It was just a stupid thing. It feels wrong now. Please, Zoe. I lost my mum too, remember . . ." But he struggles to find more words to explain what he means by that, and it frustrates me when he fails.

"What?"

A pause, as his eyes search mine, reading my impatience, then: "It's complicated. It's personal."

"You're doing my head in," I tell him, which is something everybody at the Unit used to say. Then I ask him, "Have you ever seen a counselor about your mum dying?" because I wonder if I'll have to. I don't mind, if they're good like Jason kind of was, but I do mind if they're just patronizing and give me sad eyes.

"No." I feel like he's lying when he says that, though, because his eyes sort of dart.

"Why not?"

"I don't know. Dad, just . . . Dad said we could help each other, that we'd be better on our own. It was fine."

I can see that it wasn't, though, because of the way he bites his bottom lip, and then when he holds his hand out for my phone again, and says, "Please, Zoe?" I hand it to him, because I'm soft. He taps away at it before giving it back to me, and when he does, I say, "They can find anything you delete, you know that, don't you? They'll find the panop messages you sent me."

I say that even though I know that it doesn't really matter if they do, because they'll know about my history anyway, as soon as they put my name into their computers, and sending a panop message like the ones Lucas sent isn't a crime, but for some reason I still feel like having a go at him a bit. He doesn't get a chance to reply to me though before Uncle Richard interrupts us.

"The police are coming," he says. "They want to talk to everybody again."

We talked to them a little bit this morning, but as a group, not one by one, which is what I know they like best.

"Initial accounts," I say. "That's what they want."

RICHARD

KEEP CALM AND CARRY ON.

It's a slogan you see everywhere these days, it's even printed on one of the tea towels that's draped over the radiator in our kitchen. It might have recently become part of popular culture, but that slogan has its roots in wartime strength and self-sufficiency, and today I vow to be its living embodiment, because Maria's death is a tragedy that has thrown our family into crisis, and somebody needs to keep their head.

My head is actually gripped in a vise of white pain, the worst kind of almost-migraine hangover, and I'm as parched as if I'd trekked the Kalahari, but action has always been a better kind of pain relief for me than anything you can buy from the chemist. It helps keep feelings of shame at bay too.

The bereaved family has been in our house for only about an hour, but already it's the baby who is proving most difficult to handle, so I've decided to take charge of her.

She's a gorgeous creature, utterly charming, and I'll admit to feeling quite fond of her already. The au pair was tending to her but she's rather uselessly gone to bed, though the poor girl did look beyond exhausted, and I suspect that she and I are possibly suffering similar symptoms from the after-effects of alcohol this morning, although I have the benefit of having slept.

Tessa didn't come home last night. It's a very heavy thought because you'd have to be born yesterday not to work out that it's likely she spent the night with another man. If she hadn't reacted so defensively, I might have believed that she'd crashed out at the house of a girlfriend. She's in shock, of course, and that will have modified her normal behavior, but she and I dance such a game of accusation and recrimination that I know guilty and defensive behavior when I see it. I'm an expert in it myself, after all.

As I cradle her baby daughter, my thoughts keep traveling to Maria, and the secret knowledge that I never warmed to her. She was a beautiful woman, like both her girls, but I found her prickly and, if I'm honest, shallow.

Tessa disagreed fairly strongly, so we didn't discuss it for fear of a row, but I didn't like the way Maria and Philip pushed Zoe so relentlessly on the piano. As far as I could see, the poor girl never got to climb a tree or feed a chicken on that farm if she could have been practicing her arpeggios. Philip wasn't as bad as Maria, but he was guilty of it too. I don't know why Tess excused her sister and Philip this behavior. My best guess is that she carried around guilt about being the high achiever, the good girl, and she felt happy because Maria might finally have a chance to match those achievements, albeit via her daughter.

The invasion of our house is strange. Where yesterday I lost the battle with the urges, compounded by the silence of the place, today I find my self-control is performing fairly well. Odd, given the circumstances, and the levels of tension that are prevalent, but welcome nevertheless.

When I take the baby upstairs to attempt to change her nappy, I waste three of the damn things before I get one on her. It's not easy to fit a clean outfit thing on those slippery limbs either, but I rather like the way she grabs my hand as I try. It stops the dratted tremor.

On the way downstairs, I pause by the bathroom door. I have a bottle or two of vodka stashed under the bath in there, tucked away behind the cladding. My throat wants it, my lips want it, and my head wants it. It has even stolen my heart.

As I prevaricate, the baby puts her fingers in my mouth— she's obsessed with doing that, for what reason I cannot guess—and I pull her hand away and lick my parched lips. Come on, Richard, I tell myself. Pull yourself together. Somehow, it feels wrong to drink with her in my arms. She's the antithesis of my grubby preowned path in life; she's fresh and new and unspoiled and I will not sully her.

I move on past the bathroom and down the stairs.

Later, when Tessa is up to it, we must talk, she and I, about where she was last night, and the conversation will no doubt be as sad and bitter as so many of our others, perhaps worse.

In the meantime, I shall try to be of practical use.

"Most Gracious Grace," I say to her, "would you care for something to eat?"

As we arrive in the kitchen, I feel strengthened by the fact that I resisted taking a drink, and I make some firm resolutions. I shall look after this baby so that the others don't have to. I shall try to resist asking my wife where she was last night, because she has just lost her sister.

I will not let this bereaved family down, and I will not let my wife down.

I have my first small success when Grace appears to relish eating mashed banana.

SAM

As soon as Zoe Maisey and her uncle Richard have left my office, I shut the door and look at my watch.

I have a scan booked at 11:30, and a bit later an appointment with the consultant to discuss the result. This is what they've described as a "fast-track" service, which was not what I wanted to hear.

I can walk to the hospital from my office, so I have plenty of time to make a phone call, even though I shouldn't.

I take a deep breath as I flick through the contacts on my phone and find Detective Sergeant Nick George. He's an old school mate, and I'm wondering if he'll do me a favor. I can't ring anybody else, because I shouldn't be doing this at all; I'm a potential witness.

Before I dial, I decide that this call is best made outside. As solicitors we trade in discretion, but walls have ears, and this isn't a phone call that should be overheard.

On my way out, my secretary says, "In or out for the rest of the day, Sam?"

"Out," I say. "Definitely out."

"He works too hard," I hear her say to one of the other

admin staff as the doors swing shut behind me. "It's supposed to be his day off today."

They don't know about my appointment, nobody at work does.

Nick George works in the Criminal Investigation Department in Bristol. We met for a drink when I first moved here and I heard about how he'd got married and had twins via IVF and how his wife had struggled to cope with the babies when he worked nights. We'd got on well at school, never close, but friendly, and both of us ambitious. Secret swots. Our paths hadn't crossed through work yet, but that was probably just a matter of time.

Outside, the streets are already hot. I try Nick's number as I'm walking through the city center, keeping to the patches of shade beside the buildings, and he calls me back a few minutes later as I'm wandering along the edge of the canal and looking for some prettiness in the smooth surface of the water, but instead being distracted by bits of rubbish lapping the concrete edges and reflections of the corporate buildings around me.

"What's your interest, Sam?" Nick asks me.

I come to a stop in the shade beside a waterside bar, where the sidewalk is sticky from the drinks that were spilled the night before. Next to me, a huge area has been cleared in preparation for some sort of building project. A couple of shallow puddles linger in its center after the rain, but mostly it's a vast expanse of dust and rubble.

"I know them." I think it's best to be forthright with him from the outset, but I suppose I'm not entirely honest, because I don't tell him that I might be a witness.

"Not much I can tell except that the body was found outside the front of the house, in some kind of outbuilding."

I'm relieved to hear that, because I understand immediately that it's a scenario that could throw up a vast number of suspects, both from inside and outside the family.

It's important to me that it could be somebody outside the family, for obvious reasons. I want to ask a thousand other questions, like if he knows the cause of death, but that would be definitively crossing a line, and I mustn't do it.

"You close to them?"

"I know the sister of the woman who died."

"Oh dear, sorry."

We both know the conversation is over and that it probably shouldn't have happened at all. I ask after his wife and kids, and just as I'm ready to hang up, he says, "I heard that you weren't well?"

"From who?"

"My mum." His laugh is a bit embarrassed. "The Bideford grapevine is still thriving."

I did tell my parents about my symptoms and about the doctor's suspicions. They're the only people who know. Or the only people who I thought knew. They've obviously been talking.

"I'm OK."

"Is it true?"

And suddenly, looking out over the empty site beside me and missing Tessa, I feel like telling somebody.

"I have a scan today to help confirm the diagnosis. It's complicated."

"Is it likely?"

"They're pretty sure."

"I'm so sorry, mate."

"It's OK."

"Will you carry on working?"

"For as long as I can."

He clears his throat. "Drink soon?"

"Sure. Look I've got to shoot off, I'll call you."

"Make sure you do."

I probably will call him.

TESSA

Richard's carrying the baby. He's walking around the house with Grace on his hip as if he was born to it, and I'm not sure how I feel about that.

It's been a while since our friends had babies and we would occasionally carry them, and I don't think Richard has ever had Grace in his arms before. He's transformed into the image of a benevolent uncle, and because I've wronged him, I resent that he's a spectacle of goodness today. I almost feel he's taunting me with it.

I try to reject that thought, though, because I know that grief is a strange and unpredictable thing, and I recognize that it's provoking great surges of anger in me. If I'm honest, what I really want is for Richard to be looking after me, and me alone.

Or do I want Sam to do that? I'm confused, and the truth could be that at this moment I want them both.

"Katya's resting," Richard says. "The poor girl was just about finished. I think she's had the baby all night."

He's pretending not to be feeling the effects of yesterday's binge, but I've seen the empty ibuprofen packets in the bed-room.

We have a moment to ourselves, apart from the baby.

"Where were you last night, Tess?" he asks me.

"I needed some time alone."

He lets this comment settle, visibly hurt by it. There are arguments that we've had so many times that he knows the score: he's an alcoholic, therefore I have the moral high ground. Almost always. So he makes a submissive response.

"I was worried," he responds eventually. We stare at each other across the room, and Grace tries to put her fingers in his mouth.

"Oh, don't try that again," he tells her, waggling her fingers. "You'll find some ancient fillings or some other kind of horror in there."

She tries again. "Stop it!" he says, shaking her hand, and he laughs. Only a little, but the sound of it and the look of amusement on his face jolts me because I'm not sure when I last heard Richard laugh.

When the detectives arrive at the house, the atmosphere changes immediately. Where before we were roaming the rooms like lost souls, and the family liaison officer busied herself locating the kettle and the tea, like a mother hen, now we all become constricted, nervous, hyped up, and we feel under scrutiny.

Chris responds to the detectives by putting on as good a version of his professional self as he can manage under the circumstances. Shaking hands, trying to find the words to ask practical questions. But he reminds me of a faulty robotic toy: you can see what it's meant to be doing, but it just can't manage it properly.

The detectives ask if there's a suitable room that they can use for interviews.

I install them in our dining room.

In the sitting room, Zoe is curled up in a corner of the sofa, her eyes watchful and guarded behind that hair.

Beside her, Lucas looks catatonic.

Richard has taken Grace upstairs to try to settle her for a nap in our bed; I can hear him singing a nursery rhyme that I didn't even know he knew. Katya has passed out on one of the beds in our small spare room, from shock, or exhaustion, or from an excess of whatever she indulged in last night, it's hard to tell.

I clear the dining room table to make space for the detectives. My work had been spread out all over it, mostly admin from the surgery, and I push all that to one side, as well as another of Richard's models in progress, this one at least partially constructed with all the precision and care he can be capable of.

I offer to make the detectives tea, as if they're plumbers just in to service the boiler. They decline. They're very business-like: crisp shirts tucked into shiny leather belts. Short back and sides for both, and one with salt-and-pepper speckles around the ears. They remind me of the Jehovah's Witnesses who sometimes come to the door in all their smartness.

They ask to speak to Chris first and we all wait nervously and almost silently with the family liaison officer, as their voices grumble away indistinguishably for forty-five minutes, separated from us by the hallway and the shut dining room door. When Chris finally emerges, he looks strained.

They ask for Zoe next, but she doesn't move; those eyes, which belonged first to my sister, look at me instead.

"I want Sam to be there with me," she says. "Please can we phone Sam again?" and I understand that I'm her go-to person right now, and the responsibility of that makes my stomach lurch.

"You don't need him, love. You really don't."

Still she won't move from the sofa. I wonder if the police have powers to manhandle her into the dining room to answer questions.

"Why don't you just have a little chat with the detectives," says the family liaison officer. She's a dumpy woman who has a bit of a wheeze going on that I'd want to treat if she were an animal. "As soon as they've heard from you they can crack on and get to work finding out what's happened to . . ." She trails off. Zoe's stare is ferocious.

"It won't do any harm." I'm trying to be reassuring, but it's a struggle.

"Just do as you're told on this occasion," says Chris and his words interject sharply like the crack of a whip. "It's not negotiable."

Zoe stands up abruptly, and her clothes hang off her in a ghoulish sort of way for a moment or two before she wraps her arms and her garments tight around herself again and shuffles toward the dining room. I see her slump into a chair opposite the detectives and then one of them gets up and walks around the table to shut the door behind her.

ZOE

Mum was my protector. Even when she got it wrong you could never fault her for trying. I knew that, and Jason banged on about it all the time. She wouldn't have let them interview me without Sam.

Mum was a bit taller than me, and had shiny blond hair, which everybody admired and which she gave to me and Grace.

When I was little, she was cuddly and firm and soft, and she smelled of woodsmoke and cooking. In the flat we lived in after the accident she smelled of cigarette smoke and in the Second Chance House it wasn't a smell, but a scent, and Chris gave it to her in posh bottles that she kept in a row on her dressing table. Her frame was thinner by then too. Not cuddly, like it used to be, but she looked great because it was *so slim*, everybody said so.

On the floor of the shed her body looked and felt cold.

Now, I just have my dad, and I have Tess, and I have Richard, I have Sam and I have Chris. But I'm very much not sure of Chris; in fact all I'm sure of is how much I don't really know him when Mum isn't here to be a bridge between us. The only thing I'm sure of is that he called me a slut yesterday evening, and that there was darkness in his eyes.

Tess and Richard love me, but they won't defend me the way my mum would.

Sam doesn't think I need him.

My dad isn't here yet, and I don't want him to come anyway.

So when I sit down in front of the investigating officers I decide that I must protect myself, and I know what I'm going to do.

The policemen look exactly the same as each other, as if you'd popped them out of a PEZ detective dispenser. I've met a lot of police, and these two are definitely the most businesslike. They remind me of some of the men who come to the house to meet Chris: you want to unwrap them out of their perfect suits to see if they've got real beating hearts and breathing lungs underneath.

"We're very sorry for your loss," one of them says.

I don't reply at first, because I'm thinking about the Unit.

When I got to the Unit, I thought everybody was going to be thick, and I was right in a way for many of them, but only if you're just talking about exam success. Second Chance Family type of success.

The kids on the Unit weren't thick at all if you're talking about being smart. They knew stuff about police interviews and legal advice and courtrooms that nobody tells you in your before life.

Right now I'm not being charged with a crime; I know that.

But even though I'm not being charged, what's ringing in my head is what the kids in the Unit said about giving "no comment" interviews. It's the best strategy for not letting yourself get stuffed up by something that you say. What nobody tells you is that even if you're not under caution, even if you're just "having a chat" with the police, you can make what they just have to decide to call a "significant statement," and then they can ask you about it later in a proper, recorded interview, and that interview can be quoted in court.

Ergo: no chat you have with police is a "safe" chat.

Ergo: I decide to run my own "no comment" defense.

Because then, even though they'll tell me that this could be seen as uncooperative behavior, and it could be frowned on, etc., etc., all scare tactics, I'll avoid the trap of delivering myself into their hands, because a "no comment" interview dumps the burden of proof on the police if they want to charge you.

Why am I giving so much weight to what the kids in the Unit said? Partly it's because as well as finding out they were cleverer than I thought they would be, I also liked and trusted them, a few of them anyway, though not all obviously, because some were proper psychos. It's also because there's one more thing nobody ever talks about in my life anymore, and that's how totally screwed-up unfair my verdict was.

Eva Bell robbed me of a chance at getting the not guilty verdict my mum wanted because she lied to protect her brother. At the time, my mum sobbed and said, "It's a miscarriage of justice," and Sam looked white and said how sorry he was, and my dad accused Mum of persuading me to make the wrong plea. In the Unit, I talked to Jason about it a bit, but it was never a long chat because everybody in the Unit basically believes that they've been screwed over in some way, so the key workers are fed up of hearing it.

When I first got out of the Unit and we were in the flat, my mum used to talk to me about it and she was still really bitter, but since she met Chris I was never allowed to say how it was wrong. It was time to "put it behind me," Mum told me. The "miscarriage of justice" had no place in the Second Chance Life because it didn't exist there. It was erased, even though the unfairness of it had burned inside me since the trial, and still does.

What I can do right now, though, is to use what I've learned from it; and what I've learned is that you can't be too careful and you can never trust the system. Never.

It's difficult to do what I've decided to do, I know that from before, because early interview is the softly, softly stage, when you feel like the police are your friends, that they understand, and it's so tempting to talk, you even want to talk, and after the accident I told them everything, and I didn't realize that each word was another scoop of the shovel in Project Digging My Own Grave.

So I tell myself to be strong and I put my strategy into action straightaway. When the detective says, "We're very sorry for your loss," I reply: "No comment."

There's a pause before one of them says, "You're not being charged, love, we're not taking a formal statement from you. All we're hoping is that you can tell us a bit about what happened last night, just give us an initial account."

When I hear that I think: knew it, knew they were going to say "initial account," but all I say is: "No comment."

He puts his notebook down on the table and drops his pen

onto it. Then he leans toward me. "You don't need to reply 'no comment' in an interview like this. We're not asking you to account for yourself, it's just a chat."

"No comment."

"Can you at least tell us how old you are?"

"No comment."

"We gather you played the piano at a concert last night," says the other detective.

"No comment."

His eyebrows shoot up his forehead. I'm not always good at knowing when I'm annoying people, but I can tell that I'm royally pissing him off now.

"You're very good at the piano, I hear?"

"No comment."

"It's quite a thing to publicly perform at your age, isn't it?"

It's harder than you think to run a "no comment" interview. The urge to reply, especially when questions are friendly, or flattering, is very strong. The normal answers to their questions form in your mouth, but you have to swallow them back, and instead spit out the two words that they have to pretend don't frustrate them.

"No comment."

"Would you say you're a prodigy?"

"No comment."

"Do you enjoy playing with your brother?"

That one is especially hard not to reply to, because they've got it wrong, and I hate it when people get things wrong. "Step. Brother," I want to say, and in my head I would add "imbeciles." Jason didn't like me correcting people, but my mum and dad never minded. It made them laugh.

"No comment."

I can see that I'm annoying the quiet one as well. He keeps trying tactics on me. He smiles, and then does a hard stare, and then looks quizzical as if he can't possibly understand why I might be saying "NO comment."

Now he clears his throat and says, "You do know, Zoe, that we're just trying to get to the bottom of what happened last night, don't you? It would be for everybody's good if you tell us what happened last night, because then we can focus on really finding out what happened to your mum. You'd want that for her, wouldn't you?"

"No comment."

He tries not to be frustrated, but a little twist of his lips tells me that he is and I have to bite my own lips so I don't smirk.

In the Unit, if you get to smirk at the expense of the police, you would get an A star, or a sticker on your chart, or a shiny trophy, or whatever.

I don't think the detective notices my lips twitching, though, because the door of the room opens suddenly enough to make me jump and there is my actual, real dad.

TESSA

I'm standing just beside Philip Guerin when he and Zoe first come face-to-face, and my impression is that they might as well have the Grand Canyon between them because neither of them seems able to move at first, but when he finally opens his arms to her she gets up from the chair and runs into them, and the force with which she does that makes him gasp.

The first thing he says is "Why is Zoe being interviewed without an adult present?"

The detectives stand up and the one on the left says, "We understood that Zoe is seventeen years old."

"It's a gray area," says her father, "and you know that." He says this wearily, as if the knowledge he has about the rights of children in the legal system is something he doesn't really care for, which is probably the case.

"It's perfectly acceptable"—the detective holds his ground—"particularly as she's not being charged, this is just an informal interview; and you are, sir?"

"Her dad."

Philip Guerin has aged since I last saw him, terribly. I heard from Maria that he hadn't done well since the accident, that his elderly mother was turning up at the farmhouse to cook for him, and you can see that despair in the way the lines on his face have set, and his defeated posture, though that is, perhaps, also a result of the news he's heard this morning.

In spite of that, I can't help feeling a substantial twinge of resentment toward him because he abandoned my sister and Zoe, claiming that the outcome of their shared existence was too much for him. He absolved himself of blame, hurled accusations of hothousing Zoe at my sister, but I'd seen him do it too. I'd heard him use the full armory of parental weapons to encourage her to play the piano: threats, copious amounts of praise when she'd done well, and buckets of emotional blackmail—"You don't want to let your teacher down, do you, or your mum? She's given up so much so you can perform."

The detective holds out his hand, says he's sorry for Philip's loss, and they shake awkwardly, and introduce themselves formally, with Zoe's body still sandwiched against her father.

"I don't want you to think we're getting ahead of ourselves here, Mr. Guerin," says the detective. "I understand that Zoe's had previous experience in the justice system, but I want to reassure you that she's not under suspicion at this time, and we're just trying to get her account of what happened last night so we can start to get to the bottom of it."

And from her father's chest, her voice distorted by his clothing, Zoe says, "I was asleep."

Philip lifts his hands as if to say, *There it is, she's told you everything*, but he doesn't then clamp them around his daughter. As she clings to his chest with what I can only describe as ferocity, his arms simply drop to his side in a gesture that looks a whole lot like defeat, and I have a terrible feeling that he's not going to be much help to Zoe at all.

SAM

Nick George calls me back unexpectedly, just as I'm sitting down in the waiting room at the hospital. They're running late, so I'm killing time by looking up the news on my phone to see if there's anything out there yet about Maria.

BODY FOUND AT STOKE BISHOP HOME, it says on Bristol 24/7.

The only development on that is on the police breaking news website, which identifies the body as female, and in her thirties. They haven't released Maria's name yet, but it will surely be soon.

Nick doesn't bother with pleasantries this time. "Look," he says, "I'm only going to tell you this one thing, and I shouldn't even be doing that."

I put my finger in my other ear because the receptionist is talking really loudly to an elderly man whose head is sagging, revealing the topography of the vertebrae in his neck.

"What?" I ask.

"Forensics found evidence of blood spatter in the house."

"No!"

"I can't tell you any more than that, and it'll be days before they can ascertain for certain whose blood it is, or get any other results, but I thought you should know."

"God." I let this information sink in. The police forensics team does a simple test that shows up blood and semen at a scene instantly, even if it's been cleaned away. It's the only test that gives a swift result. Everything else must be sent away to be examined in the lab.

"I've got to go. I hope it's not going to get too bad for the family now."

"Where was the blood?"

"You know I can't tell you that, I shouldn't be telling you any of this at all."

I want to mine him for more information, but I don't want to push my luck. "Thanks, Nick. I appreciate it."

"It's OK. I'm sorry, you know."

I understand that it's my health he's referring to, not Maria Maisey's death. This was a sympathy call, his way of stroking my brow, a nod from one man to another man's misfortune.

Somebody taps my shoulder. It's a nurse, holding my notes and a hospital gown.

"Sorry, Nick, I've got to go, but I appreciate it, mate, I really do."

The nurse shows me into a miniature cubicle, where she hands me the gown and tells me to change into it. There's a locker in the corridor, she says, where I can leave my stuff.

I get changed, and before I put my things in the locker, I try to phone Tessa, but it goes straight to voicemail. The nurse hovers. The radiologist is ready for me, she says, we should hurry up.

TESSA

When it's my turn to sit down with the detectives my hands shake. The adrenaline that got me through the last few hours has crashed and I sit with my hands under the table, on my lap, where they keep up their involuntary motion. It occurs to me that this is what it must be like for Richard.

On the mantelpiece behind the detectives I notice a drooping vase of flowers, which I've forgotten to refresh. They were given to me by a grateful family at the surgery, but now they've become carcasses, with papery petals and shrunken stalks. Beside them hangs a watercolor that Richard and I brought back from Hong Kong and have always cherished. Elegant and simple swaths of color describe two pears on a branch and a small bird. The serenity of the scene is a world away from the mess we're in.

The first thing the detective says to me is something kind: "We're very sorry for your loss, Mrs. Downing," and so then they have to wait until I stop crying. It's usually me doing this in the surgery, waiting for the grief of others to subside after

I've offered them a kind word in a horrible situation, so it feels strange that the tables have turned. It embarrasses me.

"I'm sorry," I say. "I'm so sorry."

"Please," says the detective who first spoke, "take your time."

They stare at their notepads while I wipe my tears away and, after a decent interval, when I've stopped sniveling loudly, they ask if I'm ready.

"How was she killed?" I ask them.

"Ah, so, at this time it's hard for us to say for sure, but your sister's body has been taken into the care of the coroner for tests so we can establish exactly what happened," the slightly shorter detective replies. He has kind eyes.

"In due course," adds his partner, as if I might be unreasonably expecting a fast-track service.

Of course I'm thinking then of the morgue, of shiny stainless steel, of bodies in drawers, of the clank of surgical instruments on a metal tray and the bloodless cut of a postmortem incision. My sister is too beautiful for such treatment. I always had a protective instinct toward her, however much she resisted it, even when she chose her own, fiercely independent path through life. I felt that instinct every day of my life until today, when she's managed to elude me with absolute finality.

"Could you give us your account of what happened last night?"

"From when?"

"From whenever you feel you'd like to start." They're exuding patience, and they're purposely not leading my answers. This, I can tell. The account I give is up to me.

"I went to Zoe's concert," I say. "It started at seven-thirty but I got there at about six forty-five to learn how to use the video camera because it was my job to record the children's performances."

"And did you go alone?"

I nod, hoping he won't ask me why, and am relieved when all he does is make a note. The other man has his arms folded and his head slightly cocked to one side. He's just listening and watching and I find that unnerving. Sam flits briefly through my mind because it occurs to me that this is his world, and I've never glimpsed it before.

"Can you tell us about the concert?" says the detective who's writing.

Memories come to me vividly, and in sharp focus. I tell all. From the detectives' responses I can hear that they already know about Zoe's past conviction, and I think that either they've run background checks on us very quickly or Chris has told them, and I reckon it's more likely to be the latter.

More note taking, then they ask me to continue talking them through the evening.

My words flow until I get to the part when we're all back at Chris and Maria's house, because this is private territory, and I am, just like Maria, a private person. The invasion of our family's privacy was one of the hardest things to bear, for all of us, after Zoe's accident.

"Will the press report what happened?" I ask the detectives.

"They will report that there's been a death," the listening one answers, "and they'll report the progress of the investigation."

"What about Zoe?"

"We won't be broadcasting Zoe's history."

"Can they?"

The answer is in the expression in his eyes: it tells me that there's a point beyond which he has no control over what the press do.

"We'll do our best to make sure it doesn't happen if it could prejudice a trial," he says eventually, and the other man gives him a sharp look and says, "Let's not get ahead of ourselves."

"What?" I don't understand at first, and it's a thump in the gut when I realize that what they mean is that Zoe could be a suspect.

"Let's move on. Can you tell us about when you first arrived at the house?"

So I try, but my natural instinct to remain private means that I falter over my words and descriptions. I feel guilty when they ask me to pause while they take time to note down my words about my conversation with Tom Barlow. When they ask me why I followed him I also feel guilty when I say, "Because I didn't know what he was going to do," and then the guilt is compounded farther when I think of him at the doorway to his home, with his wife and child.

The things I'm saying about him go against my instincts that he is a good and loving man, but they also feed a suspicion that I know Chris shares: that Tom Barlow could have hurt Maria. I wonder if she met him outside the house and tried to persuade him not to publicize Zoe's actions? Did she provoke a rage in him that he couldn't contain after a long, hot night of despair and frustration? That is surely the version of events that looks most likely right now.

I also feel as if I need to defend my sister—old habits die hard—and so to an extent I gloss over Maria's poolside scene by saying that she began to feel under the weather after a glass of wine, that she was tired from being up with the baby, and she never coped well with the heat, and I tell the police that I went home after Maria came out of the pool.

"And how did things seem with the family at this point, when you left?"

"I think everybody was tired and a little rattled. The concert and the revelation had been difficult for them all. It was a complicated night."

"Do you think her husband was angry with her?"

I think about this one before I answer, mostly because I'm not sure. "I think he was upset, but he loves her, you know."

I remember Chris wrapping his arms around her, enveloping her in a towel. I remember her burying her head into his chest.

"He loved her," I say.

"OK." He notes something down, but as he does, I wonder whether I'm sure of that.

"Do you have something to add?" The detective watching me notices something in my expression.

"No."

My sister had a good life, I'm sure of it. It's what we all wanted for her, after everything, it's what she deserved.

"Just one more thing," he says. "We're asking everybody who was at the house if they would mind letting us have their phones. Just to help us crack on with ruling things out; speeds up our inquiries. Would that be OK?"

I think of all the texts between Sam and me on my phone, and all the emails too, but I try not to let those thoughts show because the officer is watching me.

"No, that's fine," I say, and I get my phone out of my pocket and pass it to him.

He hands it to his colleague, who puts it in a bag, and writes my name on the outside of it. I see they already have Zoe's.

"Have you arrested Tom Barlow?" I ask them, because I feel as though they should be more interested in what he did.

The detective looks at me as if he's assessing me in some way. Then he says, "Mr. Barlow has been interviewed, but he has a solid alibi. He did not murder your sister."

ZOE

Me and Dad sit in the garden. There's a bench there that my mum would have had pressure-washed because it's got lichen and bird mess on it, but we ignore that and we sit on it anyway.

Dad is wiping his eyes because tears are leaking out of them slowly and oozily, the way tar used to seep out of the old railway ties we had in the yard at the farm. I know he's crying because of Mum, but I'm also used to the sight of it because it's what used to happen after the accident when he sat for long hours at the window of our farmhouse and looked out toward the fold in the landscape that allowed you a small glimpse of the ocean.

Nobody spoke to us, you see, in the village after the accident. Even though some of them had known Dad since he was a baby. We were shut out of all the communal arrangements too. Nobody bought our produce, shared costs for oil, or anything like that anymore. That's what really broke my dad, Granny Guerin said. Not what I did but how other people treated him after it. It tore the soul out of him.

"I can't believe it," he says. "Out of the two of us, I never thought she'd be the one to go first."

He's thinking about Mum, but I don't know what to say to that because it feels irrelevant to now, to the problem of now, which is who killed her and how scared I feel.

"Amelia Barlow's dad came to the concert," I tell him. "We didn't know there was a stone for her in the churchyard."

"I know what he did last night, but that man's not a killer," my dad says.

"How do you know that?"

"Because I know his family."

"How does that tell you anything?"

"He's from good stock, Zoe."

"Why? Because he's from Devon? What difference does that make to anything? Reality check, Dad, I'm from Devon and I killed people, but you never stand up for me!"

I've snapped. It doesn't happen often, but when it does, I feel like I'm exploding with anger at all the people who won't accept that what I did was just an accident, and I should never have gone to jail, and I get frustrated that people who are supposed to love me can't keep up with all the things in my head, and I get angry too with the ideas themselves, the strength of them, the way that they race around and multiply and keep me up at night.

When I'm angry I am, according to Jason and my mum, my own worst enemy.

I'm standing up and facing Dad now and I know I must look ugly because I can feel that my face has contorted out of shape. If my mum were here now she'd hold my shoulders and look into my eyes and tell me to calm down, and tell me to count to ten with her and try to access my techniques for keeping in control of my emotions.

My dad just buries his face in his hands and I can't stand

it, so I start to hit him. I don't hit him hard, but my hands slap at his shoulders and the top of his head, and they keep slapping until he stands up and catches my wrists and bellows: "Enough! Zoe! Enough!"

And I feel my knees crumple until I'm down on the brittle grass on Tess's lawn and it's spiking into my shins and my forehead and my hands, and pieces of it get into my mouth.

I don't want my dad with his leaking eyes and his permanent look of disappointment and defeat that I know I caused. I want my mum.

Out of the corner of my eye, I can see the twin trunks of Dad's legs as he just stands uselessly over me, and then I hear the voice of the family liaison officer saying, "Is everything all right, Mr. Guerin?" and my dad says, "No, it's not, I don't know what to do with her," and then they both help me up, but I keep my body as floppy as possible at first, because sometimes that's the only way you can keep protesting how you feel when people have resorted to manhandling you.

RICHARD

Zoe is making a scene in the garden. I notice it happen from the kitchen window and the detectives in the dining room see it too, because one of them interrupts the interview with Tessa and calls for the liaison officer woman to go out and help. Grace and I are struggling somewhat to find something else suitable for her to eat, but we settle on a biscuit, which she seems to enjoy hugely, and somebody has put a bottle of her milk in the fridge so I heat that up the way I saw the Russian do it earlier: small saucepan, water heating, bottle floating in it. I feel quite professional when I squeeze some of the milk out of it onto the inside of my wrist to test the temperature, as I also observed.

"It's perfect, darling," I say to Grace and she stuffs it into her mouth even before I've got us settled down properly in the sitting room, and guzzles it with the rather unnervingly greedy intensity of a lamb at the ewe's udder.

We disturb Lucas. He's looking through my collection of DVDs, and he jumps out of his skin when we enter the room, as if I'd caught him with his hand in my wallet.

"You can borrow one if you like," I say, to put him at ease.

"I mean, not today, but when things are more . . . although if it helps to watch something now, then feel free."

"No, thank you, I was just looking." He sits back down, plunges his hands into his pockets.

I'm not really sure what to say to him, though I feel sorry for him. He probably had become fond of Maria, had maybe even come to love her, and to bear this in addition to the premature loss of his own mother is going to be hard, *is* hard. I'm also at a loss for words because I mostly talk only to other scientists at work and to Tess at home. My friends have long since slipped down the cracks between my infrequent attempts at keeping in touch. I should probably say something reassuring, or comforting, but all I can come up with is "Do you like film then?"

He nods. The movement is economical, the eye contact only fleeting.

"What sort of films do you like?"

He glances back at me and then at the door, as if he's not sure either that we should be talking like this, but I think it's OK, especially if it keeps his head above water, reminds him that somebody is interested in him.

"I like some old films."

"Such as?"

"Um. *Apocalypse Now* is a favorite."

I'm surprised that he's been allowed to watch that in their closeted household, but I try not to let that show.

"One of my favorite opening sequences," I say.

He sits up straighter, engages with me with startling intensity. "I know, it's incredible. The montage is quite confusing at first, but it gives you the whole scene, how it starts off with the slow rasp of the helicopter blades, which comes in and out like an echo, and you fade in to the palm trees with blue sky above, and then you see the yellow smoke and the helicopters coming across the trees and then, boom!, the explosion, which is so intense, and then there are loads of images overlaid on each other so you see his face in the hotel room over the images of his memories of Vietnam and then the fan above him becomes the helicopter blades and you've got 'This Is the End' playing over it, which is so intense when you see his eyes, and his pupils are like pinpricks and then the camera goes to the window and you're in Saigon. And the voiceover starts. It's incredible."

He comes alive as he delivers this speech and I'm astounded because I've never heard this boy talk so much. Granted, I've spent time with him only on a handful of occasions, but he behaved as if he was mute then, and Tessa has made the same observation about him.

"I love the scene where they brief the main character," I say, wanting to keep Lucas talking, thinking that it's good for him.

He fixes me with eyes that seem slickly alive, like black treacle. He says, in a slightly strange accent: "'Because there's a conflict in every human heart between the rational and the irrational, between good and evil . . . Every man has got a breaking point.'"

"What?" I say, feeling rather unnerved, before I appreciate that he's quoting the film, and in fact the scene I just mentioned. In truth, I have very scant recollection of it, but I don't want to discourage him, so I say, "Oh sorry, yes! Bravo, Lucas. Yes, very good. It's a very dark film, I think." That, I do recall.

"I think it's his best film," he says.

"What is?" Chris has crept up on us, but he makes no move

to take his daughter from me. The poor man looks absolutely shattered.

"Can I get you anything?" I ask him. "Cup of tea?"

"Just keep doing what you're doing." He gestures toward Grace, who hasn't really reacted to him, because she's still too busy sucking at the bottle, which is nearly empty now. "I hope you're not being a film bore," he says to Lucas, rather harshly I feel, though everybody is, of course, under pressure.

"No, not at all. He was very helpfully answering a question of mine." I brush it off while Lucas reverts to staring at the floor.

We're distracted by the sight of Zoe being led in through the hallway, and escorted up the stairs. She's leaning on the arm of the liaison officer and her father is in their wake. They ascend extremely slowly and we watch.

"She's a bit overwhelmed, I think," I say to the others, because I feel the need to excuse her behavior, perhaps because she belonged to us before she belonged to them, and even though Grace chooses that moment to finish her bottle and try to heave herself into a sitting position with the last gulp of milk drooling from her lips, it doesn't escape my notice that Chris is looking at Zoe with an expression that I would struggle to describe as either friendly or caring.

ZOE

They bring me upstairs and tell me to lie on the single bed that's in Richard's office. The bedding smells of a man and it's creased as if it's been used, but it's soft and comfortable, and I feel sleep taking hold of me like it sometimes used to do at the Unit: more of a crash than a slipping away, as if your body has decided that you need time out and that's the end of the matter.

At the Unit they used to tell me it was shock that made me into a virtual narcoleptic for the first couple of months.

As I shut my eyes, I feel the weight and sag of my dad sitting down on the end of the bed. As I slip away, I hope he's not doing that "staring at me like he'll never be able to work me out" thing, but by the time I wake again, he's gone and I'm relieved.

The waking is sudden, though: it comes via a deep, sharp intake of breath, and a sudden urge to be sitting up, as if the covers were about to choke me, and then the knowledge that my mum is no longer here flows back into my conscious mind like water coursing through the holes in a colander.

The digital clock on Richard's bedside table tells me that

I've been asleep for only about twenty minutes. I can hear voices downstairs, but they're faint and indistinguishable.

I let my tears fall silently because I don't want anybody to hear me sobbing and to come with sympathy eyes. I don't like people to see me cry because that's ingrained in me since I was little. "Don't cry if you lose a competition, Zoe, that's called being a bad loser," or "If you keep crying, your practice will take twice as long as it needs to."

Not crying publicly could be seen as a little tribute to my mum.

It's also a tribute to the Unit, where prolonged sobbing could make you a target. It keeps other people awake, you see, and they shout at you that you're fucking with their heads and that they'll give you something to cry about if you like.

So my tears fall silently and I think about how my mum has always been there to tell me what to do, and now I don't know who's going to do that.

I think of Lucas, who lost his mum too, and that reminds me of the email that he deleted, and I decide that I want to read the rest of the script. The first part was kind of soppy and strange, but there must be something more in it or he wouldn't have asked me to delete it if it was just like a love story all the way through. I know it's not on my email any more, but it will be on my mum's account still, surely, because it wasn't just me he sent it to.

I don't have my phone any longer because the detectives took that, just like I told Lucas they would, so that once again they can comb through my private world and then pretend in interview that "Internet experts" have told them what all the textspeak abbreviations stand for.

They'll see the panop messages that freaked me out earlier,

but I don't mind that too much, because it wasn't illegal for me to use panop, just "not recommended" by Jason, and I can explain that Lucas found out about me and he sent them to wind me up.

At Richard's desk, which is just a few feet away from the bed I'm lying on, I click the computer mouse and his monitor comes to life silently. There's some of his work up on the screen, but I want the Internet, so I carefully reduce the windows he has open and go online. No passwords are required at any stage, and that is so different from our house where everything is password protected because of "the importance of Internet and personal data security."

My mum's email is easy to access. I haven't done it often, but just sometimes because I saw her password once and that makes it very tempting. Her password is ZoeGrace and some numbers.

Her email account is very boring, though. She mostly emails her beautician and hair salon, she gets loads of shopping order confirmation emails, and she talks to some piano people, and baby group friends, and sometimes she and Chris have incredibly boring conversations by email about paint colors or when the man's coming to trim the tree or stuff like that.

It's easy to find Lucas's email and I see that it hasn't been opened yet, so I click on it. He's sent my mum the exact same thing he sent me—it's near the top of her inbox, just above an email from Chris with the title "Appointment on Wednesday," as if my mum's his secretary or something.

Richard and Tess must have super-efficient Wi-Fi because the attachment that Lucas sent opens immediately and I start to read on from where I left off.

"WHAT I KNOW"

BY LUCAS KENNEDY

ACT II

INT. CHRIS AND JULIA'S NEW HOME. DAY.

JULIA is up a ladder, hair tied up, overalls on, in the middle of a lovely room, which has gracious and generous proportions. She's painting the intricate plasterwork on the ceiling rose.

> DYING JULIA (V.O.)
> My marriage was lovely at first, and my only sadness was settling down so far away from my mother, so I wasn't able to be with her when she died. I hadn't really had time to make many friends in Bristol before I met Chris and our life together sort of overwhelmed me, so I threw myself into making our marriage a wonderful place. We renovated a beautiful house, which Chris bought for us, and very soon we discovered that we were expecting a baby.

We see JULIA pause in her painting, rub loose strands of hair from her eyes, and put a hand to her stomach. She has felt a twinge, and we see in her eyes that she knows.

**INT. KENNEDY HOUSE, CHRIS AND JULIA'S
BEDROOM. DAY.**

The room is beautifully decorated and a
lined crib sits at the end of the bed.
Sitting in bed, her newborn baby in her
arms, is JULIA.

> DYING JULIA (V.O.)
> The pregnancy went swimmingly.
> I was healthy and energetic
> throughout it. And on a warm May
> day, my baby was born. We named
> him Lucas. Chris chose the name.

We see the baby close up. He's beautiful.

> DYING JULIA (V.O.) (CONT'D)
> The problem was, Chris never
> bonded with the baby.

As the camera pulls away, we see CHRIS
standing at the end of the bed. He's
looking at his wife, who is entirely
absorbed in her young son, and the
expression on his face is blank. He feels
nothing. He turns and leaves the room,
and JULIA, lost in her son's eyes, is
oblivious. It's only when the door closes
behind him that she raises her head.

                          JULIA
        Chris?

**INT. CHRIS AND JULIA'S HOUSE, SITTING ROOM.
DAY.**

It's Christmas Day, a few years later. We
see a lovely tall tree and a fire in the
hearth. The Christmas decorations are
tasteful, restrained, and conservative.

                    DYING JULIA (V.O.)
        After Lucas's birth we still gave
        the impression of being a happy
        family, and we often were. But
        something had changed.

CHRIS, JULIA, and LUCAS are opening
presents. It's not an especially warm
scene, there's too much formality about
the little group for that, but they're
going through the motions cheerfully
enough, although the three-year-old
LUCAS seems to be rather a quiet,
guarded child. When he's given a
present he looks to his father for
permission before opening it.

                    DYING JULIA (V.O.)
The problem was that since Lucas
had been born, Chris had become
prone to losing his temper. At
first it wasn't too bad, but as the
years went by, it got more serious
and more frightening.

LUCAS has opened his present and is
looking at it on the floor. JULIA is
on a chair beside him and she too is
opening a gift from CHRIS. She gasps when
she unwraps it, as it's clearly a very
expensive ring, bigger and more flashy than
her engagement ring.

                    CHRIS
What's the matter?

                    JULIA
Nothing's the matter. It's
beautiful. I'm just shocked, in a
good way, of course, that's all.

                    CHRIS
You don't like it.

JULIA

Darling. I love it. It's just so
much more than I was expecting.
It's wonderful, really.

She takes the ring out of its box and
tries to slip it onto her finger, but it
won't fit.

JULIA (CONT'D)

Oh dear!

She pulls it off and tries it on another
finger, but the ring is too small. She
laughs nervously. CHRIS is watching her
like a hawk. LUCAS plays on the carpet,
oblivious.

JULIA (CONT'D)

Do you think they might be able to
swap it?

CHRIS

Put it on.

JULIA

Darling, it's just a little bit
small. I'm sure if we asked them
they would be able to loosen it,
don't you think?

                    CHRIS
        Put it on. Not on that finger.
        Rings don't go on little fingers.

JULIA glances at LUCAS, and then back at
CHRIS, who gazes at her impassively, arms
crossed.

                    JULIA
        Don't you want to see what I got
        for you?

                    CHRIS
        I want to see you put the ring on.

We see from JULIA's face that she
knows there's no point in arguing with
CHRIS, that she fears an escalation.
CHRIS watches without flinching as JULIA
forces the ring over the knuckle of her
second finger. It takes time and JULIA's
clearly in pain as she does it, though
she stays silent, so LUCAS will not
notice. When the ring is finally on,
JULIA holds a trembling hand out to
CHRIS to show him. CHRIS takes her
fingers and turns them a little from one
side to the other to examine the ring.
It's impossible to ignore the red, scraped
and bruised skin that bulges around it.

> CHRIS (CONT'D)
> It looks beautiful. Well done.

CHRIS leans in to kiss JULIA and she
submits to this with an attempt at a
smile.

> DYING JULIA (V.O.)
> I kept the ring on for a week
> before going to hospital to have it
> cut off and receiving antibiotics
> for the infection that had crept
> into the broken skin underneath.
> When Chris found out, he pulled a
> clump of hair out of the back of
> my head and told me I was lucky
> that was all he did.

**INT. KITCHEN IN THE KENNEDY HOUSE.
EVENING.**

Six-year-old LUCAS is finishing his supper
while JULIA prepares something for herself
and CHRIS. LUCAS and JULIA exchange a
smile and we see that the atmosphere
between them is sweet and lovely.

                    DYING JULIA (V.O.)
          Chris didn't always behave like
          that. In fact he was mostly very
          generous and loving, but there
          were triggers. And, as time
          passed, I learned to recognize
          them.

The peaceful scene is interrupted by the
sound of a car pulling up outside and
then the slam of a car door. JULIA glances
anxiously at the kitchen clock.

                        JULIA
          Oh! I think Daddy's home early.
          Lucas, do you think you could run
          and play in your bedroom while I
          finish making supper for him?

The dinner she's preparing consists of
piles of chopped ingredients. It's nowhere
near ready, and we see that makes her
nervous. LUCAS gets up and she ushers him
out of the room and into the hallway.

                    JULIA (CONT'D)
          Well done, poppet, I'll be up to
          give you a kiss later.

                    LUCAS
Will Daddy?

                    JULIA
I don't know. He might be a bit
tired, but I will, I promise.

She's speaking urgently now, time is
running out. We hear the back door open.

                    CHRIS
Hello? Julia?

                    JULIA
                 (whispering)
What do you need to remember
to do?

                    LUCAS
Put my story CD on.

                    JULIA
Good! And what else?

                    LUCAS
Lock my door.

                    JULIA
Well done, darling. You're a
clever boy.

When JULIA is sure he's gone upstairs
and she's heard the lock of his door
sliding into place and the beginning
of a story CD playing, she straightens
her outfit and her hair and goes back
to the kitchen.

                    JULIA (CONT'D)
          Hello, darling. How are you?

                    CHRIS
          Where were you?

She shuts the kitchen door behind her.

INT. KITCHEN IN THE KENNEDY HOUSE. NIGHT.

It's just an hour later and there's carnage
in the room. Food and glasses have been
overturned and it's clear that something
violent has occurred.

                    DYING JULIA (V.O.)
          But even as things escalated,
          after every act of violence, Chris
          was sorry.

CHRIS and JULIA sit on the floor, both
in disarray. JULIA's blouse is ripped,
her cheeks are flushed high with panic,

and her hair is very tousled, but she
and CHRIS cradle each other, though
he grips her more tightly than she
does him.

                    CHRIS
        I'm sorry. I'm so sorry. I love you
        so much. I don't know what I'd do
        without you.

                    DYING JULIA (V.O.)
        And every time, I forgave him
        because, if I'm honest, I could see
        no way to leave him. I was afraid
        of what he might do to us if I
        did. And I felt shame. Oh, the
        shame I felt. Shame kept my lips
        sealed.

Unseen by CHRIS, we see the desperation on
JULIA's face as he strokes her hair.

**INT. PRIVATE HOSPITAL, CONSULTANT'S ROOM.
DAY.**

JULIA and CHRIS sit together on one side
of a desk, and a DOCTOR on the other.

                    DYING JULIA (V.O.)
The problem is, that a life lived
in fear takes its toll on you, so
by the time I had a diagnosis of
a brain tumor, five years later,
all my confidence and most of my
strength had sapped away.

                    CHRIS
Is there anything that can be
done?

                    DOCTOR
We can try to treat the tumor, to
control it, but we can't cure it,
and surgery is far too risky.

                    CHRIS
How long would she have, with
treatment?

                    DOCTOR
It's hard to be precise. Treatment
could extend life by one month,
or maybe even as much as three.
But, and it's a significant but,
treatment can have some extreme
side effects.

There's a beat while CHRIS and JULIA
absorb what this means.

                        JULIA
So it's a quality-of-life issue.

                        DOCTOR
Yes.

                        JULIA
Be treated and be very sick for
more months and then die anyway,
or turn down treatment and die
more quickly but more comfortably.

                        DOCTOR
That's probably what it boils down
to.

                        CHRIS
Is it worth getting another
opinion? Are you sure?

                        DOCTOR
You're most welcome to get another
opinion, but I will put my
reputation on the line here and
tell you that I'll be absolutely
staggered if you're told anything
different.

EXT. A HOSPITAL CAR PARK. DAY.

CHRIS and JULIA get into the car, each in
their own world.

> DYING JULIA (V.O.)
> We got another opinion anyway, it
> wasn't as though Chris couldn't
> afford it, and as the first doctor
> predicted, it was identical to his.
> Chris didn't take the news well.

We see CHRIS thump the steering wheel
of the car, and we see him turn on JULIA.
He grabs her hair in what looks like a
familiar routine, and goes to smash her
head against the passenger window, but
stops just before it makes impact, and
holds it there, less than an inch from
the glass.

> CHRIS
> What am I going to do?

> DYING JULIA (V.O.)
> And, for the first time in my life,
> I stood up to him.

JULIA

Just this once you are going to
let go of my hair, and you are
going to drive us home and we are
going to break the news to Lucas
together.

We see surprise on CHRIS's face, and then
we see that he is hugely tempted to bash
her head against the window even harder
than at first, but he lets go and the hard
expression on his face cracks. He starts
the ignition.

Camera stays on JULIA's face as they drive
away, the car lurching too quickly as
CHRIS reverses and then speeds out of the
hospital gates.

DYING JULIA (V.O.)

I don't know why it worked when I
stood up to him for the first and
only time that day. He drove too
fast, as usual, because he knew
I hated speed, and he continued
to bully me in small ways. But he
never touched me again. Maybe it
was because he feared that the
medical staff would work out what
was happening now that they had
ownership of my body.

We see JULIA sneak a glance at CHRIS,
searching the desperate expression on his
face for clues.

> DYING JULIA (V.O.)
> But, you know, in the end, I think
> it was a fear of death, of death's
> power. Death was going to take me
> so he couldn't have me anymore, so
> perhaps that meant I wasn't worth
> bullying. Or maybe it was fear that
> if he touched me again I might
> somehow infect him, bring him
> into death's orbit. I didn't dwell
> on it, though, because the bigger
> question was this: in a family
> like ours, how could I ever leave
> Lucas?

As CHRIS and JULIA arrive home they see
LUCAS, looking out of a front window. He's
obviously been waiting for them.

ZOE

I am fully freaking out by the time I've read this bit of the script. I feel sick to my core. I want to read on, I'm desperate to, because I can see that there's another section, but I'm suddenly aware that the family liaison officer is peering around the door.

"Zoe, are you OK to come downstairs to be with the others?" she says, but then she sees that I'm on the computer, and she moves across the room in a solid sort of way that reminds me of a Henry Hoover vacuum: round and squat and sort of gliding, and with a fixed expression on her face.

The next thing she says is in an *I'm-handling-you* tone of voice. It's the voice they use at the Unit before they get shouty.

In the Unit there was a progression of voices, and it went like this: first, *I'm-handling-you-calmly* voice, then *don't-mess-with-me* voice, then *I'm-warning-you* voice, then *shouty* voice, and by then the key workers would have gathered in numbers and they'd go in with the restraint holds, the ones where kids who don't have enough sense or have too much panic end up getting throttled just because they've made a scene.

It happened to one of the boys just before I arrived there. Everybody kept talking about it in my first few weeks.

The family liaison officer's *I'm-handling-you* voice is quite a good one, but it doesn't manage to lose that holier-than-thou tone that people have when they think that they're more sane than you.

I can't deny that I'm online because she's probably not stupid, but I have managed to click off the windows my mum's email and the script were on, and even do a quick browsing history delete before she gets close enough to bother getting her reading glasses out of a top pocket and peer at the screen. I'm quick, you see, at covering my tracks. There are so many rules in the Second Chance House that you have to be.

"What were you looking at, dear?" she says.

"Just YouTube."

We're having a different conversation with our eyes than the words we're speaking. Underneath a disapproving fore-head that's collapsed into wrinkle lines above her nose, hers are saying, *What the hell were you looking at?* and mine are saying, *There would have to be a planetary collision before I tell you that.*

"Anything special on YouTube?"

"I was looking for a recording of a special piece of music."

"You don't need to stop it because I'm here."

"It's a piece my mum loved. I don't really want to share it today, if you don't mind."

In spite of, or maybe because of, all the lectures about not crying in public, since I was little I have been able to turn tears off, but also on, and on this day it's even easier than usual because they're lurking anyway, in a real way.

I snivel my way out of this one and she escorts me down-stairs, saying, "Oh, pet, it's not easy this, is it?" although I know she's not dumb and I think this is a definite attempt to get me to "open up," but there's more of a chance of me becoming Henry VIII's seventh wife before I do that.

TESSA

My interview seems interminable, the only respite when we notice Zoe laying into her dad in the garden and one of the detectives asks the family liaison officer to intervene, but it moves on relentlessly after that.

They question me at length about any relationships Maria might have had outside the home and I feel hotter and more tired with every question. When one of the detectives' phones begins to buzz, I feel like it wakes me up a bit, before he silences it.

But then his partner's phone starts to buzz too. They exchange a glance and his partner says, "Excuse me, please," and slips out into the hallway, answering with a curt statement of his name before the door has shut behind him.

He leaves a newly created sense of tension, or perhaps it's expectation, behind him like a wake. The man interviewing me glances at the door once or twice before resuming his questioning.

"Did you know who your sister socialized with outside the home?"

I open my mouth to reply, but actually I realize that I have no idea, because Maria never mentioned friends. After Grace was born, I asked her if she was going to join any mother and baby groups, but she told me in no uncertain terms that she'd done all that with Zoe in Devon and had moved on. "I'm in a different place now," she'd said, and I'd thought how that was true in many ways, but of course I didn't articulate that because her well-being was so precarious at that time.

"I think she might have belonged to a tennis club," is the best I can manage. "Maria sometimes played on a ladder there. It was in Clifton, I think, the club in Clifton."

But even as I say it I'm not really sure, though I think I recall seeing Maria in tennis whites one day. "Chris or Katya, the au pair, will have a better idea than I do about what she did day to day," I say, to cover up my embarrassment at knowing so little about my sister's life. There was a time when I knew everything about her, because we shared a bedroom, clothes, secrets, everything. But that was when we were teenagers.

"And I think she might have belonged to a book club," I say, as another memory comes to me: Maria in her kitchen, dressed in figure-hugging jeans and a silk shirt, heels on, putting plastic wrap over a plate of hors d'oeuvres, issuing instructions to Katya and to Zoe, and telling Lucas that his dad would be back in an hour or so. Me following her down the hallway and saying: "Sorry, I was just passing, I didn't know you were going out."

"I'm dreading it," she said, as she wedged the plate of food into the back of the car. "Do you think that's going to be OK?"

She didn't wait for an answer. Maria never liked taking my advice.

As the trunk slammed shut, I said, "Why are you dreading it?"

"Because the book we're supposed to read is really long and *really worthy*, and I couldn't finish it."

"Will they mind?"

"Yes! They will! And I don't want to humiliate myself."

"Do you have to go?"

"It's run by the wife of one of Chris's colleagues. It's good if I go."

"Oh. Have you read a synopsis?"

"I'm not as stupid as I look."

She winked, and smiled, and I knew she'd be OK that night. It was a typical Maria comment to make, a brief flash of her feisty, much younger self, and the kind of thing she'd probably never have said in front of Chris. For him, she smoothed away all of her insecurities, and appeared fresh and calm and purposeful and content.

"I'll phone you," she said and I waved her off before clambering back into my own car and wondering what the book was, before remembering with a smile the dog-eared copies of Jackie Collins and Jilly Cooper novels that we'd once shared.

I didn't report that conversation to the detective, of course, because it was irrelevant, but he told me, with one of those annoying sniffs that jerk the side of people's mouths up, that Chris had already told him about the book club, and given him names.

Our interview got no farther because his colleague returned and beckoned to the detective interviewing me, from the door.

"Would you mind if we resumed this later?" he asked me, a veneer of professionalism barely masking an urgent tone.

"No," I say. "Of course not."

I'm relieved they haven't got around to asking me where I was last night.

Once I've gone out of the room, I realize the interview has left me feeling thoroughly jangled; I feel as if I'm starting to question everything I ever thought.

I want to phone Sam and I go to use our landline, which is a useless, old-fashioned thing that's not even cordless. It lives in our kitchen, but I find Philip sitting in there.

He still has his mobile and I guess the police aren't bothered about taking it because he wasn't in Bristol last night. He's talking on it now, in a low voice. When he sees me, he mutters an apology to whoever he's speaking to and ends the call.

Philip always did wear all his emotions on his sleeve—I think that was one of the things that attracted Maria to him in the first place—and now is no exception.

The emotion he's displaying now is guilt, and there's a certain neediness there too, which is typical of him. That quality of extreme emotional availability and the urge to share and talk that made him attractive in his youth hasn't developed as he's aged, but rather lingers as a sort of immaturity that I know is about to annoy me beyond measure.

"I'm not sure what to do tonight," he says.

"None of us are sure what's happening tonight," I say. "But if you need somewhere to sleep I'm sure we can muster up a duvet and a few sofa cushions at the very least."

My irritation levels are swelling because I don't want to deal with domestic trivia like sleeping arrangements at this moment, and they increase farther still when I see from his face that that wasn't the answer he was hoping for and I suspect he might have had something else in mind.

"You can't drive home tonight," I say. "What about Zoe?"

"I'm not sure what I can do for her."

"You're not sure what you can do for her?"

"Well, what can I do for her, Tess? We're estranged. What comfort can I offer her?"

"You're her father!"

My hands are plunged into the hair on either side of my head. I've forgotten the advice of every people-handling seminar I've ever sat through for work. I am beyond being reasonable or understanding. Philip Guerin's attitude is absolutely inexplicable to me, and if he doesn't respond properly, right now, I'm not going to be responsible for my actions.

"I'm sorry," he says. "I'm sorry. I just don't know how to be her father! How can you be a father to somebody like Zoe?"

I slap him.

I hit him hard, across the cheek and his head snaps to one side before he steps away from me and stands with his hand to the hurt cheek.

"You deserve it," I say.

"It's how I feel." There's a wobble to his voice, the sound of self-righteousness bubbling up and demanding attention, but I am absolutely unrepentant.

I believe that if you are lucky enough to have a child, then you should love them, whether or not society labels them as flawed, whether or not you label them as flawed.

"You have a duty to your daughter," I say.

"I've met someone new," he tells me. "I don't know if we can have Zoe."

My heart sinks. Philip, like Maria, has embarked on a new life, and he obviously thinks that damaged Zoe constitutes a threat to its success.

"Are you serious?"

His head bows.

"Then the least you can do is tell her yourself, but not today, Philip, not today."

"All right," he says.

"And I don't know who you think she's going to want to be with. Have you even thought about that?"

"You?" he asks, and I can hardly believe my ears.

"Is everything all right?" Chris speaks from the doorway. He looks from one of us to the other, searching our expressions for clues as to what's going on. I have no idea how long he's been standing there, or what he's heard.

I want to lash out at Philip, to say something that will shame him, to ask him what is wrong with him, to tell him that he must have lost his mind and his daughter is his responsibility, not mine, but what stops me is that Chris is the father of Zoe's sister.

Whatever happens, Zoe is a child whose future we must consider, and Grace must be a part of that future, because she means the world to Zoe, and even emotionally retarded Philip Guerin would be able to recognize that if he'd seen them together before this day. Relationships with Chris, then, need to be managed. I know it's what Maria would want.

"It's difficult for everybody," I say.

I wonder how much Chris knows about Philip. I know that Maria told Chris that they had a spectacularly messy divorce, which is why there isn't much contact between Zoe and her father. But that was before the concert. Chris might have more thoughts on that particular version of events now.

Chris says, "I understand," but before we're forced to continue like this, Richard enters the room with the baby.

"Could I give her to you for a bit, old man," he says to Chris, handing her over. "Just need to pop to the bathroom."

I hate that phrase when it comes from Richard. It can mean anything from the truth, that Richard's bladder is full, to a euphemism for the bottle of something alcoholic being dragged out from the "hiding" place under the bath and slugged back, at top speed, before a redundant flush of the loo tries to disguise the onset of the inevitable fumy breath and strained veins across his face.

Chris takes Grace, who gives him a look of surprise as if to say, *Fancy meeting you here*.

He sits her on the crook of his arm in an easy motion and they look at each other.

"So like your mother," he says. He buries his face into her neck and she responds with a squeal of delight and wraps her arms around his head. Grace is good at hugging. They are intense, baby hugs, but all the better for it.

"Thank God for you," Chris says to his daughter, with tears in his eyes, and I feel a bit of a lurch in my stomach, as I understand that Grace, who has my parents' blood coursing through her veins, might live a life that's very separate from our family now, and that thought is, if I'm honest, terrifying.

Will Chris raise her and Lucas together in that big house? And where will Zoe be? Will Philip accept that he needs to raise his daughter, or will she be better off with us, or even with Chris, so she can be near her sister?

"We have a lot to discuss," I say.

"I know," says Chris.

But neither of us can bear to start the conversation just then, and so we move away from each other, to the safety of different rooms. Philip stays sagged in his seat.

SAM

I can't do up the strings of my hospital gown because they've got lost around the back of me somewhere. I'm humiliated by having to shuffle along holding it together to avoid everybody being able to see my underwear.

The MRI scanner looks familiar to me from television, but I'm not prepared for the noise once I'm inside it, or the discomfort of staying still for such a long period, my hands held above my head.

Amid the darkness of the machine and the thumping sounds that penetrate in spite of the headphones they've given me, I try to think about what Nick has told me and what it means for Tessa and Zoe.

It means that unless somebody broke into the house, the chances are extremely high that somebody in Maria's household murdered her, and the police will adjust their investigation accordingly. I think back to Tess's arrival at my flat the night before, and her silence, and I wonder what it was she didn't tell me.

I think of Zoe in my office this morning and I hope to God that she was telling me the truth.

I think of the magnetic waves that are passing through my body.

I think of all the people in the waiting room and how almost all of them had family with them, or a friend, somebody to hold their hand or at least to talk to. Self-pity creeps in and ratchets up the feelings of desperation and claustrophobia I'm experiencing.

My relationship with Tessa is the best thing and worst thing about my life. I want nobody else, but while she stays with Richard I can't have her.

There is nothing I would like more, at this moment, than to know that she would be there when I emerge from this machine.

It's a terrible effort to keep still, but I tell myself I must because the very last thing I want is for this scan to have to be repeated.

A voice comes through the headphones I'm wearing and tells me that they're moving on to my spine now. The scan of my brain is complete.

I wonder what the radiologist can see.

ZOE

The family liaison lady, who tells me to call her Stella, is everywhere I go. She has what she calls "just a little word" with Richard, even though it's more of a bursting fishing net of words if you ask me. She tells him that I was online on his computer and then says to him and to me, like twenty times, that it's probably a good idea if I don't go online at the moment because I might read something that wouldn't be good for me to see.

But I know that's not just what she means. I know she's watching me for signs to see if I've done something. And the thing is, I'm desperate to read the end of Lucas's script.

My dad's in the kitchen, and even though I'm still angry with him I figure he's my best chance of reading the script because he still has his phone. He's sitting in there on his own at Tess's little kitchen table, which looks like it should be in a diner, with a cup of tea in front of him that he's not drinking. He raises his eyes slowly and looks at me like he's afraid that I'll go off on him again.

"Can I borrow your phone?" I ask him.

"What?"

"Just for a minute."

He takes a deep breath, and I think he's going to say "no," but instead he says, "Zoe, I think it's best if I stay in a hotel tonight, so it doesn't put too much pressure on Tessa."

"Can I come with you?" It would be good to get away from here, from the police, from Chris, and Richard, and all of the people. It would be good to be just me and Dad.

"I don't think that's a good idea. You should probably stay with the others."

"Why?"

He can't seem to answer that even though I'm standing right in front of him waiting for him to say something.

"Why, Dad?"

"Well . . ." he says eventually, but I'm fit to burst by then because sometimes I feel like I can read his mind, and I know what he's going to say, so I shout at him.

"I didn't do anything! Honestly, I swear it, what do you think I'm like?"

"That's not what I'm thinking; but there are other things to take into account if we're talking about you coming back to Devon," and that sounds like he's getting ready to tell me that he doesn't want me, and it makes me feel as if some big heavy teeth have sunk into me.

I try to blink back tears and to focus only on what I want, which is his phone. I've already made a sore patch inside my mouth from the biting and I dig my molars into the soft, sore tissue there again and pull myself back into togetherness. Jason would be proud.

"Can I borrow your phone, please?" I ask him again. "I just want to look something up."

He hands his phone over to me, because he feels obliged

now. Guilt is a good way to leverage people. Jason didn't tell me that; nobody needed to tell me that. I learned it because my guilt about what I've done makes me bend the shape of myself to fit what other people want every day of my life.

In the hallway I meet Stella, who reminds me of the sheep-dog on the farm, always trying to round everybody up.

"I'm just going to the loo," I say. I've slipped Dad's phone under the waistband of my trousers, and my cardigan's wrapped over it.

I walk up the stairs, dragging my hand up the banister purposely slowly, so that she doesn't think I'm rushing.

I lock the bathroom door behind me and sit on the toilet.

I can't get onto Tessa's Wi-Fi on the phone because I don't know the password for it and the phone doesn't log in automatically like the computer did, but that's OK because my dad is getting a 3G signal here, so it takes no time to log into Mum's email and access the script.

The ending is so sad.

"WHAT I KNOW"

BY LUCAS KENNEDY

ACT III

INT. LUCAS'S BEDROOM. NIGHT.

JULIA is sitting on LUCAS's bed, reading
him a bedtime story. She is very unwell.

>   DYING JULIA (V.O.)
> At first, I lied to Lucas about
> my prognosis, because it was too
> painful to tell him the whole
> truth. I simply told him that I
> was unwell. But Lucas is a clever
> boy, and he very quickly worked
> out that it was worse than that.

>   LUCAS
> Mum?

>   JULIA
> Yes.

>   LUCAS
> Are you going to die?

>   JULIA
> Well, sometimes people who have
> this disease do die.

>   LUCAS
> Can you get medicine to make you
> better?

                    JULIA
I have some medicine.

                    LUCAS
From the doctor?

                    JULIA
Yes, from the doctor.

                    LUCAS
And will it work?

                    JULIA
                (struggling)
No, my love, it probably won't.

They look at each other. JULIA is willing
LUCAS to understand but wishing he doesn't
have to all at once.

                    DYING JULIA (V.O.)
He didn't reply to me, but he never
wanted to leave my side after
that.

INT. CHRIS'S OFFICE. NIGHT.

CHRIS lies stretched out on his sofa,
staring at the ceiling. We see from the

clock on the wall and the darkness outside
that it's very late.

> DYING JULIA (V.O.)
> Chris took it hard too. But
> instead of sticking close to me,
> he withdrew. My illness repulsed
> him. He spent every hour possible
> out of the home.

INT. HALLWAY OF THE KENNEDY HOUSE. DAY.

The doorbell rings and LUCAS runs to
answer it.

> DYING JULIA (V.O.)
> This left us with a problem.
> Because, as a result of Chris's
> behavior, and in spite of the
> excellent nursing help that he
> organized, it was Lucas who
> inevitably became my main carer.

LUCAS opens the door and a NURSE is there.

> LUCAS
> Hello, Annie.

> NURSE
> Hello, my friend! How's she doing?

                    LUCAS
She's a bit sad today. I think it
hurts.

                    NURSE
OK, let's see what we can do about
that, shall we?

Upstairs, LUCAS stands at JULIA's bedroom
door and watches as the NURSE greets her
gently and begins to work around her.

               DYING JULIA (V.O.)
And the fact that Lucas was seeing
and doing things that he was too
young for became unbearable to
me. As was the fact that he was
old enough to realize that Chris
should have been there with us,
caring for me too. So I decided
that something had to change. I
could think of only one thing to
do, and it took all my strength to
do it. It was time to be cruel to
be kind.

INT. THE KENNEDY FAMILY KITCHEN. MORNING.

CHRIS is waiting in the doorway, holding
a set of car keys and watching JULIA and

LUCAS. JULIA is sitting down and LUCAS
stands in front of her while she adjusts
his uniform. JULIA's arms and wrists look
frail.

                    DYING JULIA (V.O.)
            I forced him to leave me so that
            his life could be as normal as
            possible. It was the only way I
            could think to show him a way to
            go forward. He didn't want to.
            He wanted to stay at home from
            school, to crawl into bed with
            me, spend every one of my last
            minutes with me, but I made him
            go to piano, to sports clubs,
            and to school.

                    LUCAS
                  (tearful)
            I don't want to go.

                    JULIA
            You have to go.

                    LUCAS
            Please.

                    JULIA
                  (snaps)
            Lucas, don't argue with me!

LUCAS is shocked and hurt by her tone of
voice. He turns and follows his father
out of the door wordlessly. The door shuts
behind them and we see JULIA, alone in the
room, utterly crushed.

> DYING JULIA (V.O.)
> And it broke my heart to do it.
> But I knew that if he was going to
> survive life with his father, he
> had to be strong, and so I had to
> force him away. And I knew, too,
> that things couldn't carry on like
> this.

INT. CHRIS AND JULIA'S BEDROOM. DAY.

JULIA is in bed, looking even worse
than before. The NURSE is in her room,
unpacking medication.

> JULIA
> Could you do me a favor? Could
> you get me a pen and paper and
> something to rest on. You'll
> find them in my desk drawer,
> downstairs.

> NURSE
> You going to draw me a picture?

JULIA
(smiles, though really
she's too tired for jokes)
No. I want to write a letter. Could
you get me an envelope too?

NURSE
Of course I will. Do you need a
stamp?

JULIA
No.

NURSE
How's Lucas?

JULIA
He went to school today. I didn't
think he would.

NURSE
That's good. First time I've had to
let myself in I think, so that's
what I was hoping. It's not good
for him to be here all the time.

JULIA
I know.

NURSE
He'll be all right, you know.

> JULIA
> (we see her pain)
> I hope so, I really do.

> NURSE
> He's a good boy, bless him.

> JULIA
> He is.

INT. CHRIS AND JULIA'S BEDROOM. NIGHT.

JULIA is propped up in bed, alone, and we see her finish writing something.

> DYING JULIA (V.O.)
> I wrote the letter. It was my "Do Not Resuscitate" order.

JULIA seals the letter in an envelope, carefully, and then laboriously places it in the top drawer of her bedside table, an action that costs her a large amount of effort. Inside the bedside table there's a box, which she takes out. When she opens it, we see it contains a large number of pills.

> DYING JULIA (V.O.)
> And I counted the pills that I'd
> been hoarding, to make sure I had
> enough.

Satisfied, she replaces the box in the
drawer, beside the envelope, and turns out
the light.

**EXT. A STREET NEAR CHRIS AND JULIA'S
HOUSE. MORNING.**

LUCAS is walking to school. It's a
different day and he's wearing a hat and
coat. The camera follows him on his way.

> DYING JULIA (V.O.)
> After that, it was a matter of
> waiting for a school day.

We see LUCAS sitting in a lesson at
school, unable to concentrate. He stares
at his book while the TEACHER drones on.

> DYING JULIA (V.O.)
> It was a harsh thing to do, I know,
> but I saw it as a way of releasing
> him from the last few weeks of my
> life, saving him from seeing me

racked with pain and out of control
of my body. I wanted our parting to
be cleaner, tidier, and easier for
him to bear.

We see LUCAS in the school dining hall,
picking through his lunch box, rejecting
everything in there. He checks his phone,
sends a text to JULIA, and waits for the
reply.

> DYING JULIA (V.O.)
> But timing is everything, and
> Lucas texted me just after I'd
> taken the pills, and lain back
> in my bed, and placed the letter
> on my chest. And, when I didn't
> answer, he sensed that something
> was wrong.

LUCAS stares at his phone. Then he tries
to call JULIA on her mobile and on the
landline. There's no answer. LUCAS runs
from the school dining hall and out of
the main school doors and starts to sprint
home.

> DYING JULIA (V.O.)
> I don't know how he sensed it, but
> he did.

LUCAS bursts into the house, and pounds
up the stairs, and tries to enter JULIA's
room, but she has locked the door. LUCAS
calls to JULIA; he bangs and kicks the
door and then throws his body weight
against it. When that doesn't work he gets
out his phone and dials 911.

                    LUCAS
    Yes, hello, ambulance, please,
    yes, and fire brigade. Please come
    quickly. It's my mum.

**INT. PRIVATE HOSPITAL ROOM. VERY WELL
APPOINTED. NIGHT.**

We find everything exactly as it was before,
in the first scene. LUCAS and CHRIS continue
their vigil by JULIA's bedside.

                 DYING JULIA (V.O.)
    I didn't want Lucas to find me.
    The idea was that it would be the
    nurse who discovered my body, and
    that I would be dead by then.
    But even this is better than the
    lingering weeks of decay that
    Lucas would have had to endure
    otherwise. My end in this hospital
    will be as controlled as possible.

And it will be soon. But, before
I go, I understand that there's
probably a question on your lips
right now. How could I leave my
son with his father? With the man
who isolated me from people, who
pounded my head against walls and
reduced me to putty in his hands.
My answer: I had no choice. My only
solace: Chris had never touched
Lucas. Yet. And I hoped, I prayed,
that if my son understood he must
be strong, then Chris never would
touch him. It was all I could do.

The machines suddenly begin to beep again,
and NURSES and a DOCTOR rush in. CHRIS
and LUCAS are ushered away from the bed
and can do nothing but watch helplessly as
JULIA slips away. The DNR order prevents
intervention and her end comes quickly,
and we know this because the NURSES and
DOCTOR step away from her bed.

                    DYING JULIA (V.O.)
          I had tried my hardest to give
          my son the best of me, broken,
          bullied, mocked, little old me. My
          attempt at suicide, and the DNR
          order, well, they were a final act
          of love, and the hardest thing I've

ever done, and I did it because
the end, after all, was inevitable.

LUCAS watches blankly, in shock, as the
DOCTOR records the time of JULIA's death,
but CHRIS's face collapses into grief.
CHRIS puts a hand on LUCAS's shoulder,
almost as if he is so surprised by the
strength of his own feelings that he
needs supporting.

But LUCAS steps away from him.

THE END

RICHARD

I should be fighting my demons by now.

Usually, my emotions when I'm sober consist mostly of a cocktail of anger and desperation, garnished with emptiness, and they feel as if they're embroidered into every cell of my body, as integral to me as my DNA.

And when I feel like that, alcohol is the only cure I know, the only thing that can wash the misery away. I think of alcohol as being like a slick waiter, clad in black and white, weaving his way through a crowd with a silver tray held aloft, bearing upon it a generous helping of respite and oblivion, just for me.

Who could refuse?

Not I. Not on a normal day, when all I want is some peace; when I would do whatever it took to escape those emotions. Any choice made on a normal day would be a choice to drink. To have a drink seems necessary, unavoidable. The taste of it might not appeal, but the feeling as it goes down your throat is oh-so-good, a physical numbness that anticipates luxuriantly the imminent longed-for dulling of your mind.

But today, with the baby in my arms, I feel something different. I feel invigorated.

It's such an unusual feeling for me that I'm careful around it, especially as this would be the most inappropriate moment conceivable to tell Tessa that I'm feeling a bit better.

When somebody arrives from the police station with DNA testing kits and they call for us to come and be swabbed one by one, the others look appalled, so I get to my feet and announce that I'll be happy to be the first.

The newly arrived officer has a bad shaving cut on his jawline, which I notice as he pulls on blue plastic gloves and scrapes a sponge on a stick around the inside of my cheek. He winces a little as he does it and I feel a tad self-conscious that my breath might be slightly on the rich side.

When I'm done, Tessa goes in, after passing the baby to me like a relay baton, and Grace and I make our way upstairs to wake Katya, whom they want to include.

She's asleep facedown in our spare room, and doesn't take kindly to being woken.

She descends the stairs and enters the dining room with her chin held high, and it takes just a minute or two before she reemerges with an expression of distaste on her face.

She's just in time to hear Chris say to one of the detectives, "I take exception to being asked to take an invasive test without an explanation of why," and as the detective begins to talk about "routine investigations" and "helping with our inquiry," Katya exclaims loudly: "I am giving mouth swab even though it is not in my contract, because of deep situation."

Chris is momentarily taken aback, and she takes the opportunity to shoot a few more barbs:

"People must do right thing. You must do right thing. You

are always business talk yadda yadda yadda, and you never put arm around son."

I look at Lucas. He's watching them anxiously, and his leg is jiggling up and down.

"Make test!" Katya is shouting now, and pointing toward the room where the young officer sits with his pile of plastic-wrapped kits.

A dark cloud passes over Chris's face and I think that this can only end in tears. What man could lose his wife to violent death and then hear this?

Zoe's mouth is agape too, and I imagine that this shocks her because it's an outburst the likes of which she probably hasn't seen before in this new family of hers, where everything seemed to be buried all the time, emotions included.

"Katya," I say to her. I put my hand on her arm because even her stance is confrontational, and, as I do so, the baby leans toward her, arms outstretched. Katya can't resist this. She turns and takes Grace from me. Behind her, Chris sits back down, a tactical withdrawal that I'm glad to see.

"We're very grateful to you, this is a horrible situation," I tell her. "Please know how much we're sorry that you have to be part of this."

"I want call my agency," she says. "I have talk to police, I have make mouth swab, and now I wish to leave and stay somewhere else because sadness is making a strong feeling in my heart."

She presses her fist to her breastbone as if in some kind of salute, and Grace puts a clumsy finger to a tear that's dropping down Katya's cheek.

Thinking that she's probably right, that it's a good idea if she goes, and that I've more or less mastered the basic requirements of the baby so we can do without her, I usher her out of the room, and direct her to the phone, taking the baby back from her as she lifts the receiver.

Behind us, Lucas says: "Dad, are we going to take the test?"

I can't resist a quick look back to see Chris respond with a tight nod.

Crisis averted, my secret satisfaction grows just a little.

TESSA

I give the DNA swab, but I want to know why they're doing this and why my interview was interrupted so suddenly earlier.

It wasn't a dramatic interruption exactly, but there was certainly a frisson of something—suppressed excitement perhaps—among the police.

My mind's racing like a greyhound out of the gate, and I think that I really need to phone Sam now, more than ever, because he might be able to interpret the situation better than me.

Once Katya has finished speaking to her agency, Richard ushers her back upstairs as if he's a mother hen, and I take the opportunity to try to get through to Sam.

He doesn't answer. He has a day off today, so I can't imagine why not. I try a couple of times and eventually leave a message saying that I'll try him again later.

I try not to feel upset with him for not answering, but part of me thinks it would have been nice if he was on standby, in case I needed him. It's not like he doesn't know what's going on.

As I replace the handset, I notice that Richard is in the doorway.

"Who are you phoning?" he asks.

The best lies are those that are closest to the truth. This is a thought that pops into my head, though I'm not sure from where. I don't consider myself dishonest, in spite of my affair. My infidelity is the only thing I hide; in all other areas of life I'm squeaky clean.

"I was phoning Zoe's solicitor," I said. "Because I wanted to know why they might be taking DNA swabs from us."

"What did he say?"

"He wasn't there. They said he's out." I think quickly enough to pretend that I phoned Sam's office, not his mobile.

"He was very hard on Zoe," Richard says. "Very hard indeed."

"They know each other well enough for that, I'm sure," I tell him. Richard was learning to consume alcohol in previously unimaginably large quantities during the time of Zoe's trial, because he had only just discovered that his professional status had fatally stalled. He never once came to Devon to support them. He never witnessed any of it. That is, of course, yet another source of resentment for me.

I hold Grace while Richard begins to heat some food from the fridge for her.

"Katya told me she likes this stuff," he says, showing me a teaspoonful of intensely orange goo.

Grace is watching him intently. I can tell that she likes him, and he makes faces for her that make her giggle, but I can't share the moment because all I can think about is the fact that Grace probably won't even remember Maria, and may not even be part of our lives in the future.

"I hope we get to see Grace," I say.

"What?"

"Well, she'll go with Chris, won't she?"

Richard stands, aghast, looking at me. "Will she?"

"He's her father! What did you think?"

"I hadn't really thought about it." He turns around to stir the puree, and I notice his shoulders have fallen.

"Well, hopefully she can come and stay with us when she's older," he says. "And how will Chris cope?"

"I don't know."

"Will Zoe go with them?"

"I very much doubt it. Why would she do that?"

He catches my tone of irritation.

"Give Grace to me," he says. "I can do this on my own. You take some time."

I'm feeling tetchy because all of this will need to be worked out, and it will be complicated and painful for the children, and probably for us too, and I can't deal with it now.

I can't ignore either the small doubts about Chris that have begun to tug at me. It's dangerous to let my mind wander down this path, I'm very conscious of that, but I'm beginning to reassess some of his behavior; in particular the way he folded my sister up in a towel and ushered her away at the end of the evening. To me, that looked loving at the time, but in the light of what's happened I can't help but put a more sinister reading on it now. Was it loving or controlling? His aggression with Tom Barlow at the house and his treatment of Lucas, the way he told him off in front of us all, would certainly edge me quite firmly toward a more negative reading.

I want to ask Richard what he thinks, because in spite of

everything he's a good judge of character, or he used to be, but we're interrupted by the doorbell.

"That'll be the au pair agency, I expect," he says.

"I'll get it."

He tries a small spoonful of Grace's puree and winces. "This is too hot," he tells the baby, "we might need to wait a bit."

"What was the number of the solicitor's office?" he calls after me as I leave the room. "I might try him again. I think you're right to ask his advice."

"Oh, I don't remember offhand," I say.

"No problem," he calls as I reach the front door. "I'll just do redial."

Before I can stop myself, and as I'm opening the front door, I shout, "No!" at him, because I know the call will go through to Sam's personal mobile. The representative from Katya's au pair agency gives me a quizzical look, as does Richard.

"Sorry," I say to her.

She offers me her hand. "Tamara Jones, West Country Elite Au Pairs. We always aim to respond to emergencies immediately."

Behind me, I can feel Richard's gaze on my back and, as I take Tamara Jones upstairs to find Katya, I can see that he has the baby in one arm and the phone in the other.

ZOE

I don't want to be near Chris after what I've read.

I don't want him near me, and I don't want him near Lucas and I never want him near Grace again.

I wish he'd never, ever been near my mum, because I have a horrible feeling creeping over me that he might have killed her with his violence.

I'm struggling really hard to stay calm with that thought filling up my head. I desperately want to talk to Lucas about the script, to tell him that I understand now why he wanted me to read it so badly, and to say how I'm so sorry about what happened to him and his mum. But Lucas won't even look at me right now. All he's doing is sitting and staring at his fingers and picking at the red skin around his bitten nails.

I also want to tell somebody else, I'm desperate to, so they know what Chris is really like, but I don't know who to choose, because I don't know if they'll believe me. Right now, I'm not one hundred percent sure that Lucas would want me to share the script, because I can see that Chris can be very bad, but he's also Lucas's dad.

While I'm trying to think about it, we're all sitting to-gether on the sofas: me and Lucas and Chris and Tess and the liaison officer, who's eating a sandwich that stinks of fish, and nobody is speaking. Richard's feeding Grace in the kitchen. My dad's gone back out into the garden with his phone. When I came down and gave his phone back to him, I tried to tell him about what I'd read in the script but he said, "Not now, Zoe."

The detectives have gone for now, but they said they'd be back later to "have a bit more of a chat." Katya has just gone too; she was collected by a lady from her agency. I'm sad and also not sad about that. I don't like her, obviously, but her going made everything feel even more real and even more final. It made it all squeeze around me just that little bit tighter.

That panicky feeling is rising now, making me want to scream out what I know, and to flee from the room so I don't have to sit near Chris, so I'm looping a bit of advice from Jason in my head: "Don't always react to everything the instant it happens, Zoe. Think before you speak."

The problem is that I'm afraid I might not be able to hold any of it in any longer, so I go for the person I think is safest to tell.

"Aunt Tessa . . ." I start to say, because I want to ask her to come out of the room with me, so I can tell her about it in private, because I think she's the best person, the one I trust most. I feel like I blurt out her name when I say it, but my voice must have actually been quiet because Tessa just turns to look at me as if to say, *Did you say something?* and, before I can explain, I'm interrupted by Chris, who says: "Can I use your phone, Tessa? I think it's probably sensible if I book a hotel room for us tonight."

"Us?" she asks him.

Chris frowns, as if that's a stupid question, and then says, "For Lucas and Grace and me."

"You're welcome to stay here," she says.

"It might be easier if we got out of your hair."

"It's fine, really."

"No, I won't hear of it. You've done enough already letting the police in here, and having us all."

"Well, do you want to leave Grace here?"

"She's my daughter."

"But it might not be easy looking after her in a hotel room. Very cramped. We're happy to keep her here for now, with the garden, and Richard is enjoying looking after her, I know he won't mind."

"I plan to book a suite. We'll be fine, thank you."

It's a pretty final statement.

"May I use your phone?"

She waves her hand toward the kitchen. "Go ahead."

She looks as gutted as I feel, and I wonder if her heart is pumping as fast as mine is, and I think that if it's not now, it definitely will be when I tell her what I know about Chris.

I don't get to talk to her about it though because Richard appears in the doorway just as Chris is about to leave the room. He's holding Grace and she's covered in orange puree. It's on her face, her clothes, her hands, and in her hair. It's on a lot of Richard too.

"Bit of a catastrophe," Richard says.

Chris looks at Grace. She shows him the palm of one of

her hands, which has food all over it, and then she squeezes it into a fist, demonstrating how the orange goo squishes out between her fingers. She's delighted. Grace loves mess.

Chris makes no move to take her from Richard, but I get there in two strides from the sofa.

"I'll take her for a bath," I say. I look at Chris. "You can't take her like this."

Because he mustn't have her.

"Take her where?" I hear Richard asking, but I don't hear the answer because I carry sticky Grace up the stairs and into the bathroom as fast as I can, and I lock the door so it's just me and her, and I turn on the taps of the bath and I let her help me squeeze some bubble mixture in. When that's done we sit on the mat on the floor together and I say, "Grace, you are so gross," and I imagine that my mum would have laughed if she could have heard me say it.

And I wonder how long I can keep us locked in here so that Chris can't take her away.

RICHARD

Zoe grabs that baby out of my arms as if the house is burning down and they must flee. She pounds up the stairs and we hear the bathroom door slam shut.

"All right if I use your phone then?" Chris asks Tessa.

"I said go ahead."

"Lucas," Chris says to his son before he leaves the room, making the boy's head snap up, "go and get your stuff together, and Grace's."

"Where are you going?" I ask Chris, but he doesn't hear me, or pretends he doesn't.

"Where are they going?" I ask Tess in their absence.

We're alone. The liaison woman has gone somewhere or other, doubtless roaming the house like some kind of shady private eye, as she's been doing all day, and Lucas shambled off obediently in response to Chris, in that way he has, as if he's embarrassed by the mere presence of himself in a room.

"To a hotel."

"With the baby?"

"She's not our baby, Richard."

That annoys me. I might have my weaknesses, but I'm not an imbecile, and I've been trying to be patient with Tess.

"I phoned the solicitor. On redial. I left a message," I say.

She blinks rapidly. "Oh?" she says, but I can tell that she knows what I'm going to say.

"Funny thing though: it was a mobile phone number. It went to a personal voicemail message."

She's breathing heavily through her nose as she looks at me. Her face is masterfully still but I can read panic behind it, however carefully hidden. Her mind must be racing but all she manages to come up with is "Are you sure it wasn't a wrong number?"

I start to quote the message: "'Hi, this is Sam, please leave me a'—"

She interrupts. "I know his number from before, OK? From the trial?"

"You remember his number from, what, two and a half, three years ago?"

"Yes!"

"So why did you say that you phoned his office?"

"I said it wrong. It's not the best day for me this, in case you hadn't noticed."

I don't appreciate that. "What are you hiding, Tess? Where were you last night?"

"Not now, please. Not this, now."

We sit in silence, and I try to sort out in my head whether her explanation is a plausible one. It definitely could be. It definitely might not be. I think that I may be too tired to tell.

Tess moves from her chair opposite me to sit beside me. For a moment I wonder if she might be going to express some physical affection toward me, and my heart beats nervously in anticipation, for it's been a long time since we offered each other that kind of solace, even with a simple touch, but she leans toward me instead, and whispers: "I've been thinking."

I wait for her to carry on, but before she does, she gets up and closes the door and then sits back down just as she was before.

She says, "If the DNA tests mean that they're considering us as suspects, it surely has to be Chris, doesn't it?"

"Chris?"

"If somebody in the house killed Maria, it surely has to be Chris, don't you think, surely?"

I can hardly hear what she's saying; she's dropped her voice so low.

"*If* it was somebody in the house," I say.

"Why else are they taking swabs?"

"I don't know."

The door opens and we both sit back like guilty children.

"All booked," Chris says. "I'm going to gather up our stuff and we'll go when Grace has finished her bath."

The thought of the baby going is surprisingly painful, but there'll be work to do still, I think to myself, supporting Zoe and Tess, and that's some consolation. I'm determined to hold on to this new sense of usefulness.

Behind him the liaison officer says, "Do you want us to organize a lift for you, Mr. Kennedy?"

"No, I don't want to arrive in a police car, thank you. I'll phone a taxi."

Could he have done it? I think. He's so pleasant, so polite. He's worked so hard for everything he has, and has been through so much.

That thought begs another question that I haven't had time

to really consider yet, with all the minute-to-minute distrac-
tions of taking Zoe to the solicitor and being at the police
station and worrying about where Tess was last night, and
looking after everybody once we got here. That question is: if
Chris hasn't done it, then who has? Is this the moment that we
all start to look for signs of guilt in each other? Was Zoe right
to flee to her solicitor this morning? Was she ahead of the
game, knowing more than most about blame and accusation,
and has Tess caught up with her thinking now, and should I?

ZOE

Grace's bath doesn't take long to fill up, because she doesn't need it very deep. While it's running, I try to persuade her to lie down so I can take off her clothes but she won't, so I have to improvise and undress her first while she sits, and then while she stands and bangs the soap dish against my back. She's so chubby without her clothes on, and her thighs are almost thicker than my arms.

I put her in the water and then hang on to her tightly because there's no grippy mat in Tessa and Richard's bath to stop her sliding around, and she's like a slippery otter. We have a few dodgy moments when she slides under water and I have to pull her back up, though she doesn't even notice the danger, she's having so much fun.

I work out that I have a problem when the water goes cold, and she's splashed every bit of me and the bathroom. It's finally time to get her out, and I need a towel to lift her, because her skin is so smooth that her body is totally slimy from the bubbly water and I'm afraid I'll drop her without one, but I can't see one anywhere. The towel rail is bare. I can't let go of her and leave her unattended in the bath even for a second while I find one, because she keeps trying to stand up, and I know she would fall and hit the taps.

So I shout for help. I shout for Tessa, but it's Lucas who comes, and I can just about reach over to the door to unlock it for him while I'm hanging on to Grace.

I hope I don't look at him funny, though I probably do. It's because I need to tell him I finished the script, but I'm not sure how to bring it up, and at the same time I realize I'm changing in my head some of the things I thought about him before I knew what Chris was really like.

I tell him what my problem with the towel is and he leaves the room and comes back with a bedspread.

"I couldn't find a towel," he says, and I'm thinking that my mum would never have had no towels in the bathroom, in fact I can hear the "tsk" noise that she would make if she could see us now, but here we are, and I think the bedspread will do fine.

Lucas drapes it over his arms and reaches down into the bath and gets Grace.

She thinks the bedspread is amazing because it's so big. When Lucas gently lays her down on the floor on it she plays with it, shaking the edges around and nuzzling it onto her head as if it's catnip and she's a kitten. We sit on either side of her and watch her; it's almost as if we were her parents.

I get up, and I lock the door again, because I know that I have a chance to talk to Lucas right now, and my heart begins to pound when I tell him: "I read the script. All of it."

He doesn't look up at me, but I can see that his face goes sort of still. He carries on pushing the bedspread over Grace's face and then pulling it back in a sudden movement. It makes her give a throaty giggle. He says nothing.

"On my dad's phone," I say, in case he's wondering, and so he doesn't think I'm making things up.

When he looks at me it's as if a layer of secrets has been peeled away from his face, and showing in his eyes is the deepest, saddest expression I've ever seen.

"I wanted to warn you," he says, "and your mum. I wanted you to know what he's like."

I find that I can't reply, because I feel like my worst fears are true, but it's OK because he keeps talking.

"Because if my mum or me had told somebody about him, it might have stopped him, and then she might have stayed alive for longer; she wouldn't have done what she did."

"Did he kill your mum?" I hardly dare ask it but it sounds like that's what he's saying.

"No. My mum killed herself, and she was dying anyway, but if her life was better, if he hadn't ruined her life and hurt her, she would have stayed alive for longer, she would have fought the disease better. I know she would have."

I feel a cold shudder run over me, from the crown of my head to the very tips of my toes. It's a ripple of revulsion and sorrow, fear, and, I think, certainty.

I say, "Do you think your dad killed my mum?"

TESSA

Philip Guerin has crept in from the garden, his face flushed from the heat, and joined us in the sitting room. The family liaison officer is in the kitchen washing up teacups.

Philip has overheard Chris booking a hotel and wants to know where they're going to be staying, and wonders out loud whether he should do the same thing.

"There's plenty of room for you here now," says Richard, but Philip pushes on, asking Chris questions of utter pointlessness, about where the hotel is located and how far it is from here.

Chris tells him the name of the hotel, and I know as soon as I hear it that Philip Guerin wouldn't be able to afford to stay there in a million years. I can see that Chris knows that too. He seems irritated, his answers short and his mind clearly elsewhere, though Philip doesn't seem to be picking up any of these cues. He drones on and on about a hotel that he stayed in once on a trip somewhere else, and it's the most boring kind of small talk. I want to scream at him to shut up because I'm trying to think. I'm also trying to be normal around Chris, which suddenly isn't easy, because all I find myself able to do is wonder what he's capable of.

Our landline rings. It's always an unfamiliar sound these days, though Richard tells me that cold calls are a frequent annoyance during his long days at home, and I have to bite my tongue to avoid making a sarcastic reply. He doesn't have much else to do all day, let's face it.

As the phone trills, my eyes meet Richard's.

"That's probably the solicitor," he says.

Chris is alert. "What does he want?"

"I'll get it," I say, and I bolt from the room. I don't know whether that will look suspicious to Richard, but I don't care. I need to hear the calm warmth of Sam's voice; I need somebody to offer me respite from my family. I want his advice, yes, but right now I also want his affection too.

By the time I get to the kitchen, the phone has stopped ringing, and the family liaison officer is replacing the handset.

"That was Sam Locke," she says. "He says to tell you he didn't have time to speak because he's going into an appointment, but he'll call back later."

I feel bereft, unreasonably so probably, but I can't help myself. Annoyed too, because what appointment could possibly be so important that Sam wouldn't at least take the time to exchange a quick couple of words with me. I pick up the phone and hit redial and pray and pray through the first few rings that he's going to answer.

"Sam Locke," he says eventually, and I hear caution in his tone. Probably he's not sure whether it's Richard or me phoning.

I wait a second or two to reply because the family liaison officer is carrying a plate of biscuits out of the room.

"Hello?" Sam says.

The family liaison officer moves very slowly, as if she wants to hear what I'm saying, but I wait until she's gone and I ease the door shut behind her.

"It's me," I say to Sam.

"Richard phoned me."

"I know, I'm sorry, we wanted your advice."

"I'm really sorry, Tess, I've got to see somebody in a minute, I haven't got long."

"If the police are taking our DNA, do you think that means we're under suspicion?"

There's a pause, and then he says, "They've found evidence, in the house, so yes, I think family members are under suspicion. I shouldn't tell you that, Tess, so please don't say that I did."

"Oh my God. What evidence?"

"Blood. That's been cleaned up. It's the only thing that would show up this quickly, and there might well be more evidence down the line, it's just that the other tests take time."

"That's why they're taking swabs from us," I say.

"That would seem likely, yes," he says. "They'll want to know whose blood it is."

"It'll be hers," I say.

"Be careful of making assumptions at this stage."

"Well, whose else could it be?"

"All I'm saying is that we won't have confirmation of that for days."

He sounds a bit distant; his tone seems more professional and less reassuring than I would like, because I feel very afraid. I want to tell Sam that I'm feeling increasingly certain that Chris has hurt Maria, but I'm afraid that if I talk in here, Chris might overhear me.

I think of Philip's mobile phone. The one he's been anxiously passing from hand to hand for most of the day, as if it's a lifeline connecting him to another world, one he'd rather be in.

"Sam," I say. "I'm going to borrow a mobile phone and call you back but it won't be easy to do it privately, so please make sure you answer."

"I have an appointment," he says. "I can't miss it, but it won't take long."

"I'm afraid," I tell him and there's a long silence, and within it I hear him swallow and I think I can also hear the echoing of footsteps as if he's walking down a corridor.

"Where are you?" I say. "Sam?"

Another voice in the background: "Mr. Locke? They're ready for you now."

"I have to go," he says. "I'm sorry. I'll try to answer, I promise."

"Chris is going to take the baby away," I say, but I'm too late, because Sam has hung up.

I'll admit I feel very stung by that. I'm not used to it. Usually, it's me who has to end a call prematurely, or behave furtively. Sam has always just been there for me, waiting patiently for me to have time to visit him, picking up the phone whenever I have the chance to make contact.

I try to calm myself down, to rationalize the fact of his appointment, whatever it is, but in truth I'm upset. If it was that important, I tell myself, surely he would have mentioned it to me?

I can't help feeling abandoned.

ZOE

Lucas stares at me full on when I ask him if he thinks his dad killed my mum, and the way he does it makes me sure that he knows the answer, but before he says anything there's a knock on the bathroom door.

"Everything all right in there, my lovely girls?"

It's Richard. I don't think he knows that Lucas is with us, and I don't want him to, because this is our chance to talk without the others.

"Yes, we're fine," I call.

"Do you need a hand?"

"No. We'll be down in a minute."

I look back at Lucas. His expression is sort of cracked now, and he's holding the bedspread above Grace's face, his hand frozen in the air, while underneath him she tries to reach for it. He starts to speak, but I put my finger on my lips because I want to make sure that Richard's gone.

After a few seconds pass, I'm confident that he has, so I say, "Did your dad hurt you?"

He winces, and he starts to fight back tears, so I think I know the answer to that.

I ask again, "Do you think your dad killed my mum?"

"No," he says, and he whispers it, and now his eyes are full up with a huge, tremendous sorrow. He looks down at Grace, who's still trying to reach the bedspread, a tiny frown puckering her so smooth forehead. A tear falls from his cheekbone onto the fabric, and darkens it.

A strange expression crosses Lucas's eyes as he gazes at our sister, and it triggers an impulse in me to snatch the bedspread away in case he plunges it on her face and smothers her, but before I act he lowers it gently down so that it's within her reach and Grace's reaction is practically ecstatic.

Lucas says, "I was trying to protect her."

"Your mum?"

"No. Your mum."

"What?"

"I'm so sorry," he says. "I just need to tell you it was a mistake. I killed her, Zoe, but it was by mistake."

My eyes are brimming hotly now and I feel my lips and chin collapse hopelessly and the muscles in my body seem to dissolve, and I find that I have nothing in me, no words at all that I can give back to Lucas.

"I'm sorry," he says again. "But it was an accident, I swear it was, and I've decided I'm going to tell them everything."

I find myself choking with sobs, convulsed with them. I cover my mouth with my hand to mute them because they're so violent.

Lucas picks Grace up and holds her close to him, and he sobs too. We sit there like that for what seems like forever and then he hands Grace to me and says, "I'm going to miss her. She's so perfect."

His cheeks and upper lip and forehead are glistening with

tears and snot and sweat from the heat of the day, and he stands up.

And, as he reaches for the door handle, the phrase that circulates around my mind, and makes me hold my sister to me as tightly as I possibly can, is this: "Lucas killed my mother."

SAM

The consultant sits behind a desk that he's clearly using just for the purposes of this clinic, because he's opening and shutting drawers crossly, picking things up from the desk and slapping them back down. I'm afraid that his actions might dislodge the rimless reading glasses that are balanced precariously at the end of his nose.

"They put things in a different place every time," he says. "Take a seat, please."

"Sam Locke," I say, and we shake hands just before I sit.

I'm not used to being on this side of the desk in situations like this, and I feel as if I need to show him somehow that I consider myself his equal, even if it's just with a handshake.

I chide myself immediately for the feeling, though, because it's not going to change anything he's going to say to me; it's no more than a futile attempt my pride is making to assert myself as a fellow professional, and anyway, the doctor seems oblivious to it. He must see this twenty times a day. To him, I'm just a patient, somebody to keep at a safe professional distance, just as, I suppose, my clients are to me.

"I only want a pen," he says, eyebrows raised. "Ridiculous, isn't it?"

I hand him a pen from my own pocket, and he scribbles something on a fat, dog-eared set of notes, bursting out of their cardboard wrapping, before he puts it to one side.

"Right! Sorry about that. They always show everybody in too quickly. Always rushing."

He takes a slim brown folder from a neatly stacked pile. It's pristine, and on the front of it is my name. When he opens it, I see a letter from my GP, a referral, and only one or two other sheets of paper.

"Aha," he says. "Yes. You've just had a scan."

I nod.

"So we need to take a look at that."

He begins to tap at the computer keyboard. He has to watch his fingers to find the right keys.

"Let's hope the system is going to be kind to us today," he tells me. "There are many hurdles we can fall at when we want to access scans."

I'm silent, I just watch him. I must not dislike him, I think, because this man is going to be looking after me. On his head there's just a shadow of hair around the back and sides, cropped extremely close, and petering out on the crown, where there's a shine that I suspect he wouldn't like if he could see it. His suit is an expensive one, and his tie is extravagantly knotted and certainly made of silk; there's a thick gold wedding band on his ring finger and an expensive watch clamped ostentatiously around his wrist. I suspect he has a lucrative private practice.

He must be feeling the heat in all that finery, I think, because I am.

"Ah yes! Here we are," he announces finally. "Got it."

And I see his face collapse into a frown as he studies it and I feel as if I'm watching a piece of my world detaching itself and falling into a void.

ZOE

I want to tear Lucas's eyes out.

But I want to hold him too.

Grace is still in my arms and I have squeezed her so close to me that she has started to cry. Lucas is still standing over us, looking down at us, not moving, though his hand is on the bathroom door handle.

"What were you trying to protect my mum from?" I ask.

"From Dad."

"Why?"

"Because he was about to hurt her, and I tried to get her out of his way, because I could see him coming for her. I pushed her, because I didn't have time to do anything else, but we were at the top of the stairs, and she fell down and hit her head. I didn't mean it to happen, I was trying to help her. It was an accident; I swear it, Zoe. I'm sorry."

And before I can say anything to that he unlocks the door, turns the handle, and he's gone, and the movement of the door sends a hot barrage of air into the room. I'm left sitting there in all the wet that Grace has made, just holding her while she frets. The force of what he's just told me makes it feel difficult even to breathe, let alone to try to understand what's happened, but I must.

Lucas says he tried to protect my mum from Chris, and he killed her instead. He said the same words to me that I said at my trial: "It was an accident."

"How are you getting on?" It's Richard, standing on the landing; it's like he's appeared out of nowhere. "Are you all right, lovey? Have you been crying again?"

"I don't want Chris and Lucas to take Grace," I tell him. I blurt that out, because it's how I feel, but also because something tells me not to tell him what Lucas just said, and I think it's because I don't want it to be true.

Richard is looking at me a bit oddly, and for a moment I wonder if he was listening at the door before, whether he heard what Lucas said.

"Is Lucas OK?" he asks.

"He's fine. He was just helping me."

He stares at my face for a second, and then his eyes fall to Grace.

"I understand why you don't want her to go," he says. He strokes Grace's head and she reaches out her arms to him and he takes her from me.

"I want to stop them."

"I don't really think we can."

"But Grace belongs to me and Mum. She always has."

"Listen, I know it's really, really hard, but Chris is her dad. There's nothing we can do."

"Help me. I want her to stay here, just for a bit."

Uncle Richard looks even more red and sweaty than he did this morning. He sits down on the side of the bath, holding Grace on his knee.

"What if we offer to keep Grace for the day, just until they've checked into the hotel and got themselves sorted out?" he says. "Then we can take her over there later."

"She needs a nap."

"Then I'll say that. She can nap here before she goes."

I look at Grace. She doesn't often settle down quickly or quietly, and if that happens then Chris might just take her anyway. He's never patient about that kind of thing.

"I'll put her in the buggy," I say. "If we push her around she'll fall asleep."

Grace has a buggy that's padded like an emperor's chariot. When she's tired, she never lasts five minutes in it before nodding off, because it's way too comfy and Mum says she likes the feeling of being in motion.

"Can you tell Chris?" I know he won't listen to me, and I don't want to say even a single word to him.

"Leave it with me," Richard says.

He puts a hand on my shoulder and I feel like I can trust him, and that he's on my side, and I suddenly understand that there's something even more important that I should be doing: I need to find Lucas before he talks to anybody else.

The stairs make a sound like thunder as I run down them and I'm lucky because I find Lucas straightaway. He's standing in the hall, in front of the sitting room door. There's nobody else there, and the door is semiclosed. He looks like he's steeling himself to open it and tell everybody what happened.

I take his arm. "Come with me," I whisper.

He shakes my hand off. He's psyched up.

"I have to do this." His words sound as if he's having to force them out from between his clenched teeth.

"I need you first. Please."

I take his hand again and pull it to my mouth, and put my lips on the back of his fingers, just very gently. It's the only thing I can think to do. I want him to feel my touch, because after my First Chance Life ended I felt like nobody wanted to touch me because of what I did, because I wasn't worth it.

They all talked and talked to me and at me about what I did and how to "move forward" and guilt, and reparation, and sentences served, and future opportunities, and I understood all of that; but the reason I never felt encouraged by it or strengthened was partly because I was sorry for what I did, so sorry that it hurt me every day, and partly because I was angry about what happened at my trial, but mostly because I felt I would never be worth anything, ever again.

"Your self-esteem," Jason told me, "is at rock bottom, and I don't like to see it that way."

"Go figure," I said back to him. It was at the end of our second-to-last session, it was nearly the last conversation we ever had, the last nice conversation, anyway.

Lucas starts to shake, and his fingers relax against my lips.

"Once you've told them," I whisper, "they'll take you away, straightaway and we won't ever get to see each other again for a very long time, maybe never. I just want to talk to you one more time before you tell them, please."

He looks nervous of that. Or is he nervous of me, and of what I might do to him now I know what happened.

"I want to hear your story," I say, because that's the other thing I never had, the chance to tell my story without people always lecturing me around it. Sometimes I think I would have liked to tell my story to the mums and dads of the children I killed, that they might not mind so much if they heard it from me, away from court and judges and solicitors.

"Bad idea," Jason said. "Reparation justice does recommend meetings between victims' families and prisoners in some situations, but this doesn't qualify as one of them."

"Lucas," I breathe the word onto his hand, terrified that we'll be interrupted, or overheard, that I'm too late. "Please." My breath feels hotter than the day even as it spreads across his fingers.

His shaking intensifies. I play my final card. I put down my ace.

"I understand," I say, "I promise."

I hope I can keep this up. My impulse to punish him, attack him, rip him to shreds, bend and break his body like the kids who were in the car with me is strong, and it's fighting a hard battle with my sensible head.

"Where shall we go?" he says just when I think all is lost, and he'll confess and go to prison and Chris will disappear out of our lives with Grace, and I'll have nothing.

I exhale with relief and tell him that there's one place I can think of.

TESSA

Chris and Philip and I are sitting more or less in silence, as the family liaison officer makes many and varied attempts to engage us in small talk, or any kind of talk. She talks about cups of tea, she talks about the process of grief, she talks about the structure of police investigations, and she talks about the weather.

Chris is managing to offer her a few responses, which she leaps on as if they were scraps thrown to a dog. I think she must have been taught to try to engage with us, to become our friend. I want to tell her that I don't give a fig's leaf how many times a day she has to water her geraniums in the heat wave, but instead I manage to zone her out, so that her words become a wall of white noise, against which I try to think.

Philip is in our most comfortable armchair, head back, mouth open, snoring gently. The drive, he told us, and the early start, have worn him out. I have no words to describe my anger at his selfishness.

I watch Chris out of the corner of my eye as he talks to the family liaison officer. I wonder if I should say something to her about my suspicions and, if so, what. If I make them known to her, and Chris guesses who has done so, and if I'm wrong, we'll never recover from that, and I don't know if I'm sure enough to risk that.

In a way, I'm grateful that Chris wants to go to a hotel. It'll give me a chance to speak to Richard about him and to get advice from Sam. And besides, Chris isn't behaving like a guilty man; he seems devastated.

I also can't deny that I crave the space that he and Lucas and the baby will leave in my house, because it might give me a chance to mourn my sister, and give Zoe a chance to mourn her mother.

So when Chris stands to look out of the window, to see if his taxi has arrived, I find that I'm willing it to be there.

"Any sign?" the liaison officer asks him.

"No," he says, and then, "Oh wait, yes, I think this is it."

It occurs to me then, as he begins to move to answer the door, that if he is guilty of something he might flee, but that immediately seems a wild, stupid thought, and something for the police to be concerned about, not me. This is not television, I tell myself, where people can just disappear in an instant, especially not with a successful business that needs running, a reasonably high public profile, and a baby and teenager in tow.

"Lucas!" Chris calls up the stairs. The three of us are gathered in the hall now, though there's no sign of Richard or the kids.

"Lucas!"

None of them answer.

"I'll find him," I say.

Chris opens the front door and there's a driver there, smart in a crisp open-necked shirt and chinos. It's definitely not the usual comfortable attire of the shift taxi driver, and behind him I glimpse a sleek black vehicle. Chris has called one of his work drivers, I realize; "taxi" wasn't quite an accurate description. It reminds me once more how little I've understood about the life he and Maria have been leading.

I run upstairs to the bathroom to see if anybody is still there with the baby. There are signs everywhere that Grace has been bathed: water on the floor and bubbles gathered around the plughole, but the room is empty of people.

"Zoe?" I call. "Richard?"

Again, no answer.

"Lucas?"

I see that his backpack has been slung onto one of our spare beds, all zipped up.

Then I glimpse them through a window; Lucas and Zoe are out in the garden, and it looks as if they have the baby in the buggy. They're patiently pushing her backward and forward in the shade of our patio.

It's a lovely sight, as if they've come together to form surrogate parents for Grace, and I know Maria would be happy if she could see them. I watch as they peer at Grace together, under the sunshade, and then, carefully, they begin to walk up the garden with her, although the uneven slabs and the tufts of tough, desiccated grass that protrude between them make it slow going.

I hear talking in the hall and make my way down.

"She just conked out," Richard is saying, "absolutely blotto in my arms after her bath, so we've put her in the stroller, and we thought you might prefer to go on ahead to the hotel and get settled in and come and collect her later. Or we could bring her to you?"

Chris doesn't look happy. He checks his watch impatiently.

"I don't want to be going backward and forward later on, so how about I send the driver to work to pick up some things for me, because I need to do that anyway, and by the time he gets back she should have had an hour or so of sleep. Do we think that would work?" he says.

"Of course," I say. That sounds like a fair plan to me, and besides, I'm flat out of the energy required to make any other kind of response.

ZOE

I lay Grace down, cover her with the sunshade, and tilt back her chair. After that it's just a few turns around the patio and she's out like a light. She puts her hands up above her head, a fist by each ear, and looks really sweet. Her tummy is bare and the whole of it goes up and down as she breathes.

Lucas and I walk her down to the end of the garden, pushing the buggy carefully over the bumpy bits, and we park it in the shade underneath a leafy tree that's grown tall beside Uncle Richard's shed.

I beckon to Lucas to follow me into the shed. It feels boiling-point hot inside, and it smells of wood shavings and paint and glue. I shut the door behind us anyway.

There's a workbench along one side with tools and stuff on it, and above that is a shelf where Richard's models are displayed. Mostly, they're airplanes made out of balsa wood, but there are also Airfix models up there, painted really perfectly, and some complicated-looking Meccano-type things with engines and wires. Some of the plane models are hanging from the ceiling on transparent threads and they turn a little after we come in.

Lucas doesn't look at any of it; instead he sinks down so that he's sitting on the floor and then looks up at me. "What do you want?" he says. "Don't you hate me?"

I kneel down, right up close to him. We don't have much time before one of the busybody adults finds us and wants to know what we're doing.

"Lucas," I say, and I take his hands, one in each of mine, and I squeeze them because I want to make him concentrate on me, completely and entirely. "This is really, really important."

"I'm ready to tell them everything." The sobbing begins again. "I'm so sorry."

"No!" I say. "No, you mustn't. Not yet."

"I have to," he says and his sobs are so choking that I shake his hands to try to make him snap out of it, but nothing works, so eventually I slap him as hard as I can across his cheek. It really stings my hand, that slap, and it knocks his head from one side to the other.

"Lucas," I say. "Listen to me. Stop crying."

His eyes are bloodshot and there's still dampness around his lips and under his nose. He looks wrecked. His expression has so many things going on in it, but I'm super focused and I block everything out except for the thing that I want to say to him.

"Does your dad know what you did?" I ask.

"Yes."

"What does he say?"

"He says we have to protect each other. We both have to say we were asleep, and we know nothing. Nobody can prove otherwise."

"Tell me exactly what happened."

"After we went to bed last night, I couldn't sleep. I heard

you come up, and then I was lying in my bed for ages, until I heard them arguing in their bedroom. It sounded like he was bullying her, and I was afraid he was so angry about the lies you both told him that he was going to hurt her, so I got out of bed and I went and opened their door because I wanted to tell him to stop. He had hold of her, but when he saw me he let go, but then he started coming for me, and he was very angry. I stepped back onto the landing to get away from him, but he caught me and he pushed me back against the wall, by the top of the stairs. And your mum . . . your mum came after him, and she caught him by surprise and managed to pull him off me just for a second. She was standing between him and me, but she turned her back to him, to check that I was OK. Behind her, I could see that he recovered really quickly and he was coming to get her, so I tried to push her right out of his way, onto the ground. But when I pushed her she hit the banister post at the top of the stairs, and she sort of bounced off it, and she fell down the stairs."

I can see it all in my head; I can see her lying broken on the stairs.

"There was blood," he says. "She hit her head when she fell, and there was blood."

And all this while I lay in my bed sleeping, with Chopin playing on my iPod and Grace in my arms. That thought almost stops me in my tracks completely, almost robs me of my courage.

"He made me clean the blood up," Lucas says, and he retches at the memory. "He made me clean it up while he carried her outside. I didn't know he was going to put her by the bins. I'm sorry. She deserved so much better than that."

It takes me a while to find the words to ask my next question because it's the hardest I've ever had to work to keep my emotions under control. But I do it for Mum.

"Why did you want me to delete the script?"

"Because Dad said we have to cover up for each other. He didn't know about the script, but I thought it would make the police suspicious of him and then he might tell them that I did it. But I want to tell them everything because I can't take it anymore."

I'm so close to Lucas that I examine his face almost forensically, wanting to understand every line and curve of it. I look at every pore, I see the arc of his damp, clotted eyelashes, and I recognize that the smell of him is the same one that hung in the air of the Unit sometimes.

It's the smell of fear.

"He hurt your mum too."

"Yes."

"Did he kill her?"

"No."

"But she died because of him?"

"She killed herself because he made her feel useless."

I know that feeling; it inhabits every cell in my body.

"But she was dying anyway?"

"She never fought the disease. She might have fought it if her life wasn't so shit. She had no reason to want to live. I told you that."

I put my finger to Lucas's mouth. "Shh," I say.

I don't say, "But she had you," because sometimes I understand that it's best to keep things to yourself when they are a hundred percent guaranteed to hurt others.

His breath smells sour, but it doesn't gross me out. I realize that I love the way that only I can see into his soul. Lucas has been carrying a secret around with him, just like I have, and that's a powerful thought. It makes my heart begin to beat a little faster.

I press my cheek against his where the wetness of his tears seals us together, and then I rest my head on his shoulder while he cries and cries again, like his sadness is never going to end, and all the time my mind is working, and my thoughts are becoming very, very clear.

Then he says, "I filmed it on my phone. I filmed him hurting her when I opened the bedroom door, because I was going to show you what he's like."

"Is it still on your phone?"

The police will find it there, surely, if it is.

"I deleted it at the same time as the script."

It might take them a little bit longer, but they'll still find it. The thing is, I want to act quickly.

"But I uploaded it," he adds, "before I deleted it. In case I had to prove that I was trying to help her, because Dad was hurting her."

He describes the film to me and, as he does, my thoughts crystallize. Perfectly.

I take Lucas's hands in mine, once again, and I take a deep breath.

Then I say to him, "I forgive you," because those are the words that I've always wanted to hear. I give them to him right here and now, because I know, even if he doesn't yet, that they're the greatest gift that I can give him, and I just hope that they're enough.

For, you see, I've suddenly understood something even more important than knowing what Lucas did to my mother; I've understood that Lucas is my only chance of keeping Grace.

Because otherwise Chris will have her.

And he will hurt her.

I know it in my bones.

SAM

The consultant says, "I believe you've had a conversation with your GP about what to expect today?"

"I have."

"As we suspected there might be, there are lesions visible in your scan. They're in both the brain and the spine."

He swings the computer monitor around toward me, and I see an image of my skull.

"This shows you a slice of your brain," he says, "as if we were looking at it from the top of your head down toward your feet," and with my pen he points at several different areas on the screen. "There are lesions visible there, there, and there's one more, which you can probably see here." He's pointing out small smudges, which are pale gray and look distinct from the rest of the scan, as if somebody had left several small, dirty fingerprints on the inside of my head.

"For me," he continues, "taken in conjunction with the rest of your symptoms, this goes significantly farther to suggest a diagnosis of multiple sclerosis, but I would like to do a lumbar puncture to confirm it. Do you know what that is?"

I struggle for a second to find words because my throat has gone dry. "Taking fluid from your spine," I say.

"And we do that because we're looking for things called myelin proteins. If we find them, then your diagnosis will be confirmed. If we don't, it won't unfortunately mean that you don't have the condition, just that there were no proteins in the sample, so we might need to repeat the test. But based on this scan, I think it would be sensible to prepare yourself for an MS diagnosis."

He starts tapping on his computer again.

"I think the best thing to do now might be to discuss how we can alleviate the symptoms you're having. Can you describe them for me?"

An hour and a half later, after a long wait at the hospital pharmacy, I leave the building holding a bag of medication and an appointment card for a lumbar puncture for the following week, as well as the contact details of the hospital's specialist MS nurse, whom I've just met.

Out on the baking-hot streets, I feel affronted by the bright glare of the sun, the way it glints off car hoods and roofs and the windows of the surrounding buildings.

I'm told the medication should ease the symptoms of numbness and joint pain soon, and I'll be grateful for that because it makes me feel vulnerable when I'm out, especially in crowded situations, and it's becoming increasingly difficult to hide it from others.

I knew the diagnosis was likely, and though it's not confirmed, I don't think the doctor would be advising me to prepare myself if he wasn't certain.

Even standing in the shade, I feel overwhelmed by the

heat, and by the momentous news I've just received. I take my phone out. Tess hasn't called me back yet.

"Sorry," I say to her, even though she can't hear me, and I turn the ringtone to silent.

I approach one of the taxis that are waiting outside the hospital and ask the driver to take me home. I don't answer any of his chatty questions, and in the silence that I've imposed, I see him glancing in the rearview mirror, wondering what's just happened to me.

At home, in the empty flat, I wish more than anything that I had somebody who would come home to me tonight, somebody I could tell, somebody who would be with me through it to the end.

ZOE

When your world explodes, all the pieces of it shatter and spread, and you don't see some of them ever again, and nothing is ever like it was before.

I lost the world I had before the accident and my mum helped me to build a new one. Now that world has gone too, and I will never see my mum again, but I don't want to lose all the other bits.

Before I left the Unit, Jason taught me one last thing. We'd just finished our final session, two days before my release, and I asked him why all of us kids were locked up like animals when what some of us had done was just a mistake, or unavoidable, because we were stupid, or young, or had other excusable reasons for what we did, like a witness who lied and a judge who didn't believe the truth when he heard it.

"Punishment is considered an effective deterrent," Jason replied, and he adjusted the neckline of his Bowling for Soup T-shirt, which was a gesture he always made when he was feeling awkward.

"That's the theory anyway," he added. "Look, it's an imperfect system, and we know it is, but that's why these sessions are important, because they're when you get a chance to unpick what happened to you and understand the reasons for it, so that we can try to find a way forward."

"I told the truth at my trial and they put me in jail anyway," I said.

"Well, as I said, it's imperfect, but you know kids didn't even used to get therapeutic sessions at all, so you're lucky in that sense."

The clock high up on the wall told both of us that our time was up. As a way to end our last-ever session, it felt like an anticlimax, because he'd said this stuff to me loads of times before.

It wasn't the final thing he taught me.

I stayed sitting because I wondered if Jason might be about to say something cheesy and nice as a goodbye, actually I kind of wanted him to, but instead he said it was time to go, and he started to walk me back to my corridor in the Unit as usual.

There were places in the Unit where the surveillance cameras couldn't see you. Most of us avoided them, because they could be frightening places to be alone in. You learned that very quickly after you arrived.

Jason stopped in one of those places, between two sets of doors, which linked separate areas. I was waiting for him to swipe his security pass and push open the next set of doors so that we could carry on as usual, but instead he paused and put his hand on my upper arm. There was nobody else around, because it was a time when most people were in lockdown.

"Zoe," he said. "You're leaving in two days, and I think you've got every chance of not coming back here, I really do. I'll personally be very disappointed if you do."

"I won't."

I said it quickly because I didn't like the way his fingers were pressing into my arm. I stepped away from him but I couldn't move far, because the space was so small, and every muscle in my body seized up with fear.

It meant that I was frozen to the spot even when he released his so-tight grip, and he ran his fingers down the side of my arm, over the sleeve of my sweatshirt, and across my cuff until they reached my wrist. They made contact with my skin there, and I held my breath as they burrowed up an inch or two under my sleeve. The pad of his little finger rested lightly on my wrist bone and I wished my bone would dissolve away, because it was a sickening feeling.

"You're so beautiful, and so talented," he said, and his voice sounded as if his tongue had grown thick. "You don't belong here."

His hand traveled up from my wrist to my cheek then, and it moved slowly and brushed against the side of my breast on the way there. I forced my head back even farther and felt my face quiver when he ran a finger across my cheek.

His breathing was loud and unsteady.

"I'll scream," I said.

"My word against yours, Zoe. Who do you think will win?"

There was no reply I could make, because I knew the answer to that. It would be him.

He brought his head toward mine and his lips grazed my neck and then he said, "Your life will be like that from now on, and you need to remember it."

He stepped away from me suddenly then, and swiped the door with his pass and held it open for me to walk through into the bright white lights of the communal area as if nothing had happened. I walked slowly because I felt as though I might stagger, and I hardly registered that Jason was saying hello to Gemma, who was on duty, and asking to see his next person, because I was feeling as though I needed to gasp for every breath.

I went to my room and curled up on my bed as tightly as possible. I felt cold, and I was shaking, and the only thing that stopped me from ripping up the sheet and wrapping it around my neck was the thought that I had only two more days in that place before my mum came to get me, and then I would never see Jason again and I would be able to have another life, a Second Chance Life.

I remember pretty much every single thing that Jason told me when I was in the Unit, because I have excellent recall, but it was that final message that he delivered in that cameraless space that lodged itself most deeply in my mind.

I already knew that life was unfair, and that structures society puts in place to protect you don't always work, but what Jason taught me there and then is that what happened to me had marked me permanently, turned me into somebody who could be pushed and pulled around, like a toy for other people to play with, somebody without a voice and without the right to a normal life.

Unless.

Unless I'm brave enough to take control.

In the baking heat of my uncle's shed, a perfect idea has formed in my head: I want to save Grace from Chris and keep her with me so I can make her into the girl that Mum wanted her to be able to be.

I look at Lucas and I try to assess whether I can make the idea work. It'll be a challenge, I know, because he's like a whipped dog so much of the time, and especially now. The thing I'm thinking of can't happen without him, though, so I desperately need him to be brave as well, and that's because I need him to lie about what happened.

I whisper it to him, the idea that I've had, but as I feared, when I've finished telling him what we need to do, he says, "I can't."

"You can."

"No."

"If you tell the truth, they'll lock you up, Lucas, like they did me. You don't know what it's like in there. And then your dad will take Grace, and he'll hurt her. And I might never see you again. Ever."

I try to stand as tall as I can. I put my shoulders back and shake my hair down the back of my neck. I stand the way my mum stood when Chris and Lucas got back from the concert. I stand the way she stood every day during my trial, when she was strong. I stand the way I want Grace to stand when she's older, no matter what's happening to her.

The problem is that however strong I am, the fear in Lucas's eyes looks as if it has run deep for a very long time, and I'm sure that it has. I also understand that right now he probably feels the same as I did just after the accident: like a trapped animal, full of panic and pain and shock about what's just happened, but I have to make him snap out of it, and see as clearly as I do that we need to do this.

"Do you want Grace to have a life like yours?" I ask him. "Living in fear of your dad?"

He shakes his head, but he says, "What you're asking me to do is wrong."

"It's not wrong if it ends up being right. Think about it."

I'm starting to feel desperate now, because if he doesn't agree to do as I ask, we'll lose everything we have left, both of us will. I think of the script and I know he must feel the same kind of anger deep down that I do.

"Anger can be a release," Jason told me once, though he was simultaneously advising me not to display it quite as much as I did then.

In desperation, I snatch one of Richard's models from the shelf beside us and I hold it out to Lucas and say, "Wreck it," because it's the only way I can think to tap into the rageful feelings he must have inside him, and that might be the only way I can make him agree to my plan, right here and now.

"What? No!"

"Come on!" I shove it toward him, but he bats it back roughly, and in that gesture I think I can sense his anger starting to fizz, and I wonder if he has ever once let it out before. It's enough to convince me that my tactic is a good one.

"I'll do it then," I say. "I'm not afraid to."

Right in front of his face, I hold the wing of the plane and bend it slowly, the tension in it ratcheting up incrementally beneath my fingers.

The model is intricate and lovely. It must have taken hours and days to make.

"Don't!" Lucas says. He makes to snatch it out of my hands and I just give it up.

"Break it," I say.

"No!" He's holding it as if it's fine porcelain, but his hands are shaking.

"It represents your life with your dad," I say. "Break it, and you'll be free of him. Break it for your mum. Break it, and we can do what we have to do to get justice for her and for my mum."

"Why are you doing this to me? I tried to warn you, didn't I? I sent you the script."

"You sent it too late!"

He looks down at the plane in his hands.

I think of what Jason said to me with his hot breath buffeting my face—"My word against yours, Zoe. Who do you think they'll believe?"—and I know that if Lucas doesn't agree to do this with me, then I can't do it on my own.

"They'll believe us; I know they will. This is the only way now," I tell him.

"But what about the panop messages I sent you? The police will find them on your phone."

"They know about my past, Lucas, they won't care if you know too. Think about it. That's all the panop messages prove."

The clarity I'm feeling is incredibly pure and I'm getting increasingly frustrated that he can't feel it too. It's like there's mud in his brain, and he's thinking about all the wrong things. "They won't bother looking at our phones anymore anyway," I say, "if we do this right."

He says, "Maria didn't deserve my dad. And nor did my mum. Nobody does."

"Grace doesn't deserve him either."

He moves the airplane around in his hands so that he's holding it by its wing like I did, and then, just as I think he's going to put it down and leave the shed and I'll have failed in this as well as everything else, he starts to bend it. I hold my breath as the tension in the wood builds and it begins to split.

Lucas gasps, and I say, "Don't give up now," and it's like

that comment is a sort of release for him, as if all his rage has suddenly boiled over.

He snaps off the wing of the plane, and then its tail, and I have to step backward because he starts to bash the airplane against the walls of the shed until it splinters and shatters into smithereens and still he keeps on bashing it until I'm afraid that he's going to break his hand and he's saying, "I hate you. I fucking hate you," and we both know he's not saying that to me, he's saying it to his dad.

When he's finally finished, he looks at the few shards that remain in his hand as if he's not sure how they got there, and I say, "Will you do it?" and he says, "OK," and my heart flips in relief.

RICHARD

Once Chris has decided to stay for a bit longer while he waits for Grace to finish her nap, he asks to borrow my computer. "I just need to tie one or two things up for work so they don't bother us for the next few days," he says. His face is grim and stressed.

"Be my guest," I tell him.

I take him upstairs and show him the setup in my office.

Could he have done something? I wonder again as I leave him to it. I have to resist the temptation to peer over his shoulder. Tessa has her suspicions, clearly, but that could just be guilt talking, because she is somehow convinced that she could have saved Maria if she'd made more effort to remain close to her after the marriage.

I notice as I cross the landing that we all left the bathroom in a somewhat destroyed state in the wake of Grace's bath, and I decide that I'll tidy it up, to make it nice for Tessa. I mop up the spilled water with the already wet bedspread, and then put it out in the hallway with the idea of hanging it up to dry in the garden, and I wash the dried-out bubbles from the inside of the bath.

As I scrub, I begin to feel confused about something I

thought I overheard when Grace was having her bath. I thought I heard Lucas say something about Maria's death, but I'm sure I must be wrong, or Zoe would have reacted differently when I spoke to her immediately afterward.

I wonder if I'll be able to persuade Chris to let Grace stay here for her tea. He'll struggle to organize that in a hotel. I wonder if she eats soup. I wonder when she's going to start missing her mother.

It appears that Grace has played with every plastic bottle that was gathered neatly around the edges of our bath, and so I begin to retrieve them from all corners of the room and stand them up in their allotted places. We're not used to things moving around, Tess and I. Ours is a quiet life.

I'm kneeling on the floor to reach a shampoo bottle that has somehow got stuck behind the stand that the basin sits on when the craving hits me. First, a wave of exhaustion, then a rush of all the emotions that I cannot bear.

Beside me, built into the cladding that surrounds the bath, is a small door. If I push it, it'll open, and behind it there's a hidden bottle of vodka. Cheap, nasty vodka. Beautiful, anesthetizing vodka. Just one push of my fingers and I can have it.

But I try to be good. I sit there, on my knees, in our nice little bathroom, and think of that beautiful baby, and Tessa's broken family, and of our shambles of a marriage, and although it takes me every ounce of strength, I manage to leave the room without touching the bottle.

Walking away is so hard. There's some payoff though, I can't deny it, because as I make my way slowly downstairs I force myself to acknowledge that resisting the bottle is also a triumph of sorts, however grim I feel.

TESSA

I'm pacing downstairs. The detectives have vacated the dining room for now and I walk around it as if it can give me some clues, or help me to think.

I'm too restless to stay there for long though and, as I go back into the hallway, I almost collide with Zoe.

It shocks her, and she gives a little scream. She seems pent up and extremely agitated, and she won't meet my eye properly, which is unusual for her. She tells me in a nervous voice, as if she's finding it hard to breathe properly, that she wants to gather everybody together in the sitting room.

She wakes up her dad, and she calls Richard in from outside, where he's been checking on the baby. She gets Chris down from the upstairs bedroom, and she asks us all to sit down, though she saves a seat in the middle of the sofa, beside Chris, which she insists the liaison officer take.

Lucas is there too, and he's doing something with the TV. He's turned it on and holds the two remote controls and he's navigating through a series of screens that look unfamiliar to me.

Once Richard arrives in the room he of course asks Lucas

what he's trying to do, and offers help and expertise, but the boy brushes him off a bit brusquely. It's clear to me that he more than seems to know what he's doing, though undeniably he's giving off nerves in exactly the same way as Zoe is.

As everyone's getting seated, Zoe stands beside my chair and I rub her slender wrist. "What's happening, Butterfly?" I ask her.

She doesn't look at me, and she doesn't reply; she's fixated on what Lucas is doing.

It reminds me of how she used to be at the time of the trial. It broke my heart, because she always seemed to be some-where else in her head, as if the core of her had curled up in fear, and though perhaps it shouldn't have, that did make her somehow untouchable to the rest of us.

"Zoe?" I ask again, because her behavior is scaring me a little, but Lucas says, at the same time, "It's ready," and then, as if she's taking a cue from him, as if it's something they've rehearsed, she turns to everybody and delivers a short speech in a voice so laconic it sends a chill running through me.

"Lucas and me were afraid. But now we've decided to tell you what we know. This is a film from last night."

We all turn to face the TV.

Lucas seems to have got it to link to the Internet, and it's displaying a video site. I wonder if it's the film from the con-cert that he's about to play, but it doesn't look as if it is.

The picture that suddenly appears on the screen looks just like the inside of Chris and Maria's house.

LUCAS

I filmed this on my phone, in secret, last night. I held the phone down by my leg and my dad didn't notice.

As we watch the footage in front of my dad and all of the other people in Tessa's sitting room, the only way I can force myself to stay there and watch it again and go through with what me and Zoe agreed is to think about how, if I was going to shoot this scene for an actual film, I would do it differently.

The secret way I had to film, before I dropped the camera and all it showed was the ceiling, means that the footage has a kind of *Blair Witch Project/Paranormal Activity* feel to it. It's a kind of indie low-budget terror look, which might work. But I'd like it to be more stylized, so I'd do it like this:

First shot would follow me along the landing, a tracking shot probably, using a handheld camera and looking over my shoulder from behind me, so you could see that I was approaching my parents' bedroom door and you could see it from my point of view.

As I walk down the corridor, the soundtrack would be a long, low note—low strings maybe—like a drone. The muffled sounds of an argument would be audible through the closed bedroom door.

As I stop outside the door and listen, the camera would swing around to show my face, so you could see how I'm trying to be brave.

Cut to a close-up of my hand opening the bedroom door. The door swings open.

The drone of the music is mounting, but not too much yet.

We see into the room. It's lit up by a small bedside lamp only, so there are powerful long shadows reaching across the space, and they make my dad look terrifying, like the evil guy on the front of a comic book.

My dad is standing over Maria. He's holding her by her hair and he's pushed her head back against the wall so you can see the smooth stretch of her neck.

Then there would be closeup shots: the back of my dad's hand, Maria's hair poking out between his fingers, the skin stretched across his knuckles and then her face, her jaw tense with pain and fear.

The drone of the soundtrack builds, adding more strings, higher pitched and clashing, so that it sounds discordant now.

I would be happy with that opening; it would show everything exactly as it happened.

When he works out what he's watching, as we all sit there in Tessa's sitting room, my dad starts to make a lunge for the TV before all the people can hear what he's going to say on film. But Zoe's dad is sitting beside him, and so is the police lady, and Zoe's dad grabs my dad by the arm and tells him to sit down in a voice that is deadly polite. Zoe's dad has a wrecked face, but he's big and strong and my dad is no match for him.

We're reaching the bit in the film where everything happens very fast. All the people in the room are totally fixated on it.

The footage gets more wobbly here, because I was frightened, but again I imagine it in my reshoot:

Dad turns to me, sees me at the door. "Get out," he says, and I would be sure you could see the vein that's bulged red and angry on his temple.

I might show my face on-camera then, the way that I'm feeling even more fear, but I'm trying not to let it drive me out of the room as it's done so many times before, so I stay where I am because I want him to stop what he's doing.

A close-up of Maria's face, as she tries to turn her head to see me, even though Dad's still holding her hair. Her eyes are full of messages that I can't read because I don't know her as well as I knew my mum. They fall shut as Dad lets go of her hair and she drops to the floor like a rag doll.

Another tracking shot, still with a handheld camera, to show Dad walking toward me. I stay where I am.

Maria says, "Don't touch him!"

"Shut up," Dad says.

"It's over if you hurt him," she says.

The music stops here too. A sudden silence would be effective, I think.

He stops, and then he turns to face Maria and laughs. We see her raise her chin defiantly, but she looks small and fragile in comparison to him, the same way my mum used to.

"Are you trying to threaten me?" he asks her. "Is that what you're doing?"

I want her to keep staring him out, but she drops her gaze.

"And if it's over," he says, "where do you think you're going to go? Another city? Another filthy little flat? Are you ready to be on your own with your daughter again? With not a penny to your name? Or will you crawl back to Devon and live among those people whose children she murdered? You'll never cope, Maria. You're not capable of doing it on your own."

A close-up of her face would show that she's realizing something.

"You wouldn't," she says.

It's then that I understand what she's understood, which is that Dad is implying that he would take Grace from her.

"What I wouldn't do is let my daughter be raised in a home with just you and her," he says. He looks at Maria in the same way he used to look at my mum, as if she was worthless, and could never be anything else in his eyes.

Then he turns back to me, and this time his face is so full of rage that I step backward onto the landing. One, two, three steps.

On the TV in front of us, we see how the phone camera wobbles, and it shows the back of my leg as I hide it, and then we see only scraps of action, but everybody watching who knows our house can easily tell that I'm walking backward toward the top of the staircase.

I don't want to be backing away from him, I want to be standing my ground, and to be shouting at him, shouting all the things that I see in my films. I want to tell him who he is and what he is and ask him why he is a monster and why did such a monster ever want a child? Two children? I want him to dance while I shoot bullets at his feet. I want him to sweat with fear when he understands that I'm not here to do a deal with him, I'm here to kill him, but he's like Colonel Kurtz in all his glory, a towering maniac, a power-riddled Goliath.

He haunts my dreams with his violence, and my days with his softly spoken words that are full of menace.

But I'm afraid, and my courage has trickled away. And he has me now; his hand's on my chest, pushing me against the wall right at the top of the stairs.

Behind him, Maria begins to stand, though she has to drag herself up as if she feels mostly weariness, and there's only the faintest spark of defiance left to propel her. Dad doesn't notice. My eyes are on his eyes, and I can see that his other hand is balled up into a fist.

I don't know which to look at, his eyes or his fist, because I'm not sure if he's going to strike, because you see he never has struck me. Yet. He's pinched and pushed, but mostly he's just used words to keep me subjugated.

What disgusts me most is that I've let him do it to me all my life, and I let him do it to my mum. He never left bruises visible on her, though. Never. My dad was too clever for that. That's why none of the doctors who treated my mum ever got suspicious.

The guilt and anger at myself that I never stopped him hurting her is the thing that fills my mind all day and every day, the thing I hear when I play piano, the thing that echoes in my head when I watch films and when I'm in school, the thing that never leaves me. Nothing makes it go away, except maybe Zoe. Because she is like me: she has bad secrets too.

I saw a counselor at school. Nobody knew that I did that. The problem was, when I got to the meeting, I couldn't actually say what I wanted to, so I talked a load of crap about being stressed about exams. The counselor gave me a ton of leaflets, which were useless, but she did say one good thing. She said, "Why don't you write about what makes you anxious? As a diary maybe? It can help." I told her I didn't want to write a diary, so she said, "What about a song?" and I asked her, "What do I look like, a boy band wannabe or something?" She said, "Well, what do you like?" and so I said, "Film."

"Well, why don't you try writing a script then?"

The script is what I sent to Zoe, and Maria. I put my heart and soul into it, I pieced it together from things my mum remembered, I pictured the scenes in my head based on stuff my mum told me about when she and Dad got together, and old photos, and I sent it to them because I wanted Maria to know that I knew what he was like, so she didn't feel alone.

I wanted to warn Zoe too, because my mum couldn't stand up to him alone, or even with me; you need more people than that and I thought Zoe could help me help Maria.

But Zoe was right: I sent it too late.

I don't look at Dad while the film is playing on the TV. I do stop thinking of ways I would have shot it and I look instead at the faces of everybody except him and I see the horror there, as they witness what I have witnessed all my life.

On the TV we suddenly lose the moving images. I dropped my phone right after Dad slammed my back against the wall, which was the moment just before Maria caught him by surprise and managed to pull him away.

All you can see on the film when that's happening is the ceiling of our landing, the chandelier glinting with dim reflected light from the bedroom.

But you can hear the scuffle as she pulls him away, and then she says, "Are you OK?" to me, which is hard to hear because as soon as Dad has recovered himself, which only takes a second or two, he says, "You little bitch," and then there's the sound of movement from when I tried to push her out of the way, and you hear Maria gasp, and then there's the sound of her hitting the banister post, and then the fall.

I started to scream then, but Dad put his hand over my mouth before I could make much of a noise, and we both watched the blood seeping out of the back of her head and pooling on the varnished wood on the stairs.

Just a few moments after that, the film stops. I picked up the phone and stopped it recording while Dad clattered down the stairs to see if he could save her.

The really important thing is that you can't see that it was me pushing Maria out of the way of Dad that sends her falling down the stairs. To listen to the footage, it's exactly as if he has done it. It's the inevitable result of his violence.

To make that extra clear, just like Zoe told me to, I turn to the room and I look the family liaison officer in the eye, and I say, "He pushed her."

Then, for the second time in twelve hours, Dad advances on me with his hand clenched into a fist.

I put my hands up to protect my face and curl up in my seat.

He never hits me, though, because Philip stops him in time.

"Don't you dare," Philip says. "Don't you dare!" He pushes Dad back down onto the sofa and holds him there.

"Are you really going to do this?" Dad asks me. "Lucas? Have you thought this through? Do you think you'd like to tell the truth?"

I have to look away from him then, and to force myself to do it, to keep myself strong. It's so incredibly hard not to reply, but I mustn't. Zoe said all we have to do is to stick to our story, and I will.

Zoe does her bit then, she says, "I saw it. I came out of my bedroom when I heard Chris shouting. My mum was trying to protect Lucas, and Chris pushed her down the stairs. He pushed her so hard, and he hurt me too," she says. She pulls down the side of her trousers to show the family liaison officer a large welt on her hip. "He pushed me too."

The liaison officer separates me and Zoe from my dad then. She stays with him, and so does Philip, and we leave the room, and tell our story again, to Tess and Richard. They believe us, both of them do, and the relief is incredible.

When the detectives have arrived and talked to Dad, which seems like only minutes after the liaison officer has called for backup, I'll admit that my stomach lurches when I see them lead him away.

I run to the open front door as they take him to the police car. I can't help myself.

"Dad!" I shout, but he doesn't turn around, or look at me at all, not once, until he's sitting in the back of the car and it's backing out of the drive, and then his eyes lock onto mine as he's driven away.

SAM

It's late when I finally phone Tessa back. I try her mobile but it goes straight to voicemail again, and I'm loath to phone the landline in case her husband answers.

Outside the windows of my flat, I can see that the evening crowd has turned out. They're on their way to the pubs on the riverside, or wandering home from work.

I sit on a chair on my balcony with a beer in my hand, but back from the edge, in the shade, where I can feel concealed but also watch the people below.

I'm in that frame of mind where your own life feels as if it has been sucked so hollow that every detail of the lives of others seems designed to wound you. I resent the pair who wander, holding hands, beside the water. I resent the young office worker who walks jauntily along, phone to his ear, chatting to somebody he's going to meet later.

I even resent the old woman who walks along with a small dog trotting in her wake. I've seen them before. They take the same route every day. The dog is never on a lead. It knows where they're going and they're happy to be in each other's company.

I'm shy. I'll never be the rowdy guy having beers in a big crowd at the riverside pub, like the one I can see across the water. I'll be the man in the corner meeting a carefully chosen friend or my lover.

But will my lover want me now?

I was her refuge, but now I'll be a drag. There will be attacks of my disease when I may not be able to move, when my pain might be excruciating. They'll probably worsen over time, so what use will I be to her then? I'll be more like her husband, with his alcoholism, which drains her. My state of mind and physical capabilities will be no better than his in time, and will inevitably become worse.

I poke at the palm of my left hand, willing the numbness to be gone, desperate to be able to feel more sensation there, but of course nothing has changed.

I pick up the bag of medication that I brought back from the hospital, which has been sitting at my feet, and I peel away the sticker that's sealing it and peer into it.

It contains three different boxes of pills.

"Diagnosis is often the trickiest time for our patients," said the MS nurse whom I went to see after the consultant. She was heartbreakingly lovely. "Do you have somebody at home with you tonight?"

"Yes," I lied. I didn't want her pity.

She gave me leaflets with titles like "Coping with MS" and "Information for Patients." Leaflets that I still believe are for other people, not me.

I drink my beer slowly and think about the frailty of life. I think of Zoe Maisey and her poor mother.

I must begin to take these tablets tonight. I must take careful note of dosages.

I must try not to wallow too much in how little I appreciated my life before the passage of time was marked by the popping open of pill packets, the rattle of a bottle full of tablets being picked up, and the tearing sound as a nurse liberates a new syringe from its packet, just for you.

I can't face taking the tablets yet. I will, but not just yet.

My parents will take this hard. They'll phone soon, to ask me what happened at the appointment, and I'll have to tell them.

I think of the other messages that were left on my phone, from both Tess and her husband; the ones they left hours and hours ago.

I wonder if the police have made any progress.

I look online, idly really, to see if anything has happened, because it would be pushing things too far to phone DS George again, and I sit up straighter when I read that an arrest has been made.

"The suspect has not yet been named, but he's believed to be a member of the family," a news website tells me.

"He." So it's not Zoe. Thank God.

Did I think it was Zoe? No. Do I work in criminal law and see what's possible, however little you want it to be? Yes. So I would never have ruled it out.

More Internet searching turns up a grainy long-lens photo that shows a man in the back of a police car. I'm pretty sure it must be Chris Kennedy, Maria's husband. No surprises in a way; he would naturally be a prime suspect for the police.

Tess will be absolutely shattered because she thought that marriage was saving her sister.

I try her mobile, which goes to voicemail, so I have no choice but to brave the landline.

I don't know if I'm going to tell her about my diagnosis, but I want to know how she is, and what's happening and I want to hear her voice, and tell her how sorry I am and that I'm thinking of her. And, if I'm honest with myself, I also want to know when she's going to be able to see me again, because I need her.

TESSA

We sit in the garden after everybody has left. It's evening, and it's still hot and we want to escape the confines of the house that's had us trapped all day, and which feels sullied now, as it's where we had to learn what Chris did to Maria.

There are some generous patches of shade that have appeared as this awful day has progressed and the shadows have inevitably lengthened, but the sun still pours across the garden fence in places and heats up our patch of ground.

I sit on the bench with Richard. Around my ankles the parched grass feels prickly, and beside me on the bench Richard sweats and is mostly silent. We are both profoundly shocked.

My sister walked into a new marriage to escape her old life. She was vulnerable and I should have protected her more.

I say this to Richard.

"She was also ambitious," he says. "And you weren't responsible for her happiness."

"I should have done more, I should have known her better."

"She didn't want you close. I think she knew what she was doing."

"But what must she have been going through?" We're speaking very quietly because the children are in the garden with us, all three of them. "It's such a high price to pay."

"The highest," he says.

The kids have spread out a rug in the shade a few meters away from us, and filled the washing-up bowl with water, and they're playing with Grace. Philip Guerin is sitting with them.

On another day, it would be a perfect scene.

Our apple tree is dying. The trunk splits into two near its base and, while one side has produced a decent crop of apples this year, the other is barren.

Philip Guerin is sitting close to Zoe, but not very close. I know he doesn't want her to live with him.

She shifts position on the rug and is backlit by the sunshine, her hair a cascade of white, which so reminds me of my sister when she was young. The golden light silhouettes and burnishes Zoe's delicate arms and slender shoulders, and makes the drops of water sparkle in the air when Grace splashes.

Something is bothering me, a detail.

I look at my lovely niece. I see her point out something to Grace.

It's a butterfly, the source of Zoe's nickname.

And, as I watch it, I work out what's troubling me.

It's the injury to Zoe's hip, because I am fairly certain that I remember her hip clashing with the piano as she fled from Tom Barlow in the church. Fairly certain, but not positive. I wonder where the film of the concert is, because that would tell us. I wonder whether I have the stomach to watch it, and whether I even want to know, because Zoe told the police that Chris did it, that he pushed her.

Among the evening midges, the butterfly flutters on, looking for somewhere to feed. I recognize it as a fritillary and I think that it's a beautiful creature. Its wings are patterned in shades of orange and black that look magical in the wash of sunlight and against the intense blue evening sky, which the sunset won't tint for at least another half hour. Fluttering among the flaxen stalks of our dried-out lawn, the butterfly brings to mind more exotic locations than this.

The lavender spikes along our garden path are mostly desiccated by now, but I know where the butterfly will go, and so it does. It continues on its path, crossing the grass. It flutters right up to the children, causing Grace to pump her arms with excitement, and then past them and toward the corner of our garden, where a rogue buddleia seed has over the years grown into a huge, magnificent plant. It's bathed in sunshine. Huge sprays of dark purple flowers arc away from it, and it's covered with butterflies and insects.

I watch the fritillary approach the buddleia, its path undulating yet somehow preordained, and sure enough, it finishes there, alighting weightlessly on one of the generous racemes. Its wings close, and it begins to feed.

It will bathe in the honeyed sunlight and feast on the nectar until dusk begins to nudge away the daylight, and then it will find somewhere to settle in the dark, close by, and it will wait there until the light rises again in the morning, warming its wings and its body, so that it can make a foray out into another day.

This is the way of the world, I think. It's the natural order of things that so fascinated me as a child, and still does. But there will be only so many new daybreaks for this butterfly. It has a short life-span. Some species can hibernate through the winter, but not this one.

Richard puts his arm around me, and I let him.

And I think, if Sam told me he wanted me, would I ever be able to leave now?

I say to Richard, "Philip won't have Zoe, you know."

"I know," he replies. "I know he won't."

Richard is crying; he does that a lot. His depression is severe.

Our telephone rings.

RICHARD

There's an image that feels as if it's just within my grasp; it's an idea that's forming and then wavering, threatening to disappear, as if it's a mirage floating in the hot evening air.

I have not had a drink today, and this means that the idea is real, even if I can't quite make it solidify.

The idea is this: that Tessa and I will take on these children. I've spoken to Philip Guerin and he wants to go back to Devon without his daughter. He's met a new partner and she's from the local village, close to the families who lost children because of Zoe. Their relationship will not work with Zoe in their midst, and Philip will not consider moving away and starting again.

I expect we could try to persuade him, but why would we, when an alternative might be available?

Mentally, I remove him from the scene in front of me and I reimagine it.

There are Tess and I, on the bench. I have my arm around her and she has remained in her seat and not squirmed out from under my touch, as usual. In front of us there are three children on a rug: two blond princesses and a dark, clever boy.

They are two damaged teenagers and a perfect baby girl who will never remember her mother, and we are looking after them. They will fill our days and nights and we will fill theirs. I will cook for them and organize them, and drive the older kids to music lessons, while Tess works as normal. We'll give them patient care and love and help, and their lives will be as good as they can be. We'll give them ordinary, we won't be seduced by their talent or upset by their histories.

There's only one thing that makes this mirage shimmer, and threaten to dissolve into the air.

It's what I thought I overheard while Zoe was bathing Grace earlier.

It was Lucas saying, "It was an accident," and "I'm going to tell them everything." It sounded like a confession, but maybe he was just talking about what they witnessed. It must have been.

I won't mention this to Tessa, but I expect that if I did she would say, "Well, what does that mean? Are you sure you heard it right? Had you had a drink?" So I won't.

I've already cleared up the broken model that I found in my shed. If one of them smashed it they would be doing nothing worse than I've done in the past, when all the sadness I've felt has occasionally driven me to an act of destruction like that.

To make sure I'm fit to take on these children, I'll go around the house and take every bottle and tip it down the sink. I'll never buy alcohol again. I'll go to AA. I'll be a perfect father to them. Even if Lucas doesn't want to stay with us, he'll always be welcome here to see his sister, Grace.

Today is not the day to say this to the children. Nor will to-

morrow be, and perhaps not even next week, but it's the offer
I want to make them as and when they're ready to hear it.

If Tessa will agree.

I'm willing to bargain.

If she'll agree to this, I'll not ask questions about how she
knew, by heart, the personal mobile phone number of Zoe's
solicitor. I'll not phone her friends to ask if she stayed with
them last night, because I think I know where she was. I think
she was with him. She herself told me, her defensiveness when
I phoned him. I'm not one hundred percent sure, I have no
idea how it might have happened, but I can live with a little
uncertainty. It's a lesser demon than the ones I've been cohab-
iting with for the last few years. Tess's infidelity is probably as
much as I deserved, and it's certainly no worse a thing than
what I've put her through.

This is what I want to say to the children, this is what
makes me feel invigorated, strong, hopeful: *Stay with us. We'll
look after you. We'll make sure no more harm comes to you. We can
be your family.*

From inside the house, our landline rings and I feel Tess
tense up beside me.

"I'll get that," I say.

SAM

I try Tess's landline because I feel I have to. I don't want her to feel abandoned.

It rings and rings, and I'm about to give up when Richard answers.

I'm tempted to hang up, but that would be childish, and this is not a day for infantile behavior.

"Hello," I say. "It's Sam Locke, Zoe's solicitor, returning your call."

I say that because I suspect he doesn't know that Tess and I have spoken since he left his message.

He says, "Thank you, Sam, but we don't need you any longer, the police have made an arrest."

"Yes, I saw that on the news. I'm so sorry. Is everybody all right? It must have been a terrible shock."

"It is a great shock, yes."

He draws out his words as if there's something else he's thinking of saying, and I'm suddenly alert to the fact that he might know about Tess and me.

"Well, I won't keep bothering you any longer, but if there's anything I can do, please just phone me."

"I think you've done enough, don't you?"

"I beg your pardon?"

"Don't contact my family again. Don't contact Zoe and, most important, don't contact my wife."

"What?"

"I think you understand me very well."

"I . . ."

"Leave us alone."

"Sorry, I . . ." But my words fall into the ether because he's hung up.

I sit with my phone in my hand and wonder if Tessa has told him about us, if she had to tell him. I'm still sitting there many minutes later, speculating, and shocked at the ferocity of his tone, when my phone rings.

Tess, I think at first, but it's not. It's my parents, and I can't ignore them. Not today. My mother cries when I tell her that my diagnosis is one step nearer to being confirmed.

"How will you manage, love?" she asks. "Will you move back home?"

"I don't know, Mum, we'll have to see."

I've had no intention of doing that, but after I hang up I drink another beer and watch the river some more and feel the beginnings of what feels like mourning for Tessa, and then I'm tempted by my mother's suggestion. I'm tempted to walk away from this city and this life and this relationship that's brought me the greatest feelings of joy but also the most profound feelings of guilt. I'm tempted to nurse my sorrows elsewhere, to rethink my life.

If I take myself back to Devon, where I'll still be in pain, and my condition will inevitably degenerate, and I'll miss Tess every day, there will at least be sea air and beautiful countryside and people who know me and love me. It'll be a return, sure, but also another chance.

Because what is there for me here now?

And these thoughts circulate as I watch the reflection of the setting sun burning brightly in the windows of the boat-yard opposite my flat, until it sinks down far enough that it disappears.

After that, the city lights and their reflections on the water have to work hard to pierce the darkness.

EPILOGUE

An Evening of Winter Music

Friday, February 20, 2015
7 P.M.
Clifton Music Club, Bristol

Zoe Maisey
plays
Chopin, Bach & Mozart

In a solo performance

Tickets: £4

*Please contact Tessa at tessa.downing1@gmail.com
for bookings and details of future performances.*

ZOE

I'm standing at the side of the stage waiting to go on.

Outside there's ice on the sidewalk, and when we arrived, Uncle Richard had to catch my arm because I nearly slipped over when we got out of the car.

Lucas is in the crowd, manning the video recorder. He doesn't perform in public anymore, though sometimes he bangs out a tune. That's how he himself describes his playing nowadays. He's so into filming and that's his thing now. He spends hours watching films with Uncle Richard. Richard doesn't make models anymore, he says he never really liked them; he gets into the whole film thing with Lucas instead.

Grace is here, but we don't think she'll last long in the audience.

Richard says that he wouldn't bring her along at all, but he's sure that she's got an unusual interest in music for a child her age. She's captivated by my playing, he says. He's sitting at the end of the back row with her so he has an easy exit and can take her home when she makes her first squawk. But he wants her to be here at the beginning at least. It's my first concert since Mum died, and I think we all know in our hearts it's a kind of tribute to her.

My piano was brought over from the Second Chance House and moved into the dining room at Tess's house. Richard has converted his shed into a kind of cinema and film room where he and Lucas edit films and watch them on a pull-down screen.

"It's tech heaven," says Tess when she looks in there.

I tried to phone Sam once, at work, but they said he'd left, gone back to Devon. They said he was poorly. I tried to tell Tessa, but she didn't want to talk about it. She reminded me of Mum then, pushing a subject away, lips tight and holding back feelings that I couldn't read.

I'm playing a short program tonight, but it contains some of Mum's favorite pieces.

Because of the cold I'm wrapped up warmly, gloves on, and a cardigan, and I've been pressed against the heater that's in the shabby little greenroom. We've been careful with the venue we've booked on this occasion, so very careful. It's not a church; it's a music club. The piano on the stage is a beautiful Steinway and there's seating for around eighty people. This time, I shall make my entrance from the side, not down an aisle.

In my head there's a mantra: This is your Third Chance.

I don't think I have nine lives, but I hope I have three.

I hear my name called from the stage, and just before I go on, in my head I send a message to my mum. This is for you, Mummy, is what I think, and I have to wipe a small tear carefully from my eye.

I take off my cardigan and my gloves.

I'm looking good, in a dress that Mum chose for me

before she died, a black silk dress with a high neck and three-quarter-length sleeves. I've brushed my hair until it's silky, just how she would want me to. As I enter the room and mount the stage, there's a round of applause.

Before I sit down, I do a small bow to the audience, and then the clapping stops politely. Tess is in the front row and she gives me a thumbs-up. Behind her, almost all the seats are full. My reputation has preceded me. As Chris might have said, if he hadn't been sentenced to fifteen years in jail: No publicity is bad publicity.

I sit. I adjust the stool, controlling my breathing, and I place my hands over the keys.

The piece is a nocturne by Chopin. It's achingly beautiful, soul-pulling music, which can make your insides ripple. It's for my mother and for Lucas, who doesn't want to perform anymore, but loves to listen. It's for Grace too, because she's going to be just like me, I know it. It's for Richard and Tess, who are looking after us now. It's for my Third Chance Family.

As I pull the first note from the piano, I'm instantly lost to the music, trapped inside it, living every delicate, haunting phrase of it, and I feel like my mum is living it with me.

And I know it's going to go well, brilliantly, in fact.

ACKNOWLEDGMENTS

A great deal has happened in the year since I started to work on this book, and I'm indebted to all the people who've supported me along the way.

A super-sized thank-you must go to Emma Beswetherick, my editor in the UK. Her extraordinary enthusiasm, her tireless support, and her razor-sharp editorial guidance and clarity are all things I could not have done without. More thanks must also go to Tim Whiting, Charlie King, Stephanie Melrose, Aimee Kitson, Dominic Wakeford, and Ceara Elliot at Little, Brown UK.

An extremely important thank-you is owed to Amanda Bergeron at William Morrow in the United States—the most delightful, smart, and supportive editor you could hope for. It's been an absolute pleasure working with Amanda and the whole team at HarperCollins, and more heartfelt thanks must go to Jennifer Hart, Julia Meltzer, Elle Keck, Kim Lewis, Molly Waxman, Lauren Truskowski, and Elsie Lyons for a stunning cover design. I'm very proud of this edition and grateful to you all for making it happen.

Another enormous thank-you to my amazing agent Nelle Andrew, who is always there for me with the right words of advice, and bucketloads of support. I feel very lucky to have you on my side.

Huge thanks also to the fabulous Rachel Mills, Alexandra Cliff, and Marilia Savvides at PFD, who have sent my first book out into the world with wings on. Lovely Rebecca Wearmouth completes the foreign rights team, and it's been so much fun to work with all of you.

To all the international editors and publishers who took on the book: thank you so much, you've also given me the courage to throw myself into *The Perfect Girl*. It's been a joy to work with and to meet many of you over the past year.

Thank you to my writing partner, Abbie Ross, for being there every step of the way. Your tireless support, friendship, and determination have kept me going and inspired me too.

Thank you so much also to Annemarie Caracciolo, Philippa Lowthorpe, Bridget Rode, Janie and Phill Ankers, Jonathan and Cilla Paget, Andrew Beck and Vonda Macmillan Beck for always being there with words of encouragement. Annemarie, you get the trophy for the best pep talks.

My two retired detectives, who helped me so much with *What She Knew*, were once again extremely generous with their time and advice for this book, and in particular they helped me devise a crime scene and timeline that would work with the intricate plot that I had in mind. Thank you so much to you both.

I also undertook research in the worlds of criminal law and incarceration to support elements of this book. Rob Rode and Margaret Evans were both extremely generous with their time and knowledge in this respect, and I'm very grateful to you both.

Any legal or police procedural mistakes are mine alone!

On the home front, another massive thank-you must go to my family, who has been very patient with me while I disappeared into my basement office for days, weeks, and months on end to tackle this book.

Jules Macmillan. Thank you for feeding the children, the dogs, and the fish while I wrote. Thank you for listening when I needed to talk about the book (which was pretty much all the time), and helping me reverse out of many a plot cul-de-sac, and for your brilliant and thoughtful suggestions. Thank you most of all for being unstintingly supportive of this book, and of me.

Rose, Max, and Louis Macmillan. Thank you for everything. You've never once complained as your full-time mum became a full-time writer, and that's something. Thank you too for patiently answering all my questions and letting me feed some of your own interests into my story. And not forgetting, most important, a very big thank-you to each one of you for making me smile every day. I'm so proud of you all.

Insights,
Interviews
& More . . .

Meet Gilly Macmillan

Gilly Macmillan

GILLY MACMILLAN is the Edgar-nominated author of *What She Knew*. She grew up in Swindon, Wiltshire, and lived in Northern California in her late teens. She worked at the *Burlington Magazine* and the Hayward Gallery before starting a family. Since then, she's worked as a part-time lecturer in photography and now writes full-time. She resides in Bristol, England.

Inspiration for *The Perfect Girl*

THE IDEA FOR *The Perfect Girl* began to evolve in my mind a long time before I started to write the novel. Many years ago, I was told a true story about a teenage girl that I simply wasn't able to forget. The girl in question was from a good family and had every opportunity in life, but there was something unusual about her. One night she made a very grave mistake and did something that caused the death of one teenager and severely injured another. She was around seventeen years old when it happened, and as a result of what she did she was sent to jail, destroying her chances of finishing school and going on to have the "normal" life that was expected. While incarcerated she began to take drugs, and by the time she was let out she had become dependent. In spite of her family's best efforts, she took to living in hostels and remaining on the margins of society. Her life never recovered its original trajectory.

I was shocked by the tale. I felt sorry for the girl and her family, and her story raised all kinds of questions for me. What would it be like, I wondered, if your chance of a "normal" life was destroyed in this way before it had effectively begun, based on one rash decision? How likely would you be to get a reasonable second chance at life after such a thing had happened, and what would that second chance be worth to you and your family? ▶

Inspiration for *The Perfect Girl* (continued)

These questions felt pressing enough that I began to develop the novel thinking that similar events might make a fascinating, if difficult, backstory, and that it might be even more interesting if the girl in question was some sort of prodigy, because that could raise the stakes even higher for her and for her family. The question of which talent to give Zoe— my perfect girl—was an easy one to answer, as one of my own children is an extremely good musician, so we've inhabited the world of competitive piano playing for many years. It's mostly a very sociable and fun world, but sometimes, on the margins, you glimpse a child or young person who you suspect might be intensively schooled to play and under tremendous pressure to win, just as Zoe is.

As the novel developed I felt that I wanted to use Zoe's character to explore the ways in which teenagers are often extremely emotionally developed and intelligent, yet very far from being in control of their own lives. Zoe's personality and life contain many similar contrasts. Her mind is brilliant and it races wildly and imaginatively, yet she has also developed extraordinary strength and discipline from her piano studies. She's spent time in prison, but now lives in luxury and privilege. She's developing a public profile as a pianist, yet that talent has also made her feel isolated from her peers. I was fascinated by those juxtapositions: what they could do to a young person, how they might affect her feelings and behavior. I often thought of Zoe as a caged bird: lonely, brilliant, beautiful, brave, and not to be underestimated.

I set the book over a very short time frame and used just a few locations and a small cast because I was hoping to give it the intensity and claustrophobia of a chamber drama—a format I absolutely love. I also adore films and books in which the actions of one person trigger another's and so on, causing events to spiral unstoppably as they do in *The Perfect Girl*. For this reason, I also used a number of other narrative voices in addition to Zoe's. I hoped it was a device that might allow the reader to experience the story almost cinematically, as the characters move in and out of focus and the reader is able to see the action developing from the point of view of each of the main players. It was a device that would also, I hoped, reveal each of the characters in more depth, peeling back their public faces and laying bare their real motives and thoughts. I felt that letting the reader into the head of more than one character could only raise the stakes for each of them, and would show how their motivations interplay with Zoe's.

It was a daunting but exciting challenge trying to bring all the elements of this novel together, and I hope you've enjoyed the result. ❧

Reading Group Guide

1. What advantages do Zoe's abilities give her? Can you understand why Maria pushed her daughter musically? What responsibility do you think parents have to a child who shows strong aptitude for something? What is fostering and what is pushing too hard?

2. Zoe makes a very difficult decision toward the end of *The Perfect Girl*, one that will certainly have significant and long-lasting consequences for both herself and others. Do you think she did the right thing? How much sympathy do you have for her?

3. To what extent do you think of Maria as a victim, or as somebody who is deliberately deceiving others?

4. What does the character of Zoe's solicitor add to the novel?

5. What is the importance of music and its redemptive power in the novel?

6. At the end of the book both Tess and Richard seem to have an inkling that Zoe has deceived everybody, but they don't discuss this. Do you think they will talk about it eventually, and work out what might have happened, and, if so, what do you think they'll do as a result?

7. Lucas is a quiet character. How do you feel about him? Do you think he'll thrive in his new family, or

could he be in danger of ultimately remaining loyal to his father and telling the truth about what happened?

8. A number of novels deal with the burden of a deadly secret—how well do you think this idea is handled in *The Perfect Girl*?

9. Do you recognize some of the pressures that the family finds itself under more generally? Is that urge to keep up with others, to be a successful unit, to put on a good show familiar to you?

10. "My mother: who never talks about what really matters . . ." How far is this observation explored in the book?

11. The ending is both satisfying for Zoe and morally ambiguous. How successful do you think it is, and did Chris deserve what happened to him? ✐

Ten Books That Inspired *The Perfect Girl*

WHILE I WAS WRITING *The Perfect Girl* I wanted to read any books that did one of three distinct things. I searched for novels that featured a strong teenage voice, took place over a very short time frame, or had multiple narrators. I read very widely in those categories, and more, over the nine months that I took to write the novel, but the following are ten of my favorites.

The Catcher in the Rye, by J. D. Salinger

A classic, obviously, but there is undeniable power in teenage narrator Holden Caulfield's voice, and the insights into his feelings of alienation and his struggle to understand his identity that the book provides. I love the quirky stream-of-consciousness writing style that makes you feel like Holden's confidant, and the way Salinger brings his wild, powerful, and clever mind alive so vividly.

The Outsiders, by S. E. Hinton

This is a classic coming-of-age story but also a wonderful, heartbreaking novel that perfectly illustrates the way in which teenagers can be victims of their circumstances. In yet another powerful first-person narrative, the story is told via the character of Ponyboy Curtis. He's a character who has stayed with me ever since I first picked up this book. I still feel a pang of concern for him now, and I'm writing this a good thirty years since I first read it!

Special Topics in Calamity Physics, by Marissa Pessl

Blue van der Meer is the clever, academic teenager who narrates this novel, and I loved her energy and the way her mind spills out all over the page as she tries to work out why one of her favorite teachers committed suicide. It's a smart, insightful story, full of challenges for the reader, and a great whodunit, too.

We Are All Completely Beside Ourselves, by Karen Joy Fowler

Rosemary is the narrator of this novel, and although she's not quite a teenager (because she's at college), much of the book describes her early years, and her fresh, quirky voice hooked me in right from the start and led me through the pages at a gallop. It's a witty, brilliant, and unusual book in which the action grips but some very thoughtful and important themes form its heartbeat. I defy anybody not to have a richer understanding of love and family after finishing it.

The Fault in Our Stars, by John Green

How I love Hazel Grace Lancaster, the teenage narrator of this wonderful novel. *The Fault in Our Stars* was originally written for teens, and passed to me by my daughter after she had read it. ▶

I'll admit I picked it up with some skepticism, but once I had, I simply could not put it down. Hazel's wit, kindness, and perceptiveness, combined with the unusual perspective on life that her illness gives her, and of course all of her normal teenage vulnerabilities, make this a very lovely, if sad, story about family and life, and absolutely essential reading.

As I Lay Dying, by William Faulkner

This novel tells the story of the death and burial of Addie Bundren, who has been the matriarch of a large family in 1920s Mississippi. It's told from about fifteen different viewpoints in intense stream-of-consciousness narratives that intersect and almost seem to weave through one another. As the book progresses, each narrator reveals more about Addie's life and the lives of her family members and others. It's a demanding read, and a bleak story, but it's incredibly powerful, compelling, and, above all, humane.

Chronicle of a Death Foretold by Gabriel García Márquez

This short novel is a masterpiece. Set over just one day, it tells the story of the final hours of Santiago Nasar. We learn in the very first line that by the end of the novel he will be dead, yet are gripped by Márquez's extraordinary observation of both the ordinary and the extraordinary as we learn how, against the odds, death stalks Santiago through those hours until it finally catches up with him. It is a tour-de-force study of human nature, love, fate, and revenge.

The Mezzanine, by Nicholson Baker

This novel has the shortest time frame of any that I discovered while I was developing *The Perfect Girl*. It takes place over a single lunch hour and we spend this time in the mind of the narrator, Howie, hearing his every thought. The extraordinary attention to detail is a marvel, as is the rendering of the paths our minds can wander along, and if nothing else the novel makes a virtue of the mundane. Not a book to race through, it's a demanding yet strangely relaxing read.

The Dinner, by Herman Koch

This is a gripping novel. The action takes place over just one evening at an elegant dinner where the protagonist and his wife must meet his brother and sister-in-law to discuss what they should do about their teenage sons, who have done something very shocking indeed.

Ordinary People, by Judith Guest

This powerful novel inspired a film that is one of my all-time favorites. It tells the story of a well-off suburban family who is struggling to live normally again in the aftermath of two life-shattering events. Narrated by Conrad Jarrett, a teenage boy, it's a sensitive exploration ▶

Ten Books That Inspired *The Perfect Girl*
(continued)

of depression, love, grief, and guilt, and it illustrates in painful detail the tremendous psychological strains of keeping up appearances when life is never going to be the same again. ∿

Discover great authors, exclusive offers, and more at hc.com.